Painting Bananas

Cherry Dene
Book 2

AMANDA PAULL

ISBN: 9798524317339

Also by Amanda Paull

Women's Fiction
The Cherry Dene Series

Pictures in the Sky
Painting Bananas
Colouring Outside the Lines

Romantic Comedy
The Scott Family Short Story Series

Let's Dance
A Christmas Day Kerfuffle
Fenella's Fabulous Fountain Fondue
Pedalo Pandemonium
Wedding Wobbles

For my mother

Chapter 1

The click-clack of Alison Riley's heels fell silent as she stepped from the corridor into the consultation room. She glanced down and suppressed a laugh. The brown swirls on the threadbare carpet had once been vibrant orange. Why, she wondered, hadn't young Dr Smedley redecorated after his father retired from the practice?

She froze at the sight of a clump of wispy grey hair, sticking up from behind an ancient computer console.

'Sit,' said a faceless voice, followed by the sound of clumsy keyboard hammering.

'Good morning.' Dusty air wafted onto her face as she sat down on a flimsy chair. A nostalgic flash of bare young legs peeling off plastic made her wince. Infection Control at Saint Mary's hospital where she worked would have a field day in this room.

'So,' said Dr Smedley, 'It says on here you can't sleep.'

'That's part of the reason I'm here. The insomnia has been much worse since a new manager moved into the office.' She squirmed in her seat. 'The thing is… I want to kill him.' There, she'd said it out loud. No going back now.

'Stupid…'

Alison gasped. 'I beg your pardon?'

Dr Smedley's bespectacled face appeared from behind the

1

computer. He cocked his head sideways at the screen and raised an eyebrow. 'Idiotic new-fangled rubbish.'

She laughed. She could remember her mother calling it 'state-of-the-art', though she had been too young to know what that meant.

He peered at her, a puzzled expression on his face. 'And what do you want me to do?'

The heat cranked up as the old motor whirred. 'Help me? It's not normal for me to want to harm people – even horrible ones – I hate any type of confrontation.' She took a measured breath. 'But I have flashes of ripping his throat out. It scares me.'

Dr Smedley gave a sage nod and leaned on the leather-patched elbows of his tweed jacket. He scrutinised her face through grey, bleary eyes. 'Don't worry, my wife was the same.'

Alison let out a sigh of relief. 'She wanted to kill her boss, too? Thank goodness. I thought I was going mad.'

'No, don't be silly,' he laughed. 'Snappy. Irrational. Flying off the handle for no reason.'

'Excuse me?'

'Not long before the divorce.' He gave her a stern look. 'So, watch your step, my dear. Or else Mr Riley will be off.'

She opened her mouth to speak, but words failed her.

He wheeled his chair along the desk to rummage in a drawer, fishing out a dog-eared pad and a fountain pen. There was an awkward silence, barring the scratching of pen nib against paper. A faint whiff of Brylcreem took her back to childhood – sitting in that seat next to her mother while he scribbled away, his hair shiny with the hair product. It made her feel smaller.

She cleared her throat. 'This is a serious matter to me. I'm concerned I might hurt my boss. And the insomnia has reached an unmanageable level.'

He raised one eyebrow and continued to scribble. She watched his huge, gnarly hands as he wrote. The same hands that had clumsily wielded a wooden tongue depressor and made her gag as a child. On that occasion she had left with a pink antibiotic syrup that tasted like bubble gum. And her mother had rewarded her bravery with a Cadbury's Finger of Fudge from the newsagent's shop on the high street.

The snap of the pen cap brought Alison's focus back into the room. He sighed. 'Ah, the problems of the worried-well.'

'The what?'

Then, as if he had read her thoughts, he said, 'How's your mother these days?'

She stared at him in disbelief. 'Dead.'

He coughed. 'Oh, yes. Yes, I remember.' He gave a nervous laugh, pulled off the pen top and finished what he was writing with a flurry of over-zealous dotting. He ripped the sheet from the pad and waved it at her. 'Perimenopause.'

Alison gasped again. 'I'm only forty-one,' she whispered, reeling from his insensitivity. 'And the insomnia started after the twins were born. They're twenty years old.'

He checked her records. 'Hmm… Your mother used to say you were a worrier.' He studied her face. 'Very ageing.'

'She didn't say that.' Alison took a deep breath. 'With respect, how can you recall what my mother said, yet forget she'd died?'

He waggled a finger at her and pushed his spectacles further up the bridge of his nose. 'To be fair, I can't remember everyone. I see a lot of patients.'

'Mangled up in car parts?' She ran her fingers over her brow – the skin was smooth. 'Anyway, it can't be the peri–'

He shook the prescription at her.

'I don't need hormone replacement therapy.' She reluctantly took it and squinted at the untidy scrawl. 'Seriously? B vitamins…?' If she didn't already know him, she'd think he was a clown doctor, like the ones she had seen around St Mary's. She glanced at his enormous hands – all he needed was a pair of white gloves and a red nose.

3

He gave a solemn nod of his head. 'Low levels can affect mood.' He leaned towards her. 'You should have brought Mr Riley; I'd have been most interested to hear hubby's side.'

Alison slowly exhaled through pursed lips. 'My husband's side?'

He leant on his elbows again and steepled his hands, his bushy eyebrows knotted. 'I expect he's noticed the change in you. Must be trying for him.' He shook his head and pulled a tooth-baring grimace. 'I know I had a dreadful time with my missus.'

She looked towards the door, half expecting someone to burst through shouting, 'Candid Camera' – another throwback from the era Dr Smedley was clearly trapped in. 'Martin and I are fine. It's only my boss, Billy Chapman, who I can't stand. And wouldn't I need blood tests to check my hormone levels before making that diagnosis?'

He gave a weary head shake. 'Now, now, Alison. I don't tell you how to fill in forms, do I? This is my job.' He reached over and patted her hand. 'It'll pass – in a few years. These will help in the meantime.'

She pulled her hand away. 'Fill in forms? I'm a senior Patient Services Coordinator.'

He chuckled. 'Is that what they're calling it these days?'

The Newton's cradle on the desk clacked as his arm brushed against it. When she was little, the momentum and sound of the shiny chrome spheres used to mesmerise her. Right now, she wanted to clack the tarnished old eyesore off the wall. 'And what about the insomnia? I can't go on like this.'

'As you said, my dear, you've had it for years.'

My dear? He stared at her, an inane grin on his face, oblivious to the inappropriateness of his behaviour. 'I know it started when the twins were babies and wouldn't sleep, but I don't know why it didn't get better. I've tried everything to put it right over the years, yet now it's worse than ever. There must be something that could help?'

'We all get weary from time to time. I mean, it's not as if you have cancer, is it?'

Her eyes widened in shock. 'What on earth…?'

Dr Smedley stood up and laughed again. He gestured towards the door. 'Take the vitamins for your little mood-swings. As for the insomnia, well I can't give you a magic pill. And even if I could, we wouldn't want you becoming a slave to drugs, now would we?'

She remained in her seat. 'I don't want drugs. But vitamins can't possibly stop me from wanting to throttle my boss.'

He nodded at the prescription. 'Try them.'

Alison picked up her bag and reluctantly tucked the prescription into her jacket pocket. 'Surely –'

Dr Smedley opened the door and waved her through. 'Bye-bye, my dear. Give my best to Mr Riley.'

On the way out of the health centre, the patient feedback screen caught her eye. 'How was my experience today?' She thumped the red, unhappy-looking face. 'Bloody awful.'

She stormed along Earlby High Street, muttering to herself and cursing Dr Smedley's incompetence. She had wanted to kill Billy Chapman before her appointment but would now happily do it with her bare hands. If he wasn't such a horrible boss, she would have been able to continue coping. 'Vitamin B,' she fumed, marching into the newsagents.

Alison stepped out onto the busy street, clutching a Cadbury's Finger of Fudge and a packet of red liquorice shoelaces. Glancing up, she caught sight of the wrought iron entrance gates to Cherry Park. Her mood lifted. They had also gone to the park after the tongue depressor incident. She didn't recall seeing Dr Smedley again. Her mother must have requested another doctor after that.

'Perimenopause. I'm forty-bloody-one,' she muttered, wandering through the gates. If she were a vindictive, or maybe braver person, she would report him.

The park opened out onto vast grassy areas, bordered by

cherry trees, with a small man-made lake at the far end. She recalled happy trips there with her parents as a child, and then with her twins. Chloe used to love feeding the ducks. Jack liked to eat the bread himself.

Alison set off along the pathway running the perimeter of the park, pleased she had booked the entire morning as annual leave. She had expected to leave the surgery feeling positive after plucking up the courage to get help for her problems, and she had planned to celebrate with a bit of shopping and a coffee in Caffè Alessandro on Earlby high street. But the prospect of no end to her sleepless nights or murderous thoughts had quashed all hope of a happier future. She couldn't face the shops.

She was pleased there weren't many people around, barring the local junior school team who were practicing on the football pitch, and the odd dog walker. It was peaceful. As she marched along, she replayed the conversation with Dr Smedley. She gave him a mental ear bashing for his patronising manner and inept medical practice, and she chided herself for not standing up to him.

Alison wondered why her mother had entrusted her child's health to him, then rationalised that he'd have been much younger and his knowledge more up to date for that time. Thankfully, she had registered Chloe and Jack with one of the other GP's in the practice.

The sight of an odd-looking man heading her way made her stop in her tracks. She assumed it was a man because of his gait, though it was difficult to tell due to the copious layers of clothing. Despite the mild weather, he was dressed more for the Antarctic than a stroll around the park, with heavy waterproof trousers, jacket and scarf. His zipped-up collar covered the lower half of his face, so that all Alison could see were his eyes beneath a hood which, on closer inspection, sat on top of a woollen balaclava, further unnerving her.

The nearest people were a couple of hundred metres away.

Her heartbeat quickened. As she stood worrying about a pending attack, a little white Westie in a tartan coat hurtled out of the bushes and shot off across the park towards the football field.

'Angus come back here this minute,' called the well-spoken Antarctic man.

She felt guilty for assuming the worst.

The Westie carried on tearing across the pitch, disrupting the game as he chased after a football almost as big as him. The referee blew his whistle to halt play while the team dealt with the ensuing mayhem. Alison laughed at the scene, made more comedic by the sound of the man's waterproofs, rustling into the distance as he darted off after Angus.

Danger averted, she carried on along to the lake and sat down on a park bench to watch the ducks and eat her sweets. Although there was no one around, the public footpath on the other side of the bushes behind her seat gave her a sense of security. She pondered over how she could be such a coward yet spend so much time fantasising about murdering another person.

She pulled out the prescription and stared at Dr Smedley's scrawl. She wondered how her mother would have reacted. She'd no doubt think it was a load of rubbish, too. In fact, she'd be in fits of laughter at the very idea. But she'd more than likely try them, if for no other reason than to prove the doctor wrong, before telling him so.

She knew one thing – vitamins would not stop her from wanting to throttle Billy Chapman. Until he had turned up in the department, Alison hadn't given him a thought since her first day at Saint Mary's. She had only been twenty-one. Leaving tiny Chloe and Jack had been heart wrenching, but she'd had no choice – a family of four couldn't live off Martin's student grant.

Billy had plonked himself next to her in the lecture hall on induction day and irritated her from the outset – with his noisy gum-chewing and domination of the shared armrest. She never expected him to turn up as her boss so many years later – or for him to pick on her so much. He had started out in Sterile Services, so how he had ended up as Team Lead for Patient Services, she had no idea. She remembered him boasting about having only two GCSE's, and how he had blagged his way through the interview to get the job. He had planned to scale up the career ladder doing as little as possible. His tactics had obviously paid off.

Until Billy burst into the office and rolled his eyes at the sight of her, she had coped with the insomnia.

She bit into the Cadbury's finger of fudge and closed her eyes in delight as it melted in her mouth. At least, she thought, she had a supportive husband. Martin had said on many occasions that he wished he could swap places with her, so that she could have a good night's sleep. He reckoned that would solve the problem with Billy, too. But he didn't believe she was capable of murder, even without sleep. To a certain extent she could understand it – it was completely out of character for a placid, people-pleaser like herself. But Martin also knew she wasn't a liar, so why didn't he believe her?

Alison watched a family of ducks glide across the pond and pulled out the liquorice shoelaces. She sighed in resignation – there was nothing anyone could do to help her.

Chapter 2

Christopher Barker rolled over and gently cocooned his wife Sandy with his body for an early morning snuggle. He nuzzled the back of her neck, inhaling the sweet smell of her skin, delighted he had woken before the alarm. 'Good morning, beautiful.'

Sandy stirred and nestled herself into him.

He opened his eyes and spotted the clock over her shoulder on the bedside cabinet. 'Crikey.'

'Ear… loud...' she grumbled.

'Sorry.' He bolted out of bed. 'It's eight-thirty. I didn't hear the alarm. I'm late.'

Sandy rolled over and stretched. 'I switched it off. You're at the health centre this morning.'

'Yes, but I have to go into work first.'

She pulled the duvet over her head. 'Shh.'

Christopher shot out of the bedroom, then popped his head back around the door. 'Remember we're meeting for breakfast after my appointment.' He disappeared into the bathroom without waiting for a response.

The sound of the shower drowned out the scutter of Sandy's feet on the stairs.

It was as he crossed the landing to his dressing room that Christopher smelled bacon. The neighbours must be having a cooked breakfast, he thought, assuming the aroma must be wafting in through an open window. His stomach rumbled.

It was unheard of for him to sleep in. His job as a troubleshooting, quality control assessor for Henleys Bank took him all over the United Kingdom. He was usually based in a noisy city-centre hotel or apartment, where there was no need to set an alarm.

The smell of bacon grew stronger as he stole down to the kitchen, taking care to be quiet in case Sandy had dozed back off. He did a double take. She was standing at the cooker in her dressing gown, her long blond hair tied in a knot on top of her head and a spatula in her hand.

He stood, puzzled, in the doorway. 'What're you doing?'

She turned and laughed. 'What's it look like? I'm making you a bacon sandwich.' Fat dripped from the spatula onto the floor.

'Why?'

'You said you didn't have to fast for the blood test.'

Christopher pulled off a wad of kitchen roll and stooped down to mop up the grease. 'But you don't cook.'

'Rubbish.' She peered down at him and frowned. 'Leave that. Yvonne will get it later.'

'No need to create extra work for her. And we don't want her thinking we're Clampits.'

Sandy threw her head back and guffawed. 'What are you like? She's paid to clean.'

'Is there a cuppa on the go?'

'Sorry, I've been busy making your breakfast.'

He filled the kettle. A cup of instant would have to do. 'I don't understand why you're cooking when we're going to Alessandro's. That's why I was going into work early, to get a head start.'

She looked at him, nonplussed.

'I just reminded you, upstairs.'

'Must have been half-asleep.' She yawned. 'Anyway, you're

the boss, you set your own hours.'

'I had a couple of things I wanted to do.' He took two mugs from the cupboard. 'It's strange – I know I've only been at the Earlby Street branch for two months, but I really like it there.'

Sandy studied his face without saying anything.

'What?'

She picked a bread bun from the packet and tore it open with her hands. 'It's not like you to become attached to a place.'

'I know. And I love living at home.'

Sandy smiled at him. 'It's been fantastic having you here for longer than a weekend. Such a shame you'll soon be off to Milton Keynes.'

Christopher sighed and nodded. 'I'm not looking forward to moving on at all this time.'

Sandy gazed at the ceiling, as the bacon sizzled in the pan. 'If I hadn't met you, I might have had a chain of beauty salons by now.'

He felt a familiar twinge of guilt. Sandy could have stayed in one place and continued with her business plans when they got married, but she chose to move around with him. It was only when Emily was on the way that Sandy had agreed to settle in one place. And then, with a baby to care for and a husband only home at weekends, her career plans were shelved indefinitely. He would always be grateful for the sacrifices she had made. It was one of the things that drove him to do well, to provide the best life possible for his wife and daughter. 'You can still do it.'

'I will. I can't wait to set up my own business. It'll be great. Once Emily's grown up.'

He chuckled. 'She's living with her fiancé. If you're serious, you could speak to an adviser at the bank. We have a start-up course for small businesses. You know, brush up your knowledge and consider you options.'

She shot him a sideways glance. 'Maybe after the wedding, there's still so much to arrange.'

He checked his watch. 'Would you be able to drop me at the health centre, please?' In hindsight, he should have dropped the car into the garage for its MOT this morning rather than last night.

'Sorry, babe. I've got an early appointment with the wedding coordinator.' She gave a little sniff. 'That's why I can't meet you.'

'I was looking forward to that.' He poured water and milk onto the instant coffee and took a mouthful. 'Are you picking up Emily on the way?'

'She doesn't need to be there today. I've got a few things to go over with Margot.' Sandy shot her mug a look of disdain. She left the bacon cracking and spitting in the pan, while she filled the coffee machine with water and popped in a pod.

Christopher took another mouthful of his and picked up his briefcase. 'Sorry, love. It's a lovely gesture to cook for me, but I'm going to have to dash.'

Sandy looked at him, her huge blue eyes filled with disappointment. The abandoned bacon continued to sputter.

He was itching to switch off the hob, but he didn't want to offend her further. 'It's just with my car being in the garage.'

'Can't you eat it on the way?'

He eyed the blue smoke swirling up from the frying pan. 'Okay. I might make it if I cut through the park.' Earlby Health Centre was a two-mile drive but half as far on foot across Cherry Park.

Christopher felt his whole body relax at the sound of the hob clicking off. He reached into the fridge for the butter and picked up a knife, just as Sandy plopped the frazzled meat into the dry bun.

'Here you are,' she said, proudly holding it out to him.

Abandoning the butter, he accepted the burnt offering. The top of the bun had a thumb-shaped hole in it. 'Mmm, lovely. Thanks.'

Christopher kissed her cheek. 'See you tonight.'

He closed the front door to the sound of the coffee machine percolating into action. As he strode off along the street, a neighbour waved from her garden.

'Morning, Mrs Graham,' he called, waving his bacon bun. He briefly considered throwing it over the hedge to her dog which was sniffing around the garden. Guilt stopped him – that would be ungrateful.

He continued on his way, feeling lucky to have such a caring wife. How many men, he wondered, had wives who would drag themselves out of a cosy bed to make them a lovely breakfast?

Christopher bit into the bun and winced as he felt a piece of rock-hard rind pierce his gum. Should have brought a bottle of water, he thought, as he set about trying to unstick the bread from the roof of his mouth and chew it into a swallowable form.

Chapter 3

Breathy grunting sounded from the bushes behind Alison's seat, sending an icy chill through her. A flock of ducks took off down the park. She jumped up, grabbed her handbag and went to flee, but a rasping, puce-faced man flung himself into her path.

She screamed and clutched her bag tighter.

The man sucked in a toothy breath and reached for her with a clawed hand, his blood-shot eyes wild beneath a heavy brow.

'Get away from me,' she yelled in a booming voice she didn't recognise as her own. Her heart banged against her ribcage and her legs trembled as she grappled in her bag for her attack alarm. One firm squeeze set off its piercing siren.

The man lurched forward, his arms flailing around as he lumbered towards her, his eyes mad and drool running down his chin.

'Gerrof you perv,' she shouted, through chattering teeth.

The man's eyes widened. He turned his head and hacked out something brown onto the grass.

She tried to scream again, but this time no sound came out. In utter panic, she threw the alarm at him. It clipped his brow, rebounded off and ricocheted along the footpath.

He clapped his hand to his head and growled.

No, I've angered him. She wanted to run across the field to the safety of the footballers, but her feet were stuck to the concrete.

The alarm continued to scream from its resting position ten metres away. Her attacker staggered forward. Alison noticed he was clutching his chest. He stumbled towards the seat.

'Are you all right?' she asked, her voice tremulous.

The man shot the alarm a panicked look as he grappled for the arm of the bench. He emitted a wheeze through blue-tinged lips and nodded. 'Cor Blimey,' he gasped, flopping onto the seat, his chest heaving.

Alison immediately felt less afraid. Her father used to use that phrase. He hated profanities. 'Are you unwell?'

He shook his head.

'Sorry, I thought you were a pervy lurker, about to attack me.'

He gawped at her with horrified, round eyes and garbled something incomprehensible. Then he hacked up another gruesome chunk. 'No. Dear me, no.' He pulled a cotton handkerchief from his jacket pocket and wiped his brow and mouth. 'Excuse the spitting.'

His politeness surprised Alison. She noticed his sharp suit. 'Yes, I realise that now.'

The alarm continued to scream at an ear-perforating pitch. He shot it another, desperate look. 'Do you think –'

She hurtled over to retrieve it. 'Sorry,' she said, clicking it off and dropping it into her bag. The silence was almost audible. She turned, ready to apologise to anyone dashing to her aid – there was no one. The people dotted around must have heard; she could hear the boot of the football across the park, quiet compared to her alarm. She shuddered as she realized she'd ventured out and about for years, with the misapprehension that help was only ever an eye-watering siren away.

Alison turned back to the man, who looked ropey. 'Do you need medical help?' She held out her empty hand as if to offer an invisible lifeline of some sort.

The man drew in a deep breath and exhaled through pursed lips that had started to pink up. 'I feel *stupid*.'

'St Mary's hospital is opposite the park. Shall I help you over to Accident and Emergency? Or if you don't think you can walk, I'll call an ambulance.' Alison reached into her bag for her mobile.

He shot the bag a nervous glance. 'No. Honestly, I'm fine. Thank you.' He held out his hand. 'I'm –'

'Oh, sorry.' Alison took his hand with both of hers, planted one foot firmly behind the other and put her full body weight into trying to haul him to his feet.

The man resisted her efforts and remained on the bench, his face turning crimson. 'Oh heck.' He rested his elbows on his knees and buried his head in his hands.

Alison noticed his wedding ring. 'Shall I call your wife?'

He shook his head.

She leaned over, rested her own hands on her knees and peered at him, checking for signs of respiratory distress.

'Are you in pain? Can you speak?' She spoke in slow, measured tones. 'Tell. Me. Your. Name. Please.'

The man's shoulders started to shake.

Alison stepped back and glanced around, not knowing whether to leave a potentially poorly man, or stay only to discover he was dangerous after all.

He let out a hearty laugh then wiped his eyes and smiled up at her.

She noticed the colour, a striking green, flecked with hazel. There was something strangely familiar about them.

'I was about to introduce myself.' He stood up, straightened his suit jacket and offered Alison his hand again. 'Hello, I'm Christopher Barker. Thank you for trying to help me.'

'Oh, I see.' She blushed. He was taller than she expected. His handgrip was firm but gentle. 'Alison Riley, how do you do.'

'Sorry I scared you. And please forgive all that unseemly hacking. It was a piece of half-chewed bacon sandwich.'

Alison grimaced.

'You didn't need to know that disgusting bit of information…' Christopher looked at her, his eyes filled with mirth. 'I'm having a dreadful morning. Sandy, my wife, made me a bacon sandwich. But I have an appointment at the health centre, and I didn't have time to eat it. I didn't want to hurt her feelings, so I shot out of the house, thinking I'd save time if I ate it on the way. My car's in for an MOT today.'

Alison nodded in comprehension. 'Ah, I see. And that set off your angina?'

'Crikey, no.' He stood up taller. 'There's nothing wrong with me.'

'Sorry.'

'I was chewing and hurrying along the path when a piece of bacon got stuck in my windpipe. It was awful. My life flashed before me. I was doubled up behind those bushes where no one could see me, panicking at the realisation I was about to die a terrible death. I had to get out into the open in case I choked.'

'And that's when you stumbled out of the undergrowth, and I thought you were a pervert who'd been lying in wait.'

Christopher shook his head and held up both hands. 'I can assure you…'

Alison clapped her hand over her mouth and giggled. 'Yes, I know. But you have to admit, you were rasping on a bit… The bushes and the mad popping eyes… I didn't know what to think.' She broke off to guffaw.

He raked a hand through his hair as he watched her cackle. 'It's a wonder somebody didn't call the police. I could've been arrested. That alarm is rather… alarming.' He started laughing again. 'I'm going to buy my wife and daughter one each.'

'I wouldn't bother,' she cackled. 'It's rubbish. No one batted an eyelid. I'd have been on the evening news –

murdered in plain sight.' She wiped her eyes with the back of her hand. 'Actually, you've cheered me up. I've been to the medical centre myself this morning. What a debacle that was.'

Christopher checked his watch. 'I'd better crack on.' He smiled at her. 'Lovely to meet you, Alison.'

'I hope you're not seeing Dr Smedley,' she said, noticing how clean his teeth looked considering he had just eaten.

He gave her a wave as he set off towards the park exit. 'Practice nurse. It's only for a check-up for an insurance plan, nothing wrong with me. Cheerio.'

'Bye.' He did have rather lovely eyes.

The vitamin pills rattled in their over-sized container as Alison stepped out of the pharmacy onto the busy high street. The thought of having to return to the office without any understanding of why she'd been thinking like a psycho of late, or hope for a better night's sleep was depressing.

She consoled herself with the fact that she wasn't trapped in her job forever. In two years, she would be at university, picking up where she left off when she fell pregnant. It was more starting from scratch than resuming her studies. Alison didn't care. She loved studying and she would love being a physiotherapist. A flurry of excitement somersaulted in her stomach.

Alison smiled to herself. In two years, the twins would have graduated from university and she and Martin would have amassed enough money to pay for her course. Maybe she would sleep better, too. Feeling inspired, she decided to pop along to Henleys bank to withdraw some money to treat herself and Martin to fish and chips for tea. She could check the balance of the savings account while she was there. There were cashpoints dotted along the way, but she preferred the indoor type. She felt more secure inside the bank, with its heavy doors and real people.

After withdrawing money for the fish and chips, she found she couldn't access the savings account. Her login attempt failed – three times – resulting in getting locked out altogether. A fruitless conversation with an unhelpful bank clerk yielded nothing but a call centre telephone number. Martin liked dealing with that clerk, he reckoned he was on top of his game. Alison didn't. She thought there was something odd about the man – the substance on his hair and shifty look in his eyes. He reminded her of a dodgy second-hand car salesman.

There was no real need to check the account; she had kept a record of the savings since she received her first wage packet. At first, they had only been able to afford a couple of pounds a month, but as their earnings increased, so did the savings. Most of it came from Alison, as she liked to hunt for bargains so she could make extra deposits. Martin liked nice things. 'Buy cheap, buy twice,' he'd say, if she objected to the price of his Hugo Boss suits.

As she left the bank, she hitched her bag strap onto her shoulder and the container of pills clanked out onto the ground. A young lad in a scruffy grey tracksuit spied it rolling towards him. He drew on the cigarette hanging from his mouth and kicked the tub away, roaring, 'Goo-aal', with a jump and an air punch. Alison scurried after it, her outstretched hand just missing it as it disappeared beneath a display of fruit and vegetables outside the greengrocers.

'Sorry missus, I thought it was rubbish.'

She looked up to speak but tripped and landed on her hands and knees with a thud. He bent down as if to help her then thought better of it and scarpered.

By the time she'd retrieved the container, it was covered in a smelly gunge from something rotten and unidentifiable. The same goo had clagged to the knees of her trousers and a decaying cabbage stench had wrapped itself around her. If she'd wanted to harm Billy before, she'd have taken great pleasure in beating him senseless right now. Not one passer-by offered to help her.

Her knees and hands stinging, she hobbled back into the pharmacy for anti-septic wipes. Someone commented on a 'smell of drains' in the shop. She made the purchase without making eye contact and scuttled out of the shop. Once outside, she paused to clean her hands, gently picking out gravel from her palms, the antiseptic smarting as it seeped into the wounds.

Glancing up, Alison noticed she was outside Caffè Alessandro. She peered through the window, it looked vibrant and cosy at the same time. Despite his penchant for expensive clothes, Martin said Alessandro's was too pricey and the coffee bitter. He'd never been in, but to him, their Fairtrade products were leftovers after the giant, unethical companies had taken the best stuff. He had no such qualms about consuming expensive 'unethical' products.

Alison had planned to end up there, but not in this state. Taking out a fresh wipe, she scrubbed at the knees of her trousers. 'Sod it.' She rummaged in her bag, gave herself a generous blast of Chanel Chance and pushed open the door to Caffè Alessandro.

The warm, welcoming atmosphere immediately calmed her frazzled nerves. And by the time she had placed her order and tucked herself away at a table in the corner, she was able to see the funnier side of some of the morning's hideous events. The delicious aroma of fresh basil wafted up as the waitress set down her meal.

What a treat, she thought, dropping the few pennies change from a twenty-pound note into her purse. The buzz from the double-shot latte perked her right up. The first bite of the chicken and pesto baguette tasted like heaven, and never had she seen such luxurious caramel on shortbread.

Despite his criticism of the place, Alison knew Martin would love the baguette. Feeling inspired, she decided to pop into the bakery on her way back to work for a nice fresh bread stick. She'd make him one for his lunch the following day.

Martin could get a decent meal at work. Being a private school, the food at Saint Paul's primary was excellent and certainly a cut above state school dinners. But this would be a lovely treat for him.

She inspected the caramel shortbread – she might even make a tray of it that night – it would help to pass the time if she couldn't sleep. *If*, she thought with a wry smile. There was never an *if* about it.

When the children were young, the insomnia hadn't seemed such a big deal. In fact, once Chloe and Jack had finally fallen into an exhausted sleep, she had been glad of the extra time to get through the chores. At first, when they lived in the tiny flat above the Pizzeria, she couldn't do anything that made too much noise for fear of waking them. But getting the ironing and dusting out of the way was a great help.

They had loved that little flat at the start. Once the shock of the pregnancy and having to leave university had subsided, they set about creating a home. On weekends, they'd decorate or browse the second-hand shops in town, searching for furniture and ornaments to create a cosy haven. And then they'd snuggle up on the sofa with a pizza to watch a film on an old portable television. But once the twins were born, the reality of their situation set in. It wasn't nearly as much fun living on a shoestring, with crying babies, no sleep, and the stench of garlic and cheese permeating the whole place and everything in it.

At one point, she'd feared Martin might leave them. They were both sleep-deprived, but he struggled to stay on top of his studies. Though he'd kept on his room in the student residence for during the week, the constant crying affected his studies on the weekends. Alison knew the insomnia was a result of trying to cope alone with the babies all week, and then keep them quiet when Martin was home. She had somehow managed adjust – sort of. But he hadn't.

It was after a particularly nasty row, ending in him storming off with a holdall to his mother's house, that the insomnia ramped up. Two heartbroken days were enough to turn her into a nocturnal coiled spring, jumping from sleep to wide awake whenever one of the babies so much as whimpered.

Once they were married and in the new house, the enormous kitchen extension was the perfect place to escape. Far enough away from the bedrooms not to be heard, she could get on with whatever took her fancy. Because she was working, being wide awake in the middle of the night was a godsend. And the only window of time she could get to fit in an odd Pilates routine.

Mostly it was chores, rather than a downward dog stretch she busied herself with. She couldn't otherwise have held down a full-time job and look after her family. And that job enabled them to take on the sizeable mortgage loan for their house in Farnby Close.

'Eugh… What's that smell?' said a voice nearby.

Alison's heart sank. A shifty side-glance revealed two elderly ladies, veering away from the next table and across the room – one of them, to Alison's mortification, openly nipping her nose.

Desperate to escape unnoticed, she scanned the immediate area. If only she had sat near the door. Pretending to stoop down to retrieve a serviette, she surreptitiously grabbed her perfume and spritzed it over her knees. She should have dashed home to shower. It was too late now. For a moment, she contemplated calling in sick, then dismissed it. That would be wrong. Besides, there was an important team meeting with their service manager later. They had to decide where to place the QC code on the patient feedback cards. She had spent the previous Sunday afternoon making dummy cards to practice, to make them user friendly for someone with an injury or vision impairment. Her stomach churned at the prospect of going into work stinking of drains.

She wrapped the caramel shortbread in a serviette and

checked the way out was clear. Glancing out of the window, she saw Christopher from the park striding towards Henleys Bank. Despite her current unbecoming plight, the sight of him powering along the street, straight-backed and confident, after his earlier stumbling, made her smile. He carried himself with an air of authority.

There was nothing pervy about him. A flush of embarrassment warmed her cheeks.

With his dark, grey-flecked hair, Christopher reminded her a little of Martin. He was self-conscious about his grey, but Alison loved it. They both suited a well-cut suit, though Martin wore his better, thanks to his daily gym workouts. She felt a fuzzy warmth in her tummy. Twenty-two years together and they still loved each other. Few people could count themselves so lucky these days.

Christopher made a sudden detour towards Alessandro's.

Crap. She crouched down and pretended to busy herself with the shortbread and her bag.

He flung open the door and marched towards the counter.

After another glance around, she stole away. 'Phew,' she said, as she scarpered past the window, momentarily relieved to have escaped unseen by Christopher. She checked the time. The stomach churning returned. Her only option was to get to work and try to sort herself out the best she could with soap and water in the toilets.

As Alison turned back along the street, she remembered the little boutique on the corner. They had a customer toilet. Perfect, she thought. She'd clean herself up and buy a smart new pair of trousers.

'What a thoroughly awful morning,' she muttered to herself as she hurried towards the boutique. Christopher's eyes popped into her mind. Well, maybe not *all* of it, she thought, with a little smile.

Chapter 4

Christopher watched the health care assistant mouth the words as she wrote. A yellow name badge pinned to her tunic said, *Hello, my name is Beverley*, in a black jaunty font. He thought she looked more the cheesed-off than jaunty type.

She arched an eyebrow. 'You work in a bank? No doubt you'll be slouched at a desk all day.'

Christopher sat up straighter. 'No, not at all,' he said, wondering if he had misheard her.

She pressed her lips into a straight line and glanced at him out of the corner of her eye. 'Your body mass index is twenty-nine.'

It sounded like an accusation. 'Is that bad?'

Beverley spun around in her chair and pointed to a wall chart.

He could see that twenty-nine hovered between the overweight and obese categories. 'Is it true that if you're over six feet tall, those charts aren't accurate?'

Beverley spoke in a flat tone. 'Can you grab handfuls of fat from your torso?'

Christopher gingerly picked up and dropped a generous handful of something he cared not to classify. 'Yes, but –'

She gave a swift nod. 'That's why your blood pressure and blood sugar levels are raised. You're becoming insulin resistant

– borderline diabetic.'

It was like something his mother used to say to him. 'Christopher Barker, you've become cheeky and impudent. Go to your room. You're grounded.'

She tapped her pen on the desk. 'If you don't want to end up on medication for the rest of your life, you need to lose weight.'

Christopher noticed the red rings around her upper arms where her uniform cuffs had cut into her flesh. 'Beverley are you trying to scare me?' he said, in an attempt to lighten the sombre atmosphere.

She looked momentarily taken aback on hearing her name, then regained her air of superiority. 'No. I'm being honest. You're at risk of a heart attack or stroke. Do you realise diabetes can lead to amputations?'

Christopher stared at her, flabbergasted.

'I didn't think so,' she said with a jab of her pen in his direction.

Her fingers reminded him of the gigantic maggots in an old *Dr Who* episode. He found himself transfixed at the way her double chin puffed out a third one, as she dipped her head when she wrote. He wondered if *she* was insulin resistant. 'Surely I'm not that unhealthy? *Am I?*'

She shot him a non-plussed look, then air-tapped the pen at him again. 'You came here to find out why you don't feel well, and I am telling you.'

'I didn't. I needed a check-up to renew my life insurance policy.'

Sandy had recently been on at him about his lack of energy, but he wouldn't tell Beverly that. He hadn't been concerned; it was normal to have a period of stress whenever he moved into a struggling branch to troubleshoot the problems. This job was a doddle compared to those he usually had to tackle. The difference this time was that he wasn't working away from home, so Sandy had noticed.

Beverley scribbled on a form. 'I'll refer you to *Healthy Choices*.'

'What's that?'

'It's our twelve-week diet and exercise programme.' She spun to the right and pointed to a poster. A group of tubby people in baggy track suit bottoms and T-shirts stepped out as they high fived the air, wide smiles fixed on their faces. 'With commitment from you,' she pointed the pen at him again, 'it might be possible to undo some damage.'

Christopher wanted to snap the pen. 'Would you mind not pointing that at me, please?'

Beverly pursed her lips and plonked it onto the desk. 'It's up to you to take responsibility for yourself.' She pointed a maggot finger at him. 'No one can do it for you.' She reached into the desk drawer and pulled out a small box and pushed it across to him. Blood pressure machine. Four times a day. Fill in the card – instructions in the box.'

If a member of his staff spoke to a customer the way this woman was speaking to him, they'd receive a verbal warning. He would have expected the health service to ensure frontline staff had undergone communication skills training before letting them loose on the public.

'No, thank you.' He stood up and looked her up and down. 'You obviously don't think it's worth doing. I'll explore other avenues.'

Christopher strode out with as much dignity as he could muster, given his humiliation. He wasn't used to being reprimanded. Up until that disastrous morning, he had always commanded respect in both his private and professional life. As he passed through the entrance vestibule, he stopped at the feedback booth. He tapped the unhappy red face. A question flashed onto the screen asking if he would recommend the practice to his friends or family. 'No, I blinking-well would not.'

He stormed across the car park and onto the high street,

cursing Beverley under his breath. Then he caught his reflection in a shop window and had to do a double take – he looked like he was wearing a fat suit. Before going into the surgery, he hadn't thought for one moment they'd find anything wrong with him. Clearly, there was something very wrong – he was a fat, lazy flump; a stroke waiting to happen. And if Beverley had her way, he'd be a one-legged flump for good measure.

Alison's concerned face flashed into his mind. He cringed – no wonder she thought he was having an angina attack. If only he had choked in front of someone less attractive. His pride plummeted to an all-time low.

He paused on the corner next to the Post Office while he came to terms with his overnight transformation from fit to decrepit. He was a trouble-shooter by profession, trained to seek out and resolve problems. *How had he allowed this to happen?*

'Hello, Mr Barker,' said a wobbly voice.

He looked around to find an old lady, walking towards him with a tartan shopping trolley. 'Good morning,' he said, conjuring up a cheery smile. Christopher didn't know her name but had seen her in the bank. He was touched she knew his. 'Are you off shopping?'

'After I've collected my pension. I hope there isn't a queue.'

'Would you like me to walk down with you and show you how to use the cashpoint machine?' He spoke slowly and offered his arm for her to link. 'It's quicker than going to the counter.'

She shot him a fierce look. 'No thank you. I'm not stupid. You can't trust those things. They put cloning devices in them during the night.'

'Sorry,' he said in a business-like tone, inwardly chiding himself for patronising her. It had to be the discombobulating effects of his shenanigan of a morning. 'Ours are secure. They undergo rigorous checks.'

'I'd rather queue.' She started to rumble off, then stopped

and turned towards him. 'Mind you, I hope that bloke with the greasy hair's not on the counter.'

Christopher assumed that she was talking about Frank Budle. He was rather heavy-handed with the hair gel. 'Rest assured, you can trust the team at Henleys. They're a grand bunch.'

'He's got a shifty look about him, that one. And that wife of his… disgraceful. Can't wait to swipe your house from you.'

He had no idea what she could mean and thought it best not to ask. 'It's a beautiful morning, isn't it?'

She narrowed her eyes at the sky. A cloud scudded across it. 'No, it's going to rain. I'd better get a move on,' she said, trundling away.

Christopher wondered what it was about Frank's hair that women disliked. Shirley, his secretary, had said something similar. He checked his own hair in his reflection in the Post Office window but was distracted by the chunkiness of his neck. Worse than that… *Where the devil had his cheek bones gone?*

As he continued to work, the sign for Earlby Family Undertakers caught his eye. His mind wandered back to Doug Lancaster's funeral the previous month. Doug was the first of his old university rugby team to die. When he thought back to the wake, he realised that most of the gang had thicker necks than they'd had at university. They had all agreed Doug must have had dodgy genes. But what if he hadn't? thought Christopher. Any one of them could be heading for a premature death. And if Beverley got her wish, he would lose a leg along the way.

Distracted by his newfound ill-health, he stepped out into the road without checking. The blast of a car horn sent him racing to the other side. He stood on the pavement, his lungs burning and blood pinballing around his body. Two careless, near-death experiences in one morning. He was in a bad way for a man in his early forties.

Enough was enough, he decided. He would tackle his health

with a strategic approach, like he would any other project. He had resolved trickier problems than this one in his time. Feeling more positive, he strode on in confidence. And the next time he choked in front of a pretty lady, at least he would look good, not decrepit.

He would turn this around in no time at all, starting with an overhaul of his diet. Then he would implement and exercise programme. Once he had made a plan, there would be no going back. As he passed the bakery, a delicious aroma of freshly baked pastries hit him. Before he knew it, he had made a sharp turn and was heading towards Alessandro's. Well, he thought, it couldn't harm to devise a plan of action over one last tasty treat.

The counter assistant gave Christopher her usual cheerful greeting and reached for a plate. 'You're in early today. Ham, cheese and pesto panini, cinnamon swirl and a cappuccino with extra chocolate?'

'Yes, please.' He might as well, it would save him returning at lunchtime. Beverley's face flashed into his mind. 'No. I think I'll have a change.'

The assistant's eyebrows shot up to her hairline.

Was he so predictable? He perused the contents of the food in the chiller cabinet. 'I see you have the calorie and carbohydrate values on the labels. Is it a new initiative?'

She glanced down at the copious selection of savoury and sweet fare and shrugged. 'No, they've always been there.'

So predictable he had never bothered to look in the cabinet. He pulled in his stomach. Little wonder his weight had crept up. He couldn't remember the last time he'd considered the composition of food. But looking at the choice available, he suspected he might have been consuming an entire day's calories for lunch. When did portions become so huge? Concluding that there wasn't anything for someone with high blood pressure and borderline diabetes, he stuck with his panini and decided to sort out a proper plan later. If he was to change his eating habits, he might also have to look for an alternative venue. 'Strike that, I'll have my usual after all.'

The assistant nodded and laughed.

Christopher noticed that she had already picked out his regular panini. When had he become an old stick-in-the-mud? Drastic action was called for. 'But I'll have it to go, please.' There, he thought – a change. A small one, but better than nothing.

The assistant leaned towards him and lowered her voice. 'Do you think it smells okay in here today?' She wrinkled her nose. 'There was an unpleasant smell around before.'

'I noticed a bit of a whiff when I came in – I assumed it must be the parmesan.'

'We think it was a customer. A woman – she snuck out.'

Christopher sniffed the air. 'It's fine now.'

'Good.' She handed him his order. 'See you tomorrow.'

He stood outside Alessandro's, his food in an array of paper bags and his cappuccino in a disposable cup. He preferred not to eat meals at his desk and using the staffroom wasn't an option. When he was a graduate trainee, his old boss used to have lunch with the rest of the team. 'If you don't get yourself into the staffroom from the start, you'll never be able to venture in there,' he'd said. But they all hated it. Christopher made it a rule not to intrude – his staff were entitled to relax on their breaks.

The word 'his' took him by surprise. The Earlby Street posting felt different from the start. At first, he'd assumed it was because he was able to live at home, rather than in a faceless hotel, in a city he didn't belong. But he was enjoying the role of manager there, now that just about everything was sorted and the branch was running efficiently. At one time, he'd have balked at settling for the restriction of a manager post. It had only been two months, but this time it felt like his branch and his team.

He headed back into Cherry Park, his usually razor-sharp mind full of jumbled thoughts about his health and career. Perhaps fresh air would help, he thought, wandering over to a bench near the football pitch. It was only ten-thirty, but he tucked into his food, anyway. He watched the local school team practice and thought back to his own school days. He'd been like those youngsters, bombing up and down the field, taking his youthful fitness for granted. Who'd have thought he'd become a chunky, middle-aged bloke in a boring work suit who had to eat his meals from a paper bag on a park bench?

There was a *whoosh,* followed by a tartan and white blur hurtling past. 'Crikey.' Christopher stared at his empty hand, as the blur shot off across the park, his panini hanging from its mouth.

A man in winter clothes appeared in the entrance to the path leading up from Cherry Dene, shouting, 'Angus, where did you get that? Get back here now.'

Angus stopped in his tracks and wolfed down the panini, before the man reached him.

'Well, that's that then,' said Christopher. He held onto the cinnamon swirl with two hands and did a bit of wolfing himself, this time keeping his eyes peeled. As he wiped flakes of pastry from his mouth, he felt a twinge of guilt – no wonder he was borderline diabetic.

He decided on a brisk walk around the park before going into work. Another spontaneous action – he was on a roll. By the time he had completed one circuit and was heading towards the exit, he was clammy and huffing and puffing more than he would have liked. He was rubbing his sternum to quell the acidic rift from the cinnamon swirl when a football came speeding through the air towards him. Without missing a beat, he took aim and booted it back. He felt exhilarated.

'Thanks, mister,' called one of the young players.

Christopher acknowledged the lad with the confident wave

of a man who knew his way around a football pitch.

There was life in him yet. He wondered when he'd started to let himself go. He enjoyed good food, but it also served a purpose, fuelling him to work hard. He and Sandy had a grand life – a house on the exclusive Naunton Hall estate, platinum golf memberships at the Ackley club, not to mention a villa in Portugal, an apartment in Durham and luxury holidays abroad. Admittedly, Sandy and Emily benefitted more than he did, due to work taking him away for much of the time. He felt his stomach with the flat of his hand. *But when had he lost his abs?*

Crisis management was what he excelled in – he'd tackled trickier problems than middle-aged spread. And he liked a fresh challenge. He picked up his step. Despite the rubbish morning, he felt more inspired than he had for some time.

Ten minutes later, a smiling, rosy-cheeked Christopher walked into the bank vestibule feeling like a new man. He inhaled the fragrance of the wood. There weren't many of the old banks left, most having been sold off for conversion into trendy bars. He looked up at the high ceiling and admired the well-preserved ornate coving and original brass light fittings. Yes, he thought, there was something different about this branch.

Or perhaps it was he who had changed. Whatever the reason, for the first time since leaving university, he wasn't eager to push on to the next project. This place didn't feel like an assignment. It felt like home. He grinned as the seeds of an idea began to form in his mind.

Chapter 5

Alison stepped out of the clothes shop in a pair of black, what she could only describe as, *slacks*. She had already had two static shocks while paying for them at the metal-edged cash desk, and one on the way out when she touched the door handle. Glancing up at the shop sign, she wondered when the trendy little boutique had become The Nylon Shop.

She spotted Christopher heading towards Henleys Bank and wondered if he worked there. She'd heard the old manager had retired. He didn't see her, no doubt deep in concentration, like Martin, constantly chewing over work projects.

Alison was immensely proud of her husband, whose dedication to his work had earned him a deputy head teacher position before the age of forty. His commitment was one of the things she admired most about him. He was also an excellent provider, and it was thanks to him that they enjoyed a very comfortable standard of living. Not that she held too much store in material things – she was happy if they could pay the bills, anything more was a bonus.

She, on the other hand, knew she'd coasted along in her career for years and often felt as if she was letting them down. Her job was a means to an end. Things would have been different if she'd finished university, but she hadn't. She smiled to herself – not yet anyway.

As Alison turned the corner to Trafalgar Place, her good mood waned. By the time she had climbed the steps to the main entrance, a cloud of doom had descended on her. She sighed and walked inside.

When the Patient Experience Department had first moved down the road from St Mary's Hospital to the old town hall site, she'd loved it. Unlike the hospital – a bland nineteen sixties concrete block – this building was beautiful. It oozed history and tradition, especially in the entrance hall, with its high ceilings and oak fixtures. A master crafted reception desk took pride of place, complete with its original brass call bell. Alison couldn't get enough of the smell in the entrance hall, a unique mixture of wood and stone, reminiscent of an old university or museum.

But everything changed with the arrival of Billy Chapman. Now she dreaded coming into the place.

The ground floor lift doors dinged open and Ashley, the Patient Services Manager, stepped out.

'Alison,' he said, his tone betraying a touch of surprise. 'You *are* here.'

'Yes, I am.' It seemed like a silly thing to say, but she couldn't think of anything more appropriate.

'You didn't send your apologies.'

'No, I'll be at the team meeting this afternoon.'

'This morning.'

She felt herself go hot. 'No, my email said this afternoon.'

'The meeting was this morning. Billy asked for the time to be rescheduled.'

'I didn't receive notification –'

Ashley shot her a sceptical look. 'Everyone else was there.'

'I'm so disappointed, I had an idea about where the QC code could go on the patient feedback card –'

'We got it sorted.' He started to walk away. 'Check your inbox next time.'

In her mind's eye, Alison reached for Billy's throat.

She stepped into the lift and thumped the button to the second floor, sending a bolt of static zapping up her arm. Her hand was still throbbing as the lift came to a standstill. The doors opened to reveal Peggy, the cleaner, singing at the top of her voice as she mopped the corridor floor. There was another crack of static energy as she stepped out and brushed the metal lift frame.

Peggy started in surprise. 'What was that?'

Alison rubbed her arm. 'Did you hear it? I got an electric shock.'

Peggy rummaged in her trolley and ambled over with a wet cloth. She opened the doors and proceeded to dab all the metal parts that her four-foot-nine-inch frame allowed her to reach.

'You know, Peggy, if there was anything wrong with the electrics, touching it with that wet cloth could be dangerous.'

'Yes, Julie, Angela–, oh heck erm, thingamabob…' She tapped the air with her index finger. 'Alison! But it's a good test.' She cackled. 'You'd soon find out if it was faulty.'

An image of a blue-lipped Peggy lying dead on the corridor floor flashed into Alison's mind. She couldn't remember from mandatory training whether it was safe to touch someone who had received an electric shock. Did that require wellies? she wondered. Or was that if they were lying in a pool of water? What if the wet cloth was still in her hand?

Katie would know. She project-managed the training videos used throughout the hospital. Like Billy, Alison met Katie when she started at St Mary's. Unlike Billy, Katie had gone on to become a dear friend. Now it was only Katie and another friend, Sharon, who made coming to work bearable.

Peggy had another root in her trolley. Alison spied a wooden door chock in a box of bits and pieces. She hoped Peggy had removed it from somewhere and wasn't planning to use it. The fire officers went ballistic when they found a door wedged open. She returned with a can of air freshener and sprayed inside the lift.

'Some people stink, don't they, hinny?' She sniffed around Alison and wrinkled her nose. 'My God, the stench is clinging to you…'

The sound of a raised voice from the office interrupted them. Alison dashed towards the ruckus, followed by Peggy who, for someone with such short legs, was pretty nifty.

Billy was leaning over Sharon's desk, his glasses perched on top of his head. They couldn't hear what he was saying to her, but Sharon was glaring at him in contempt. He reached for the phone handset. She batted the phone, along with its cable across the room. A junior clerk screamed as it thwacked off the side of her desk.

'They should sack you for that,' said Phyllis Cheery in her scratchy voice, her mousey corkscrew hair rocking from side to side like a car dashboard dog.

Phyllis, a recent addition to the team, had taken a dislike to most people in the office, except Billy. She had tried to get along with Phyllis, but she couldn't find a single redeeming quality about the woman. She seemed to relish causing havoc, enjoying nothing better than twisting the knife Billy had plunged into someone.

She heard the distant crack of bubble gum and Billy's conceited words echoing down the years – 'If you and I went for the same job, I'd swipe it from under your nose. I'll be your boss one day.'

And there he was, Billy Chapman, her boss.

'What on earth is going on?' said Alison. She strode over to her desk and dumped her bag on it. The tub of vitamins rattled.

Phyllis shot the bag a suspicious glare, her eyebrows, set only millimetres apart when wearing a relaxed expression, now merged into a unibrow.

Billy looked over and smiled. 'Hello, hope you got sorted out this morning.'

So sly.

Peggy peered up at Alison, her eyes wide with intrigue.

He wandered over, his smile changing to a sneer when only she could see. 'What've you got in there? Maracas?'

Alison turned her head away in disgust as his fishy breath caressed her face.

Phyllis had sidled over to earwig.

'Why didn't you tell me about the meeting?'

'You should pay more attention.'

'I know you did it deliberately.'

'Prove it,' he whispered.

A giggle sounded from behind Billy. He shot around. 'Oh, bloody hell, Phyllis. Go away.'

Phyllis traipsed off to her desk, her head down and shoulders hunched. She slumped onto her chair and sat looking daggers at the other women.

'You can't say things like that,' hissed Alison.

'Why not?'

'It's abuse. And anyway,' she whispered, 'there's clearly something *wrong* with her.'

Billy looked from Phyllis to Alison. 'What the hell are you on about? She's got a degree. Geography, but still… There's nowt *wrong* with her, stupid.'

Alison glanced at Phyllis, who was glaring at her, an evil glint in her eye. 'Really?'

He swaggered off to his office, clearly pleased with himself.

Alison turned to Sharon. 'What happened?'

He'd just eaten a tuna sandwich. It was all over his hands and he was purposely trying to pick up my phone because he knows I hate tuna.

'It's harassment,' Alison said, logging on to check her emails.

'Don't be ridiculous,' chimed Phyllis. 'You're making that up, I was here.'

The email facility was set up to show a list of messages down the left-hand side of the screen, with a preview on the right, making it easy to scroll down and read them without having to click on them. As she searched for the one that Ashley insisted she had received, a new message pinged in from Billy.

Ha ha ha. You and your mates are idiots. And you're the worst of the lot of them.

She gasped and looked over to Billy's office. The door was ajar. He was pointing at her with the arm of his glasses, laughing. He's the idiot, she thought. Now she had proof he was a bully. Smiling, she tried to save it, but he recalled it before she had the chance.

'Oh no.'

Billy wandered out of his office and along the corridor to the beverage bay, whistling 'The Winner Takes It All.'

'I shouldn't have to put up with this,' muttered Alison.

Phyllis unlocked her desk drawer and took out a tiny food storage box. She unclipped the lid, picked out one brazil nut, and for the next ten minutes stared at her computer screen, nibbling the nut and chuckling.

Alison tried to block out Phyllis's squirrel-like gnawing and get on with her work. Only two more years. Perhaps then she'd love her job too, like Katie and Martin.

Billy stomped along the corridor to his office, ensuring everyone knew he was back.

'Idiots,' said Alison under her breath.

Phyllis shot her a crazy-eyed look, then turned back to swoon at Billy's office door.

Two short years.

An eternity.

Chapter 6

Christopher stood at his office window, watching the busy high street below as he waited for Sandy to pick up.

Shirley tiptoed in, placed a cup of weak milky coffee and a Hobnob biscuit on his desk, then crept back out. He waved his thanks. She was having terrible trouble accepting his top-of-the range coffee machine. He'd wait until she left her desk then nip along to the beverage bay to dispose of it. He peered at the undissolved granules floating on top of the insipid liquid.

'Hello…'

'Sandy, I'm pre-diabetic and hypertensive and—'

A gasp sounded down the line. 'Oh, my God. Did they keep you at the health centre? Are you all right?'

'What? No, I'm fine. Sorry, listen—'

'What is it then? I've got to meet Emily to show her the sample invitations.'

'Didn't they go out ages ago?' Christopher spotted Frank Budle leaving the building and wondered why he was going for lunch at three in the afternoon, for the second time that week.

'Did you hear what I said?'

'Oh, sorry. Yes – more invitations.'

'No, those were the save-the-day cards. Why did you call?'

'Right, yes. I wanted to run an idea by you. But it can wait until tonight if you have to lea—'

'Is it about Barbados? She gave a little squeal of delight. 'You booked it, didn't you?'

'Barbados?' *What the heck had she said about Barbados?*

'I knew you weren't listening. I'm just white noise to you, Chris. No wonder I'm looking for a therapist.'

'I thought you wanted to go to Mexico. Hang on… a therapist?'

There was a pause, then Sandy laughed. 'Sorry, love. Yes, we changed it to Mexico.'

'Anyway, it's not about Mexico either.' There was no way he could take time off in June if they were to go to Portugal for a fortnight in July. 'Look, you're busy, we can talk tonight. And you can tell me about the therapist.'

'Never mind about that. What's your idea? But can you hurry up.'

His enthusiasm had waned. He ran his hand over the polished surface of his desk as if to glean some support. 'How would you feel if I were to change my role? If it meant I'd be able to live at home full-time?'

Silence.

'Are you still there?'

'What do you mean by "change your role"?'

'This branch is almost sorted. All it needs is a new manager.'

Sandy gave an impatient sigh. 'Chris, would you get to the point? You know I can't be doing with work stuff.'

'I am. I would like to apply for the post myself. What do you think?'

The sound of a sharp intake of breath.

'I know, it would be great wouldn't it. I'll never have to go away again.'

'A branch manager? Why the hell would you want to be a *manager*?'

'What's wrong with that?'

'It's a downgrade, for one. And secondly, how would we live on a manager's salary?'

'The salary package is competitive. Admittedly, it's less than my current one. But I earn way above what we need. Just think, we'd finally live together full-time.'

Quiet sobs sounded down the line.

'Sandy, what the heck? I thought you'd be happy.'

'But I love our home. Don't you? I don't want to move.'

Christopher's tone softened. 'We won't have to. This would be a wonderful thing. I'll explain it all when I get home tonight. But don't fret.' He gave a little laugh to lighten the atmosphere. 'You'll still have your John Lewis account.'

Silence.

'Honestly, love… You won't even notice the difference. I promise. Sandy…?'

The line was dead.

Chapter 7

The dining table was strewn with paper, a calculator, a laptop and the caramel shortbread from Alessandro's. Alison sipped coffee and waited impatiently for Martin to return home from his workout.

She heard him sneeze as he turned the key in the lock and dashed out to greet him. She flung her arms around him and planted a big kiss on his lips.

He turned away to sneeze again 'Has that filthy animal been in here again?'

'I've missed you too, darling,' she laughed. 'Sammy was waiting on the doorstep to say hello when I got home.' As Alison went to close the door, she spotted the neighbour's ginger tabby, watching from beneath the garden hedge. She Suppressed a giggle. He loved her, but for some reason no one could fathom, he'd arch his back and hiss whenever he saw Martin. To make matters worse, Martin was allergic to cats, especially tabbies.

'I'm going to get some lion's poo. That'll scare the little sod away.'

'You're not – it'll stink. He knows you don't like him.'

Martin dropped his gym bag on the floor and draped his jacket over the banister. 'Anyway, why are you in such a great mood tonight?' He kissed her cheek. 'Good day?'

Alison picked up the jacket and hung it in the coat cupboard under the stairs. 'No, it's been bloody awful. Dr Smedley was a waste of space, and Billy was horrible, as usual. But it spurred me into action, and I think I've cracked it.'

He wandered into the kitchen and opened the fridge. 'Fancy a cold one?'

She sat down and beckoned him over. 'No thanks. Come and see, I've got it all worked out.'

'I haven't seen you this enthusiastic about anything for ages, it must be good.' He studied her face. 'You're pretty when you smile.'

She scrunched up a ball of paper and aimed it at him. 'So, I'm not normally?'

'You're as gorgeous as the day we met in the Student's Union bar.' He kissed the top of her head and stole a bite of the caramel shortbread. 'This is divine. You can always tell when they use good-quality ingredients.'

She gave a wry smile. 'Indeed.'

'Do I have one?'

'Sorry, it was left over from a café in town.' She pushed the plate over. 'You have the rest.'

He pulled out a seat, popped the remaining shortbread into his mouth and washed it down with her coffee. 'If I was single and saw you in town, I'd ask you out straight away. Would you say yes?' He opened his can and took a long drink. 'Ah, that's hit the spot.'

Alison eyed his caramel-coated teeth. 'Hmm, maybe.'

'Only maybe?'

'Well, I'd wonder what was wrong with you to be single at your age,' she laughed.

'Hadn't found the right woman yet. Anyway, what is it you've worked out?'

'Well, after the Smedley debacle, I met a scary man in the park, and I fell down. And then –'

Martin clunked the can down and shot over to her. He

hugged her so hard he squeezed the breath out of her. 'Are you all right? Oh my God, what did he do? Did you get the police? Why didn't you call me? I'll kill the pervert.'

Alison giggled. 'Nothing. He was fine.'

'What were you doing in the park alone?'

She rolled her eyes. 'I'm allowed, it's a *park*...You didn't let me finish. I was so frustrated after Smedley practically dismissed me, I went for a walk to calm down. The man, Christopher Somebody-or-other, jumped out from the bushes, and I thought he was going to attack me.'

Martin's face clouded. 'What the hell was he doing in the bushes?'

Alison held up her hand. 'No, listen. He was choking on a bacon sandwich on the footpath. I fell after I came out of the Pharmacy and a lad kicked my vitamins away –'

'Vitamins?' He returned to his seat and took another drink.

'Dr Smedley prescribed them to stop me from killing Billy Chapman. He also told me I was going through the perimenopause.'

Martin spluttered on his lager.

'I know...' She grabbed a dishcloth and cleaned up the mess. 'I fell in some rotten vegetable gunge which added to the rubbish morning.'

His shoulders shook as he laughed. 'Oh, Ali, bless you. You don't need vitamins – not with the amazing meals you cook. Your problem is that you're too nice. That's why bullies like Billy take advantage. You've bottled everything up and ended up wanting to kill the dickhead.'

'Well, anyway... By the time I got to work, Sharon was kicking off at Billy for being a prat. He ended up saying I was the worst out of everyone. I wasn't even there when it all started.'

Martin looked at her with a puzzled expression. 'So why are you so happy?'

She held up a dogeared notebook. 'I couldn't check the

savings account balance at the bank, but I keep a running total in my book –'

'I don't know why you have that old thing. Not with online banking.'

'Just as well I do – my login didn't work. I've got to call the helpline.'

Martin waved his hand in dismissal. 'No need, I'll check for you.'

'It's all in here. Nearly twenty years' worth. But I can do the techie stuff, too.' She turned the laptop screen to show him a spreadsheet.

He scanned the document. 'What am I looking at?'

'Our predicted income and outgoings. Billy was the last straw. The prospect of being stuck in that office for another two years… It was overwhelming.'

'Can't you get another post, or transfer to a different office?' He pointed to a column. 'No need to worry about the twins' university fees, we've got them accounted for, remember?'

'Not theirs – mine.' She grinned in satisfaction and pointed to a column detailing the total remaining after all expenditure.'

Martin examined the screen. 'But these figures will be out of date when it's time to apply for a place.'

'I've been going through the household and savings accounts, and we can afford –'

Martin looked at her without moving, barring a flex of the tiny muscle in his jaw. 'What do you mean "you've been *going through* them"?'

She pushed a sheet of A-four paper his way, on which she'd plotted a timeline. 'I've worked out dates for major bills and fees and set them against your salary and our savings. If we tighten our belts a little…' Alison could barely contain her glee, 'I can go to university this September.' She watched him for a response, her hands clasped together and her eyes round and shining. 'I'm treating us to fish and chips to celebrate.'

Martin shot her a worried glance. 'But you said you haven't

even checked the actual balance.'

'I did try. I spoke to that greasy clerk. He's the one who told me to call customer services.'

'And did you?'

'Yes, but I failed security clearance – they said I got the answer to my favourite place wrong.'

'Filey – the caravan site you used to go to with your parents.'

'Exactly. The lad insisted I must have changed it at some point – which I haven't. Anyway, it's reset, but I had another call come in, so I got distracted. I'll check tomorrow.'

'You'll never get on the course this year. We're into February, entry will be closed.'

Alison gave an excited squeak. 'It isn't. I've had a look at the online form.'

Martin drummed his fingers on the table and perused the list of figures. Then he gently took hold of her hands. 'But why rush? It's only a couple more years. Does it really make that much difference? We could have another nice holiday first. Or at least get the driveway done, before we lose your income.'

She pulled her hands away. 'Martin, what's wrong with you? We've already saved nearly thirty thousand pounds for my fees. We'd hardly be poor – you know fine well we could live comfortably on your income. It's three years, and then I'll be earning again.'

'But why *now*?'

'I'm struggling' She threw her hands up in exasperation. 'It was always the plan – our plan.'

Martin caressed her cheek. 'When the twins got through university.'

'Because that's when we thought we'd have the money.' Alison was desperate to make Martin understand. He wasn't usually so slow on the uptake. 'We can afford it now.'

'The plan was later, not right now. Another year or two won't make much difference, but it would mean we'd be more financially able to withstand the loss.'

'I can't bear it at work any longer. It's awful. Billy Chapman is intolerable. He hates me.'

'But there are arseholes in every workplace. Do you want to have to scrimp out an existence because of an office idiot?'

She stared at him in disbelief. 'We can afford it. I don't understand why you're creating obstacles.'

Martin turned back to her calculations. His eyebrows shot up to his hairline. 'You've cut down the holiday fund by two hundred pounds a month.'

'Don't you think three, four-star holidays abroad every year is excessive? Especially if I have to go through misery to pay for them?'

He clicked his tongue against the back of his teeth. 'It's risky with the twins at university.'

'As you said, their fees are accounted for. Martin, we've been saving since the day I started work. We've got pots and savings accounts for everything. We're bloody experts at saving. We've got more than enough.'

'But to lose your salary.'

'What are you talking about? How was I ever going to return to university without losing my salary? We agreed - you build your career first, and then I start mine. The way you're going on, you'd think I came up with the idea on a whim.'

Martin watched Alison fetch a can of lager from the fridge. 'I thought you didn't want a drink?'

She opened it and took a swig. 'Well, I do now.' She leaned against the worktop and raked her hand through her hair. 'Look, the sooner I qualify, the sooner I get on to the career ladder and pay-scale. It's not as if we'll starve. There are entire families living off a hell of a lot less than what you earn.

His tone had an irritated edge to it. 'Are you even sure you want to go ahead with this course?'

Alison's eyes widened. '*This course?*'

'Could you be looking at the past through rose-tinted glasses?' He moved over to her and slipped his arms around her waist. 'I mean, things always seem better in hindsight. It was a different time back then. We were different people, kids really. Now we're grown-ups.'

Alison sighed. 'I'm not stupid. It's not as if I want to whoop it up in the student union bar like a teenager.'

'Now you're being silly,' said Martin in his teacher's voice.

'Well, you're treating me like I don't know my own mind. And as if you didn't sit down with me when I was pregnant and *promise me*, that if I gave up my course, you'd help me return to it as soon as I could.' She freed herself from his embrace and slumped down at the table. 'Anyway, teaching's changed since you were a student, but you're still a teacher.'

'Deputy head.' He pressed his lips into a flat line. 'Anyway, that's different. I never left. I stuck it out and built a career.'

Alison looked at her husband, barely recognising him. 'You didn't *stick it out*. You got to stay because *I* was the one pregnant with *our* babies, not you.'

He rubbed his face with both hands. 'I'm sorry – this is coming out all wrong. I want you to be happy in your work. And I do appreciate what you sacrificed for our family.'

'It's physiotherapy I'm returning to. University is a means to get there. I don't understand. What's changed?'

'Well, to be honest, I thought you might not bother. People always talk about what they wish they'd done with their lives, but most wouldn't change anything even if they could.'

She felt tears prick the back of her eyes. 'Do you even *know* me?'

'I just need to get my head around it.'

Alison leaned back in her seat, gutted. 'I had another idea, about earning a bit of money. I'm not sure I want to share it with you after the way you've reacted.'

He looked at her with trepidation. 'Go on, tell me…' He reached across for her hand again. 'I promise not to criticise.'

She gave him a wary glance. At least he couldn't say this would deprive him of his next holiday. 'I thought I might go back to teaching Pilates.'

His brow furrowed, he opened his mouth to speak, then he paused, as if choosing his words with extra care. 'Will you have the time?'

'I could fit it around the course. Physiotherapists often study Pilates.' She gave a little laugh. 'I'd be ahead of the game for once.'

He sighed. 'Promise me you won't do anything rash, like firing off your application? You've had a grim day. Sleep on it and make sure it's the right thing for you. If it is, I'll support you. Even help you with the form.'

She felt a twinge of irritation. 'I can fill in the application. I got in last time...'

He looked at her, his expression sheepish. 'There'll be lots of good-looking young men on the course.'

Alison's irritation dissipated as the reason for his panic dawned on her. 'Irish physio students...' Northumbria attracted Irish students because of the proximity of the North East to Ireland. Martin used to hate them. He'd fake friendliness, with his teeth-baring-half-grimace smile.

'They were so fit. You used to say you loved their sexy accents. He met her gaze, his eyes full of insecurity.' You won't run off with a strapping young Irish student, will you?'

She laughed. 'You're forgetting about all the young girls.' He continued to look anxious. 'I'm pulling your leg. Why would I look at anyone else when I've got a gorgeous husband at home?'

She walked round to him and sat on his lap. She felt him relax, as he snuggled into the crook of her neck. Behind him, Alison noticed a carrier bag on the floor. 'What's in that?'

'A couple of tablecloths for the meeting tomorrow night. Will they dry by morning?'

'Yes, if you get them straight into the washer.'

Martin peered up and shot her a mischievous grin. 'Could you do it for me, please?'

'Why didn't you set the machine off before you left for the gym?'

'I had a pile of marking to do...' He nibbled her ear. 'Go on, please?'

'Oh, all right. But you owe me one. What's the meeting?' She went over to the bag and pulled one tablecloth out, scattering debris onto the floor. 'Someone could have given them a shake.' A musty smell wafted into her face. 'Eugh, they're mouldy. How long have they been festering in here?'

He grimaced and shrugged. 'It's a senior management meeting to prepare for the Ofsted inspection. It'll be a late one, so we're having food. I don't suppose you'd knock up your delicious chocolate gateau for dessert, would you?'

She glanced up at him from her crouched position at the cupboard beneath the sink, where she was rummaging for stain remover. 'You've got to be joking?'

'I know it's a bit late now, but if you can't sleep and you're up and about during the night?' He gave her his *poor me* look. 'When you go back to uni, you might not have much time for baking. Do you think you could do your nice cherry sauce to go with it?'

He scarpered from the room, just in time to miss the wet tea towel she hurled at him.

'So, we're agreed then...' A flutter of excitement somersaulted in her stomach. I'm going to uni this year.'

Alison grinned so widely her mouth hurt.

Chapter 8

The branch staff had initially regarded Christopher with suspicion. It didn't faze him – he was used to it. Typically, people who couldn't normally stand each other, would unite against him – the enemy sent by Head Office to make redundancies and closures. However, after a period of adjustment, he'd gained their respect and cooperation.

It was the same here. Once the old, incompetent manager had gone, things had quickly turned around, and they'd wholeheartedly taken on board every initiative Christopher introduced. But this time, the idea of handing over the branch to someone else didn't sit right with him. He closed his office door and set off for home, certain he was making the right decision.

Christopher was also sure that, once she understood properly, Sandy would agree with him.

She was applying lip gloss at the mirror above the fireplace when Christopher got home. He walked over and kissed her cheek.

'Hi, I've left you a lasagne in the kitchen. And there's salad in the fridge. I've got yoga tonight.'

'Lasagne, lovely.' This caught him by surprise. It was rare for her to cook. 'What time will you be back? We didn't finish our conversation earlier.' He caught her scowl in the mirror.

'I thought we'd finished discussing that.' Her tone was light and at odds with her expression.

'Hanging up on me won't make it go away.' This wasn't how he had planned to talk about it. 'The thing is, I had a real wake-up call at the health centre this morning.'

Sandy turned to look at him, a concerned expression on her face. 'You said you were fine.'

He gently touched her shoulder. 'I will be – the blood pressure and pre-diabetes are reversible. But it made me take a good look at my life.'

'Well lose the weight and join a gym, like normal people.'

'That's a bit harsh, love.'

Sandy kept her back to him while she fixed her long blond hair into a chic knot with a purple band that matched her gym vest. 'I'm not being awful, but you've sort of brought it on yourself. It would be easy for me to let myself go, but I don't. It's about choices. Making health a priority.'

'Exactly. And work is part of the equation.'

Anger flashed from her eyes. 'Other people manage to hold down a job and stay healthy.'

'With respect, it's not something you've had to do in a long time.'

She gasped. Christopher knew he'd gone too far.

'I put a bloody good career on hold for you.' She rubbed a smudge of gloss from her perfect veneers with a tissue.

'I'm sorry. I know you did.' He stepped towards her, but she brushed him away. 'Could you just sit down for a minute, please?'

She sighed and flopped down on the sofa. 'I told you I'm on my way out.'

'Sandy, I don't want to continue in my current role. I no longer enjoy it – the moving around, the cut and thrust, I –'

She splayed her hands. 'What are you on about? You thrive on stress.'

Christopher loosened his tie and sat down beside her. 'I

used to. I love the Earlby branch. I know I could be happy there. And look what happened to Doug.'

'What's Doug got to do with anything?'

'He's dead, for goodness' sake. It's over for him. He'll never have the chance to wind down, enjoy life. I do – if I make the right changes.'

Sandy's head snapped round. 'You can't give up a good salary. Come on, Chris, we haven't built this life to throw it all away on a whim.'

'A *whim*?' This wasn't the reaction he'd expected. Christopher couldn't understand why she was acting so out of character. 'Sandy, for as long as I can remember, we've been paying fees for Emily – nursery fees, school fees, extra tuition, university fees. And now there's the wedding. But once that's over, an awful lot of money will be freed up.'

'Exactly,' said Sandy, her eyes shining as she expressed her sudden excitement. 'Think what we could spend it on.'

He was flabbergasted. 'My funeral?'

'Don't be facetious.'

'The point I'm trying to make is that we haven't missed that money, so if I don't earn it, we would theoretically be no worse off.'

Sandy grabbed her gym bag and threw her mobile phone into it. 'Of course, we'd miss it.'

'No, we wouldn't because our outgoings are about to drop significantly. Why can't you understand?'

'I do get it, I'm not stupid.' She looked directly at him; her deep-blue eyes filled with disappointment. 'But I thought we might buy a holiday home in California.'

'*What*? You want to sell the villa?'

'Absolutely not, I love Casita Emilia.'

'The Durham flat?'

'No.'

'So, you want another holiday home? And I'd continue working the same as now?' He threw up his hands in frustration. 'I barely get to Portugal as it is.'

'I'd go with Emily, or Mum or the girls.'

'What about me?' Christopher's stomach was churning. It was bad enough that his wife seemed not to care about his health, but it sounded as if she wasn't fussed about spending any time with him either. He took a breath to quell the rising panic. 'I feel as if I'm working to pay for things we don't need.'

Her mouth fell open. 'Like our only daughter's wedding?'

He rubbed his face. 'Please don't twist my words. I don't begrudge a single penny we've spent on Emily since the day she was born.' He sighed. 'Aren't you concerned about me at all?'

She narrowed her eyes at him. 'You're not the only person in this marriage. I work my fingers to the bone in this house, to make it nice for you.'

Christopher glanced up at her, bewildered once more.

She pointed at him with a perfectly manicured nail. 'You think a house this size runs itself?'

'We have a cleaner. And we had a nanny when Emily was little.'

'Who slaves over a hot stove for you?'

It was on the tip of Christopher's tongue to say, 'Nobody.' Then he remembered the lasagne in the kitchen and thought better of it. 'But now we're heading towards middle age, and we need to take care of ourselves so we can enjoy it.'

'I'm nowhere near middle age. And I *do* enjoy my life.'

The front door opened. A breathless voice sounded from the hallway. 'Can't stop, bag by the door. See you tomorrow, Bye.' The door banged shut again before either Christopher or Sandy had a chance to respond.

He looked at his watch. 'What's Fiona doing here at this time?'

'Dropping off dry cleaning.' She shot him a sideways glance. 'Don't look at me like that. She was going into town anyway on her way home, before taking her kids to some after-school club.'

'Couldn't you have picked it up yourself?'

Sandy, her eyes like saucers and arms outstretched, turned a full circle. 'No. Typical man. Do you think that paying Fiona two measly hours a day, is enough to keep a six-bedroomed house like this clean?' Her voice notched up an octave. 'And look at the size of the garden.'

'The gardener –'

'Never mind, forget it. You don't understand because you're away half the time.'

'Exactly.' He shook his head. 'I mean being away, not the not understanding.'

She pulled on her new training shoes. 'I'm not ready yet...'

'For what?'

Sandy garbled something incomprehensible, then quickly gained her composure. 'More changes. Isn't it enough that Emily's grown up and leaving home?'

He refrained from inflaming the situation by reminding her that Emily had moved into the Durham flat when she'd first gone off to university, and that she'd lived there with Simon since graduating.

She sniffled. 'I won't be a mother any longer. I feel useless.' She stood looking at her feet like a sad child.

Christopher was filled with empathy and love for his wife. He took her in his arms and pulled her close. 'You're a smashing mum, Emily will always need you. And I'm going to be around in future, too.' He stroked her hair. 'And I promise, you won't notice the change in finances.'

Her voice softened. 'I don't want you to be ill and miserable.' She relaxed against his chest. 'You used to say you were lucky I married you.'

'Crumbs, I hit the jackpot with you.'

He meant it. When Christopher had first seen Sandy, she'd taken his breath away. He'd never had trouble asking girls out in the past, but Sandy's beauty had rendered him speechless.

She worked in the beauty salon at the hotel hosting Henleys annual conference and awards ceremony. It was a three-day event, and he'd been invited, following nomination for the 'most aspiring trainee' award. Although he'd spotted her on the first day, he was too intimidated to even smile at her until the second. When she flashed her perfect smile back and looked at him with those baby-blue eyes, his legs had buckled.

It wasn't until the last evening that he plucked up the courage to speak. Still buzzing after winning the award and emboldened by alcohol, he'd spotted her at the bar. He walked over with as much confidence as he could muster, which wasn't much, and prayed he didn't look like a dork. His heart almost beat out of his ribcage when she accepted a drink from him.

Later, after a couple of glasses of Champagne, Sandy told him that attending the events was a perk of her job, but she confessed she'd only stayed on in the hope of bumping into him. She told him he looked handsome in his evening suit, like a green-eyed Adam Sandler. He was completely in awe of her. He knew there and then she was the one for him.

'You said you'd always look after me.'

'And I will.'

She sighed and pulled away from him. 'Sorry, I'd better get going. Let's talk again later.'

As Sandy drove off, Christopher changed out of his work clothes. He felt exhausted. And ravenous – he was looking forward to his meal. What an awful evening it had been. He didn't know what he'd do if Sandy stopped loving him, he couldn't bear it. Thank goodness that wasn't the case. She did love him. And she'd even cooked for him. He wandered into the kitchen and opened the oven door.

There was nothing inside.

Christopher found his lasagne in the fridge – an M&S meal for one. He jabbed the cellophane and set it away in microwave, then gathered ingredients from the salad drawer and reached for the chopping board.

Chapter 9

Martin snapped shut the cake carrier lid, pulled Alison away from the toaster and twirled her once around the kitchen. 'You're a star.'

A familiar warm fuzziness filled her – along with a deluge of relief that things were back to normal.

'No one can match your gateau.' He reached into the cupboard for two cups. 'I'm a lucky man.'

'It helped to pass the time.'

'I wish you could sleep.' He handed her a mug of coffee then rummaged around in the freezer. 'Where's the smoothie mix?'

Alison gave a little laugh. He made it sound like a supermarket ready-made mix, not one for which she had chosen and painstakingly washed and chopped ingredients. 'Blue container, top shelf of the fridge, next to the cherry sauce for the gateau.'

He emptied the contents into the blender. 'There's kale in it...'

'The spinach didn't look very nice this week. Don't worry, I added mango to balance out the bitterness.'

He spilled some almond milk onto the bench. 'These cartons are useless for pouring.' He clattered around trying to force the bladed lid onto the beaker. 'Bloody thing.'

Alison gently nudged him out of the way. 'Give it here, I'll show you. You have to line it up –'

He'd already sat down at the table. 'It leaves bits anyway.'

'Not if you blend it for long enough,' she shouted over her shoulder above the whirring motor.

He took the glass of smooth liquid from her and nodded. 'You're naturally better at this stuff than me.'

'Yeah, I was born with a blender in one hand and an iron in the other... Anyway, I also did a bit of Googling last night. There's a smart health and fitness studio ten minutes from the university. I'm thinking of going for a look around, maybe arrange to have a chat with someone. You never know, there might be an opportunity to teach a Pilates class.'

Martin frowned. 'Don't you think it's a bit soon for that? Why don't you concentrate on getting the insomnia sorted out first? Go back and tell old Smedley you want a referral to see a specialist. After all, you've tried everything you can to put it right yourself, and he had nothing constructive to offer you.'

Alison looked reflective. 'Remember those lavender pillows that set off your allergies?'

'They were worse than next door's mangy cat.

She didn't mention that Sammy had visited the previous night and had kept her company while she baked.

'And those weird herbal tablets that had you slurring for two days.'

'Ooh, yes, I liked those.' She sipped her coffee. 'I couldn't have carried on driving, though. It's a wonder Dr Smedley didn't tell me to count sheep or something.'

Martin laughed. 'Have you tried?'

'Yes, their little hooves got caught in the barbed wire, and they all ended up in a tangled pile on the other side of the fence.' She grimaced. 'Well, the ones that weren't stuck dangling from the wires.'

Martin cackled. 'Why did it have barbed wire?'

'Because they do in the countryside.'

'But you could have imagined it without the barbs.' He took a bite of toast. 'Could you get some apricot jam next time you go shopping?'

'You know I like to do things properly.' She shuddered. 'Blood and guts all over the place. And so noisy – all that bleating and baa-ing. My stomach's churning thinking about it. Try the Tesco Express next to the school.'

'No worries, it's not urgent.' Martin looked at her and shook his head. 'I don't know why you can't relax and go to sleep. It's easy.'

She shot him a mock-angry glare. 'Do you want that gateau, or not?'

'Sorry. Seriously, why don't you see one of the other doctors, and if they can't offer anything either, ask for a referral?'

'If I'd known Dr Smedley was still working – alive even – I'd have asked for someone else. He reckons Mam told him I was anxious –'

'Well –'

'No, hang on… He couldn't even remember she was dead.'

Martin shrugged. 'I suppose a lot of his patients have died in his time.'

'In a car crash?' She pushed an image of the accident from her mind. She hadn't witnessed it, but she had created a vivid mental video that would play on a loop in her head if she allowed it to.

He looked at her as if he was searching for the right words. 'Dr Smedley's incompetence aside, do you think… Could it be your tendency to over-complicate things that stops you from sleeping?'

Alison jerked her head towards him. 'No. You seem to have forgotten that it was being up all night with incessantly crying babies that messed up my sleep in the first place. Nothing to overthink there.'

Martin sighed. 'It wasn't easy for me either.'

'Yes, I know.' Alison watched him butter another slice of toast. She tried to recall an occasion when he had fed or changed the twins during the night, but she couldn't. 'Actually, I don't. You didn't get up.'

He shot her an indignant look. 'That's not fair. I had to sleep. I had to be on the ball to build a future for us. You weren't working.'

Alison felt herself rankling. 'Yeah, babies are so easy to look after – twenty-four-seven.'

'Having babies is natural. Other people cope.'

'You didn't.'

'I did. I simply organised life around them. Anyway, my mother used to call in to help you.'

She spluttered on a mouthful of coffee, as she recalled the flood of disappointment on opening the door to one of her mother-in-law's unexpected visits. *Don't worry about me Alison,* she'd say, handing over her coat, *I know it's lunchtime. I'll just have a chicken sandwich and a milky coffee.* 'I ended up having to run around after her, on top of the children.'

'For goodness' sake, Alison. You can be ungrateful sometimes. Chloe and Jack are twenty years old now.'

'Exactly. Twenty years without a decent night's sleep. If you'd been the one –'

'Oh, don't start with that now.' He checked his watch. 'I have to get off to work.' He grabbed a piece of toast and barely brushed her cheek as he kissed her goodbye.

Alison felt flat as the front door banged behind him. Then she heard him come back in and cheered up. She hated bickering, it set the day up wrong from the start.

Martin bounded into the kitchen, picked up the cake carrier and cherry sauce and turned to leave again. 'Remember I'm staying late for the meeting tonight,' he said over his shoulder. 'Think on about the jam if you get the chance – apricot.'

Disappointment replaced the earlier warm fuzziness in Alison's stomach. 'Get your own jam,' she muttered to herself as she quickly cleared away the breakfast dishes. She picked up her work bag. 'And you can tell your mother what she can do with her chicken sandwiches.'

'You're joking… *More* time off?' shouted Billy down the phone.

A quiet scrunching crackled over from across the office, like Rice Krispies popping as the milk hits them. Alison glanced up and started. Phyllis's eyes were boring into her.

'Billy said you have to collate this month's negative patient feedback comments and send them to me. I will review the document before forwarding it on to him.'

Alison held the phone away from her ear while Billy continued his rant. She suppressed the urge to laugh at Phyllis's head and neck, which reminded her of an apple impaled on a twig. She pointed to the handset and mouthed, *I'm on the phone.*

'Did you hear what I said?' scrunched Phyllis.

Sharon could hardly suppress her giggles as she pretended not to eavesdrop.

Alison flapped her hand at Phyllis to signal she couldn't speak. She lowered her voice. 'Billy, I took annual leave last time. I'm entitled to see my doctor. Check the policy.'

Billy hung up.

She shot his closed door an angry glare and replaced the handset. She could feel Phyllis's eyes on her. The once professional office now felt like a madhouse. 'Why are you snapping orders at me? The comments are nothing to do with you. I'll send them on myself.'

Alison had realised Phyllis wasn't to be trusted soon after meeting her, when she'd helped her get to grips with spreadsheets. Phyllis had passed the work off as her own and then whined to Billy that no one had been willing to show her what to do.

'I'm simply following instructions.'

'If you concentrated more on your own work, we'd be closer to meeting our departmental targets.' Alison turned to her computer screen.

Phyllis got up and went off for a walk around the perimeter of the office, for no apparent reason as far as Alison could tell. The sound of her Scholl sandals slapping off the soles of her feet grew quiet and then louder again, until it stopped behind her chair.

Alison felt shallow breathing on her neck and looked around. Phyllis fast-blinked down at her, saying nothing.

'Do you mind? You're in my space.'

'Send the report to me by the end of the afternoon.' Phyllis's lips made tiny clicking sounds between each word, as if they were stuck and had to be forced apart.

'You're not my manager.'

Phyllis's perm barely moved as she shook her head beneath it. 'This afternoon.'

She took a measured breath. 'Go away.'

'If you speak to me like that again, I'll report you to Human Resources.'

'Wait there, I'll get the number for you.'

Phyllis's sandals fast-slapped over to her own desk. Alison looked at Sharon, who was trying to suppress a giggle. 'What the heck?' she whispered.

Sharon wiped tears from her eyes. 'Ignore her. She's got a crush on Billy. Silly fool.'

Phyllis got up from her desk and stormed towards Billy's office, briefly pausing to straighten her twinset cardigan and scrunch her perm before knocking crisply on the door. She came back out, looking smug. She'd left the door open and Alison could see Billy smirking to himself. He opened out a paper clip and used it to pick his teeth, then he pulled out a set of scales from beneath his desk, kicked off his shoes and weighed himself. He glared down at the scales then booted them under the desk and stormed through the doorway.

'Alison, would you send a summary of the patient feedback comments to Phyllis, please.' He smirked and returned to his office.

Phyllis tittered in delight.

Alison reached for Billy's throat in her mind's eye.

Until Billy and Phyllis had joined the team, Alison had enjoyed work. She'd even stepped up as a temporary line-manager herself for a while and applied for the post when it was advertised. It wasn't that she resented someone else getting the job – she was planning to leave after all – it was that such an imbecile like Billy had got it. And how he made the shortlist with two GCSE's, was baffling. The pay grade required a degree, or at least evidence of working towards one. She had achieved it because of her time at university.

She had to admit he was a skilled networker; forever delivering some presentation or other to a corporate bigwig gathering. But she'd heard snippets of gossip that, like Phyllis, he wasn't averse to taking credit for the work of others, presenting it as his own. She could well believe it. Even so, he was now her manager, and she had tried to treat him in a professional manner. At least at first – he made it so difficult.

The office fell into a subdued silence for the rest of the morning, and by the time lunchtime came around, Alison was itching to get out. At one point, Phyllis had taken almost forty minutes to nibble noisily on one brazil nut. It was like nails scratching down a blackboard to Alison. She'd wanted to scream, 'Just swallow the bloody thing.' Anyone would think she had no teeth.'

Alison knew she did have teeth – strange ones. She'd seen them once, when Phyllis had accidently smiled at her – most unnerving. It looked as if all her teeth had been extracted and replaced by little square Tootie Minties. All the same shape and size, and so even you'd think she'd taken a file to them. Alison used to love Tootie Minties when she was little. Three pence a packet, and her favourites after a Cadbury's Finger of Fudge.

The sound of the clip going on Phyllis's box brought her focus back into the room. Time for lunch, she decided, unable to face the prospect of more nut nibbling. On her way out, Billy shot her a snarky glance.

She paused at his door. 'Billy,' she said, in the nicest tone she could muster, 'did you get Trust funding for your degree?'

He tilted his head and stared at her as if she'd said something odd. 'I didn't need to. I wouldn't bother applying if that's what you're thinking. There's no money in the pot.'

Billy's expression clouded. 'What are you looking at?'

'Nothing.' Alison was convinced he must have lied about his qualifications to get the job. She wouldn't say anything – for now.

Katie hung her coat on the back of the chair and sat down. 'I love it in here. Scrumptious food.'

Alison hadn't been back to Alessandro's since the bad smell episode. 'Thanks for coming down with me. It'll stop me obsessing over what to say. I hope she's better than old Smedley. It's unusual to get an appointment on the day you phone. Fingers crossed it doesn't mean she's rubbish too.' Katie knew about the insomnia, and her dislike of Billy, but not the murderous thoughts. Alison was ashamed of those – or at least ashamed of admitting her thoughts to her friends.

'Well, if she is, try our practice. Dr Oliver is excellent. Good-looking too. Married, unfortunately.' Katie bit into her pastry. 'This is delicious.'

'Everything in here is yummy.' Alison checked her watch for the umpteenth time. 'Ten more minutes. To be honest, Dr Smedley's incompetence aside, I'm not sure any doctor can help me.'

'It's a wonder you reached adulthood with him though. That health centre is famous for being useless,' said Katie. 'I can remember the stories that used to go around when his old partner was there.'

'Why don't I know this?'

The door opened and Christopher walked in wearing a serious expression, until he spotted Alison. He waved over. 'Hello there.' His whole face, and the room, lit up as he smiled.

He pretended to stagger, grasping at his throat and pulling a silly expression. Alison flapped her arms and made a high-pitched beeping sound, which sent them both into fits of laughter, and left Katie bemused.

'Who the heck's that?'

Alison wiped her eyes with a serviette. 'It's Christopher. He jumped out of the bushes at me in the park.'

Katie shot Christopher a look of disgust. 'Did you report him to the police? Pervert.'

'It's fine. He was just choking.'

Katie craned her neck to get a better look at Christopher. She raised an eyebrow. 'He's not bad looking. Bit like that actor… What's his name again? He was in that rom com we saw, with Jennifer Aniston.'

'*Along came Polly*. No, he's nothing like Ben Stiller.'

'Not him. Erm… Adam Sandler, yes, that's him.'

'Can't picture him.'

'Nice eyes, cheeky smile. He was in the film we saw in The Gate in town and then ended up hammered on two-for-one cocktails in Pleased To Meet you afterwards. What was it called again?'

'Oh, yes… *Just Go With it*. Adam Sandler?' Alison sneaked a surreptitious glance at Christopher. 'Possibly, though he has a squarer jaw.

'Who, Adam Sandler?'

'No, Christopher.'

'He's attractive – shame he's wearing a wedding ring.'

Alison laughed. 'Hawk-eye. He doesn't look like your type…' She lowered her voice. 'Isn't he a bit old and podgy for you? He must be in his mid-forties.'

'To be honest, the young ripped ones can be miserable. They're always so *hungry*. And you can't eat anything *normal* in front of them. You don't know how fortunate you are to have your Martin.'

Alison bit into her caramel slice. 'He has his moments, too,' she mumbled. 'Especially lately.'

'What's wrong?'

She shrugged. 'Oh, I don't know. He's just been a bit snappy –'

Christopher stopped at their table. He was holding a paper bag. 'No cinnamon twirl for me today.'

Alison was glad of the interruption. She'd already said too much.

He sighed. 'Apparently, I've been having too many of them.' He patted his stomach and grimaced.

'Was it that rubbish Dr Smedley, doling out insults again?' said Alison. 'Take no notice, you're fine.' Out of the corner of her eye, she caught a hint of a smile from Katie. She flushed up.

'Not him. It was a rude, obese nurse who told me I'm obese.'

Katie looked him up and down. 'There's no way you're obese.'

Alison noticed Christopher's awkwardness under Katie's scrutiny. It was endearing. Martin would have puffed out his chest.

'Well, thank you both very much. It's extremely gracious of you to lie through your teeth. You've cheered me up no end.' He turned to Alison and grinned as he went to leave. 'I'll try not to scare you next time I see you in the park.'

'That was a dazzler of a smile you flashed him, Ali,' said Katie, as Christopher left.

'Rubbish,' snorted Alison.

'Nice eyes.' Katie followed him with her gaze as he walked towards the park. 'He's got a silver fox thing going on. Quite distinguished-looking.'

Alison checked the time again. 'Five more minutes and then I'll go. I hope this doctor believes insomnia is a real problem. I hate people thinking I'm a malingerer.'

Katie looked reflective. 'You know Judy who lives further along the bay from me? The one who met a sexy Spaniard on holiday?'

'Yes.'

'I'm sure she has a friend over at St Mary's who's a sleep nurse. I remember thinking it was funny because Judy said she had a sleepy condition but couldn't sort herself out.'

'Was she the one you said had an affair with a married man who had an alcoholic wife?'

'Yes, that's her. Some women are stupid. Men are bad enough when they're single.'

'You've just been ogling a married one. I would kick Martin to within an inch of his life if he was unfaithful to me.'

Katie gave a wry laugh. 'I'm never with anyone long enough for them to cheat on me.'

Alison watched her friend as she spoke. Katie was an enviable combination of smart and beautiful. She was financially astute too, having bought her house on the quayside when the market had dipped. It was now worth double what she paid. With her slim figure and high cheek bones, she was never short of handsome admirers. But no matter how great her boyfriends seemed to be, she could never settle with any of them.

Katie sipped her coffee. 'The older I get, the more irritated I become with men. They're all so, I don't know… *disappointing*. Have you ever read that book *Who Moved My Cheese?*'

'Is it a recipe book?'

'No, it's written by some doctor. It's about two mice and two little people who find their cheese store has gone. The mice scurry off in search of a new supply, but the little people keep returning, hoping in vain that the cheese will be there. I think I'm stuck going back to the same type of relationship and expecting to find something different.'

'Do you know what you're looking for?'

'No. But it's never there, whatever it is. Maybe it's like you going to bed and hoping to sleep?'

'You mean, I put on my pyjamas, climb into bed and expect to drop off, but the cheddar has gone?' laughed Alison.

'Yes, something like that. Perhaps I need to look for a different type of man. I wonder if Christopher has any single silver fox friends.'

'Maybe I've been tackling the insomnia all wrong.' Alison had an unsettled feeling. Had her relationship with Martin changed? she wondered. Was she trying to force it to be what it no longer was?

'Don't look so worried,' said Katie. 'You'll be fine if you remain calm and refuse to be fobbed off.'

Alison pulled on her jacket. 'Wish me luck. I'll let you know how I get on.' As she left, she made a mental note to find out how *Who moved my cheese* ended.

Chapter 10

'There must be some mistake. It's with Dr McPhee.'

Morven, the old receptionist who had been there since the year dot, peered over her glasses at Alison. 'No, it's definitely with Dr Smedley.'

'It can't be.'

One of the younger receptionists leaned out from behind Morven, gave Alison an apologetic smile and mouthed, 'Sorry'.

'He's a blithering idiot.'

Morven gasped.

Alison felt the space around her expand as she realised she'd said that out loud.

'I'm sorry. Dr Smedley couldn't help me, you see. I was hoping Dr McPhee, being so young, might have some more recent experience.'

'I remembered that your mother used to like to see Dr Smedley.' Morven tilted her head and adopted the look of pity Alison had grown to hate after the crash. 'Such a *polite* lady. I swapped you to him.'

'That was thoughtful of you, but I'd like to see Dr McPhee, please.'

'She's full. Dr Smedley is an extremely experienced consultant general practitioner. His knowledge goes back years.'

'I know.'

'You're lucky he had a free slot.'

'I don't agree. If the truth be known, I'm going through a particularly unlucky period in my life.'

Morven checked the computer again. 'She has a free appointment a fortnight today.'

'Never mind. I'll see him – this time.'

Alison sat down in the waiting room. She took out her diary and listed the things she wanted to discuss, in case she became distracted by one of Dr Smedley's patronising comments.

Her name flashed up on the board and she trudged down the corridor to Dr Smedley's room. She took a calming breath and knocked on the door.

Once in the consultation room, Alison carefully stated her case, ticking off the points on her list, then awaited Dr Smedley's response. At least she couldn't be disappointed, her expectations were too low.

He rested his elbows on the desk and steepled his hands, then leaned to the side and scanned the space between Alison and the door. 'No hubby today either? I expect he's busy – shaping the great minds of the future.'

Stick to the point, she told herself. 'Martin sleeps fine and has no desire to kill his boss.'

He stared at a corner of the ceiling and sucked on his teeth. 'Hot chocolate.'

She blinked slowly. 'It doesn't wor –'

'I find that a nice mug of hot chocolate helps me.'

'Surely you don't think an old wives' tale can resolve a twenty-year-old problem?'

Dr Smedley turned to the keyboard. 'Aggr-ess-ive.'

'I certainly am not.'

'As I said last time, it's the perimenopause. Anger, not sleeping, weight-gain.'

A gasp caught her breath and made her cough. 'Weight-gain?' Her cheeks burned in indignation.

'I see you're having a hot flush right now.'

'No, I'm not.' She gripped her pen so tight her knuckles whitened.

'It's the lack of sleep that's causing you to be angry with your boss. Try the hot chocolate.' He raised one eyebrow. 'Maybe the low sugar option.'

She had to summon up everything she'd learned in the Dealing with Conflict workshop to remain calm. 'So, it's not a lack of B vitamins that makes me want to kill my boss after all then?'

'Are they helping?'

'Of course not. And hot chocolate won't help me to sleep.'

'There's the "counting sheep" exercise.'

This was exhausting. Alison was on the point of giving up when she heard Katie's voice in her head, telling her not to allow herself to be fobbed off. She took a deep breath. 'I believe there's a sleep clinic at St Mary's hospital. I'd be grateful if you could refer me there, please.'

Dr Smedley sighed. 'I don't think –'

Crack. The pen launched its inner spring across the desk. It pinged off the Newton's Cradle then twanged off Dr Smedley's forehead and into his mug of tea.

Her face burning with shame, she stood up to leave.

He cowered. The man actually cowered. What was the *matter* with her? 'I'm so sor–'

Dr Smedley held up his palm. 'I'll refer you.'

He disappeared behind the computer screen and hammered at the keys more quickly than ever before. The ancient printer cranked out a form and he ripped it off and flung it at her. 'It's a Choose and Book system. You'll need to quote the reference number to make an appointment.'

She took it without looking him in the eye. 'I really am –'

'Goodbye.'

***

Peggy, wearing fluorescent pink ear buds, was pushing her cleaning trolley along the corridor when Alison, still in a state of mortification, jumped out of the lift after yet another static shock. The nylon trousers had been banished to a British Heart Foundation charity bag, awaiting pickup on the doorstep, but she'd continued to receive shocks from any metal object she inadvertently touched.

Peggy's trolley was making an eye-watering screeching sound.

'Hiya, erm, thingamabob… Alison,' she shouted. 'Have you seen the blinking wobble on my wheel?' She pushed the trolley back and forth a couple of times, setting Alison's teeth on edge. Peggy removed one bud.

'I don't know how you can stand that,' said Alison.

'I've got no choice. They won't give me any WD-40. That's why I've got these in. I'm listening to the news – miserable it is.' She pushed the trolley off with an almighty squeal then paused. 'Eeh mind, I'm pleased they're starting to get those bairns out of that cave. Their parents must be beside themselves with worry.'

'Yes, I heard they'd rescued another two this morning.'

'If you ask me, it shouldn't have happened in the first place. They should play baseball on a proper field.' She pushed the trolley back and forth a couple of inches, like a mother rocking a child in a pram.

Alison winced.

'I can't run on the sand at the seaside.' Peggy raised one foot. 'I don't know why.'

Alison glanced down at the tiny Velcro-strapped black shoe. She guessed her feet would be about a size two – completely out of proportion to the rest of her body – and wondered how Peggy didn't topple over.

'On holiday, me and my sister-in-law play rounders with the grandkids on Blackpool beach. My Alf has to watch – blockages in his legs. My brother used to join in before his coronary.' She crossed herself and looked up to the ceiling.

Alison nodded and lowered her eyes in respect.

'Eeh, I love Blackpool. Roll on August.'

'Have you booked up?' A family holiday to their favourite B&B was the highlight of Peggy's year.

'This weekend.' Peggy rubbed her hands together. 'We're meeting at my daughter's house for a fish and chip supper. Her man can work that interweb thingamajig on the legtop. You have to book up early, Blackpool gets packed in August.'

'Sounds exciting,' Alison said, internally balking at the thought of a crowded resort full of screaming kids and hen and stag parties.

'I was after some overtime for spends. Can't get any for love nor money. Miserable so-and-so's here. The bairns like to go to the amusement arcades.' She winked and tapped her nose. 'Keeps them busy, while we're in the bingo.'

A childhood memory of playing on penny slot-machines in the Spanish City at Whitley Bay floated into Alison's mind on a wave of nostalgia. The old machines were long gone, like her parents. If only she'd known she'd lose them so soon…

'Have you been to Blackpool?'

'No, I haven't.' It was a world away from the spa hotel holidays she and Martin enjoyed. But seeing Peggy's excited expression made her realise that she was no happier on her expensive holidays, than Peggy was in Blackpool.

Peggy shot the office a glare. 'Mind you lot in there get overtime. Plenty of money for office workers – nothing for us.'

She had a point. Alison had noticed that lately, there always seemed to be someone in on a day off, covering sickness leave. She had half wondered if it was something being transmitted by the old air conditioning system.

Replacing her ear bud, Peggy squeaked off, singing 'I do like to be beside the seaside' at the top of her voice.

Alison made a mental note to bring in some WD-40 from home. A voice boomed out from the beverage bay, making her jump and go over on her ankle. Her heart beating against her ribs, she glanced up to find one of the fire officers, Rick Shannon, shaking a wooden chock in his hand.

'Thirty-two years in the fire service – went in a fireman, came out a firefighter. Dunno what that was all about, like.'

It was the door wedge Alison had spotted on Peggy's trolley days before. He shook it at her. Unable to fully weight-bear, she leaned against the wall, on one foot, to let the pain subside. Getting into the office was beginning to feel like tackling an assault course. It really shouldn't be this difficult, she thought.

'Why would anyone wedge open a fire door?'

'No idea. We all do the annual mandatory fire training.'

Rick turned to the door and gently caressed it as he gazed at it with love-filled eyes. 'Look at the depth of that wood... And the bristles,' he said, running his fingers along them.

'Hmm, lovely,' Alison said, for want of a better word. She tentatively attempted to stand on both feet.

His attention returned to the door wedge. 'Have you seen this?' He pointed to the bold black wording along the side and his voice notched up. 'Someone's even labelled it... *B e v e r a g e B a y.*'

Alison shook her head and pulled her mouth down into a supportive grimace as she made to slope away. 'Terrible.'

'This type of thing put the lives of my men in danger.' He shook his head at the chock. 'I've got a box full of these things in my office. I take them away, but they *replace* them, would you believe...?'

Alison shook her head and tutted. 'I'll remind everyone in the office.'

Rick retreated into the beverage bay and closed the door behind him. Alison limped off to the sound of his muffled, increasingly high-pitched ranting... 'A fire blanket, extinguisher. A beautiful, ninety-minute fire door... And they *wedge it open...*' There may have been more, but she surmised only dogs could hear it.

Before going into the office, Alison pulled out the sleep clinic referral form and dialled the number. For the second time that day she was offered a cancellation appointment, for later in the week.

With a renewed sense of hope, she returned to her desk. She passed Billy's office and caught him picking his nose while eating a Mars Bar. To her surprise, this merely invoked a throat-scraping retch, without any desire to physically injure him. She had a feeling that things were about to change for the better. All she had needed was the opportunity to get some help. Her cheery greeting visibly disarmed Phyllis, who bit clean through a brazil nut.

As she set about collating the patient feedback comments for her report, which she had no intention of sending to Phyllis before Billy, she thought about little Peggy and wondered how much she earned. She knew her husband was medically retired, so they couldn't be well-off. She and Martin were rich in comparison.

Despite her problems, Alison felt blessed for the good things she had in her life. There was a lot to be thankful for – a husband, two wonderful, healthy children and a great group of friends. The things money couldn't buy were the most precious.

The thought of her children made Alison swell with pride. She'd enjoyed every moment of their childhood. Perhaps not so much the crying nights. But even then, once they fell into an exhausted sleep after hours of inconsolable howling, she'd stand, bushed, between their cots, her heart melting as she watched them sleep. Now that they were grown up and starting out on their own pathways, the doors were opening for Alison to step back onto hers, too. Feeling much more positive, she glanced up smiling and caught Phyllis scowling at her, which made her smile even more.

It was nearing the end of the afternoon that an email pinged in from Ashley. He wanted to see her immediately in the seminar room upstairs. She racked her brain for something she might have missed. As she got up to go, so did Sharon. They were followed out by Phyllis and Billy.

'What do you think this is about?' whispered Alison to Sharon, as they made their way up to the seminar room.

Sharon looked ashen. 'Tuna-telephone-gate.'

Alison gave Sharon a sideways glance. She lowered her voice to no more than a whisper. 'Do you ever want to beat Billy's head to a pulp?'

Sharon gritted her teeth. 'Like right now?'

The atmosphere in the seminar room hung heavy with glum expectation. Ashley sat at the top of a long table, with someone from Human Resources on his right. Ashley's expression was grave. Billy sat down, grinning inanely.

Ashley glanced at Billy. 'Thank you all for coming. Please sit down.'

Billy stopped grinning.

'We've received a complaint from a member of staff, stating that the working environment in your office has become intolerable.'

Everyone looked at everyone else. Billy narrowed his eyes at Alison.

She looked directly at him. 'It wasn't me.'

'I know,' said Ashley.

Alison felt stupid.

'I can't name the member of staff, but I can tell you that it's no one in this room. However, the complaint concerns two cliques, who apparently dislike each other and can't get on at all.'

Billy opened his mouth to speak.

Ashley raised his hand. 'If I could finish, Billy. A decision has been made to relocate one of you to another area.'

By the time Ashley had delivered the plans, Sharon and Alison were devastated. Billy and Phyllis delighted.

'But I don't understand,' said Alison. 'The working

environment has become unpleasant for everyone, yet you leave me with the people who have caused it and move one of the victims out. And why leave *me*?' she continued, panic rising in her voice.

'To be honest, Alison, you're staying because you seem to be able to cope,' said Ashley.

That was what she got for stooping to childish murder fantasies instead of following Trust procedure and reporting Billy's behaviour. 'But that's not true. I'm the one who wants to bea–' A sharp kick from Sharon silenced her.

As they walked back to the office afterwards, the girls were shrouded in a cloud of disappointment. 'I can't believe it's come to this,' said Alison. 'It's like he can do nothing wrong.'

Billy strode past and cracked a bubble with his gum.

'I hate him,' said Alison under her breath.

'It's so unfair,' said Sharon. 'I'm going to be working in that death-trap of a portacabin at the back of St Mary's. And why do *I* have to stop people smoking on the grounds? I'll get my head kicked in…'

Alison turned to her friend. 'Listen to us. A few months ago, we were professional women with careers. Well, you were – I was biding my time. All the same, I wanted to do a good job. We've allowed a bully to get us into trouble.'

'That's exactly what he wanted.'

'I don't know why he dislikes me so much,' said Alison.

'It's because he knows you'd have done a better job than he's doing.

'I wish he'd leave me alone.'

It was as if, as soon as something positive happened, something else popped up to spoil it and drag her back down. She really did try to be a good person. Alison couldn't understand why she brought out the worst in some people – at work and, more recently it seemed, at home.

Chapter 11

Christopher was in his usual spot, people watching at the window, as he sounded out head office about his proposal. His manager was shocked. Although he agreed to the request, he suggested doing an eighteen-month stint, with the option of reverting to his current role at the end of it. Christopher agreed to think about it.

In the current financial climate, it would be financially beneficial for the bank. Christopher was on top increment of his pay grade. They would make a significant saving by seconding someone onto the bottom of the grade below, and it would be an excellent opportunity for an ambitious young banker.

He did a double take at the sight of Sandy, striding towards the hairdresser's opposite. He rapped on the window, but the reinforced safety glass muted the sound to the outside world. It was unusual for her to be in Earlby, she shopped in Newcastle, where there was more choice – and pricier salons and boutiques.

He laughed to himself, it must be an emergency, no doubt a snapped nail, or something equally catastrophic. He loved it that she wanted to look pretty for him after over twenty years of marriage. But as far as he was concerned, she was every bit as beautiful without the make-up and designer clothes. She knew she was attractive, and that most men would be proud to have her as their wife. And so did he, she had no need to keep reminding him. He could hardly miss the looks she attracted wherever they went. Just as well he wasn't the jealous type. She might enjoy the attention, but he knew it was him she loved – though he had to admit a bit of doubt had crept in the previous night.

Christopher tried calling her, but she didn't pick up. He texted to suggest she call in for a coffee when she had finished.

A knock at the door interrupted his thoughts.

'Come in.'

A heady scent wafted in, followed by Frank Budle, holding a plastic pocket file and looking shifty.

Christopher indicated for Frank to sit down. He opened the window. 'It gets warm up here.'

Frank took his seat and fumbled with two sheets of paper.

'Good, you've prepared your appraisal documentation. Not everyone does. Coffee?' He popped a pod into the machine.

'Please. I find it saves time. Not that it takes long to zip through anyway – tick a couple of boxes, prove you've jumped through the right hoops etc.'

'It'll take the full hour.' He passed Frank his coffee and sat down.

'Really? Shall I run you through the way we do it here?'

Christopher laughed and ignored the offer. His opinion of Frank plummeted. If he ignored correct appraisal procedure, what else was he ignoring? 'It's taken longer than I would have liked to pin you down. You're a busy man to get hold of.'

'Yes. I like to keep occupied.'

'Tell me how you think this year has gone for you.'

Frank looked taken aback. 'Well… I haven't thought about it.'

Christopher leaned back in his seat and looked directly at Frank. 'How can you set objectives for the coming year without first appraising the previous one?'

Frank coughed and shuffled. 'I've been here so long, one year is much the same as the next. Nothing really changes.' He nudged his paperwork across the desk.

'As you know, Henleys is committed to the career development of its staff through programmes of life-long learning. So, tell me – what have you embarked on this year, and what do you hope to do over the next twelve months?' An uneasy fifteen minutes passed, during which Christopher attempted to draw Frank into a genuine conversation, and Frank squirmed in his seat and avoided speaking about anything on more than a superficial level.

'Do you see yourself working towards a management role?' asked Christopher. He took a sip of coffee and could have sworn it tasted of aftershave.

Frank batted away the question with his hand. 'No.'

'You've must have gained a great deal of experience in your ten years here.' Though not of the calibre Christopher had previously assumed.

'My wife, Patricia, manages Earlby Care Home – a stressful job. We value our down time together.'

Christopher thought back to the old lady's accusation about houses. She must have been referring to people having to sell their homes to pay for residential care.

'So, when we're off work, we like to get away on holiday. You know, forget about the daily grind. That would be difficult to do in a management post. Too much responsibility.'

It was interesting to Christopher how people could look at the same thing from such different perspectives. Frank's idea of too much responsibility was his own of a stress-free existence.

'I also dabble in property development. Nothing grand, but it helps to afford the holidays.'

And the sharp suits and pricey Grenson shoes, thought Christopher. Frank didn't need to move up the ladder. 'Tell me about the goals you'd like to aim for.'

'I'm happy to continue as I am.'

It was like pulling teeth. 'Okay, if you prefer not to set your own, I'll do it – though at your level, this shouldn't be necessary.' He had clearly been coasting along contributing very little to the branch.

Frank's eyes widened.

'How about identifying one or two areas for development and get yourself booked onto the appropriate training days. I suggest you start with time management.'

Frank looked puzzled.

Christopher nodded over to the window. 'I've spotted you, going out for lunch mid-afternoon. Take a look at your schedule. It may be that we need to delegate some of your work to someone else.'

Frank paled. 'No, no. That's not necessary. I'll have a look at my scheduling. As you say, time management.'

By the time Frank left the office, Christopher had a much better understanding of the way he worked – or didn't, it would seem. The cool professional exterior didn't reflect his attitude to work. He had no place on his team for shirkers. Just as well he wasn't interested in a promotion – there was no chance he'd get one.

Shirley bustled in with a cloth and spray and set about cleaning everywhere Frank had touched. 'He must get through a tonne of that awful gel.' She picked up his cup, peered at the remnants, then shot the coffee machine a stony glare.

Christopher laughed. 'Try one.'

'No thank you, I'll stick to my kettle,' she said, retreating to her own office.

He reached into his desk and pulled out the blood pressure machine. He was pleasantly surprised to find that, according to the chart that came with it, it had dropped to the high end of normal. Christopher felt more certain than ever that he was making the right decision about his own career. He sighed in contentment. He had a wonderful family, a fantastic home and the perfect job. A brilliant future lay ahead.

Chapter 12

Martin's car was on the drive when Alison returned home from work. She checked the time on the dashboard, five-thirty – he'd usually be at the gym by now.

Sammy was sitting on the doorstep, looking regal cleaning his paw. He gave her a pitiful look and meowed, as if to warn her Martin was inside.

'Hi, love,' shouted Martin as she opened the door.

Sammy hissed and shot off under the hedge back to his own garden.

'Was that that bloody awful cat again? Just wait until I get my lion's poo.' He appeared at the kitchen door holding a mug. 'Want one? I saved you some cake. They loved it at work.'

'Please.' She slipped off her shoes and felt herself relax. 'You'll never guess what happened at work.'

Over a tiny slice of cake and coffee, Alison related the details of her hideous day.

'Surely they can't do that without an investigation into the situation?' said Martin. 'It smacks of constructive dismissal to me.'

'They haven't asked for anyone's opinion about anything, other than the person who complained. But I don't think they're trying to make us leave.'

'It's ridiculous. There appear to be no professional

standards at all in that place. You should raise a grievance.'

Alison ate her last spoonful of cake. 'Drat, I forgot to have some cherry sauce.'

'There was none left, sorry. Why don't you have a word with your union representative?'

'Not sure I've got the energy to fight them.'

'From what I can see, you're the one who's come off worst. You'll be on your own with them.'

'If I went for constructive dismissal and won, I'd get a lump sum. Would be handy for uni.'

Martin looked at her as if he was going to say something but didn't.

'No, it wouldn't be right. Maybe all this has done me a good turn.'

'How so?'

'If it wasn't for the aggro, I wouldn't have been desperately searching for a quicker escape and discovered that we have enough funds for me to leave.' She reached for her mobile. 'That reminds me, I need to have another go at re-setting my login details.'

'Do it later, you just got home. I checked the balance today, it's the same as the running total in your ancient little book.'

'See, it comes in handy when the stupid website doesn't work.'

He shot her a sideways glance. 'Yeah, you reckoned it somehow managed to change your details, didn't you…?'

'I've been thinking about our holidays. The Gran Canaria one, for example. If we didn't go, we'd save four thousand pounds. And we'd still have two other holidays to look forward to.'

Martin's head snapped round to her. 'You don't want to go to the Canaries?'

'Little Peggy at work has one holiday a year – a fortnight in Blackpool.'

He looked aghast. 'Blackpool?'

'No. The point is… Well, don't you think our holidays have gotten a bit out of hand?'

'No, we love that place. The spa is amazing.'

'Oh, come on, love. We only peer through the window when we wander past. And after a couple of days, we don't notice it.' She cleared away the mugs and plates. 'Oh, by the way, I finally got a referral to the sleep clinic.'

'That's great. But getting back to your job… What kind of reference would you get if you left now, after the complaint? It might scupper your chances of getting on the course, never mind find a new job afterwards. Not to mention if you go to your union.'

Alison frowned. 'You were all for me involving the union a minute ago. If I really felt I was being constructively dismissed, I'd have to do something about it. I'd hope to have your support…'

'Of course you would, it's–'

'And if I won, that would prove I was the injured party and had a right to go to tribunal. So, I don't think it would hinder me in any way. Or it shouldn't.'

She was thankful that not every establishment was as snooty and judgemental as St Paul's primary. She sometimes thought Martin set too much store in the opinions of others. He could be very black and white – so used to telling children what they should and shouldn't do. And opinionated. Then again, she could hardly criticise since recent antics in her own workplace belonged more in the playground than in the office.

'I know something that'll cheer you up,' said Martin with a big grin. He disappeared out to the utility room and returned with a bottle. 'Look what I found. Let's crack it open and watch a film.'

'No, that's the Moet for your mam's birthday meal.'

His eyes widened. 'Oh crap. When is it again?'

'Martin, she's *your* mother. She's seventy on Saturday.'

He looked from the bottle to Alison in disappointment.

'Go on then.' She reached into the cupboard for two flutes. 'You'll have to replace it, though. I won't have time to get to the shops before the meal.'

He rattled around in the freezer for ice and popped the cork. 'You know what would go with it…? A Hawaiian pizza.'

An hour later, the pair of them were ensconced on the sofa, watching *Bridget Jones's Diary,* a half-eaten family-sized pizza on the coffee table next to the ice bucket.

Martin handed her another slice. 'It's like the old days.'

She cackled. 'Except we couldn't afford a table.' Alison looked around the lounge, with its huge corner leather sofa and forty-inch television. 'We've come a long way since then…'

'When you think of how little we had.'

'Can you remember how we used to dream of having a garden with a slide and a swing for Chloe and Jack?' Alison snuggled into Martin as she thought about cosy Sunday mornings. Shattered after the night feeds and teething, they'd whisper their dreams to each other, so as not to disturb the twins.

The garden toys were now long gone, replaced by a stylish swinging bench seat and matching John Lewis bistro set. Alison sat with her feet up on Martin's legs. 'Let's have one more glass.'

He went to replenish her drink, but only a couple of drops came out.

'Probably for the best,' she said. 'I feel a bit tipsy and Work's bad enough without a hangover.'

'Suppose so.' He cleared away the bottle and ice bucket and disappeared outside.

Alison remained on the sofa, trying not to think about the following day, while Martin clanked the bottle into the recycling bin. He returned with another. 'I see you bought two.'

'We really shouldn't,' she said, holding out her glass. 'Sixty quid they cost me.'

'I'll get another two from the supermarket tomorrow. Not

this stuff though,' he laughed. 'They wouldn't appreciate it.'

She noticed Martin's taut thigh muscle flex through his jeans as he leaned over to fill the flutes. A realisation that they hadn't made love for three weeks shocked her. It was the longest gap since they'd got married. Alison set down the glass on the coffee table and shot him a cheeky grin. 'Follow me.' She headed out to the hall. 'Bring the Moet.'

They giggled like teenagers all the way upstairs. Martin set down the drinks, then picked her up and threw her onto the bed.

She ran her hands over his firm shoulders and her tummy flipped. 'You've gone all macho. I love it.'

Martin pulled off his T-shirt and flexed his biceps. 'Brace yourself, woman.'

She cackled at the sight of her husband, a smouldering expression on his face while he attempted his best Brad Pitt imitation.

'You're supposed to go weak at the knees with desire, not be overcome by mirth.' He wiggled his eyebrows, and she laughed louder.

The landline telephone rang.

'Ignore it.' Martin dived onto the bed. 'It'll be my mam. I haven't phoned her tonight.'

Alison batted an image of Doreen's critical face to the back of her mind. 'Don't mention your mother, it's enough to put me off.'

'I've got the very thing to take your mind off her,' he said, kissing her giggles away. He suddenly recoiled, his face etched with pain.

'Cramp in your leg?' It was a recurring problem, for which Alison had suggested seeing a chiropractor, followed by a programme of Pilates. Martin seemed to prefer to suffer.

'Give me a minute,' he said through clenched teeth. 'It'll go off.' He attempted to stretch it out. 'Aargh.'

Alison tried not to laugh as Martin lumbered around the

bedroom, dragging his right leg. 'Now my foot's cramping as well.'

She peered at his foot. 'Your toes shouldn't be able to flex that far up. They're almost touching your shin. Have you been replacing your electrolytes after working out?'

'Shh. Yeow.'

'Why don't you see that chiropractor I mentioned? I'm convinced it's coming from your hip.'

He was now in what looked like the yoga warrior pose. 'I'll be fine,' he said with a grimace.

The phone rang again.

'Bloody hell.'

'I'll get it,' said Alison.

'No, don't. I'll be all right in a second…'

She reached over to the bedside unit for the handset, taking a swig of champagne on the way. 'Hello… It's Jack.' She put him on loudspeaker. 'Is everything all right?'

'Yeah, yeah. Chloe and I were wondering… Do we have to come home for Grandma's meal this weekend?'

'Of course, you do. It's her birthday.'

'Can't we send a card? It's just that there's a great new band on at the Student's Union, and we –'

'No, sorry.' Alison knew it was an excuse. Though they were both at Manchester university, they had their own groups of friends and rarely socialised together. It had been a coincidence they'd chosen the same place, but it had delighted Alison. Knowing they were near to each other stopped her worrying too much. Jack was studying Information Technology, and Chloe Business Studies and Marketing. Although they were based at different sites, they could get to each other quickly if the need ever arose.

'I suppose it was worth a try,' sighed Jack.

'I don't want to go either, but we have to make sacrifices for family.'

'Well, can you at least get Dad not to bicker with aunty Gail?

I hate it when they start.'

'I don't bicker,' said Martin.

Both Jack and Alison laughed at that.

When she replaced the handset, Martin was standing at the bottom of the bed staring at her.

'What do you mean, you don't want to go?'

Alison shook her head. 'You have to ask? Your mother starts on me as soon as we arrive, Robbie slobs around stinking the place out, you and Gail end up tearing strips off each other, and –'

'Don't exaggerate. You've always been over-sensitive to Mam's comments. She would never deliberately offend you.'

'She likes nothing better. And anyone would think Gail was your sister, not your sister-in-law.'

'It's only when our Keith gets drunk and ignores her. And Robbie's not so bad.'

'He's rude and dirty. Gail and Keith let him get away with murder. Have you forgotten how he used to mercilessly torment Chloe and Jack? I couldn't say a word without getting my head bitten off.'

He crawled back onto the bed and wrapped his arms around her. 'My cramp's gone.'

'The thought of that lot… And the furniture polish. It sets off my sinuses as soon as I walk through the door. I'm sure your mam randomly blasts it around when she knows I'm going.'

'You sound paranoid. She never stops, always cleaning and running around after my dad, what with his arthritis and everything.'

'She wouldn't need to do half as much if she allowed him to have a stairlift.' It was a fruitless argument. As pointless as the one about his ability to drive a car with a manual gearbox. 'The man can no longer bend his knees.'

Martin tried to nuzzle her neck. 'Let's not let this ruin the moment.'

She puffed out a big breath. 'It already has – I'm going to put my pyjamas on.'

He flopped back on the bed. 'I told you not to answer that damned phone…'

Chapter 13

Shirley popped her head around the office door and smiled. 'Are you free? Your –' Sandy clicked straight past on her black Versace heels, a to-go cup in each hand. 'Wife's here to see you.'

'Thanks,' Christopher said, leaning around Sandy, who'd plonked herself in the seat on the other side of his desk, blocking Shirley from view. He could tell Shirley was vexed by the way her top lip curled up ever so slightly at one side. Turning to Sandy he lowered his voice and said, 'That was rude.'

Sandy glanced at the ajar door and frowned. 'No, it wasn't. I don't need her permission to see my husband. She was being pedantic – Making me wait out there until she deigned to allow me in.'

'She was doing her job and you were disrespectful.' Christopher usually admired Sandy's forthright manner, but he'd never known her to be discourteous before.

'I was trying to be nice – I brought you coffee...' She leaned over the desk and brushed his cheek with her hand. 'I do appreciate how hard you work for us.'

He turned and kissed her hand. 'I know you do.' He noticed her nails. One had a tiny chip in it. 'Don't they do nails over there?'

'Who?'

'The salon over the road.' He took a sip of coffee. 'Latte? I shouldn't really…' He closed his eyes and savoured the delicious full fat milk he'd missed since starting his health kick. 'Did you get my text message? I also tried to call you.'

She averted her eyes and took a sip of her black Americano. 'Didn't I reply? Sorry, I could have sworn I did. I mustn't have pressed Send in my haste.'

'I was surprised you went in to be honest.'

'Where?'

'That salon. You looked like you were on a mission.' He nodded at the hand with the chipped nail. 'It's hardly noticeable anyway.'

Sandy looked down at her hands and spotted the chip. 'Oh, I erm… I wasn't going to say anything… I was checking out the competition.' She rummaged in her Saint Laurent tote bag and pulled out a paper packet. 'I got you a treat…'

Christopher peered inside. 'My pre-diabetes…'

Sandy rolled her eyes.

'He took out the fat Danish pastry from the bag and inhaled. 'I can smell the almond filling.' He sighed. 'Thank you, but –'

Sandy waved away his protestations. 'Go on, it's a one-off.' She scrunched the packet into a ball and launched it into the bin.

'Where's yours?'

She cackled. 'You don't get legs like these by eating that stuff.' She straightened out one of her long slim legs and ran her hand along her thigh, showcased to perfection in skinny black jeans.

Christopher didn't know if it was the pastry or his wife's legs that made his mouth water. He pushed the treat to one side and grinned. 'Come around to this side of the desk and let me see.'

A cough sounded from the other room, making

Christopher and Sandy giggle like naughty children.

'What did you mean about checking out the competition?' Christopher said in a more adult tone.

'Well, I said I wanted to set up my beauty and health business when Emily had grown up. But I'm out of the loop, so I decided to have a scout around.'

'Excellent idea.' Christopher felt a swell of pride at his wife's entrepreneurial attitude. 'Get a broader idea of the current market.'

She looked at him, her brow furrowed. 'What do you mean?'

'Well you see a lot of top end salons, but not so much the more middle of the range type, like the one over the road – with a different client-base. Good to build up a solid foundation of knowledge.'

Sandy drained her coffee cup. 'Yeah, that's what I was thinking. Anyway, they don't do nails over there.' She started gathering up her things. 'Right, I must get off.'

'Have you got a couple of minutes? I wanted to run you through our finances.' He noticed the corners of her mouth turn down. 'Nothing heavy.' He clicked open a spreadsheet. 'Just look at the projected income and expenditure totals at the bottom, ignore the rest. There'll be a significant positive balance.'

Sandy didn't so much as glance at the screen. 'How can you say that?'

'You'd say the same if you looked at the blooming screen.' He smiled apologetically. 'Sorry for snapping. Just look, please.'

Sandy inhaled sharply. 'That's a lot less.'

He felt himself rankle. 'Not if you consider the reduction in our outgoings. And once Emily and Simon move out of the Durham flat, we can rent it out and we'll be even better off.'

'No, I've got plans for it. It's going to be my crash-pad – somewhere the girls and I can stay after a night out.'

Christopher scrutinised her face for signs she was pulling his leg. There were none. 'Are you saying you're happy for me to do a job I no longer enjoy, and which is affecting my health, so that you and your friends can have a *crash-pad*? Will any of *their* husbands be chipping in, or will it just be me footing the bill?'

Sandy pressed her lips together and exhaled heavily through her nose. 'Us – it's *our* money.'

'Yes, of course it is. But something's got to give. You have to accept that, surely?'

Her expression softened. She walked around to him and perched on the desk. As she curled the hair in the nape of his neck between her fingers, she smiled lovingly at him. 'I was also thinking that you and I could spend some time there. Maybe go to the theatre or out for a nice meal and stay over. It would be our little love nest.'

'How? I'd be off working down the country.' He shrugged. 'We have a lovely six-bedroomed love nest a taxi ride from Durham. Emily could easily have jumped on a train to get to university – she didn't even have to move out.'

Sandy pouted at him. 'You said that flat was a good investment for the future.'

He gave a weak smile. 'It's the future now, Sandy.' He slid his arms around her waist and drew her closer. 'If you want to stay over in Durham, we can always book in a hotel.'

Sandy pulled away and looked down at him, her huge blue eyes glistening with tears.

'We only bought it, so she had somewhere safe to live. Unlike other students, Emily's had rent-free accommodation for the duration of her course – not to mention the three years since she graduated. We should be charging her, especially now she's living there with Simon.'

'Don't be silly. You can't charge your daughter rent.'

'Why not? They're both working.'

'I don't know what's happened to you lately, Christopher.

You're turning into a right old skinflint.'

'Skinflint?' He eyed her bag on the desk. 'Is that new?'

She gave it a surreptitious shove behind her. 'No, I've had it ages.'

'Face it, I'm far too young for my health to be failing – pre-diabetes, blood pressure...'

'God, you're wearing them like a bloody badge.'

'Sandy, give me a break…'

She rolled her eyes again. 'You said you'd lose weight to get your blood pressure down.'

'And I am. But this job change could also have a big impact on my quality of life.' He nodded at the pastry. 'And I'm not sure you're taking any of this seriously.'

'But you love a nice Danish.'

He sighed. 'I do. Unfortunately, they no longer love me.'

Sandy leaned in to kiss his cheek. She grabbed a handful of the flesh around his waist. 'Don't worry, once you get this under control, you'll be fine.' She jumped off the desk.

Christopher felt a surge of embarrassment. He stood up and walked over to the window, straightening up to lengthen his torso as much as he could. 'I know I'm heavier than I used to be, but do you think I'm that fat?'

'No, but if your weight is the cause of the problem, tackle that.' She ran her hand through her long blond hair. 'There's no need to throw away a successful career.'

'I'm not. I'm no longer interested in the cut and thrust of it all.' He splayed his arms and looked around the office as he spoke. 'I like it here, Sandy. They've offered me the chance to stay, and I want to accept it.'

A gleeful squeak sounded from the other room.

Sandy marched over to the door and slammed it shut. 'You can't down tools and go off on sabbatical because you are bored,' she hissed.

'Now come on, that's not what this is about.' He rubbed his face with both hands. 'I could be happy at this branch. I like the team and they like me…'

She gave a slow blink and stood with her hands on her hips. 'You'll have them sitting cross-legged on the floor singing Kumbaya next.

'Stop it, please. I miss you and Emily. I'm tired of moving around, living in temporary accommodation. I want a home, our home – with you.'

Sandy opened her mouth to speak then closed it again. She raised her arms, let them flop down by her sides and walked out of the room, leaving a trail of Versace Blue fragrance in her wake.

Chapter 14

Alison's stomach churned with anxiety as she walked along the hospital corridor to the sleep clinic. Memories of visiting her parents in Critical Care after the car crash flooded her mind. Though it was a different hospital it felt the same. An awful, twilight-zone world, where people bustled past while she wandered around like a zombie, waiting to hear that they'd died. The corridor even had the same smell about it.

She paused to look out of a window while she tried to recall happier hospital memories. As she watched a rabbit hop across the garden to a shrub, she pictured seeing little Chloe and Jack for the first time in the delivery suite. Her anxiety began to subside. And then a random image popped into her mind that made her laugh out loud – her mother-in-law's disgruntled face as she came out of the plaster room with her arm in a cast. Doreen had fallen while hurtling to the buffet at a wake. It wasn't often that Doreen got her comeuppance, but when she did, it never failed to cheer up Alison.

Feeling better, she continued along to the sleep department. If they could help her, this could be life changing. She couldn't begin to imagine what it would be like if she could sleep.

Alison pushed open the doors to the sleep department and was hit by a delicious aroma of sticky toffee pudding. As the waiting room was empty, she sat down and read a leaflet on snoring. She had been there for around ten minutes without seeing a single soul when it occurred to her that she might be in the wrong place. She wandered back out onto the corridor to check the door sign against her appointment letter. It appeared to be the right place.

She clattered the door to attract attention on her way back in. 'Hel-lo…' she called. Nothing. She coughed as loud as she could, re-checked the time and date on her appointment letter again and sat down in the same seat. When no one appeared after another five minutes, Alison tentatively went in search of a member of staff, cautiously venturing through an open door and along a corridor leading off from the waiting room.

There was no one in the first room she came to. The door to the next one was slightly ajar, so she knocked on it. As it swung open, she gasped. A nurse lay with her head resting on a pillow on the desk – fast asleep. Alison panicked and quickly turned, banging her handbag off the door frame.

'What, why, eh?' The nurse's desk chair wheeled backwards, almost toppling her onto the floor.

'Oh, I'm so sorry,' said Alison. She attempted to discretely close the door but yelped as a shock shot up her arm. Ever since the nylon trousers episode, she'd felt as if she was plugged into the mains.

The nurse jumped up, flattened down her hair with one hand and straightened her tunic. She removed what looked like an oxygen cannula from her nose and a plastic probe from her finger. 'I must apologise. Do you have an appointment?' She bustled around, bumping into things as she attempted to tidy up and remove all trace of her nap. She hurled the pillow beneath the desk and gave it a swift kick with a black clumpy-shoe-shod foot.

Alison held out her appointment letter. 'Sorry I woke you. I suspect I'm in the wrong place.'

The nurse took the letter. 'No, no. You're in the right department.' She gave a nervous laugh and smoothed her hair again. 'Electronics returned a piece of sleep monitoring kit and I had to test it. It helps if you can doze off.' She craned her neck to look towards the waiting room. 'The sleep administrator was meant to give me a knock after ten minutes. So sorry.'

'Don't worry about it. There was no one around out there, so I wandered through here.'

'They must have gone for lunch. You're the last patient on the morning clinic list.' She looked around the room and then back at Alison. 'You'll have to excuse me – I feel rather discombobulated. I'm usually well prepared.' She scratched her head 'Erm. Did you get some forms to fill in?'

Alison handed over her completed documents and smiled to herself. This must be the sleepy sleep nurse Katie had mentioned. 'I feel a bit stupid, not being able to sleep. I know there are people with much worse problems than me.'

The nurse looked at Alison with bloodshot eyes and smiled. 'Not at all. If you could take a seat out in the waiting area, I'll give you a call in five minutes. Is that all right? Sorry.' She escorted Alison back along the corridor. 'I'm Michelle by the way. Hello.' Then she darted away.

It was only as the double doors to the corridor closed behind her that Alison noticed the 'No patient access' sign in a large bold font. She cringed.

Five minutes later, Michelle, now looking well-presented and professional, called Alison back into the office, which smelled of a mixture of toothpaste and lemon air freshener. There were some leaflets about sleep neatly set out on the desk.

'Right, from your GP's referral letter, it looks as if you've tried to treat your insomnia yourself without any success.'

'Yes, I've tried everything – lavender pillows, cherry juice, over-the-counter supplements and countless other things I can't even remember. If anything, it's worse…'

The way Michelle nodded in apparent understanding made Alison want to hug her.

Michelle tapped the letter, her brow furrowed. 'Dr Smedley says you refused to comply with his advice. Did he give you a "one-stop" summary of the cognitive behavioural therapy for insomnia programme? It can work well for some people, but it requires a lot of self-discipline.'

Alison felt tears prick the back of her eyes. 'There's a special programme?' It felt like the sun was shining in the room, even though there were no windows. 'He gave me vitamin B pills and then told me to stop worrying and drink hot chocolate.'

Michelle threw her head back and cackled, then suddenly stopped and grimaced. 'Sorry, that was unprofessional. I don't know what's wrong with me today.' She coughed and turned to Alison, a more serious expression on her face. 'Let me outline the CBT-i programme. Then you can decide whether you'd like to go ahead with it.'

An hour later, a less hopeful Alison stood up to leave. 'I'll give it a go, though I've already tried most of the things you've suggested...'

'Yes, that's what everyone says,' said Michelle. 'But it's the putting everything together over a short period of time that makes it effective.' She pushed a pile of patient feedback cards to one side and stood up to open the door. 'Good luck. See you next week.'

'I suppose I have nothing to lose by trying...'

'Exactly. And remember, it's perfectly normal to feel worse for a while,' said Michelle with a cheery smile.

'What... even on a weekend?' said Sharon. 'There's no way I could do that, I like my sleep too much.'

'Yep, go to bed at one in the morning and get up at six – regardless of whether or not I've slept,' said Alison. 'The times don't worry me too much, I'm awake most of the night anyway.' She took a sip of coffee. 'It's cutting back on the caffeine that worries me. None after midday. My head's going to be banging by morning.'

Katie checked her watch. 'It's half-one now.'

'I'm starting tomorrow. But this canteen stuff won't do. If I'm having less of it, I'll have to pop out for a nice takeaway coffee.' Alison looked at her friends hopefully. 'Maybe for the exercise part, you girls could join me on a lunch time?'

Katie and Sharon shot each other sideways glances.

'Oh, sorry I won't be able to. I'll be too far away in the prefabs, at the back of bloody beyond,' Sharon said, looking suitably disappointed.

Katie gave Sharon a sly dig with her elbow. She turned to Alison and smiled. 'Could do. How about you get a routine going on your own at first? Didn't you say the nurse told you that you shouldn't be dependent on other people to help you make it work?'

Alison scrutinised her friend. 'Drat, you're so sharp.'

'I get a good night's sleep.' She laughed and bit into her chocolate chip muffin. 'Anyway, Sharon, how are the preparations for Cynthia's party going?'

Neither of the women were keen on Sharon's sister and only feigned interest out of loyalty to their friend. Cynthia seemed to delight in nothing better than putting Sharon down in public at every opportunity. 'You're piling the weight on there… You need to exercise more,' cackle, cackle. 'Stop making a show of yourself, dancing like that. You're too old to be able to do the splits…'

'Cynthia's being ridiculous,' said Sharon. 'It's like when we were kids – she always had to make things difficult. I blame Mam for spoiling her because she was the youngest. We've got to change the balloons. Ian texted me to say she wants no mention of her age. Apparently, under threat of divorce. Such a drama queen.'

Katie threw her hands up. 'How on earth can she have a fortieth birthday party without the forty bit?'

'Exactly. Poor Ian's trying to make her birthday special and she does nothing but complain. I made it worse by telling her Davey and I have booked a holiday to Greece.'

'I'd love to have a sister,' said Alison. 'It was lonely being an only child. My mam said I had an imaginary sister called Ermintrude.'

They all laughed.

'I have no recollection of it. Or where I got the name from.'

'The cow on *The Magic Roundabout*,' said Katie matter-of-factly.

As they reminisced about childhood television programmes, Billy walked into the canteen with Phyllis. Phyllis detoured past their table to have a smirk. She eyed Sharon's chocolate chip muffin. 'Do you know how many calories are in that?' she twittered, smoothing down her skirt with one hand to draw attention to her non-existent stomach. She looked Sharon up and down.

'Phyllis…' Sharon stared at her nose, 'how do you manage to breathe when you eat?'

'You can't speak to me like that.'

'What are you going to do? Have me moved from the office?' Sharon glared at her as she bit into her cake.

'You know that wasn't me.'

'Go away,' said Katie. She pointed over to Billy, who was chatting to Dorothy from supplies while perusing the chiller cabinet. 'He's getting on like a house on fire with her over there.'

Phyllis squinted over to Billy and Dorothy, standing with their heads dipped together and laughing. She sniffed her nose into a sharp point and scuttered away. When she reached the others, all three turned around and sniggered.

'She looks like a little rat,' said Alison.

'Where on earth can she be getting that perm these days?' said Sharon.

Katie laughed. 'Come on girls, let it go. Don't descend to her level.'

Sharon glared at Billy. 'It's that oaf who encourages her anyway. He loves it.'

'So unprofessional,' said Alison. 'Have you ever wanted to slap someone's face and never ever stop?' She bared her teeth at Billy.

'Not that I can recall,' said Katie.

Sharon shot Katie a side-glance.

Alison's eyes widened as she realised that they were staring at her. 'Not that I would, of course.' She gave a little cough and took out her vitamins. 'But I'll be glad to get out of this place.'

'Why don't you have a word with your bank?' said Sharon. 'Instead of getting angry and wishing your life away, go over the figures with a professional and see when it would be feasible to go?'

Katie grinned and tapped the air with her finger. 'Ooh, didn't you say you thought your sexy silver fox worked for Henleys?'

'Don't need to. I have the figures. And Martin's more than capable of understanding them.'

'Go on. I'll come with you for support,' continued Katie. 'Once you have a firm plan of action, you might feel better.'

Alison dismissed the suggestion. Though she had to admit she could do with some professional advice, she'd feel disloyal to Martin if she went without him. 'I just need to convince Martin it's not too early.'

'I thought he was on board?'

'He is, but he's playing devil's advocate about the timing.'

'You can't argue with numbers,' said Katie.

Feeling uneasy about mentioning Martin's objections, she changed the subject. 'Have you ever had problems with online banking? I've had a right carry on with my login. No sooner did they reset it than I got locked out again. I'm not sure I even used my new password. Martin's had no problems with the same account.'

'Sounds a bit suspicious to me,' said Sharon.

'I was scared I'd been hacked or had downloaded a Trojan virus on my laptop. But Martin logged on okay and said the money was all there.'

Sharon gave a little laugh. 'Were you there when he checked? Maybe he doesn't want you to get at the money.'

Alison shook her head. 'That's an awful thing to say. It's my university fees account – it never gets touched. Anyway, how could he lock me out of a joint account? That's an awful thing to say. He's fully supportive of my plans –'

'Okay, calm down. I was joking,' said Sharon.

'What the heck's the matter with you?' asked Katie.

'It's just that, Martin thinks we should save a bit more money, as a safety net. He suggested we get the drive done and have another holiday first, while I'm earning. But I hate it here more each day. And I feel like I'm going mad.'

Sharon gently touched her arm. 'Sorry, I didn't mean to be flippant.'

Alison shrugged. 'Maybe I'm being impatient. I could wait. Oh, I don't know. One minute I'm certain, the next I'm confused. My head's all over the place at the minute.'

Katie studied her face, a serious look on her own. 'You need to simplify it. Which would you regret more – putting off university, or foregoing the drive and holiday?'

'University, of course,' said Alison without missing a beat.

'There's your answer. No need to tie yourself in knots about it.

Chapter 15

'Mam, what did we get for Grandma?' called Chloe from her bedroom.

'Hang on.' Alison tied a length of red ribbon around a gift and finished it off with a neat bow. She grabbed a plastic carrier bag from down beside her dressing table and took it through to Chloe. 'Thornton's chocolates and Blue Grass perfume.' The fragrance made her stomach turn, but it was Doreen's favourite. 'You can wrap it yourself. There's paper and a card in there, too. Ask Jack to write it out when he gets back from the gym, so she thinks he remembered.'

Chloe glanced up from her downward dog position. 'Okay, in a minute.' The instructor on her tablet screen rolled up to standing, copied by a pink-cheeked Chloe.

Alison scrutinised the tablet. 'Where does the DVD go?'

'DVD?' Chloe, now balancing on one foot laughed and wobbled. 'No one uses those these days. It's on YouTube.'

'What's that?' Alison watched the instructor execute another move. 'She's not doing that right. Her leg's too high, it'll strain her back.' She grabbed Chloe's leg and manoeuvred it into position. 'There, like that. Are you all nipped in?'

'Ye-es, Mam.' Chloe looked from the screen to Alison. 'Ooh, I don't know why I never thought of it before. You could do this.'

'I was thinking about teaching Pilates again. To go alongside my course.'

'You've applied? Brilliant. About blooming time.' Chloe jumped up, threw her arms around her mother and lifted her off the floor.

'Not yet,' Alison wheezed out 'But I'm about to.'

Chloe set her down and stepped back into a leg stretch. 'It would fit around your studies. You could record sessions at home and upload them.'

Alison held up her hand and stepped back. 'Record? I couldn't do that. I know I use computers at work, but that's way beyond me. Anyway, I need to earn money from it.'

'You can earn a fortune if you get it right. Jack could help you with the techie stuff. And then you just need to get subscribers to attract advertising.'

Alison's brows knitted together. 'Now you're talking gobbledygook.'

'My little mam, an internet star.'

'Like a porn star,' laughed Alison.

Chloe cackled. 'Can you imagine Dad's face if you showed up in a porn search? He'd go mental.'

'Dad's not so bad.' Alison pulled a sheet of wrapping paper from the carrier bag and opened it out on the bed. 'You should be doing this,' she said, reaching for the scissors.

'You're joking, aren't you? He can be a right old misery. Sometimes, he sounds more like your *dad* than your husband.'

As Chloe disappeared off for a shower, Alison wrapped the gifts and watched the instructor continue with her class. She walked over to the full-length mirror and executed a roll down – correctly. Excitement fluttered in her stomach. Even though she knew nothing about internet videos, or how anyone could make money from them, she had a good feeling. With some new gear – and a bit of makeup – maybe she'd get away with it.

***

Keith's car was already on the drive when they pulled up outside Doreen's house. The red velour curtains twitched at the lounge window and the hall light went on.

Jack laughed. 'Did you see Grandma's eye – just the one – peeping out?'

'That hiding behind the curtain thing reminds me of when we were little,' said Chloe. 'She thinks she's invisible.'

Alison passed the gifts and card to the twins. 'I don't know why she doesn't wave like normal people.'

'Remind me what we got her again?' said Martin.

'The cashmere cardigan she was hinting for.' She handed him the gift. 'Here, you give it to her, she'll like that.'

'Thanks. It's a good job you remembered the date. I don't know what I'd do without you. Mam would be devastated if she knew I'd forgotten.'

'She'd find a way to blame me and then cook mince and dumplings for you, to compensate for having such a horrible wife,' laughed Alison. 'I'll give her two minutes to praise you and five to have a dig at me.'

'I bet she hugs Jack before me,' said Chloe.

'She loves her boys,' Jack said, nudging Chloe. 'You girls can set the table.'

Chloe punched his arm.

'No, not on her birthday, she'll be in a great fettle and on her best behaviour,' said Martin. He kissed Alison's cheek and grinned. 'You'll get a reprieve. Maybe fifteen for you, and five for me.'

As Martin reached up to knock on the door, it whooshed open, causing him to topple forward into the hallway. Doreen caught him in a hug. 'Hello son. Oh, I'm so glad you're here.'

Martin lifted his mother off her feet, and she squealed in mock shock. 'Happy birthday, Mam.'

Doreen tutted. 'I'm not bothered about birthdays anymore. You don't when you get to my age.' She clocked the others over Martin's shoulder. 'Oh, little Jack. Come here and give

Grandma a kiss.'

Alison gave Chloe a sideways look.

'Hiya Grandma,' said Chloe.'

'Come in, love.' Doreen spotted Alison. 'Oh, hello, Alison, are you here?' She shot off along the hall.

'Why do you put up with that, Mam?' hissed Chloe. 'And Dad should have nipped it in the bud years ago.'

Alison gave a wave of dismissal. 'It doesn't bother me, as long as she treats you fairly.' She stepped inside and coughed. 'That blinking polish catches the back of your throat.'

There was an angry shout from the lounge.

'The others are in the front room.' Doreen pulled the lounge door closed. 'Come into the kitchen first and have a catch up with me. Cup of tea, son? Jack, I got you that fruity cider you like.'

'Chloe likes that, too,' said Alison. She collected their coats and hung them in the cupboard beneath the stairs. She closed the door and screamed as a wet blast stung her eyes. When she could focus again, she noticed an automatic air freshener on one of the shelves. 'Right at bloody eye level.' Squinting, she moved it to a higher shelf.

In the kitchen, Martin clanked the carrier bag containing two bottles of Moet Champagne onto the work top. 'I've brought some bubbly to celebrate.' He shot Alison a cheeky grin.

'Mam, what's wrong with your eyes?' asked Jack.

'Air freshener. Doreen, I've moved it to a higher shelf.'

Doreen raised one eyebrow and continued chattering away to Martin. True to his word, he had replaced the Champagne they'd drank, but with a cheap and chatty alternative. Alison had forked out for more Moet. Chloe already had the others in her holdall to take back to her student digs.

'You're so considerate, Martin. You're like me in that regard.' She reached up to kiss his cheek. 'I've got some of that Sam Meegel beer you like too. I do like to see you, son.'

Martin turned and winked at Alison. 'Two minutes,' he mouthed.

'Happy birthday,' said Alison to her mother-in-law's back.

Doreen continued fussing over Martin.

It occurred to her that every other member of the family was either shorter, or taller than she was. There were three picture shelves. Only one of which was at her eye level. The idea that Doreen might want to blind her shocked her, more because she'd had such a crazy thought than it being a possibility. She shuddered, if she didn't watch herself, she'd end up like paranoid Phyllis.

Martin and the twins handed Doreen the gifts. She was like an excited child as she ran her hand over the shiny gold paper on the one Alison had wrapped from herself and Martin.

'Lovely detail,' said Doreen. She smiled at Alison. 'Look, the twins have brought me gifts, too. All beautifully wrapped. I think they must take after my Martin.'

'Mam wrapped ours,' piped up Chloe as she rummaged in the fridge for a drink.'

'So thoughtful they are.' Doreen turned to Martin and gently caressed his cheek.

Alison sighed quietly, already regretting volunteering to drive home. 'Yes, we tried to bring them up to have good manners.'

'Martin's a good father.'

'We'd have taken you out for a meal, Mam,' said Alison. Doreen's eyes narrowed. Alison knew she hated it when she called her *Mam*. It was a cheap shot, but it was all she had. She smiled sweetly. 'You didn't have to cook for everyone on your birthday.'

'You know what Mam's like, she enjoys it,' said Martin. 'Where's Dad?'

'Upstairs, faffing around.' Doreen frowned. 'He's so slow these days.'

'How's his arthritis?' said Alison. 'Has he thought any more about a stairlift?' They'd tried to persuade his parents to have one installed, but Doreen wouldn't have it.

'My old dad didn't have one, so Cyril's not getting one. Anyway, the doctor said the stairs are good exercise for me. He's fine. A stairlift would just get in my way.'

Martin squeezed Alison's shoulder. 'Might be something to consider in the future though.'

'Come on, Jack,' said Chloe. 'Grab a bottle and let's go and see Rancid Robbie.'

Ignoring the subject of stairlifts, Doreen picked up a gift then paused. 'Don't you think Martin's looking thin, Alison?' She frowned and touched his brow. 'Have you been eating properly? You look so tired.' She shot Alison a sharp look. 'No doubt he's working too hard, as always. Footing bills and what not.'

'I'm fine, and I get plenty to eat,' said Martin. 'Alison's a great cook.'

His mother's eyes widened, and she gave a tiny shake of her head. 'My Martin's a grafter – always has been.'

Alison glared at her husband. 'We both work pretty hard, don't we, darling?'

Doreen flinched at the word *darling*. Alison kept a straight face but smiled inwardly, even though she knew she was being childish. Doreen pulled out the cream-coloured cashmere cardigan and gasped in delight.

'We hope it's the right one,' said Alison. 'There's a gift receipt in there so you can change it if it isn't.'

Doreen hugged Martin, yet again. 'Thank you so much, it's beautiful. It's the one I wanted, you remembered.' She pulled a hankie from her apron pocket and wiped away a tear.

Martin squirmed and shot Alison an apologetic grimace. 'Pleased you like it. It's from both of us, of course.'

'Thanks Alison,' Doreen said without looking at her. She gripped Martin's hand and choked back a sob. 'You've matured into such a generous man.'

Alison gave up. Her mother-in-law was too good at this game. In over twenty years, Alison had never gotten the better of her.

Doreen opened the oven door and lifted out a huge casserole dish. She removed the lid, disappearing in a cloud of steam. 'Nearly ready.'

'That smells delicious, Mam.'

'Mince and dumplings, your favourite.'

As she returned it to the oven, Martin put his finger to his lips and widened his eyes at Alison. 'Lovely. Mam, you make the best mince and dumplings in the world.'

Alison gave Martin's foot a sly kick.

Doreen turned to Alison. 'A good feed, that's what he needs. He was healthy before he left home.'

'How's Cyril's cholesterol now?'

'That's all a load of rubbish if you ask me.' She threw her oven gloves onto the bench top and exhaled loudly. 'My lads were fed meat and two veg, every night without fail. They ailed nothing.'

'Don't you worry, Doreen. I make sure he eats well. Just last night he ate a whole tin of beans on his toast.'

Doreen gasped.

Martin stifled a laugh.

'Is that Gail I can hear in the lounge?' said Alison.

'Yes, they arrived on time,' said Doreen.

Alison felt her shoulders slump. 'So did we.' She glared at Martin and mouthed, *Say something.*

'They must've been early,' said Doreen. 'Gail's a considerate girl – always has been.'

Martin grabbed Alison's hand. 'Come on, let's say hello to the others. Give us a shout if you need any help, Mam.'

'Aw, thanks, son.'

'Pack it in,' said Alison, once out of earshot. 'She's on top form tonight as it is, so give me a break.'

'Relax. It's all light-hearted banter.'

'For you, maybe. But it gets a bit much sometimes. And the more you encourage her, the more digs she gets in. It's one thing her putting me down, but you need to pull her up over the way she ignores Chloe.'

'She treats the kids the same.'

'No, she doesn't. And quite frankly, it's upsetting that you can't see it. Stop wallowing in her adoration and man up.'

Martin let go of her hand. 'It's her birthday. Anyway, it's your own fault for biting.'

Alison stopped in her tracks. 'Don't defend the old bat,' she hissed. 'And your dad needs a stairlift.' She raised her eyes in the direction of the stairs. 'I bet he "decides" to have his meal up there.'

'Oh, here we go.'

She turned to face him, splaying her hands. 'What do you mean?'

'Can't we just have a nice time here, for once?'

'I'd love to, given the chance.' Alison studied her husband's hard expression. Her heart banged against her chest as, for the first time ever, she felt intense animosity towards him.

'What now? Why are you looking at me like that?'

'Nothing.' She turned the doorknob. 'Come on, let's get this over with.'

Her distress ramped up a notch. In the lounge, football blared from the television and a wet dog stench hung in the air – despite the absence of a dog. Keith and Gail sat in armchairs, bickering, while Robbie lay sprawled out on the sofa. Alison grimaced at the sight of his dirty-socked feet on the only remaining seat.

Keith and Gail looked up, said 'hello' and then resumed their sniping.

'Robbie, would you move your feet and let me sit down, please?' said Alison. 'Look, Chloe's had to sit on the floor.'

Chloe, sitting cross-legged against the radiator, glanced up from her mobile phone screen. 'I'm fine here, thanks. He stinks.'

Robbie took off one sock, rolled it up and bounced it off Chloe's head.

'Pack it in,' said Keith.

'Leave him alone,' said Gail.

'Happy days,' muttered Jack from his seat on the pouffe in the corner.

Martin backed towards the door. 'Anyone want a drink? Alison, orange juice?'

Gail glanced at Martin and gave Keith's leg a kick with her slipper. 'At least your brother's got manners. Alison's got the life of Riley; I've got a life-sentence.'

Martin laughed nervously from the doorway.

'I'll have Champagne please,' said Alison.

'You're driving.'

She smiled sweetly at him. 'Would you mind if I didn't?' She turned to Robbie. 'Oh, come on, shift your feet.'

Gail shot Alison a glare.

'Do you expect me to stand, Gail?'

'Robbie, move your feet. Or I'll send you to live with Uncle Martin and Aunty Alison,' said Gail.

Alison ignored the remark. Gail had used the same threat to control Robbie since he was little. She'd stopped thinking it was an odd thing to say years ago.

'What's up with you tonight, chipped a nail or something?' said Gail. She turned to Martin. 'I'll have Champagne.'

Alison nudged Robbie's legs further over with her foot and sat down. Robbie tutted and sat up, without taking his eyes off the football.

'I'll have Chloe's room,' Robbie said, hurling another sock her way.

'Mam, I want a lock on my bedroom door before I go back to uni.'

Alison could feel the walls closing in on her.

The meal went off like every other family get-together. Gail took advantage of any opportunity to nag Keith and snipe at Alison, who was easy prey as she was busy batting off Doreen's insults to see Gail's coming. And Cyril had his meal on a tray upstairs.

'Aunty Gail...' said Jack, after a particularly snidey comment about the dried-out state of his mother's hair.

Gail didn't hear, she was glaring at Martin.

Alison patted Jack's hand, smiled and gave a little shake of her head. 'Not worth it,' she whispered. She tucked her hair behind her ears and drained her flute.

Jack leaned his face towards her ear and whispered, 'She's a cow.'

Alison tutted in disapproval. 'You weren't brought up to speak like that. Then she leaned towards him and giggled. 'You're spot on, though.'

Gail shot Martin the look that usually preceded a verbal scrap. She accused Martin of bringing Moet to show off about how much he earned. Alison retreated to the kitchen.

The television was playing to itself – a documentary about the Bee Gee's. As she filled the sink with soapy water, an image of her father in a skin-tight white suit flashed into her mind. At the time, she was too young to know he was dressed as John Travolta from *Saturday Night Fever*, but she recalled giggling when he'd stopped to do a silly pose on the stairs, and then gasping as her mother sashayed down in high heels and the most beautiful red dress she'd ever seen. She'd watched in awe as they danced for her and the babysitter before going off in high spirits to a fancy-dress party.

'You Win Again' came on and Alison felt her heart thud with sudden, overwhelming grief. Her mother used to love that one. She'd say that Barry was a big strong hunk, like Alison's dad. Alison now watched Barry through adult eyes. Her mother was right, Barry was an extremely good-looking man. Then it hit her – in the recording, the brothers were young. Two of them had since died.

'But they couldn't have been old,' she said aloud. Panicking, she picked up her mobile phone and googled Barry's age. 'Seventy-three? He can't be.' She looked at the handsome man on the television screen, her brain frantically trying to calculate how long ago it had been recorded. 'But that makes me old, too.'

'Rubbish. You're not old.'

Alison jumped and turned, to find Keith had wandered in.

He went over to the fridge and took out a can of beer. 'Sorry, I didn't mean to scare you. Why don't you use the dishwasher?'

'I wanted an excuse to stay in here. The constant sniping and bickering drive me mad.'

He glugged the beer. 'Gail's started on Martin now, so suits me.' He drained the can and took out another.

'Is everything okay?'

Keith swayed and rubbed his face with one hand. 'She's worse than ever since Robbie moved out.'

Robbie was only a year younger than Jack and Chloe, but they were nothing alike. He'd grown up believing the world owed him a favour.

'How's he getting on?' said Alison.

'To be honest, I didn't think he was mature enough to leave home. He hasn't thought it through properly. When he sells a car, the commission's good, but it's unpredictable. And he can't grasp the idea of saving.'

'Is he managing his rent?'

'That's the thing, he keeps asking us for a sub. I said we should refuse. It's the only way he'll learn to look after himself. But Gail lectures him then gives in. It's hard enough running one home. Especially as…,' he paused and stared into the middle distance.

'Especially as what?'

'Pardon? Oh, don't mind me, I'm a bit squiffy. Dulls the pain…'

Alison noticed Keith was looking more drawn than usual. Lines had appeared on his forehead that weren't there not so long ago. Though he was a graphic designer, he now had the weathered look of someone who worked outdoors. No-one would guess he was Martin's younger brother.

'Has Gail thought about getting a job now that Robbie's left home?'

Keith spluttered on his beer. 'You're joking, aren't you? She's not like you – more like my mother. Even when Dad's knees were going, she had him out doing overtime.'

Alison frowned. 'Not good for a carpet-fitter. It's strange because your mother seems to resent Martin paying any of our bills.' She scrubbed the plate she was washing with extra vigour.

He steadied himself against the benchtop. 'And you work full-time,' Keith said, laughing. 'I love Mam, but I don't know how you put up with her.'

'I have to, for Martin and the kids. Anyway, she's not so bad – in small doses.' She gave a wry laugh. 'And she's the only mother figure I've got.'

'Your own mother would never have hidden your hair thing,' he slurred.

She looked up from the washing up. 'What hair thing?'

'Your wedding one. That was a nasty trick. If Martin had stood up to her, she'd have been different with you. He's like Dad – a right pushover.' Keith got up from his seat and grabbed another beer. 'Don't spend all night doing those, get yourself a drink and come through to the sitting room. It's awful in there.'

Alison's mind whirred. Had Doreen hidden her beautiful wedding hair comb? She wouldn't have done something so nasty, would she?

She thought back to the morning of the ceremony. Everything was going perfectly. She hadn't minded that the wedding had to be small, especially since her parents couldn't be there. Martin had said that drawing attention to starting a family without being married might have harmed his career prospects. Even so, when he'd suggested a little civil ceremony, just for family, she'd been disappointed. With no family of her own, it had left her with no one, except for the children. In the end, he'd conceded to Katie going.

The thing she'd most loved about her wedding outfit was the little Swarovski Crystal hair comb, bought well before she was even engaged. It was a coincidence that it matched the delicate belt on her ivory knee-length wedding dress. It had been on her dressing table on the morning of the ceremony, as she and Katie got dressed. Then it was gone.

Alison had bought it shortly after her mother's death. She'd been wandering around town looking for a funeral outfit, when a window display in the Swarovski store had caught her eye. She had stared at the sparkling hair decoration and sobbed. It was so small and delicate. Like her mother. Only her mother was lying in the chapel of rest in her coffin, her sparkle gone forever. Alison had bought the clip and immediately felt close to her.

She froze as she recalled Doreen popping in on her way to the venue. She'd made a special effort and was wearing her finest pieces of jewellery, including a huge ruby ring set in a surround of little diamonds, with matching necklace and earrings. It had looked spectacular against her white satin dress and jacket. It had seemed a strange choice for the mother of the groom – especially the colour. Alison had seen it in the bridal section in Harrington's department store.

Katie said that Doreen had worn it deliberately to upstage Alison. But Alison had insisted her future mother-in-law mustn't have realised it was designed for a bride, and she tried to justify it with the fact that her own outfit was ivory, so at least it wasn't the same colour.

Not for one minute had she suspected that someone among her tiny wedding party could have taken her hair comb. And

Doreen knew how precious it was to her. She and Katie had turned the room upside down looking for it to no avail. Without it, she'd felt as if her parents were missing twice over.

Alison stood at the sink, her hands hanging limply in the cooling soapy water, wishing that they were at her parent's home, celebrating her own mother's birthday. That her children were in the lounge with their wonderful, kind grandparents. As the Bee Gees sang a gentle melody in the background, Alison watched the last of the bubbles pop. She felt miserable, old and alone.

On the way home in the car Alison's head rang with snippets from the evening. She couldn't talk to Martin about her comb, not with the twins in the back. She knew she'd cry, and he'd say it was because of the alcohol. Thankfully, they disappeared up to their bedrooms once they got back.

'That wasn't too bad a night, was it?' said Martin.

'You're joking, aren't you? Your mother was awful to me. Gail was horrible, too. And then you and she kicked off, as usual. It was a nightmare.'

Martin turned to her, his tone betraying his irritation. 'What are you on about? We didn't "kick off".'

'You're like a couple of kids. Worse that Jack and Chloe ever were. I don't even understand why there's so much animosity between you.'

'You're imagining it. You go into my mam and dad's house looking for fault – every time. As soon as you step through the front door.'

'Hardly. She almost blinded me with that toxic spray.'

He laughed.

'It's not funny. I don't know what I ever did wrong to your mother.'

'You married me.'

'She's fine with Gail, and she married her other son.'

'The difference is that Keith doesn't love Gail. She's no competition.' Martin shrugged. 'Mam's harmless though.'

Alison looked at him, could he really be this obtuse? 'It's hard to make allowances for her when she's nasty towards me.'

He shot her a stony glare. 'That's unfair. She's not a nasty woman. It's the drink talking. You never could hold your alcohol.'

'Why are you being arsy? You were making fun about how she treats me earlier.'

Martin poured himself a Jack Daniels. 'Because you're going too far. It's not funny any longer.'

'Oh, let's all laugh at how your mother doesn't like me. But God forbid I tell you it hurts and ask you to support me.'

'My mother has been good to you over the years. You're being ridiculous.' He walked into the lounge and switched on the television.

Alison followed him. 'Has she really? Do you know what happened to my hair comb on our wedding day?'

Martin downed his drink in one. 'What on earth are you harping on about now?'

'Keith said —'

'He was drunk, and so are you. I'm going to bed.'

Alison sat on the sofa with a glass of water, feeling alone once more and wondering how the conversation had gotten so out of control. Martin had never reacted like this before. Then again, she'd never let herself become so openly rankled by Doreen. The most hurtful thing was that, though they joked about how Doreen doted on Martin and picked on her, she had never doubted that, if it got too much, Martin would support her. For the second time that night, she felt an aversion towards her husband.

Chapter 16

Alison sank back into the deep armchair and took in the opulent lounge – the velvet curtains hanging at the Victorian windows, the polished mahogany coffee tables and the ornate fireplace with coal crackling in the grate. She gazed into the fire, mesmerised by the changing shapes of the flames.

She hadn't intended to end up at Cherry Dene Hotel, she'd simply felt good as she jog-walked and kept going beyond her usual loop. It wasn't a place she'd have chosen to visit because it used to be Cherry Dene House, the old psychiatric asylum. Perusing the lounge, she wondered what it had been used for back in the day. Whatever that was, there was a lovely peace about it now. She closed her eyes and inhaled the subtle fragrance of fresh freesias, not quite overpowered by the earthy smell of burning coal. There was something comforting about the room, like being enveloped in a warm hug.

As she relaxed, she felt a sense of achievement at having met some of her CBT-i goals for the day. Although she found it hard to believe that the daily out-of-breath exercise would help to resolve her insomnia, she was committed to giving it her best effort. By the time she got home, she'd have achieved her daylight target too.

She hadn't yet mastered the mindfulness exercises. The previous night she'd tried counting back from a thousand in sevens but had ended up more frustrated than ever. Not only did it not distract her busy mind, she ended up more awake than ever, due to her obsessive need to ensure the numbers were correct. There were others to try, so all wasn't lost just yet.

A young waitress made barely a sound as she crossed the deep-pile carpet. Alison eyed the cafetiere she set down with great pleasure – she reckoned there'd be the best part of two cups of coffee in it. She checked her watch. Great, she thought, well over six hours before bedtime, plenty of time for the caffeine to clear from her system.

Her eyes lit up. 'A cookie, too?'

'They've just come out of the oven. Enjoy.'

She was savouring her biscuit when a young couple bustled into the room on a cloud of excitement. An officious grey-suited woman followed them in. The three of them smiled at Alison and sat down at a table at the far end of the lounge. It was so quiet that Alison couldn't help but eavesdrop as she enjoyed her post exercise treat. The couple were there to discuss the final details of their upcoming wedding. The rooms sounded lovely, and with onsite spa facilities, Alison thought it would be perfect for a girlie overnight stay. Pricey, but just the thing for a special treat.

'Not long now,' said the wedding co-ordinator.

'I know,' said the groom. 'It's surreal how fast the time has gone.'

'So excited,' said the bride. 'I can't wait.' She let out a little squeal of delight.

'How are the children?' asked the co-ordinator.

'Olivia and Ellie are excited about being bridesmaids,' said the groom. 'But it's been mad. First there was Christmas, and then we moved to a new house straight afterwards.'

Alison felt a pang of sadness. She and Martin had endured so much criticism when they'd had the twins. It was a different time back then. Or was it? she wondered. Most of it came from his family, not society. She would have loved a wedding in a venue like Cherry Dene Hotel. She imagined Jack and Chloe as page boy and bridesmaid and felt her heart might burst.

'And then Olivia and Ellie both came down with chicken pox,' continued the groom. 'Olivia picked the tops off every single one.'

'Ellie's were inside her eyes – she scratched them to bits.'

Alison remembered the chicken pox days well. The twins both caught them the week before their appointment for the vaccination. And to add to the drama, she'd caught them too. Apparently, her mother had taken her to a chicken pox play day when she was two, but she'd seemed immune to the virus – until her own children brought them home.

They'd only come through the crying-all-night stage a week and a half before the little blisters appeared. The three of them had barely slept a wink for a fortnight. The most Martin had been able to do was drop off calamine lotion on the doorstep. It didn't make sense for him to risk coming into the flat. If he'd caught them, he could have missed an essential teaching placement. Keith tried to stir up trouble by insisting Martin had already had chicken pox. According to Doreen, Keith had tried to get Martin into trouble with his 'little stories' since they were kids.

The next thing Alison knew, she was alone in the room, feeling red hot and confused. The fire had been stoked up with fresh coal. How, she wondered, had they done that without her seeing?

The waitress returned with a tray to clear the table. 'I didn't like to wake you before.'

'Wake me? I think I might have fainted.'

The waitress gave a little smile. 'Do you feel unwell? Is there anything I can do? Call a doctor?'

Alison rubbed her face. 'No, I feel fine to tell you the truth.'

'I was sure you'd dozed off. It's the fire and the comfy chairs. Lots of people have a snooze.'

Alison was flummoxed. 'But I have insomnia. I never ever feel sleepy during the day.' She yawned. 'Excuse me. Good grief, I don't know what's happening to me. I wonder if I passed out with the heat…'

The waitress laughed. 'We should put it in the brochure. "Come to Cherry Dene Hotel for a nap".'

Before Alison set off for home, she wandered into a quiet corner of the garden to pull herself together. There were some lonely pathways back up to the park, she didn't want to risk fainting again. There wasn't a soul about. The rustle of the surrounding trees created a wonderful, calming atmosphere. She wondered what an outdoor Pilates routine might look like on YouTube. Perhaps she'd try recording in her own garden, maybe in front of the apple tree.

As she walked up through the park, she tried to work out what had happened at the hotel. She hadn't felt ill either before or since the fainting episode. Could it really have been a nap? Unheard of.

'Hello there,' said a cheery voice from behind.

Alison turned to find Christopher, striding towards her with a big smile on his face. 'Good afternoon. New trainers?' she said with a nod to his fluorescent orange-shod feet.

He slowed down to walk along with her. 'Yes, they're smashing, aren't they? Rather more conspicuous outdoors than they looked in the shop.'

'Are you training for anything in particular?' He smelled nice – a mixture of aftershave and something else she couldn't identify.

'Health primarily, but also my daughter's wedding. I don't want to be a fat father of the bride.'

She shook her head. 'Like Katie and I said in Alessandro's, you're not fat.' She imagined him in a top hat and tails. The image made her blush.

'Fat enough to have diabetes and high blood pressure. According to that dumpy nurse at the health centre, I've got one foot in the grave, and the other one's in danger of being chopped off.'

Alison laughed. 'She sounds the encouraging sort.'

'I'm determined to put it right. Are you training for anything?'

'A good night's sleep.'

He looked at her, puzzled. She noticed the way the skin at the corner of his eyes crinkled. 'Part of a programme to reset my sleep pattern. Apparently, sleep is regulated over the whole twenty-four-hour period. I'm not building up my hopes. I caught the sleep nurse fast asleep at her desk, so I'm not sure she knew what she was talking about.'

Christopher gave a hearty laugh. 'I once read that marathon runners need more sleep than other people.' They came to a fork in the path and he paused. 'If I've remembered it correctly, they have to schedule naps into their training plans.'

'Thanks for that. I do a walk-jog-walk routine at the minute. Maybe I'll try speeding up.'

'Don't exhaust yourself, though. Remember that those athletes do manage to sleep to recuperate. Don't get too run down, will you?'

Alison felt all warm inside. Christopher was being so *nice* to her, it felt strange but lovely at the same time. She felt tears prick her eyes.

'Are you all right?'

'Yes, yes. Actually, I'm feeling discombobulated. The waitress in Cherry Dene Hotel said I dozed off. I can't understand it. I thought I'd fainted.'

He smiled. 'Well, I know nothing about your therapy, but could it be a sign it's working?'

Alison laughed. 'I'd never even thought about that. Wow. Maybe I'm not abnormal after all.'

'Of course, you aren't.' Christopher turned onto the path that led up to the high street. 'Keep going and good luck.'

'Thank you so much.' Feeling fortified and encouraged, she

power walked all the way home.

Martin was rummaging in the cupboard under the stairs when Alison burst into the house, windswept and excited.

He emerged, dishevelled and flustered. 'Good, you're back. Have you seen my trainers? They've gone missing. And I banged my head on that ironing board in there.'

'Can't say I have. When did you last have them?'

'At the gym on Thursday night.'

'They'll be wherever you left them.' Alison slipped off her own trainers and put them on the shoe rack. 'Something brilliant happened today. I think I might have dozed off when I stopped for a cuppa at Cherry Dene Hotel. I didn't believe it at first, but the more I think about it –'

Martin kicked a fallen jacket from the doorway into the cupboard and forced the door closed. 'For Goodness' sake. It's a mess in there.'

'Martin, this is a big thing to me. You know I can't nap.' She opened the door. 'That's my work jacket.'

'Wish I had time for a nap. Anyway, my trainers are usually on the shoe rack and they aren't today.'

Alison shrugged, irritated by his lack of interest in her good news. 'I usually put them there when I'm tidying during the night.'

'So where have you put them?'

For the second time that afternoon she felt tears prick her eyes. 'Don't speak to me in that tone.'

'Sorry. But to be honest, I don't see where the harm is in using your time productively. There are never enough hours in the day for me.'

'I'm teaching my brain that night-time is not for housework.'

Martin strode into the kitchen-diner, looking behind doors and muttering as he went. 'And I don't see how going for a walk at this time of day is going to help you to sleep. I could understand if it was high intensity interval training before bedtime and you were shattered. Twenty minutes is hardly any time at all.' He stood in the middle of the room and raked his hand through his hair.

'It's the rise in heart rate and being a little out of breath that helps. Michelle said the brain is hardwired to light and dark, so we should also get at least two hours daylight every day.' She pointed to her eyes. 'We have little sensors and that's why the bedroom has to be dark at night.'

'You're anoraking. Anyway, who on earth has two hours to spend outside?'

She gritted her teeth. 'Only if it's possible. You have that lovely big window in your office at school. Michelle has no windows, but she's got a daylight simulator. It's blinding. I've seen a small one on Amazon I could put on my desk.'

'Waste of money buying faddy contraptions.' He knocked over a bottle of washing up liquid as he rummaged in the cupboard under the sink.

Alison sniggered at the sight of him, frantically clattering bottles of bleach and furniture polish. 'I'm giving the programme a go. If it doesn't work, fair enough. But I'll never know if I don't try.'

'Where the hell can they be?'

'It helps so much that you're showing an interest.'

'How can a pair of size nine trainers disappear?'

'Would you stop ransacking the place. It looks like we've been burgled.'

'I can't find anything in this bloody house these days.'

'Martin, what's wrong with you?'

He glared at her, his mouth set in a straight line. 'I want my trainers.' He stomped off upstairs to rummage through the wardrobes.

As Alison walked into the lounge, the ceiling shook.

'Damned mess, everywhere,' he shouted. As he stormed out

of the bedroom, it sounded like he'd cracked a floorboard. One of the glass lampshade panels shook loose and smashed on the floor.

She couldn't understand why Martin, who was usually so mild-mannered, was behaving so out of character. She pricked her finger on a shard, as he clattered into the lounge, still ranting and raging.

'Look what you've done,' she said, showing him the broken glass.

'That wasn't me.' He stood in his old training shoes, with a petulant look on his face. 'Be careful. You're dripping blood onto the floor.'

Alison retreated to the kitchen to clean her finger. 'What the heck is wrong with you, Martin? You're being nasty.'

He followed her in, hands in the air. 'Mess, I hate the mess. I'm going to the gym.' And with that, he stomped off out of the house.

She was drying her finger when the doorbell sounded. She wrapped a square of kitchen roll around it and opened the door.

Robbie was standing on the doorstep.

Great. Could this day get any worse?

'Can I chill here for a bit? An hour or so will do. Mam and Dad are bickering and it's driving me mad. She said to come round. Said she'd call you.'

Sammy regarded him cautiously from the edge of the path. Robbie spotted him and drew his leg back as if aiming a shot at a football.

'Touch that cat and you're dead,' said Alison.

He tutted. 'I was only jesting.' He stepped forward into the hall.

'What's wrong with your own flat?'

He looked at her as if she had asked a stupid question. 'There's no food in it. Mam's in the huff, she's not cooking tonight.'

'Take off your boots, they're filthy.'

'So many rules in this house. Y.u should relax a bit.'

'You wouldn't say that if you had to clean the carpet.' Alison bent down to stroke Sammy, who purred then shot off home. By the time she closed the door, Robbie was sniffing around the kitchen.

He lifted the lid on the slow cooker. 'What's this? Any spare?'

'Beef casserole. Help yourself.'

'Thanks,' he said, abandoning the lid on the bench top. 'I'll have it watching the telly if that's okay?' He wandered through to the lounge and switched on a sport channel.

Great, thought Alison. Against her better judgement, she dished out a portion for him.

'Any beer?' he asked, as she set the tray down on the coffee table.

'Nope. And I'm not your slave.'

As she walked out of the room, Alison spotted Martin's trainers down by the side of the sofa. She snatched them up, stormed straight outside and stotted them into the wheelie bin. Then she marched into the kitchen, reserved herself a plateful of casserole and carried the rest outside. It was with a sense of immense satisfaction that she slopped it onto his trainers.

Chapter 17

Christopher felt his mobile phone vibrate in his pocket as he pulled on the handbrake. Strange, he thought, unable to recall switching off the ringer. Frank Budle's name flashed up on the screen. Even odder, he never added employees' numbers to his personal contacts, or gave them his number.

'Hello, Frank. What can I do for you?'

There was a pause on the other end. 'Christopher?'

'You sound surprised.'

Frank gave a nervous laugh. 'I was expecting to speak to your wife.'

'Sandy? On my phone?'

'Erm no. I called her number.' Another pause.

Christopher looked again at the mobile screen. 'Crikey, I must have picked up her phone. She'll kill me.' He felt his other pocket, and sure enough, his was in there. 'So, Frank, what are you doing calling my wife?'

A cough sounded down the line, then Frank garbled something Christopher didn't understand.

'What was that?'

'A savings account. She left me a message at work – wanted to discuss the best interest rate,' said Frank. 'I was surprised she didn't ask you.'

'I'm surprised she has savings,' laughed Christopher. In all the years they'd been married, he'd never known Sandy show any interest in saving a penny. It was good to hear she was now thinking about it. Perhaps their recent discussions had made her think more seriously about their finances. 'Hang on, Frank, I thought you'd taken a couple of hours annual leave to view a property development opportunity today. Why are you making a work call from home?'

'I thought I'd tie up a couple of outstanding bits and pieces, since I left early today.'

'No need. Worst thing you can do is work beyond your hours. Before you know it, you'll have hypertension and diabetes.'

'Pardon?'

'Leave work at work. Did you look at the training directory?'

'No, not yet. It's on my to-do list.'

'There's a course that will help you with that list. Anyway, I'll pass on your message and get Sandy to give you a ring tomorrow.'

'Okay, thanks.'

Sandy was chatting to Yvonne on the landline when Christopher walked into the lounge. She was asking if Yvonne had seen her mobile phone. He kissed her cheek and held it up for her to see. She rang off and gave a sigh of relief.

'Thank goodness. Where was it?'

'I must have picked it up. Sorry.' He put it down on the coffee table with his car keys and wallet.

Her eyes widened. 'You've had it all day? She unlocked it and scrolled through her messages.'

'Don't worry, I didn't read anything,' he said, checking through a pile of post.

'Why would I worry? There's nothing to read.'

'I was joking. You looked panicked.'

'It's just that all of the wedding plans and appointments are in my planner on here. I thought I'd lost months of preparation.'

'Save it in the cloud.'

'What cloud?'

'I'll have to show you. It's a way of ensuring nothing gets lost. Frank phoned.'

Sandy's head snapped around. She tucked her hair behind her ear. 'Who? Frank? I don't know any Franks.'

'Said you'd left him a message to call about setting up a savings account.'

'Oh, he's called Frank, is he?' She nodded and plugged in the mobile to charge. 'I thought I'd try to start saving a little. Just to be on the safe side. In case you do go ahead with the demotion.'

'It's not a –'

The doorbell rang. 'That'll be the takeaway. Chinese. You don't mind, do you?' She grabbed his wallet and shot off.

He laughed to himself and wondered which of their accounts she intended to plunder to start off her savings account. She left a delicious trail along the hall as she went through to the kitchen with the food. He followed her, his stomach rumbling.

'You're a bad influence. Did you forget I'm trying to stay off the carbs?' He leaned over a tub of beef curry and inhaled deeply. 'Mmm. I suppose I could have the curry. Maybe a small spoonful of rice.'

Sandy reached into a cupboard for plates and shot him a mischievous grin. 'Oh, go on. Allow yourself a little treat. You look great,' she said without looking at him.

He felt the flesh around his waist. There was less than before, but he still had more to lose. 'I suppose I've done some exercise today. I bumped into Alison in the park. She was exercising, too.'

'Who?'

'The woman I scared when I was choking.'

She laughed as she scooped out egg fried rice onto a plate.

'It's a good job I'm not the jealous type. I expect she'll be middle-aged and dumpy anyway.'

'No, she's got to exercise to help her sleep.'

'Weird.' Sandy opened a carton to reveal sweet and sour pork.

'Oh no, Hong Kong style.' His mouth was watering.

'Your favourite.'

'Well, maybe I won't have the beef curry after all. But it's the last time.'

'Yeah, yeah.' She piled up his plate. 'Prawn crackers?'

Christopher picked up a piece of battered pork and popped it into his mouth, such a delight after depriving himself so much recently. 'I'm serious, it's not some faddy health-kick I'm on.' He carried the plates over to the table. 'I'm making serious, permanent changes. I have to.'

'I know. It was me who said that's what you needed to concentrate on.'

'After we've eaten, I can talk you through savings accounts.'

She looked up at him, her brow furrowed. 'No, it's okay. I'll call that Frank bloke. You're supposed to be reducing your stress levels. The last thing you need is to be thinking about work at the end of the day.' She smiled at him. 'You need to think of your health.'

Christopher squeezed her waist. 'You can be so caring sometimes. It makes me feel loved.'

'Come on, let's eat in the lounge instead. We can put a film on – there's a new rom com I'd like to see. Can you bring in a bottle of red, please? Oh, and I got you a treacle pudding for afters.'

Sandy closed the front door and brought in the package the postman had delivered. She opened the gold and diamante box, her eyes sparkling and cheeks flushed. 'This wedding is going to be amazing.' She handed an invitation to Christopher. 'Look, they're gorgeous.'

The thing Christopher loved most in life, was seeing his wife and daughter happy. And right now, his wife was elated, planning the day that would be the most wonderful of his daughter's life. 'You've done a sterling job putting it all together. I don't think I've ever seen posher wedding invitations.' He ran his finger over the small jewel on the front of the ivory card before passing it back to Sandy. 'And to have them match the detail on Emily's dress… I don't know how they come up with these things. I suppose it's little touches like this that make Margot worth her fee.' Initially, Christopher had considered a wedding coordinator an unnecessary expense, but he had to admit that these invitations were beautiful.'

She smiled, thrilled. 'Margot didn't find them, I saw them in a magazine. Everyone adds touches like these nowadays, Chris.'

'Surely not? I can't imagine many people being able to afford them.'

Sandy's expression flipped from jubilant to vexed. 'Do you begrudge your only daughter her once-in-a-lifetime wedding?'

'Don't be silly.' Christopher slid his arms around her waist. He felt her tense up. 'Emily's a smashing kid. She deserves the best wedding ever.' Sandy relaxed. 'It's what it's all about isn't it.'

'What is?'

He looked into his wife's eyes. Even after all these years, he was in awe of her beauty. 'Life, sacrifices, it's —'

'Sacrifices? What do you mean, *sacrifices*…?'

He brushed some stray strands of hair from her face. 'Working so much, being away from the pair of you.'

'Yes. It gets lonely when you're away. I miss you.' Sandy ran her fingers up his back. 'I've had a brilliant idea about how to make the entrance to the venue look even more classy.'

'It's already lovely.'

'I've ordered some little shrubs.' She kissed him gently on the lips. 'And some fairy lights.'

He glanced at his watch. 'I'm sure they'll look wonderful. How about you come into the bank later and I'll take you for a nice lunch? You can tell me about the shrubs, and we'll talk more about my job. I've spoken to Head Office and they've suggested –'

'I'll see, I need to arrange to see that Frank bloke.'

Christopher checked his reflection in the mirror above the fireplace and straightened his tie. 'I can talk you through it all, remember.'

Sandy shrugged. 'I don't think of you as working in a bank. You're more of a bigwig type…'

Christopher guffawed. 'Bigwig – I'll have to add that to my curriculum vitae. I can still advise you about savings accounts.'

'But it's not what you do, is it?' She caught her reflection in the mirror and stepped in front of him to inspect her roots. 'I must get these done.' She smoothed her line-free brow then checked her side profile.

'What do you think I do all day?' He opened his briefcase, pulled out some leaflets about bank accounts and handed one to Sandy. 'And, now, it's my branch, and Frank works under me.'

She glanced at the leaflet with a look of distaste. 'Oh, come on, Chris… You're better than this.'

His eyebrows shot up. 'You look down on the profession I've dedicated my whole adult life to? Do you look down on me, too?'

Sandy shot over and started fussing with his tie. 'No, no, of course I don't. I didn't mean that at all.'

'So, what exactly do you think of my career. And me…?' He stepped back from her and splayed his hands. 'The man who works in banking, who has earned enough to pay for all this?' He pointed to the box of invitations on the table. 'And those? And your brand-new Audi, sitting on the new drive outside your six-bedroomed house? The house you can't look after because you're so busy not working anywhere at all?'

Sandy gaped at Christopher. 'I'm sorry,' she finally managed, her voice croaky. 'I just meant that…' she tentatively stepped towards him, her arms outstretched.

Fuming, he stood rigid and ignored her advance.

She stroked his arm. 'You love a challenge… Sorting out the big, important problems is what you're good at. I didn't think you'd be interested in the day-to-day stuff. And I'm worried you'll hate being stuck in the same job once the novelty wears off.'

He tensed even more as she tried to embrace him. She squeezed him harder and started to cry. 'I'm proud of you.'

Christopher hated to see her cry. He was mortified he was the cause. 'I'm so sorry.' He wrapped his arms around her.

She buried her face into his neck, her shoulders shaking.

'I feel like such a cad.' He stroked her hair as she wept. 'I thought you'd stop caring…'

'Stopped caring? I've been worried sick about you,' she cried in a muffled voice into his shoulder. 'I don't know what I'd do without you.' She reached up and kissed his neck, still sniffling.

He gave her his handkerchief. 'You'll always have me.'

She blew her nose then lifted her head and kissed his lips. 'Don't go to work just yet.' She kissed him again and then stopped and smiled sweetly at him.

As she looked deeply into his eyes. Christopher's heart melted.

She dabbed beneath her eyes with the hankie then took his hand and led him towards the stairs. 'I don't want you to go.' She stopped and kissed him again. 'I need to feel close to you.'

Unable to resist, he followed her upstairs.

Sandy paused at the bedroom door and glanced over her shoulder, her eyes sorrowful. 'I do love you, you know.'

'I love you, too.' Christopher didn't notice her eyes were

bone dry and makeup intact.

Chapter 18

'For goodness' sake, Ali. I've got to be up at the crack of dawn for work.'

Alison paused, mid-creep out of the bedroom. 'You said you would support me,' she whispered.

'It's a bit much, though – all this in and out of bed all night. You'll be shattered.'

'As Michelle said, I'm not getting less sleep than I was when I was lying in bed awake. I told you all this.' She could feel her heartrate rising and knew this meant adrenalin was pinballing around her body – the very process guaranteed to feed insomnia.

'Well, it was a lot to take in.'

'You weren't listening. I don't know what's got into you lately.'

'I'm sleep deprived.'

'Join the blinking club.'

'At least move into the spare room while you do this stupid programme. You know I can't function properly without my eight hours.' He pulled the duvet over his head.

Alison shot daggers at the quilted bulk in the bed. She grabbed her dressing gown. 'It's got to be my usual bedroom.'

'Shh…'

'I'm trying to re-establish a healthy, happy association with sleep and remove anger and frustration from the bedroom,' she hissed through gritted teeth.

A muffled voice sounded from beneath the duvet. 'As you're up, any chance of knocking up a packed lunch for me?'

'That's a daytime activity.'

'And prowling around the house is a sleep door one?'

'Window. It's a sleep *window*. And making your lunches in the middle of the night is one of the reasons I have insomnia.'

'Rubbish. You've had it for years.'

Alison had a desire to pin the duvet over his head with her body. 'I'm going to my nest.'

She stomped into the lounge and took three deep breaths, which did nothing to calm her down. Clambering into her little nest on the sofa – still warm from the previous time she'd been downstairs, she flopped back onto the cushion and tried not to scream.

Michelle was right; having a cosy, dimly-lit place to read did help her to relax – eventually. She tried not to be drawn to the wall clock. Ignoring the time was much more difficult than she'd envisioned, especially since her ability to see the time out of the corner of her eye had improved immensely.

Snuggled in the hollow, she felt secure. She pulled the blanket around her shoulders. It felt like her old 'horsey' blanket – a fleecy pink one with a picture of *Black Beauty* on it. As a child, her mother would tuck her up in bed with it, making her feel warm and safe. She felt safe now. Until a flash of nostalgia burst into her mind without warning – she was back in the hospital. Since the crash, happy memories always flipped into unhappy ones. People told her that one day she would be able to remember them without thinking about their deaths. But over twenty years had passed, and a happy memory could still flip in a second.

As Alison's mind wandered off, her heart weighing increasingly heavy in her chest, something Michelle had said suddenly made sense. These were the thoughts that replay in the mind during the night to keep you awake. She needed the distraction exercises.

Having decided on the painting exercise, she acknowledged her memories without trying to suppress them and then focused her mind's eye on a white easel. She lined up little paint pots and brand-new brushes, then set about outlining an apple. Before the brush touched the easel, the green pot spontaneously toppled over and stained the other brushes. She conjured up a jar of soapy water, but as she cleaned them, the water turned darker and thicker than the paint. Her stomach churned.

Right, acknowledge the mess and magic up another brush. Holding the new one out of reach of anything green, she managed to dip it into the red pot and start to paint an apple. As intrusive thoughts popped into her mind, she accepted them and then refocused on her painting. It was as she was praising herself for staying on task and no longer feeling angry about being awake, that her lovely apple sprouted Phyllis's permed hair and beady eyes. *Drat.*

Next, she picked up the folder she'd left as an alternative distracting tactic. Martin's old dissertation. She yawned. This might be the perfect thing to induce sleepiness, she thought. She'd had to tell him a white lie, saying she wanted to read it to prevent her from falling asleep before her negotiated bedtime, because it was interesting. She got no further than the title 'Teaching in Victorian Times' before yawning again. *Great, sleepy enough to go back to bed.*

Alison tiptoed upstairs and slipped silently between the covers. As soon as her head touched the pillow, she zinged awake.

Fifteen minutes of painting grapes yielded a mouldy bunch, covered in maggots. She silently eased back the covers and, once again, adopted her hunched creeping action, to the sound of a 'bloody hell' from the other side of the bed.

***

The atmosphere in the kitchen was frosty. Martin sipped coffee and checked emails, while Alison prepared his packed lunch in silence, wavering between apologising for disrupting his sleep and wanting to stot a banana off his head.

It occurred to her that although Martin heard every tiny movement she made during the night, he didn't used to wake up when the twins were crying as babies. He complained about disturbed nights, but he actually didn't have any. She'd never realised this before.

He disappeared upstairs for a shower, then thundered back down into the kitchen, his eyebrows knotted. 'My pale blue shirt's not hanging up in the wardrobe.'

Alison wanted to laugh at his bewildered expression, as if the shirt hadn't returned home after a night out on the tiles. She dolloped a spoonful of chutney onto a ham bun. 'Have you checked the ironing basket?'

'Why?'

She turned to him, puzzled. 'What do you mean – why?'

'You've not ironed it, yet?' He steadied himself against the benchtop.

'*Me?*'

'Yes, it's your job.'

Alison turned so swiftly, she caught the jar of chutney and sent it crashing to the floor, where it exploded its contents up the wall and cupboards. 'My *what?*'. Martin had never spoken to her in this way before. '*My job?*'

'We set up the system years ago. It works. I don't understand why that has to change as well.'

Alison stood, the spoon in her hand dripping more chutney onto the floor. '*System? What system?* Why on earth would you think it was *my job.*'

Martin looked around the chutney-splattered kitchen with distaste. 'Surely you don't expect me to come in from work and start with chores?'

'When did *chores* become my responsibility?'

'That's the way it's always been. We agreed.'

'When did we agree?' She stood, wide-eyed, completely blind-sided by his words.

'When the twins were born. You took care of the home and I focused on my career – to build a secure future for us all.'

'Martin, get a grip. The twins are adults.' She couldn't believe the claptrap he was spouting. Who was this man who was speaking to her like she was his nineteen-fifties housewife? 'Are you saying you expect me to come home after a hard day's work and start on chores?' She rived at her hair, there was chutney in it. 'And then keep going during the *night*?'

Martin shrugged and pulled a face. 'I never thought about it before. You don't need as much sleep as I do, so you've got more time. Why can't you do the ironing?' He looked at the sandwiches. 'And you used to make proper meals.'

'Yes, and according to Michelle, my brain has been waking me up for years because it's time to do the cooking and ironing. But not for one minute did I believe you *expected* it of me.'

Martin spoke tersely through gritted teeth. 'Well if you aren't doing it any longer, why aren't you sleeping?'

'Because it takes time to reset the pattern. For an intelligent man, you're being obtuse.'

'I think you like lazing around on the sofa more like.'

'When am I *lazing around*, Martin? Could it be when you're tucked up and fast asleep by any chance? Why don't you put the alarm on and get up and do my ironing if the middle of the night is such a good time?'

'Now you're being ridiculous.'

'I'd like to open my wardrobe in the morning and find all my clothes hanging up clean and ironed. And I'd like a nice meal to take to work for my lunch.'

Martin turned to walk out of the room. 'This conversation is going nowhere. I'm off to school.' He paused. 'Are you going to finish making those sandwiches?'

He managed to scarper just as a ham and chutney bun

stotted off the door frame. 'And you're getting very violent,' he called from the safety of the front door.

After he'd left, Alison slumped onto the floor, numb and unable to think straight. On automatic pilot, she opened a cupboard and pulled out a bin bag and a plastic tub, then began the task of separating chutney from glass. The most she managed to do without making herself late for work was to pick up the shards. She could have done with one of Peggy's yellow warning cones. As she got up, her slipper skidded on some onion and she jarred her knee.

Alison left the mess and limped off for a shower feeling sorry for herself, and rather stupid. She'd called Martin obtuse, but it turned out she was dimmer than him. She hadn't realised her kind, loving husband had turned into a chauvinist under her nose.

Chapter 19

Katie rested her arms along the back of the sofa and exhaled a contented sigh. 'You're right,' she said to Alison. 'It's lovely here. I haven't been down into Cherry Dene for years. Good idea of yours to take a half-day from work.'

'From up in the park, you can't even see it,' said Alison. 'It's like having the countryside on your doorstep.' She drained her cup. 'And the coffee is delicious.'

'Yeah, that dewy forest smell hits you as soon as you get out of the car,' said Katie. 'How's the reduced caffeine going?'

'I'm getting used to it, except that now every mouthful tastes like heaven.'

Alison didn't know if it was the opportunity to escape from work, combined with a break from the frosty atmosphere at home, but taking time to go to the park on a lunchtime had become the highlight of her day. 'It's good to get out for a walk and some fresh air. You tend to see the same faces in the park, like that Christopher. He seems nice.'

'I'll say,' said Katie.

'Not like that. He's a cheery face to take my mind off the miserable ones in the office.'

Sharon stared off into the middle distance, smiling. 'We used to come down to the dene on our bikes to pick blackberries when we were kids. With Jam sandwiches, and water in an old pop bottle.' Her face clouded over. 'Of course, Cynthia used to eat her sandwiches and then greed mine.'

Alison watched a blue tit hopping around the patio outside. She imagined herself and Martin sitting at one of the tables having a coffee and enjoying the garden. Her stomach churned as she tried not to think about the ironing row. He'd been cool with her ever since. To make matters more frustrating, his mother was doing his ironing. She was over the moon – more at the prospect of a hint of a chink in their marriage than ensuring his shirts were 'properly ironed for once'.

She tried to push her worries to the back of her mind. 'You can forget about the daily grind down here. Look, it's started to drizzle. Makes it feel all nice and cosy inside. It reminds me of a relaxation CD I used to listen to.' She decided to hunt it out for her nest time.

Sharon looked thoughtful. 'I'd all but forgotten about this hotel. I'm trying to think when I was last here. An eighteenth birthday party I think.'

Katie sipped her coffee. 'We had a work's Christmas do down here once.'

'Must've been before my time,' said Sharon.

'I never used to go to them. We only had Martin's mam and Gail to babysit. They were always busy whenever I asked.'

Sharon shot Alison a sideways glance. 'And Martin.'

'Hmm… You know what schools are like during the festive season.' She caught Katie rolling her eyes at Sharon. 'What was that?'

Katie grimaced. 'Hawk-eye. Sorry. It's just, you used to miss everything. It might have been nice if Martin had given you a night off now and again.'

Despite her own irritation with her husband lately, she jumped to his defence. 'He would've done if I'd pushed it, I suppose. Mind you, nights out aren't so appealing with young kids to see to at the crack of dawn.'

'Martin could have –' started Sharon.

'Let's get a bottle of something nice.' Yes, thought Alison to herself, he could have. Why hadn't he? She looked over to the bar from where the bartender, Gavin it said on his name badge, had been earwigging.

He gave her the thumbs up and rattled ice into a bucket. 'How about the house Prosecco?' he said, holding up bottle. 'I'm told it's rather nice. Reasonably priced too.'

'Perfect.'

Gavin, who had looked rather bored minutes before, perked up. 'It's nice to have a young girlie group in. It can be a bit quiet sometimes.' He glanced towards the door and lowered his voice. 'Management say it's the luxury carpeting, but I say it's the clientele.'

Sharon laughed. ' "A young girlie group" – pity Cynthia wasn't here to hear that.'

'I don't know why she's so upset about being forty,' said Alison. 'I wasn't bothered. But I was when I hit thirty. I'd expected to be an experienced physiotherapist by then…' She didn't tell the others that she'd started to feel anxious about time. Every minute she was trapped in her job was like a minute of her life wasted.

'Age is only a number.' Katie smoothed her brow. 'You can't tell how old people are anyway, thanks to Botox. Genius invention.' She leaned back in her chair an exhaled slowly. 'I can't believe how nice it is in here.'

'There's a spa, and apparently the rooms are lovely, too. We should save up and stay over the next time we have something to celebrate,' said Katie.

Gavin set down the ice bucket and three frosted flutes on the table. He went away and returned with another plate of homemade cookies. 'Shh,' he said, holding his finger to his lips. 'They're only supposed to be for the hot drinks.'

Katie laughed. 'I bet you do well in tips.'

Gavin winked and returned to the bar.

Alison scrutinised Katie as she was speaking. 'You're

looking rather fresh. Have you had something done?'

Katie turned her head to the side, showing off an extra neat profile. She ran the back of her hand up from her collarbone to her jaw. 'Yes, a non-surgical facelift.'

Sharon pinched the flesh below her own jaw and frowned. 'I'd like to have that done, but I'm scared.'

Katie pointed to her temples. 'They thread a string thing from here to here. I had it done in my lunch hour. Nothing to it.'

'New man on the go?' said Sharon. 'I'm pleased I'm off the shelf.'

Katie tutted. 'You know I wouldn't mess with my face for a man. It was for me. I've had a busy week and I deserved it. But yes, I have a new man, too. I'll bring him to Cynthia's birthday do.'

'Tell him not to mention her age, or she'll go mad,' said Sharon.

Katie gave a dismissive wave. 'Don't worry, I won't. Blokes are useless with details anyway.'

'Except Martin,' said Sharon. 'Alison, you'd better warn him, he's good with dates.'

Alison cackled. 'He forgot his mam's birthday recently. And he opened the Moet I bought for the old bat.' Shocked by her disloyalty to her husband, and the way Sharon's brows shot up to her hairline, Alison attempted to backtrack. She had never been the type of woman to openly criticise her husband – nor had she felt the need to. 'I'm being unfair… He's under a mountain of stress from that blooming school inspection. And I did drink half the Moet…'

'You're right about his mother; she is an old bat,' laughed Katie. Her eyebrows didn't move. 'Never seen her crack a smile in all the years I've known you.'

'It would kill her to smile at me,' said Alison, relieved to get the focus off Martin. All the same, she felt perturbed. Usually, when the others vented about their partners over some misdemeanour, she'd have to rack her brains for a snippet to join in with the conversation. Leaving his gym bag lying around full of dirty kit was about as irritating as it used to get. Today, it would have been easy to reel off a decent list of niggles. She wasn't ready to do that, not out loud anyway. 'So, has anyone decided what to wear for the party?'

Alison might have managed to hide her growing marital woes from the girls, but at some point, she was going to have to face up to them herself. She took a sip of Prosecco. She would deal with whatever was brewing at home, but not yet, not today.

Chapter 20

It was a shock for Alison to walk into the office and see Phyllis sitting at her desk. So, she thought, this is what she does when I'm not around. Phyllis was bubbling with excitement.

'What's going on?'

'I hope you don't mind swapping,' said a voice from behind.

Billy was standing in the doorway. He nodded at Alison's new desk and lowered his voice. 'Your things have been moved to save you the extra work. I obviously can't discuss the reason as it's confidential.'

'It's my ears,' scrunched Phyllis. 'I have a problem.'

'You heard that all right,' said Alison. 'This should have been discussed first.'

'It's the draught. Too near the door,' said Phyllis.

Alison dumped her bag on her new desk.

Billy retreated to his office, shooting Alison a smirk on the way.

Her hands shook as she hung up her jacket. It was all she could do to keep them from his throat.

Feeling humiliated, she logged onto her computer. An email from Billy pinged straight in.

You should be thanking me. The breeze through the door will stop you dozing off. Ha ha.

Typically, as she went to save it for evidence, it disappeared.

His probationary period as Patient Experience Team Lead was up, and his job was now permanent. They were stuck with him.

Alison put her head down and got on with her work. Apart from when she nipped out to fill her water bottle and give Peggy a tin of WD-40, she managed to avoid further communication with anyone for the rest of the morning.

It was a familiar rattle that made her look up from her screen. She saw Billy, dragging the scales from beneath his desk. She reached into her bag for the useless vitamins. Her stomach tightened as he kicked off his shoes. She pictured fat cheesy feet inside his grubby socks. Keys clunked down onto his desk, then his watch came off. The man was such an idiot. He wasn't losing weight – if anything, he was getting bigger.

Billy stepped off the scales, removed his sleeveless sweater, then gingerly stepped back on, seemingly unaware the door was open.

She popped two capsules into her mouth and grabbed her water bottle. Gritting her teeth, she accidently bit into one of the vitamins, causing a pungent yeasty explosion in her mouth. She retched and had to gulp down water to dilute the awful taste.

Billy looked through the gap in the door. He shot Alison an irritated glare. 'Are you eating and drinking at your desk? You know the policy.'

'No,' Alison replied curtly, suppressing another retch.

Phyllis popped up from behind her screen like a meerkat. 'Spilled fluids destroy expensive equipment,' she said in a particularly crispy voice. 'Your keyboard for example –'

'Wind your neck in Phyllis. It's medication and it's a sports top bottle.'

Phyllis gave her a beady-eyed stare. 'Your teeth are black.'

Drat.

Billy put on his shoes and sweater and booted the scales under the desk with extra force. 'Right, shall we go for lunch, Phyllis?'

Phyllis emitted a gleeful squeak and jumped up from her chair. 'Just need to get something from the fridge on the way.'

The rest of the office had already shot off for lunch. No doubt, thought Alison, to avoid having to go with Billy and Phyllis. Or perhaps it was so that they wouldn't be left alone with her. She looked at the empty desks and wondered who had reported them. It could even have been someone from another office, there was usually a temp around or someone covering sickness leave.

Billy glanced at her over his shoulder and made an odd little 'tst' sound. She'd heard a dog trainer make the same sound to control a spaniel on a television programme.

'What was that?'

He scrunched his face at her as if she was talking gobbledegook. 'Stay here and man my phone. You can go later.'

Fury whooshed through her. 'I will not man your phone. That's not my job.'

He gave her a wave of dismissal and strode off without answering. Phyllis's titters echoed along the corridor.

She picked up the phone to call Human Resources. This situation couldn't go on, she needed some advice. The doors had no sooner closed than they were booted open with an almighty bang and an aggressive roar.

Alison screamed, dropped the handset and threw her water bottle at the threatening figure storming in.

Rick Shannon stopped in his tracks. He stood for a minute, red-faced and looking dazed. He appeared to be trying to get his bearings. 'Thirty-two years in the Fire Service and no one ever attacked me with a water bottle,' he finally said with a wheeze.

She hurtled over to retrieve the bottle, where it lay next to his feet. 'So sorry. I thought you were an angry intruder. Are you okay?'

'Just about. Mind, I'm sure those stairs weren't so steep

before the wife and I went on that cruise. I'll let you off, just this once.'

'Thank you,' said Alison in a small voice. She replaced the telephone handset.

'You're a nervous wreck – you should see somebody about that. But you're right, I'm angry. Very.'

She noticed a wooden chock in his hand. 'I've been diligently checking the doors. Honestly. And I emailed a reminder to everyone. In fact, I went in to refill my water bottle an hour ago and there wasn't a chock in sight.' Alison wondered if he'd brought it with him, he seemed to like nothing better than a good rant.

'I warned you lot we'd be doing spot checks this week.' He shook the chock. 'I'm confiscating the toaster.'

'No. not the toaster...'

'Why the NHS allows toasters that don't pop up beggars belief.' He pointed the chock at her. 'Do you know how many hospital fires me and my men were called out to, because of *toasters*?'

She grimaced. 'No.'

'Too many. You shouldn't have a toaster anyway. You're not a ward.'

'No,' agreed Alison, 'I'm not a ward.

He shook his head, turned on his heel and marched off to repossess the offensive item, muttering, 'Thirty-two-years...'

With Rick Shannon's rebuke ringing in her ears, she decided to call HR later. She pulled on her new trainers – a reward for sticking to her sleep targets – and set off for her exercise. In twenty minutes, she could now make it once around the park and down to the little waterfall, leaving enough time to eat lunch. As she passed Billy's office, the phone rang. She ignored it.

By the time Alison reached the park, her mood was significantly brighter. Michelle was right about automatic associations. As soon as she smelled the grass, her body and mind relaxed. The air there seemed clearer and the sky bluer, even on drizzly days.

As she power-walked around her route, her mood lifted more and more. Angus, the little Westie scampered by, followed by his owner, still dressed for winter. He always said hello as he passed. Alison wondered if he had a condition that made him cold all the time. She had the opposite problem today – by the time she flopped down onto her bench next to the miniature lake, she was red hot.

While she ate lunch, she watched a dog training club at the other side of the football field, and a mother and baby exercise session over by the playground. She'd have loved to have joined a group like that when the twins were babies. Their clumpy old double pushchair had borne no resemblance to the nifty jogging buggies available these days.

Anyway, she'd had to get a job, so even with a speedy buggy, she couldn't have joined in. It was a different world back then. Her brow furrowed. Or was that just her world, she wondered?

A loud voice sounded next to her, and for the second time that day, she jumped and shrieked. Fortunately, this time there was no assault.

'Sorry, I didn't mean to startle you. Do you mind if I sit here?' said Christopher.

Alison looked up and smiled. He looked different – he was wearing jeans. He really did have the most striking eyes.

He was standing, an expectant expression on his face. 'Or, if you'd rather I didn't…?'

She quickly looked away. 'Not at all, I'm going soon.'

'Don't let me chase you away.' He sat down and opened his lunch box.

She eyed his chicken salad. 'You' aren't. I like a nice bit of tasty company.' *Nooo!* 'Salad. A bit of tasty salad. A nice salad.' Her body burned up in mortification. *Quick, think.* 'No panini today?'

'Sadly not. It's not tasty either – rather bland.'

Alison was too busy trying to bury her head in her own lunch to notice his little smile.

'But it's good for my health.'

'I usually make a packed lunch for my husband.'

He laughed. 'I can't remember the last time Sandy did something like that for me.' He stared into the middle distance. 'Actually, she never has.'

'The day you jumped out at me.'

It was Christopher's turn to blush. 'Ah yes, the bacon sandwich I was choking on. I honestly didn't jum—'

'I know you didn't. But I do like pulling your leg.' Alison threw her head back and laughed. 'So, Does Sandy have a busy job, too? Is that why you go to Alessandro's?'

He shuffled awkwardly in his seat.

'Martin would say I was spendthrift if he knew I went there. He prefers a homecooked meal and doesn't like paying for expensive lunches, unless he's got no option. And even then, I think he might rather starve.' She laughed heartily at her own joke. Why, she asked herself, was she criticising her husband to a virtual stranger? 'I'm making myself sound like a nineteen-fifties housewife. It was just something to do when I couldn't sleep, you see…' *Shut up.*

'Oh, right. Alessandro's… those were the days.' He looked thoughtful, fork mid-air. 'My wife doesn't work.'

'Is she disabled?' she asked, feeling a surge of empathy for the woman. She was bound to be a nice lady to be married to such a lovely man.

His head whipped around, a confused expression on his face. 'No, Sandy's very fit and well. Why on earth would you think she was disabled?'

'Because you work, and she doesn't.'

He shrugged, still nonplussed. 'I don't understand…'

'No lunch. If I didn't have a job, Martin would have me wiping his nose for him, never mind making his lunch,' she laughed.

He frowned. 'Hmm.'

What was it about this man, she desperately asked herself, that brought out inappropriate questioning and hideous wifely disloyalty? Her eyes darting around, she grappled for something normal to say. She noticed his trainers and stuck her foot out. 'We've got the same ones. I thought they seemed familiar when I tried them on.'

'So we have.' He smiled. 'They're bright, aren't they. I got some odd looks wearing them with my suit, so I've started bringing my jeans to work to change into.' He pointed to the park exit as he spoke. 'I work in the bank on the high street.'

She didn't mention she'd already worked that out for fear of looking like a stalker. She nodded at her tailored black trousers. 'I still look weird.'

Christopher crunched a piece of cucumber.

'Watch you don't choke on that,' she said, rocking as she laughed.

'I'd love a bacon sandwich.' Christopher had a wistful look in his eyes. 'On a buttered bun.'

'How are your blood pressure and pre-diabetes?'

His eyebrows shot up. 'Wow, you remembered... Both going in the right direction. Thanks for asking. How's your sleep?'

'No change yet, but I'm sticking to my targets. Martin's not keen on the changes. I'm no longer doing chores during the night.'

Christopher looked horror-stricken. 'Surely he doesn't expect you to do that...?'

'No, no. He's stressed to bits about the Ofsted inspection and the sleep disturbance is getting to him.' *Why was she telling him this stuff?* 'Well, I'd better get back to the grind.' She started to pack away her lunch box when she felt a gentle caress on her leg. She gasped; he must have thought criticising Martin was her way of flirting with him. *The pervert.*

Alison was so relieved she looked down before raising the

alarm… A small back poodle was looking up expectantly and tapping her with its paw.

'Haurice, come here,' shouted a woman, as she hurtled across from the edge of football field. She reached them, rosy-cheeked and out of breath. 'So sorry.' She turned to the dog. 'Haurice, you naughty boy.'

The poodle looked up as his owner. Alison could have sworn he raised an eyebrow. He glanced back at Alison and tapped her leg again.

She stroked his head. 'He's a cute little fella.' He had curly hair like Phyllis, only glossier.

'He's a Miniature, isn't he?' said Christopher. 'Poodles have a lovely nature. My mother had one.'

The woman attached the lead. 'Yes. I love him to bits, but he's naughty. I knew he wasn't ready to be let off the leash. The trainer said poodles are easy to train.' She wagged her finger at Haurice. 'He doesn't know you though, does he?' She looked from Christopher to Alison. 'Sorry to interrupt your lunch.' And off she went, dragged along by the surprisingly strong little dog.

Alison bid Christopher goodbye and tried not to say anything offensive.

'See you next time,' he said with a wave.

Who knew why she acted so silly around him, but she was determined to nip it in the bud.

Back in the office, Alison couldn't stop yawning. She opened her inbox and a plethora of messages filled the screen. Her body felt heavy. She blinked to focus better, bored beyond belief.

The Bee Gees drifted into her mind – the video of them singing 'For Whom the Bell Tolls,' in New York. It must have been near Christmas as there was a huge tree covered in decorations and an ice rink, where a mother caught her little girl as she stumbled. In her mind they looked like her mother and herself as a child. Time is so precious, she mused to herself with a yawn.

Alison felt something brush her face. She turned and banged her head off a tiny plastic box that had appeared like magic. Phyllis was standing inappropriately close to her. She could feel her nylon pleated skirt against her arm. She pushed her chair away from her.

'Would you like a Brazil nut?'

'How did you get there?' She looked down at Phyllis's Scholl's. 'I didn't hear you.'

'You were asleep,' she said unnaturally loud.

'I was most certainly not.'

'You should ensure you get to bed early on a work night. That's why we're behind with our targets.' Phyllis shook the box. 'Healthy fuel.'

'No thank you.' Alison eased the tub away from her face. 'We aren't allowed to eat at our desks.'

Phyllis picked out a nut and shaved off a sliver with her front teeth. 'I am.' Her Scholl's made their familiar slapping sound as she wandered back to her desk.

Alison watched Phyllis chew on the minute fragment for a full five minutes. She rubbed her eyes. They felt dry and irritated. She yawned again and wondered if she was coming down with something. She closed her eyes for a second to ease the grittiness – it was such an uncomfortable sensation. Billy chose that precise moment to walk past.

'Keeping you up, are we?' he said. 'It's a fraudulent activity to sleep while you're being paid to work.' He was chewing gum noisily.

Alison's eyes shot open. 'I wasn't asleep. It's my eyes, I think there must be something in them.' She looked up and noticed the sweat-stained underarms of Billy's pale green polo shirt.

He put on his glasses and scrutinised her face. 'They look

bloodshot.' He leaned in closer and sniffed. 'Have you been drinking?' he whispered.

She recoiled, wheeling her chair away from him. 'Get away from me. Of course I haven't been drinking.'

'Consider this a verbal warning. Asleep at your desk.' He cracked a bubble and pushed the glasses onto the top of his head.

'You can't issue a warning in that manner. Even if you had grounds, there are procedures to follow.'

There was a rustle from across the room and a snapping sound. 'I find that a healthy diet helps me concentrate during the afternoons.' Phyllis shook the food container at her. 'Are you sure you wouldn't like a Brazil?'

Alison looked from Phyllis to Billy. 'What was that rule about eating at our desks?'

He shrugged, then leaned back in so only she could hear. 'Nobody likes a jobsworth.' Billy left the room, cackling to himself as he went.

A verbal warning? Alison had never put a foot wrong in her whole career. He had no grounds. Picking up some papers, she made as if she was going out to the Xerox machine. She needed to make that call to HR.

On her way along the corridor she spotted something on the floor. Billy's glasses, the arms pointing up towards the ceiling. He was lucky someone hadn't stepped on them. Her heartbeat quickened. She glanced around. There was no one about. Easing the toe of her shoe up, she placed it ever so gently on one of the hinges. Her leg shaking, she exerted just enough pressure to bend the arm out at an awkward angle without snapping it.

The lift dinged, bringing her to her senses. She shot off into an empty room before the doors opened. *What on earth was she doing?* She should have felt ashamed, but she didn't. She tapped in the phone number for HR and spoke to Norma, her HR officer. Alison had two choices – fill out a formal grievance now, or keep a diary, collect documentary evidence and then submit a more detailed one. Either way, the verbal warning wouldn't stand, as Billy hadn't followed the correct procedure.

Alison hung up and yawned. For now, she decided, a diary would suffice. Apart from anything, she couldn't face filling out a grievance form when she felt so under the weather. She wandered back to the office, daydreaming of flopping into her lovely big, comfy bed and imagining the soft touch of her fluffy pillows against her face. She stopped abruptly, shocked at the realisation that, not only did the thought of bedtime not fill her with dread, she was looking forward to it. She shot off to the end of the corridor and called Martin.

'I can't wait to get into bed,' she gushed.

'Ok-ay,' said Martin. 'That would be nice. But I was planning to go for a pint with Keith after work.'

'No, I mean to sleep.'

There was a pause on the other end of the line. 'Good. Couldn't you have waited to tell me tonight? I'm at work.'

Alison felt her heart sink. 'It means the CBT-I must be working. I wanted to share it with you.'

'I'm sorry. I'm pleased for you.'

'Never mind…'

'Hang on... While you're there. Have you heard from Gail this week?'

'No, why do you ask?'

'Mam thinks there's something up between her and Keith. He stayed over at their house midweek. Made the excuse that he'd had a drink while fixing their floorboards, but Mam didn't believe him.'

'Couldn't blame him. I'm surprised he's put up with Gail this long to be honest.'

'She's not that bad. Our Keith can be difficult, too.'

Alison scowled at the phone. 'I don't know why you defend her, she's horrible to everyone.'

'Don't be childish, it doesn't suit you. I'll see what he says tonight. Might be late.'

'Childish? What the –'

The line went dead.

Fuming, she called straight back. It went to answerphone. As she dropped her mobile into her pocket, it occurred to her that it was herself and Martin who needed to have a chat. She'd been reasoning that the change in him was down to the school inspection and sleep disturbance, but there was clearly much more to it than that.

Chapter 21

The telephone rang at the same time as Christopher reached for it. His secretary's number flashed on the screen. 'Perfect timing, Shirley. Has Sandy arrived?'

'No. But she called to say she's sorry, she's running late and can't make it. Something to do with wedding hair arrangements. She tried to get you on your mobile.'

Mustering up joviality, he said, 'That's a shame. I was looking for an excuse to pop over to Alessandro's for a cheeky treat.'

He replaced the handset and checked his mobile – no missed calls or messages. He knew Sandy was avoiding having to talk. It was the same with his health. She ignored things that worried her, as if to face them made them real.

He leaned back in his chair and sighed. She'd had an appointment with Frank Budle, earlier. She must have shot straight off. 'Silly woman,' he said aloud, rubbing his face with both hands. If only she'd sit down with him for more than five minutes, he could allay her fears. The arguments were ridiculous. He'd had confirmation of his new salary and had wanted to show her. Alison's concerned face popped into his mind. He laughed at her assumption that it must be a disability that stopped Sandy making his lunch. If he asked Sandy to do that, it would finish her off.

He was still chuckling as he called Shirley. 'Has Frank Budle got anyone with him at the minute?'

There was a pause while she checked his appointments. 'Should be finishing with a client about now. Shall I ask him to come up?'

'No thanks, I'll have a wander down.'

It would be good to stretch his legs and touch base with the rest of the staff. Having a plush office was nice, but he sometimes felt cut off upstairs.

As he walked downstairs, he could see Frank chatting to his client. They were laughing, wrapping up the consultation. He had to admit, Frank communicated well with the customers.

The client, a professional-looking man in a sharp suit, stood up and shook his hand. 'You saved my life, Frank. I owe you one.'

'Fingers too big for the tiny keys on screen keyboards. So easy to mistype a password.' Frank glanced up and spotted Christopher, then turned back to the client. 'Just tell her to give customer services a call. Number's on the card.'

The man looked puzzled. 'Right. Thanks again.' Christopher watched him leave. He wiped his hand on a tissue once out of Frank's sight.

'Christopher, what can I do for you.'

'Did Sandy make it earlier?'

Frank cocked his head. 'Make it?'

'Didn't she have that appointment to sort out a savings account today?'

'Oh, right. Yes. I mean no. She called to cancel. Something came up.' He rustled some papers and tapped them on the desk. 'I'd better get this lot uploaded.'

Yes, thought Christopher, there was something untrustworthy about that man. Back up in his office, he asked Shirley for a print-out of Frank's appointments over the last few months.

Ten minutes later, Shirley presented him with two lists.

'These were in house, those others off-site.' She shot the coffee machine a stony look. 'Can I get you a drink?'

'No thanks. What do you mean, off-site?'

'He often goes out to see people who can't get in for an appointment.'

That service was not within Frank's role. What was he up to? 'Thanks Shirley.' He stood up and walked over to the machine. 'Let me get you a coffee. White?'

Shirley swayed. 'No. You can't make me a drink.'

'Of course I can.' He popped in a pod and switched on the machine. 'I've told you before, it's not your job to make coffee.'

She eyed the cup he passed her with suspicion. 'Thank you.' She made to leave and then paused. 'There's something, I don't know if I should mention it, I don't want to overstep the mark...'

'Please, go on... Sit down, have your coffee.' Christopher carried his back to his desk. 'I'd offer you a biscuit, but I don't have any.'

Shirley perched on the edge of the seat. 'I've never sat in here before.' She took a sip and raised an eyebrow.

'See, I knew you'd like it once you tried it,' he said with a brief smile.

'It's okay, I suppose. I still prefer my kettle. Anyway, the people he goes out to see... They aren't new customers. They should all have online accounts, so have no need for him to meet them.'

'How do you know?'

'I checked out a load of them one month. He'd spent a lot of time out of the office, so I looked up how far away the customers lived. One of them was my hairdresser's son. She used to have the salon across the road. When she was ill, her son was back and forth from the shop. I don't know why he couldn't come in here, rather than Frank going off somewhere to meet him.'

'So, why was her son doing her banking if it was her business?'

'Oh, it was all incredibly sad. She was only in her sixties. She had a big stroke and had to go into a care home.'

'Right, and he had to sort out her finances.'

'She ended up having to sell it to pay the fees. Scandalous. Over four hundred pounds a week, I believe.'

'Yes. And the private ones are even more expensive.'

'I heard the salon went for a pittance.'

'I'm surprised to hear that. Property prices in this area are usually at the higher end of the market for the region.'

'Not when people know you need to raise money. Vultures, if you ask me.'

'Did she go into Earlby Care Home?'

'Yes. It has a good CQC rating, though I don't know how. They reckon it's run down, and they can't keep their staff either.'

Christopher recalled what Frank had said about dabbling in property development. And his wife running a care home. He'd bet Frank would have no problem snapping up some old dear's home cheap as chips. 'Thanks for the lists, Shirley. I'll have a look through them.'

Chapter 22

Alison paused and inhaled a lungful of fresh air then continued down the dirt pathway towards Cherry Dene. She stopped to stretch in a clearing in the trees and let the spray from the cascading waterfall cool her face. She loved this place. Her irritations dissipated as she was mesmerised by orbs of light glinting off the water.

It was like an Enid Blyton story. Tales of children going off into the countryside to have magical adventures – saying things like 'Gosh,' and 'Run for it ….' It brough back happy memories of her mother, making the tea or chatting to her father after work. Recently, she'd stopped fast forwarding to sad times when she thought about them. Alison breathed in the mossy damp air. *The Magic Faraway Tree,* that was the one she was thinking of.

Christopher was already sitting on their bench when she got there. He was making a right racket with a Red Delicious apple. She flopped down at the opposite end.

He waved a greeting with his apple. 'Nice rucksack, is it new?'

'Yes,' she said, taken aback he'd noticed. Martin hadn't, despite nearly tripping over it that morning before work.

'You're not so out of breath,' said Christopher.

How observant, she thought. 'It's disappointing because I

need to be out of breath.'

Christopher glanced over at her, puzzled. 'Don't worry, it's a good thing. It means you're getting fitter.'

She pulled out a ham sandwich from her rucksack. 'It has to be out-of-breath exercise. But I don't like being sweaty at work in the afternoons. But if it helps me sleep…'

'It must be awful.'

'Well, I have a pack of Wet Ones and deodorant. I don't stay in these clothes all afternoon.'

He laughed. 'No, the insomnia – must be dreadful to be awake while the world sleeps. Lonely.'

Barring the sleep nurse, no one had shown genuine understanding. 'People rarely grasp how bad you feel.'

'It's not rocket science. We all need a good night's sleep. Is it getting any better yet?' He removed the lid of his shop-bought salad and looked disappointed at its wilting contents.

She gazed out across the football field as she thought about it and saw the Arctic man wave over. She waved back, Christopher looked up and did the same. 'I'm more tired during the day. And now and again, I think I've slept a little longer than usual. But I don't know because I'm not allowed to check the time.' She bit into the sandwich. It tasted wonderful. 'It's certainly giving me an appetite.'

Christopher speared a piece of avocado with a plastic fork. 'Change isn't always easy.' His fork snapped. 'Drat.' He rolled his eyes at Alison, making her laugh. 'But it can be worth the effort. My clearly diabetic diabetes nurse is pleased with my HbA1C. She said I'm less pre-diabetic than I was.'

Alison had no idea what an HbA1C was but assumed it must be to do with the condition. She gave him a surreptitious glance. He seemed fit for someone with an obesity illness.

He stabbed a piece of chicken with the fork handle. 'I'd love a ham and cheese panini.'

'That apple looked nice.'

'It was. That's why I ate it first. I was going to have a cheat meal today with my wife, but she was held up. We missed a Danish pastry the other day.' He gazed into the middle distance, then his face clouded. 'Just as well – I'm not having that nurse calling me obese again. So, salads it is for me for a while.'

'I'm missing my coffee. Michelle's funny. The first time I went to see her, I caught her asleep on her desk.'

Christopher laughed. 'The nurse told me to lose weight, while she was sitting there, spilling over the sides of her chair. It groaned every time she moved. She says I'm still overweight.'

'Not that I've been scrutinising you, but you seem to be losing weight.' Alison watched him for signs of fear. None – much to her relief. Christopher was becoming easy to chat to, she often forgot to think before speaking.

'I'm going to join Hoppington's gym. There's only so much you can fit into a lunch time.'

'Martin goes there. I used to teach Pilates and I'm thinking of starting up again. I wonder if there's a class I can join to get back into practice first.'

'According to the website, they have everything – Zumba, Spinning, Pilates. I'd love Sandy to come with me. She goes to the Elliot Spears one in town. It's too far away to get to after work for me.'

Alison winced. 'Pricey.'

'Yes. She's looking into saving at the moment, but I don't think her gym will go.' He laughed. 'She doesn't really do saving.'

'I've been saving for twenty years for university. Martin too, but mostly me. It'll be worth it.'

He paused, the fork handle halfway to his mouth. 'Wow. That's amazing.'

From his incredulous expression, anyone would think she'd done something unheard of. Alison had noticed an air of sadness about Christopher. At first, she'd assumed he was one of those people born with a permanent frown. But every now and again, he seemed to forget himself and it disappeared. She wondered if he and Sandy were happily married. Christopher was staring at her, waiting for her to speak.

'Pardon? Sorry, I got distracted for a moment.'

'I asked what you do for a living?'

'I work for the NHS. Not the clinical side. But I'm going back to university to study Physiotherapy.'

Alison detected another look of admiration. She couldn't recall the last time Martin had shown real respect for her career plans. Thinking about it, no one in his family took her aspirations seriously. Doreen had once said to her, 'You need A-levels to get to university, Alison,' ignoring the fact that she and Martin had met there.

Christopher was pensive. 'My wife wants to set up her own business. A beauty salon. She used to work in the industry before she left to have our daughter, Emily. Sandy plans to return to work though…' His voice tailed off.

Alison wanted to ask him more – whether he ever felt like Sandy didn't care about what he wanted. But he was gazing off into the distance, lost in thought. 'I like Cherry Park.'

He nodded. 'Me too.'

'I can exercise and get a good dose of daylight down here.' She inhaled deeply. 'And escape my horrible line manager.' She leaned sideways towards Christopher and lowered her voice. 'I don't normally admit this to people, but 'I sometimes think I'll kill him…'

He put his head back and guffawed. 'You're so funny.'

She had no idea why she'd confided such a disturbing personal snippet. Thankfully, he seemed to think she was joking. He looked ten years younger. 'You have to laugh, or you'd go mad,' she said, with a little chuckle of her own.

Christopher studied her as she spoke.

'You were serious… Do you think it's him per se? Or is it to do with something else in your life?'

Alison blushed. 'I couldn't really harm another person.

Martin reckons the lack of sleep makes me overreact to everything. He says I've always been over-sensitive.'

He shrugged and made an open-handed gesture. 'No disrespect to Martin, but your feelings are your feelings.'

His response took her by surprise. She didn't know what to say – all she could do was stare down at her feet.

'I enjoy working with my colleagues at this branch, but I've met some unpleasant people in my time.' He smiled. 'I usually move around the country from branch to branch. I'm planning on staying here.'

Alison felt a little bubble of happiness in her stomach. 'I expect Sandy will be thrilled to have you at home.'

'Yes, she says she misses me when I'm away.'

Alison noticed his frown return and felt a twinge of sympathy. 'I'd planned to start my course the year after next – when our twins finish university. But it looks like we might be able to afford it earlier.'

'Good for you,' said Christopher. 'If you ever need financial advice, I know a friendly bank manager in the branch on the high street.'

'Manager – Sandy must be proud of you.'

Haurice gambolled over before Christopher answered. Judith appeared in hot pursuit. Haurice ignored her calls. By the time she reached them she was out of breath.

'You should borrow Haurice, Alison,' said Christopher. 'He'd wear you out.'

'You could be right.' She smiled up at Judith. 'He likes his little routine, doesn't he?'

Judith attached the lead. 'He's bordering on obsessive compulsive if you ask me.'

Christopher stroked the poodle's head. 'He likes to pop over to say hello, don't you Haurice?'

Alison's eyes widened – she could have sworn Haurice smiled at Christopher.

'Come on, old Mrs Caudwell will be banging on the salon

door for her cut and blow dry.'

'Is that your salon opposite Henleys bank on the high street?' asked Christopher.

'I lease it, unfortunately,' said Judith. 'It's an excellent spot, but the rent's high.' Haurice tapped her leg and looked along the path. 'Okay, let's go.'

Christopher seemed pensive.

'I wish we'd thought about a buy-to-rent property,' said Alison. 'I bet we could've funded my course years ago.'

'Hindsight's a grand thing.'

As Judith and Haurice trotted away, Alison checked her watch and sighed. 'Well, I suppose I'd better get back. She packed up her rucksack. 'See you next time.'

'Don't let him grind you down,' said Christopher.

'Who?'

'Your boss. Stand up to him. You've got rights.'

'Thanks, I will.' How kind, she thought, feeling bolstered by Christopher's words of support.

He was right. She didn't have to put up with harassment at work. She'd stepped in as line manager before, she'd read the policies. Christopher had made her realise she'd allowed a stupid man of no importance whatsoever to knock her confidence.

As she walked through the gates onto the high street, Alison felt her step lighten.

Chapter 23

Christopher replaced the handset and leaned back in his chair. He laced his fingers behind his head and smiled in satisfaction. The latest blood test showed no sign of pre-diabetes. Ill-health nipped in the bud. Just about anyway. The blood pressure was on the high side at times but heading in the right direction.

A guffaw caught the back of his throat, making him cough. Who'd have thought he'd be grateful to Beverley? Maybe it was supposed to have been this way – the steely ambition to set up the ideal life – and then a sharp slap of realisation from a fat dollop to bring him to his senses. If it hadn't been for her, he might have worked himself into an early grave, without ever discovering he wasn't even happy.

He pushed his foot against the desk and spun himself around in his chair. He was good at his job. And he'd do a good job as manager here, too. And… it would be a pleasure, barely any effort at all. He spun around some more, revelling in his good fortune.

Christopher selected a coffee pod, an intense Brazilian blend, and popped it into the machine. He perused the office with fresh eyes as it filled with the aroma of freshly brewed coffee – he felt at home. He'd loved the thrill of troubleshooting and resolving a crisis, but he was now ambitious for a different challenge.

This would be the best branch in the region. And he and Sandy were going to enjoy the life he'd been too busy to partake in before.

Shirley knocked on the office door and came in holding some papers. He took them from her and sat down to read them.

'You look right sitting at that desk.'

'What do you mean?'

'Well, our old manager didn't. It was as if he didn't belong there.' She looked around the room. 'And this office had a different feel to it. I used to hate coming in here. In fact, there's a better atmosphere throughout the entire branch now.' She chuckled. 'Some days I almost like coming to work.'

As Shirley closed the door behind her, Christopher smiled, tapped the desk with his foot and spun around again.

'You look pleased with yourself,' said Sandy, as Christopher walked into the kitchen, carrying a bouquet of pink roses.

He kissed her cheek. 'I am. And these are for my beautiful wife.' He felt as if the world had been lifted from his shoulders.

Sandy sniffed the flowers. 'They're gorgeous, darling. Thank you. Could you pass me a vase, please?'

He picked one out from the cupboard above the microwave, then filled it with water and added the sachet of feed. 'The lady in the shop said to cut the stems on an angle to make them last longer.' He rummaged in a drawer and turned back around holding a pair of scissors.

Sandy plopped the bouquet straight into the vase. 'How come you're home so early?'

'I couldn't wait to speak to you. I've got two pieces of good news.' He took off his coat and hung it over a dining chair.

'Okay, but can I go first?' She left the vase of flowers on the bench top next to the discarded cellophane and bustled over to the table. It was covered with papers and a brochure.

Assuming she'd been researching salon opportunities, Christopher looked from the papers to his wife in admiration.

'It's come up for sale.'

'What has?'

She could barely contain her excitement. 'The William's house. In California.' She clapped her hands and bounced up and down on the spot.

His shoulders slumped. 'I thought we'd already discussed this.'

Her expression flipped from happy to sad, her huge blue eyes filled with disappointment.

Christopher caressed her cheek with his hand. 'Come on, love. You know we don't need a second holiday home. What's this really all about?'

'We loved that house. Think how great it would be to go over any time we wanted to.'

He felt like he was stuck in a revolving door. 'But we couldn't. I'd have to keep doing the long hours and work away from home. I'd never have the time to go.'

She flopped down on a chair like a frustrated child. 'You said you wanted to spend quality time together.'

Christopher raked his hands through his hair. 'How can we do that if I'm not here with you? Sandy, you say you want one thing, which by default means you can't have the other.'

'Huh?'

'And you also want to keep Casita Emilia and the Durham apartment.'

'Of course I do, they're excellent investments. They would help to secure our future. You never know what might happen.'

'They've got mortgages on them. You don't like renting them out, so I have to earn the money to pay for them.'

She walked over to the coffee machine and popped in a pod. 'Forget about it for now. What was it you wanted to tell me?'

Christopher's news had lost its shine. 'Well, the first thing is that my blood sugars are good. I have to have a more in-depth test in three months, but at the moment, I'm okay.'

She pressed the button and filled her cup, then took it over to the table. 'That's brilliant news. See, I knew you could put it right without downgrading.'

'I'll get my own, thanks.' He reached for a cup and made himself a coffee. 'And Head Office has sent me a draft contract through –'

Sandy sucked in a sharp breath. 'No, you can't –'

Christopher pulled up a seat next to her and put his arm around her shoulders. She bristled. 'They've suggested an eighteen-month secondment, with the option of returning to my old job if I want to at the end.'

'A secondment? Does that mean you'll keep your current salary?'

'No. Look, for the umpteenth time, nothing will change in our standard of living. The equity in the Durham apartment will pay off the small mortgage we have left on this house, and We'll be able to manage the Casita Emilia on my salary.'

'And the William's house?'

'You're like a dog with a bone.'

'But we've worked together all these years to build a wonderful life, and you want to throw it all away,' she clicked her fingers, 'just like that.' She held her head in her hands and cried.

Christopher felt himself rankling. 'I've tried to show you the figures –'

'You know I'm useless with that sort of thing.'

He got up and walked over to the kitchen. 'What would you do if something happened to me?'

She gave a wave of dismissal. 'I'd be fine. The will's up to date. All the banking passwords are on that USB stick you made for me. The solicitor would sort everything out.'

Christopher felt light-headed. He had to hold onto the

bench to steady himself.

Seeing his look of shock, she quickly added, 'Anyway, that's one reason I wanted to start a savings account. All this talk about change got me thinking. I want to contribute to our finances. And if you were ill, I'd be here to look after you, not out working because you couldn't.'

'Sounds like you'd cope better than I'd imagined.'

'You're wrong. I'm just peeved about the whole job thing. I don't think I'd cope without you.'

He gave her a side-ways glance. 'At least you'll have your new business.'

She flushed up. 'What on earth do you mean? I haven't got a business. Why would you think I had a business? Who said that?'

'Why would anyone say that?'

Her shoulders relaxed. 'Exactly.'

This wasn't going the way he'd hoped. 'I was talking about the one you're going to start up now that Emily's all grown up and getting married. And as I'll be living here, I'll be around to help with the business side until you're up and running – or I kick the bucket.'

Sandy shot him a look of disgust. 'Ah, now I see. You're sending *me* out to work so *you* can go part time.'

'Get a grip. When have I ever expected anything from you?'

She slumped into a sobbing heap. 'So, I've contributed nothing to this family?' she choked out.

Christopher, who normally felt distressed when Sandy cried, felt nothing. He waited until her cries subsided. 'You've told everyone for as long as I can remember you wanted to set up your own salon. You said as soon as Emily left home.'

'I bet a law court would say I contributed.'

'You do, of course you do. In so many wonderful ways. Hang on, why are you talking about a law court?'

She shook her head and glared at him. 'You've never appreciated me. You should think yourself lucky I chose you.'

He rubbed his face with both hands. 'Please, not this again.'

'I could've had any man. I –'

'Yes, Sandy. You settled for me.' He went towards the door, then paused. 'Why *did* you do that? If you could've done so much better than me, why didn't you?'

'Where are you going? I thought you wanted to talk?'

'It's pointless.'

Upstairs, Christopher flung his gym gear into his bag, his head full of jumbled thoughts. Maybe he should forget his stupid plan if it was going to cause so much strife. At that moment, a hotel room in a faceless city where he knew no one and had nothing to do but work, seemed an attractive prospect. He stopped. What was he thinking? Sandy had shown zilch interest in his happiness; why was he contemplating making himself more unhappy to please her? He'd wanted to believe that it was the stress of wedding preparations, and Emily leaving home for good that was behind Sandy's lack of understanding – and awful mood swings. But he had a gut-churning feeling that he simply hadn't been around for long enough before to really see her.

Chapter 24

Alison locked her bag in her desk and looked around the grim office. Without Sharon, work was awful.

Billy ambled over, eating a Snickers bar. He leaned in and lowered his voice. 'Your face could turn milk sour.' He slurped back a string of chocolatey drool.

She shot him a stony glare. 'Get away from me.'

He wandered back to his office chuckling.

Phyllis meerkat-ed up from her computer screen. 'That's not a professional way to speak to your manager.'

Alison looked over and snorted a half-choke – Phyllis had taken the straighteners to her hair. It looked like she'd drawn the fringe and sides on her head with a thick black marker pen, while the back resembled a burst couch. She was saved from having to answer by the ping of an incoming email. Billy – he'd scheduled a meeting at lunchtime. She sent her apologies and set about her usual duties.

Not optional, pinged in a reply. It immediately disappeared.

How does he do that? Alison reached for her vitamins. She emailed him, asking him to stop belittling her and telling him that she had to leave the building at lunchtime – during her unpaid break. She blind-copied in his manager and recorded it in her diary. Yes, it was sneaky, but there was a line of command and a plethora of policies and procedures. There was no way she was going to allow Billy to continue to undermine her rights.

She also raised a ticket with IT about disappearing emails.

Thankfully, Billy left her alone for the rest of the morning; or so she thought. A phone call from Occupational Health proved otherwise. She had an appointment at five o'clock that afternoon – following a referral from her line manager. The person on the other end sounded almost apologetic. She had no idea what the problem was, only that it was urgent that Alison was assessed.

With as much professionalism as she could muster, she calmly walked over to Billy's office and gave the door a confident rat-a-tat-tat.

'Come,' he boomed.

Alison walked in with the most assertive expression she could muster. 'Could I have a word in private, please?'

He sucked in a whistle and shook his head. 'Sorry, no can do. Got to see a man about a dog.'

'Occupational Health…?'

He splayed his hands and pulled a facial contortion that made Alison want to poke his eyes out. 'Asleep at your desk. I had no option.'

She left the room with the sound of his cackles ringing in her ears.

Recounting the details of her insomnia condition and CBT-I treatment to the Occupational Health nurse was one of her most humiliating experiences to date. It was as if she had no right to privacy.

Her eyes brimmed with tears as she thought about the potential effects this could have on the rest of her life. If she was declared unfit for work, it would go against her application, for the physiotherapy course. It could ruin everything.

'I've always given my best to my work – unlike Billy

Chapman. I'm not the type of person to sleep at my desk. He's constantly looking for ways to put me down.' She clasped her arms and dug her nails into the flesh as she spoke.

The nurse watched her. 'You seem stressed.'

Alison unclasped her hands and held them loosely in her lap. 'Maybe. But it doesn't stop me from doing my job properly.'

The nurse smiled. 'Given your lack of sleep, you've done well to get in for a full day's work all these years.'

'I've never thought of it like that. To be honest, I feel such a failure.'

'On the contrary. Many people would have taken sickness leave long ago. You've managed to continue working during the treatment programme, too. That must be making it even more difficult.'

Alison felt her spirits lift. 'Yes, it is. And it's causing havoc at home. The getting up and down during the night disturbs my husband.'

'Is he supportive?'

She felt suddenly embarrassed – and small. 'Most of the time,' she lied.

The nurse looked at Alison without speaking, as if processing the information.

'We're both shattered.' She couldn't bring herself to discuss her marital problems with this stranger.

'But there's less help in the work environment, I suspect,' she said, arching an eyebrow. 'If you did doze off, could it be a sign that the programme is working? As you said, it's meant to make you extra tired at first. I think we need to support you as much as we can.' She gave a wry smile. 'Let's start by protecting your lunch breaks.'

'Really?'

'And would it help if you had the option to come in later if you'd had a particularly bad night? You could start and finish within a two-hour window of your normal times and balance your hours as you see fit. Don't worry about the odd micro-sleep. If you need to take an extra break, log the times and let your manager know.'

Tears pricked the back of Alison's eyes, this time in response to the nurse's kindness. 'That would be helpful. Thank you. It won't be for long. I'm due to start increasing my sleep window soon.'

'Okay. I'll send you and your manager a copy of my report. Good luck with the rest of the programme.'

As soon as Alison left the consultation room, she allowed the tears to fall. For once, Billy's attempts to stick the knife in had failed. She realised how alone she'd been feeling lately, at work as well as at home. The silly rows between herself and Martin had been weighing heavily on her which, on top of the nasty work environment, had made her feel as if her life was imploding.

She blew her nose and let out a lungful of air, as a wonderful sense of peace washed over her.

By the time Alison met up with Katie after work for an impromptu coffee, she felt confident that all visible signs of her testing, tearful day had faded.

Gavin set down a plate of biscuits. 'There's an extra one for you.' He nodded at Alison and circled his eye with his index finger. 'You look like you're having a bugger of a day. Oops…' he gave the room a quick scan, 'sorry about the language. I forget I'm at work when normal people come in.'

'You could say that. Thanks,' said Alison.

Katie scrutinised her face. 'Have you been crying?'

'A little. Billy referred me to Occupational Health.'

'Why?'

'Phyllis told him I fell asleep at my desk – which wasn't true. He did it because I wouldn't go to a lunchtime meeting.'

'Are you all right?'

'Yes, fine thanks. I just want to pull myself together before I go home. I promised to make a bolognaise for tea and my head's all over the place.'

'Let Martin make tea, for once.'

Alison frowned at her. 'It's not his fault.'

'No, it isn't, but as you said, you've had a bad day. There's got to be give and take.'

Alison changed the conversation. 'Anyway, I was livid at first, but he's ended up doing me a good turn. I've now got protected lunch breaks, and more flexibility when I start and finish.' She gave a little grin. 'I'll tell him in the morning. It'll ruin his day.'

'Great, wish I could see his face.' She took a sip of coffee. 'Is the CBT-i helping? You've seemed quite low recently.'

Alison dunked her biscuit into her cup. As she raised it to her mouth it broke off and plopped back into her coffee. She stared at it in dismay then scooped out the mush onto the saucer. 'It's hard but I think it's starting to work. I now have a more regular sleep window –'

'Get you with the technical lingo,' laughed Katie.

'There's nothing I can't tell you about sleep. I called Michelle to tell her about being reported to occupational health. She said that if I stick to the targets, I can start moving my bedtime by fifteen minutes.'

Gavin came over with a fresh cup.

'Sorry. Don't know why I did that, my Mam used to tell me off for it.'

He winked at Katie and pointed at Alison with his thumb as he returned to the bar. 'You can't take some people anywhere.'

'The only thing is, I'm still having to get up and down during the night, which sets Martin off whinging. Sometimes I stay in bed when I shouldn't. Michelle said it's probably slowed down my progress.'

'Surely he could be supportive for a few weeks.'

'For an intelligent man, he's being thick about it all.' He complained because I hadn't done his ironing.'

Katie clunked down her cup. 'You're joking? Since when has he expected you to do that? I hope you put him right. And why are you worried about dashing home to make his bolognaise?'

It was coming out all wrong – she was making Martin sound horrible, and herself like a doormat. 'Well, I think it's my fault. I've tended to do useful things during the night. He never expected it.' Alison gazed into the middle distance. 'At least I didn't think he did,' she said in a quiet voice.

'To be honest, I never thought Martin was as into the whole equality thing as you made out. I mean you're the one who's supported him through everything your whole married life.'

Alison paused, her cup midway to her mouth. 'That's not true. Martin has worked so hard to provide for our family. Without his efforts, I would've been a struggling single-parent.'

'As would he, had you left him with the children.'

She stared at Katie, aghast. 'I could never have left my children.'

Katie raised her eyebrows, her lips pressed together into a flat line. 'They're his children, too. Yet, it wasn't him who had to move into a skanky flat.'

'But they were crying babies. It didn't made sense for him to move out of the student halls of residence. He needed to be alert for lectures.'

'How many new fathers do you think get away without sleepless nights? Anyway, you've managed to get yourself to work for years without a good night's sleep.' Katie shook her head, her brow furrowed. 'The least he can do now is support you while you work on putting it right.'

'Katie, why are you so angry with Martin?'

She shrugged. 'It's not him. It's men. They get on my nerves.'

'None taken,' Gavin called over from the bar.

'Sorry, I forgot you were earwigging,' said Katie.

Alison waved a biscuit at him. 'Thanks for these, they're delicious.' She turned to Katie. 'Are you still seeing What's-his-name?'

'No, I binned him. There was no spark. And he made this nauseating, slopping noise when he ate. It made me want to crash his head into his plate.'

She nearly choked on a crumb as she guffawed. 'I wonder if he knows Billy,' she croaked.

'Oh, God, he wasn't that bad,' said Katie, laughing.

Alison cackled. 'I could crash Billy's head into his computer screen for breathing.'

'I'd laugh, but I think you might be serious.'

Alison looked down.

'To be honest, I wouldn't blame you.'

A chic woman, who looked to Alison to be in her late thirties, sashayed into the room. Alison smiled as she passed their table. The woman smiled back, revealing perfect white veneers. She peered around the corner at the table by the fire as if searching for someone. A middle-aged man in a sharp suit came into the bar and called her over. He looked familiar, but Alison couldn't put her finger on where she knew him from.

They greeted each other with a hug and then the man ordered a bottle of Champagne, to be taken to the lounge. The woman clapped her hands and gave an excited squeal. 'Does this mean what I think it does?' He gave her a wide grin and offered his arm.

'Sounds like they have something to celebrate,' said Alison. 'She was stunning. I'd love to be able to wear wide-legged trousers. I look like an Oompa Loompa in them.'

'I wonder where she had her Botox. It's bloody good. I bet she's a fair bit older than she looks.'

'Somewhere pricey if the cut of her trouser suit is anything to go by.' She grabbed the barely-there roll of fat around her middle. 'I think I'll have to wear my black dress for Cynthia's birthday do – it's slimming. Mind you, I wouldn't allow Martin out of the house with his hair caked in that much gel. Aha, he's that useless bank clerk – I knew I recognised him.'

Katie wafted her hand in front of her nose. 'Heavy-handed with the aftershave.'

'Can I ask you something?'

Katie narrowed her eyes. 'Depends. What is it?'

'It's, well… What exactly are you looking for in a man?'

Katie puffed out her cheeks as she exhaled. 'To be perfectly honest, there's nothing I want from any man.'

'So why are you disappointed with them?'

She shrugged. 'Same old story, different bloke. It starts off great. Then they get serious and it all turns mind-numbingly boring.'

'Sounds like *Who Moved My Cheese*. How does it end end?'

'I think three of them found a new supply. Not sure about the other one, he wasn't so keen on change.'

'Maybe we all just need to work things out in our own time.'

'Maybe. I just don't want to be like my mam and dad.'

'Aren't they happy?'

'On the surface maybe. They're content. Nice home, financial security. They rub along okay together. She likes disorder, he likes tidiness. Sort of balance each other.'

'And?'

'Mam's always tried to change Dad, make him more adventurous. She says he's settled for a humdrum life.'

Alison's mobile pinged. She shook her head and sighed as she read the text message. 'Martin can't find his gym shorts. It's like he's turned into a child and I've become his mother. Sorry, I interrupted you.'

'She encouraged my brother and me to dream big and let nothing stand in our way. But look at me… I work in an NHS training department. You can't get much more boring than that. I feel like I've let her down. She didn't stand in my way, but I've settled for humdrum, all the same.'

'But you love your job.'

'Yes, but it's a typical, boring job.'

'What else would you like to do?'

Katie turned her palms to the ceiling. 'Nothing. But I can't let myself settle for a humdrum man, too.'

Alison hadn't realised Katie felt disillusioned with her life. 'I suppose the trick is in discovering what it is you want from life and ignoring what other people say you should want.'

'Hmm,' said Katie. 'That's the problem, though. You know you want to be a physiotherapist. And you found the right man. Even if he is turning out to be a bit of a chauvinist.'

'You make my life sound almost good.'

'You do have things pretty well sorted.'

Alison knew Katie was right, but she couldn't ignore the growing worry that it was more than a touch of chauvinism with Martin. She wasn't ready to share it with Katie. If she said it out loud, it would be real. Her stomach lurched. She certainly wasn't prepared for that. She kept her tone light. 'I suppose we've all got things we'd like to change. Mine is my job. Yours is your man.'

Gavin plonked his elbows on the bar and cupped his head in his hands. 'You two should think yourselves lucky. I think I've got the wrong job and the wrong man.' He rolled his eyes and sighed. 'I don't sleep so good either.'

Alison looked from Katie to Gavin and all three of them laughed.

'I've been thinking about joining the gym.'

Panic flashed from Martin's eyes. He dropped his fork; splattering bolognaise sauce across the table. 'Since when are you interested in fitness?'

She fetched a dishcloth. She was about to clean up the mess when she checked herself and handed it to him instead. 'I do Pilates. I'm a qualified instructor. I've taught classes in gyms.'

Martin scoffed. 'Oh, come on, it's years since you've taught. Anyway, we've always had our own interests. Why do we suddenly need to be joined at the hip?'

'What's wrong? Everything I do seems to irritate you.'

'It's this Ofsted inspection. Looming like a black cloud.' He licked sauce from the handle of his fork. 'The gym's where I unwind after a hard day.'

She tore off a square of kitchen roll and passed it to him. 'Can't I unwind with you? I thought it would be nice. We could do our own thing and then meet for a drink in the bar area afterwards.'

'I'm at school all day. You have to remember I carry a great deal of responsibility.'

'What's that got to do with having a drink with me? I work and I have a sleep disorder, but I'd love to spend more time with you.'

'Tell me about it. I've never been so shattered in my whole life. And now you want to rob me of my gym time? And you said the up and down thing was only going to last two weeks...'

She inhaled deeply and let out a slow breath. 'It might have done if I'd been able to stick to it every night.'

'So why haven't you? Is it too much to ask that you do what they've told you to? My mother's doing my blinking ironing for God's sake.' Martin mopped up remnants of sauce with a piece of bread.

She gritted her teeth. 'I've stayed in bed when I should have got up so I wouldn't wake you.'

His shoulders slumped. 'Look, I'm sorry. It's just that it's new to me, this sleep deprivation malarkey.' He gave her a weak smile. 'I don't suppose there's any afters?'

'When did you last cook me a meal – tired or otherwise?' Alison grabbed the spaghetti pan and tipped leftovers into the bin.

'No, stop. I'll have that tomorrow.'

She gave the bin a sharp kick. 'I've been pussyfooting

around in case I upset you because you do nothing but gripe on like a child.' She threw the pan into the sink and stood, hands on hips, glaring at him.

'You're overreacting.'

'You have a right go at me then expect me to dish out pudding for you?' Alison's eyes were like saucers. 'No, there's no *afters*.' She went to storm from the room then turned to face him. 'And since you get in from work earlier than me, it's about time *you* started making the meal.'

Martin spluttered on a mouthful of tea. 'Come on now, that's a bit rich –'

'You can keep your precious gym time. I'll take a longer lunch break to exercise. I'll be in even later from now on. Have a look in the fridge and decide what you're cooking for us tomorrow. And you can tell your mother to shove your ironing up her backside.'

She marched out of the room and tripped on Martin's discarded work shoes in the hallway, scattering them to the bottom of the stairs. In anger, she flung open the front door and gulped in a lungful of air. Sammy appeared on the step and meowed. He was chewing something. Alison smiled and stroked his head, pleased to see his friendly little face. He peeked through the door then slunk inside and sauntered over to inspect one of Martin's shoes. She watched in horror as he hacked up green slime into it.

'Oh, Sammy. I've got enough to do without having to clean up this mess.'

Sammy purred as he brushed past her legs and strolled back out and off under the hedge. Alison picked up the shoes and sighed. Then, with a wicked little cackle, she put them back where they were before she tripped and snuck off to watch TV in the lounge.

Chapter 25

The way Billy was perched on the edge of an empty desk, arms folded and smug expression on his face, put Alison in mind of a conceited boiled egg. He was regaling everyone, barring her, with his Mallorcan travel stories. Dorothy was working in their office – doing overtime on her day off to cover a sickness absence – and she and Phyllis watched him, enthralled. Phyllis hung on every word; Billy leered at Dorothy. The rest of the office had the look of people trying to meet work deadlines while feeling obliged to feign interest in Billy's monologue.

'The thing is, you've got your Mallorca and your Majorca.'

Alison flashed him an irritated glance. They'd sat around wasting time since clocking on an hour previously, which meant she hadn't had an opportunity to speak to him about the outcome of her Occupational Health consultation. She willed herself to stay silent, determined not to become embroiled in his inane rubbish.

'I preferred Majorca. Classier. The airport was better for a start. And the people are much friendlier.' He swung his leg as he perched, revealing a Micky Mouse sock. 'Mind you, they do a tasty Spanish omelette in Mallorca.'

Alison scrunched her eyes closed and clenched her fists.

'You all right over there, sleepyhead? Have *you* ever been to either island?'

Her knuckles whitened. He wasn't even attempting to hide his nasty comments any longer. 'Could I have a word when you've got a minute, please?'

He ignored her. 'Didn't think so.'

'It's the same place, Billy – and it's pronounced Ma-y-orca.'

Phyllis and Dorothy sniggered and looked at Alison as if she were simple.

'No, that's where you're wrong. I've been to both,' said Billy.

Alison tried to concentrate on her work, consoling herself with the fact that this man was an idiot, and that once she left for university, she'd never have to clap eyes on him again.

'You see,' he boomed, 'that's a common misperception among people who know no better.'

The office turned en masse towards Alison. She stared up to a corner of the ceiling and started outlining a banana in her mind's eye.

'Looks like she's having an episode,' said Billy.

As she focused on her banana, she found herself relaxing and zoning out from the titters. She laughed to herself. If the mindfulness exercises could blot out Billy Chapman, they had to be doing something to her brain. The CBT-i was working.

The school football team was out practicing when Alison arrived at the park. She buzzed with excitement all the way around her exercise route – the prospect of a good night's sleep increasingly feasible in her mind. It would make such a difference to Martin's life, as well as her own.

She ate lunch to the familiar sound of the ball being booted and the youngsters' cheers and jeers. She noticed how normal the teachers and parent helpers looked compared to those at St Pauls' primary. One mother was even wearing jeans. It looked a lot more fun than the staid atmosphere she was used to. She cackled at the thought of Martin's face if she turned up to help in trainers and jeans. She could imagine his rebuke. *Alison, you're the middle-aged wife of a deputy head teacher. You have standards to maintain.*

It had been a blessing they couldn't afford St Paul's for Chloe and Jack. Even with Martin's staff discount, the fees were too high. The place had an air of snobbiness about it that made her feel inferior, and she didn't want her children to be made to feel the same way. It hadn't harmed them, they'd both done exceptionally well and turned out fine.

She sipped coffee from her flask mug and sighed in satisfaction.

'Looks like you're enjoying that,' said a voice too close for comfort.

Alison's head snapped around in fright.

Christopher laughed and plonked a carrier bag on the other end of the bench. 'I'll have to start wearing a bell'

'Hi, I was miles away.'

'Have you always been of a nervous disposition?' He rustled around in the bag for his lunch.

'I didn't realise I was, but you're the second person to mention it lately.' She glanced at his carrier, Martin would never have his lunch in a supermarket bag, even if it was from M & S. For some reason, she liked it that Christopher did have his in one. 'Savouring my coffee. Last one of the day.' She looked down at her cup. 'I'm trying to eek it out to make the most of it.'

'Cutting down?'

'I have to get caffeine out of my system at least six hours before bedtime.' She took a tiny sip. 'It's been one of the hardest parts of the programme to stick to.'

'I didn't expect to find you here, I thought you might have swapped the park for the gym with Martin.'

'He was horrified at the thought.' She shrugged. 'You men and your *me* time. Looks like I'll be better off finding my own gym.'

Christopher raised his eyebrows. 'I'd have thought he'd be delighted to accompany you.' He clipped open his lunch box and pulled out a metal fork. 'Funnily enough, you inspired me to invite Sandy to the next open weekend.'

'What's that?'

'Once a month, members can take a guest. Hasn't Martin ever invited you?'

Alison tried to keep her expression impassive to hide her embarrassment. 'No. To be fair, he said he thought I wasn't interested in exercise any longer.' She felt stupid. Sitting there kitted out in sports gear, trying to make it sound feasible that her husband had no idea she exercised. She glanced down at her fluorescent trainers and wondered why he hadn't noticed them in the shoe rack.

'Went down like a lead balloon with Sandy, too,' said Christopher. 'I suppose she does have her own membership. And she has a lot on with planning Emily's wedding...' His voice trailed off.

'Yes, I imagine it must be tricky trying to fit all that in.' She imagined no such thing. His wife sounded bone idle.

'She does an amazing job of organising our lives and keeping the home running. It's a full-time job.'

Alison gave a hearty laugh, then noticed him looking at her with a puzzled expression. 'Oh, sorry, I thought you were joking. I've always worked and run the home.'

'It's a sizeable property that we have. It keeps her busy.'

She noticed the sparkle in Christopher's eyes had dulled as he chatted about his wife. He gave the impression they were happily married. But she wondered if he was like her, trying to keep up the façade everything was fine at home when it wasn't.

So many people she knew were either disillusioned with love or trapped in an unfulfilling relationship. Sharon was one of her only happily married friends. And even she and big Davey had their difficulties, what with the infertility issues. It must have been devastating to have finally had to give up trying just as her sister fell pregnant with her first child. Everyone else around her was miserable at the minute, especially Keith and Gail.

Despite her recent misgivings about Martin, she had to admit that he'd stepped up to support his brother. He'd spent ages on the phone the night before trying to calm Keith down. Then Gail called, half-cut, and he got stuck listening to the saga of how useless a life she had with his brother. Alison hit lucky and managed to avoid speaking to either of them – she was having a bath when Keith called and then setting up her nest when Gail phoned. Martin looked worn out by the time he'd finished speaking to Gail.

She felt a tap on her leg. 'Hello there, little man, how are you today?' Haurice licked her hand and moved over to tap Christopher.

An almighty shriek sounded from the edge of the football field. They looked over to see Judith fall to her knees – kyboshed by an old Casey football to the head. Haurice shot off. By the time Christopher and Alison reached her, a small crowd had gathered. Judith was sobbing and jabbering.

The football coach was beside himself with concern. He tooted his whistle and shouted, 'Er, right… You lot, get back.' The youngsters scampered away. He went to help her to her feet. 'So sorry.'

Judith wobbled and had to sit down on the grass. 'It's okay,' she wept. 'Accidents happen.' She brushed the hair from her brow, to reveal a muddy, ball-shaped imprint.

Alison picked up the ball and handed it to the teacher. 'Good grief. It's a heck of a weight. Judith, are you sure you're all right? Maybe you should get checked out.'

The teacher shuffled awkwardly from foot to foot. 'We're hoping to get some lighter ones in the new financial year.' He shot Judith a shifty glance. 'If you're sure you're okay, I'd better get back…'

The crowd dispersed and Alison and Christopher helped

her to her feet.

Judith looked around, discombobulated. 'I'm sorry. I'm fine.' She smiled, revealing coral lipstick coated teeth. 'It's been a hell of a day.'

Haurice ran circles around her feet, tap-tapping every bit of her leg he could reach. At one point he tripped himself up attempting to tap her with all four paws at the same time. 'Heaouw nyeaw,' he cried, launching himself into a body splay in the air. He landed with a thud on the ground.

'Whoops-a-daisy,' said Christopher. 'He's in shock.' He picked him up and held him firmly like a baby, to calm him down.

Alison felt a warm glow inside. She wished he'd been around to say "whoops-a-daisy" to her when she fell outside the greengrocer's shop. She caught herself wishing she could swap places with the poodle and blushed.

Once Haurice had pulled himself together, he reached out for Judith and scrambled up her coat, leaving a trail of mud. Then he hyperventilated little sobs into her neck before trying to eat her earring.

'Is there anything we can do?' said Alison.

'Oh, no, no.' Judith started to regain her composure. 'I've been snowed under at the salon and feeling the pressure more lately. One moment I was planning out the afternoon – I had to squeeze in a couple of extra appointments – and then, *dunch,* the football hit my head. I actually saw stars. It felt like the end of the world.' She wiped her nose with the back of her hand. 'Haurice had run off again – that dog training class is rubbish – I haven't got time for any of this. My landlady has put up the rent again on my salon.'

Christopher brushed dirt from his jacket and appeared to be weighing something up in his mind. 'Forgive me if this is too intrusive a question, but may I ask how many employees you have?'

'There's only me,' she replied. 'Oh, and Peggy, my new

cleaner.'

'Peggy?' piped up Alison. 'By any chance is she a little woman with glasses, aggressive?'

'Yes. Do you know her? She started last week.'

'We have a cleaner at work called Peggy. She said she has another job. "Lovely little hairdresser lass," she told me.'

Judith smiled.

'Looks like Jonny Vegas with glasses, in an overall?' said Alison. 'But don't repeat that.'

'Yes, that's the one,' giggled Judith.

Alison laughed. 'She's funny, isn't she?'

'Oh yes. And she gets all the gossip.' Haurice jumped from her arms and started gambolling around. He lay on the remnants of an old baguette and rolled in it, all four legs in the air. 'Stop that this minute.' Haurice jumped up and ran around in circles until he was exhausted, then he flopped down and started gnawing at his paws. 'He gets stressed if I'm upset. He likes to feel secure.'

'So, you're busy, and there's only one of you. Is that what you're saying? Have you enough space for another stylist?'

Judith began to cry again. 'Yes, four beautifully fitted work-stations. But I can't afford to employ anyone else. There's even a nail bar.'

Haurice jumped up and ran over to Alison. He clawed at her leg and looked up at her, a beseeching expression on his face. She picked him up and held him tightly like she'd seen Christopher do.

'Have you thought about renting out your chairs?' said Christopher.

'Yes, but…' she choked back a sob. 'I don't know how to find decent stylists I could trust. My dad would have been so proud if he'd lived to see my business.' She pulled a tissue from her pocket and blew her nose. 'But disappointed I'm not managing it very well. I'm good at my job. But I've discovered I'm rubbish at the business stuff.' She howled louder than ever.

Haurice whimpered and sunk his teeth into Alison's arm. She screamed.

The others gasped.

'He bit my arm.'

Haurice sprang free and clamped his teeth into her leg through her jogging tights, digging his paws into the grass and pulling back with all his might.

'Crickey, are you all right?' asked Christopher, who was doing a poor job of suppressing a laugh. 'Sorry, I know it isn't funny. Gosh, is that blood?'

Judith gasped. She apologised profusely as she unclamped his teeth with her fingers. Quick as a flash, Haurice sunk his teeth into Alison's trainer and rag-dolled it.

Alison inspected the wound on her leg. 'Oh, it's nothing. My jogging tights got the worst of it.' She smiled brightly, in a bid to hide the fact that her wounds were smarting, and she was gutted at the hole in her new gear.

'I'll replace them, of course' said Judith.

'Don't worry about it. They're an old pair,' lied Alison.

'Come here, little fella.' Christopher plucked Haurice from his crazed stupor. He smoothed his head. Haurice nuzzled into Christopher's neck and whimpered. With one hand, Christopher managed to fish a business card from his inside pocket. 'Here, give me a call and come in for a chat.'

Judith looked puzzled.

'I should have said, I work at Henleys bank on the high street. I can give you some business advice if you think it might help.'

She scrutinised the card. 'Oh, right. Thank you so much. I'll do that. Thank you.'

Judith and Haurice wandered off, as Christopher and Alison gathered up their things and set off for the exit. As they walked, Alison heard a little wheeze. She turned, to find a red-faced Christopher, quietly laughing his socks off. He had to stop and rest his hands on his knees to get his breath.

'I'm so sorry, Alison. Haurice really laid into you, didn't he?'
They were both reduced to fits of laughter.

Christopher stood up, took out a handkerchief and wiped
his face. For a second their eyes met. Alison could have sworn
she heard a crack of electricity.

Neither of them spoke.

They hot footed it to the park gates and bid each other a
hasty farewell without making further eye contact.

Alison wandered back to work feeling bamboozled. She tried
not to think about the strange events of the last hour as she
cleaned up her wounds and changed her clothes.

On her way to the office, she removed a wooden chock
from the beverage bay door.

'Not me,' said a voice from along the corridor. 'By, he's a
vindictive so-and-so, that fire officer.' Peggy stood by her
cleaning trolley, clenching and releasing a metal contraption
with her hand.

Alison dropped the chock into the bin bag on her trolley.
'What's that?'

She looked from Alison to the tool and nodded, her eyes
extra round. 'It's just the job for my wrist. I pulled it playing
Twister with the grand bairns.'

'Did you get it from the doctor?'

Peggy gave it an extra fast squeeze. 'Whey no. Those
physiotherapists left it in the clinical skills training room.' She
placed it in a pull-out drawer in her trolley and flexed her hand.
'That's better. I would've given it back, but they left the room
in a tip. Finders keepers.' She paused to glare at the rubbish bin
next to the lift. 'Some people are plain filthy,' she said to the
bin. 'Would you look at that…' She pointed to the remnants
of a tuna sandwich on the floor next to it. 'It's not even as if
the bin's full. Bone idle.' She looked at her watch. 'I can do
without this palaver; I have to get away to my other job.'

'I saw your new boss in the park. She had a fall, but she's okay.'

'She needs to slow down. Never stops. Not like the idle lot around here.' She put a new liner in the bin. 'It's good news they got those kiddies out of that cave, isn't it?'

'Yes, only the coach and a teacher left in there now.'

'You know what though, er Alison…? What I don't understand is, how on earth they got that thing in there in the first place.'

'What thing?'

Peggy looked at her as if she were simple. 'The coach of course, silly. Who in their right mind would drive a coach-load of kiddies into a blinking cave?'

Alison bit the side of her mouth. 'I think the coach is –'

'Hey, while I remember…' Peggy tapped the side of her nose with her index finger and nodded towards the office. 'I reckon he's in bother.'

'What have you heard?'

'You mark my words, lass.'

'Tell me.'

'I have to get going, I'll fill you in next time I see you.'

Alison smiled to herself, she might have no clue to what was going on, but if Peggy said Billy was in bother, you could count on it to be true.

When she checked her inbox, there was an email from occupational health with the clinic letter attached. Billy was copied into it. He shot her a furious glare then slammed his office door. Alison didn't care.

Then another good thing happened. Boris from IT called to talk her through disabling the facility that enabled others to recall emails. She was thinking how well the afternoon was going when it took an even better turn. A completely inappropriate email pinged in from Billy, demanding she took sickness leave because she wasn't fit for work. It didn't disappear. She replied to say that she would do no such thing.

Then she forwarded the chain to Ashley, with the clinic letter attached.

That night, she slept for two uninterrupted hours.

Chapter 26

'Do we have to go?'

'Oh, come on, Ali, it won't be that bad,' said Martin.

'It's a bit much. I mean, we slog our guts out all week, then plough through crappy chores on a Saturday, and now we have to spend Sunday at Gail and Keith's... Why don't we just stick pins in our eyes and be done with it?'

'You're such a drama queen.' He laughed. 'At least you won't have to cook.'

'Would you stop it with the chauvinist rubbish. It's not funny. Anyway, with Keith and Gail falling out, I'd rather not go. The atmosphere will be dreadful. You go, though. You can sit next to your mother.'

'Go on, I came shopping with you, didn't I?'

'That was for new shoes for you.'

He smiled at her. 'I'm trying to be better.' His brow furrowed. 'Are you sure that cat hasn't been in the house...?'

'No.' Alison Suppressed a giggle – the air was blue when he had slipped his foot into the green slime-filled shoe. Well, she told herself, he'd deserved it. She hadn't forgiven him, but she had to admit that he was making an effort to be more reasonable. 'I know you're trying.'

'I even let you drag me in here.' Martin curled his top lip as he surveyed Alessandro's. 'I don't see the attraction.' He took a sip of coffee and pulled a face. 'Three pounds for this? It would strip paint.'

'Just as well you didn't pay for it…'

A tap on the window interrupted the conversation. Alison looked up to see Christopher, waving at her. He nodded at Martin. Alison smiled and waved back but tried to avoid looking into his eyes. She felt relieved when he continued on his way.

Martin paled. 'How do you know him?'

'It's Christopher. Remember I told you about him? The choking man from the park. I usually see him, Judith and Haurice in there at lunchtime.'

Martin stared at her, his eyes betraying his anxiety. 'All sounds very cosy.'

'It's nice getting out of the office and seeing some friendly faces. I was thinking again about making an appointment to see Christopher.'

'What the hell for?'

A man from the next table looked over. 'Lower your voice, people can hear. I mentioned this before – to get a professional opinion about funding university.'

Martin shook his head and held up his hand. 'Alison, we're not stupid people. We've got two kids at university right now and we've managed that without running to the local bank manager.' He shot the bank a shifty glance.

Alison lowered her voice. 'Martin, are we okay?'

'Of course we are.' He reached over the table and gently brushed her hair from her face.

Alison felt her shoulders relax. She hadn't realised they'd been so tense. 'Well we've argued such a lot recently.'

He took her hands in his. 'We're both tired. You hate your job, and I've got the Ofsted inspection coming up. It's just life.'

Alison yawned. 'You're right. I'm so blinking tired. I'm going to chill out tomorrow rather than go to Gail's, before another crummy week starts.'

The flip in Martin's mood took her by surprise.

'You're going to bed at twelve-thirty in the morning and getting up at six. Of course, you're tired. It's a ridiculous bloody plan.'

She rubbed her face with both hands. 'It's temporary – you know this. Anyway, I've progressed from one a.m. to twelve-thirty. Michelle was pleased with me.'

'You're still worse than you were before.'

'This conversation is like a revolving door.' She yawned again.

'Why don't you pack it in? That Michelle's a pretty bad advert for it anyway. She can't even sort her own sleep out.'

'It's going extremely well,' she said through gritted teeth.

Martin shook his head. 'Could've fooled me.'

'I had another good chunk of sleep last night.'

'Good? You're joking, aren't you?'

Alison splayed her hands, a look of exasperation etched on her face. 'Three hours is brilliant for me.'

'It's purgatory for me.'

'And, like everything else, it's all got to be about you.' She sighed. 'Look, why don't you come to my next appointment with me? It'll give you a better understanding if you hear it from Michelle.'

'I'm sick to the back teeth of hearing her name. Anyway, I can't get the time off work, we're too busy preparing for the inspection. Can't you just pack it in? We used to be happy.'

'I'm not happy anymore.'

He rolled his eyes. 'Yes, I know. I get it. Your job, Billy Chapman, my family –'

'With you and me.' The words were out before she had time to properly register what she'd said.

Martin looked shell-shocked, but not half as much as Alison felt.

Chapter 27

Christopher sucked in his cheeks and stomach and tried to look chiselled. 'Go for it.'

The printer cranked into action and the membership clerk handed over his identification badge. On it was a picture of someone with a close resemblance to his father.

He took a closer look. 'What the Dickens?'

The girl tilted her head to the side. 'What the what?'

He waved the badge at her. 'I hope this isn't a true likeness.'

She looked at him as if she was searching for an appropriate comment but couldn't find one.

'At least no one else has to see it.'

She gave a little tooth-baring grimace. 'Could you swipe it at the turnstile to check it works please?'

Christopher passed it over the scanner and the turnstile unlocked. His face flashed up on a twenty-inch screen, suspended from the ceiling for the whole world to see. He shrugged. 'Ah well, I suppose it'll motivate me to work hard.' He tucked the badge into his wallet and picked up a list of activities. 'Bye for now.'

As he stepped outside, he saw Alison's husband heading towards the entrance. He gave him a nod as he passed, there was little point in speaking to him, the man was ignorant. To his surprise, Martin spoke.

'Hello, it's Christopher, isn't it?'

'Yes. Alison said this was your gym. Any good?'

Martin shrugged. 'As good as any other, I suppose.' He narrowed his eyes. 'Could I ask a favour of you?'

Assuming it was to do with finances, Christopher reached into his jacket pocket for a business card. 'Of course. She said you were planning for her return to university. Exciting times.' He offered Martin the card.

Martin gave a dismissive wave of his hand. 'No, it's not that. It's a bit awkward. My wife isn't herself at the minute. I'm concerned about her.'

Christopher felt a sensation of pinpricks all over his body. 'Goodness. Is she all right?'

'I don't think you're helping. Confusing her with your opinion.'

'Me?'

'The thing is,' he sucked in a noisy breath through his teeth, 'she's always been rather whimsical – weak-minded.'

Christopher laughed. 'Alison? Are you serious?'

Martin sighed and nodded. 'Unfortunately, yes. I'm concerned she could be inadvertently influenced into throwing away a twenty-year career.'

Christopher's grip tightened around the handle of his briefcase. 'I don't think –'

'So, I'd appreciate it if you watched what you said to her.'

He looked directly at Martin. 'Alison strikes me as a highly intelligent lady who has thought long and hard about what she wants. I would never dream of attempting to influence her in any direction whatsoever. Give her my regards. Good night.'

It was true, he wouldn't have. But he'd make it his business to do so in the future.

A delicious aroma of steak pie wafted down the drive as Christopher opened the car door. Anger had left him ravenous.

For a moment, he forgot he couldn't eat pies any longer. It was difficult enough sticking to his healthy diet without coming home to unbearable temptation. Sandy must have asked Yvonne to bake. Who knows why, Sandy wouldn't be eating pastry and he couldn't.

'Hi, love,' he called, as he stepped inside.

No answer. He eased off his boots in the hallway and placed them on the shoe rack. What sounded like an episode of *Midsomer Murders* blasted from the television in the lounge, so he wandered in, removing his jacket on the way.

Suddenly, he was hurtling towards the fireplace, one arm entangled in his sleeve. His mobile shot out of a pocket and landed with a crack on the glass coffee table. He broke his fall with his free hand, but not before twisting it as he tried to miss Sandy's favourite porcelain horse ornament.

The pain knocked him dizzy.

Sandy ran into the room, threw down the tea towel she was carrying and lunged towards him. 'What on earth happened? Are you all right?'

Christopher hauled himself up, in agony. 'I tripped on something.' Nursing his wrist, he stumbled into an armchair. He nodded at a massive sheepskin rug in the middle of the room. 'Where the devil did *that* come from?'

'It arrived just after you went out this morning. It's the same as one featured in *Hello Magazine*. From Italy. Took ages to have it made.'

'On account of the herd of sheep they had to slaughter first?'

She knelt on the floor and stroked the hide. 'Do you like it?'

He didn't. He thought it looked as if a skip of fur had been emptied onto the floor. 'It's got a pong about it.' He shuffled in his seat, unable to get comfortable. Apart from his pain, there was an oversized cushion occupying most of the chair. 'And what's with all these hairy cushions? There's barely room to sit down any longer.' The movement sent pain shooting up his arm, making him wince.

'They go with the rug.' Sandy shook her head. 'Chris, you've got no idea about modern furnishings.'

'But these are more like goat hair. I bet they cost a bomb.'

Sandy sniffed in a sharp breath. 'Not considering the quality.'

His wrist was putting. 'Well, that mat has probably cost me a broken arm. My finger's killing…'

She glanced at his hand and gasped. Christopher howled as she yanked off his wedding ring.

'Don't be a baby. Remember the woman on that hospital documentary who had her finger cut off?'

'Hers was black; mine's just a bit red.' He managed a weak smile. 'I'm not sure I liked the speed with which you whipped that off.' They both looked at his bare finger. 'It doesn't look right without my ring.'

Sandy gave a wave of dismissal. 'I take mine off all the time.'

His mouth dropped open. 'You do? Why?'

'For the tanning bed – white marks.'

'But why would that matter? No one sees you without your wedding ring.'

She rolled her eyes. 'You know how I hate white lines.'

'I think a white wedding band line would look lovely.'

'That's one of the reasons I'd like to make an offer on the William's house. The garden is completely private. I could sunbathe naked.'

'Please, not now with that house…'

Sandy disappeared into the kitchen, returning with a flexible bottle cooler from the freezer. 'There, that'll help.' She manhandled his arm into it and secured it tightly with the Velcro fastener.

Beads of sweat pricked his brow. 'Thanks love, but I think I need to get it checked out at Accident and Emergency. I suspect it's broken. Could you drive me there, please?'

'I've got yoga this evening.'

Christopher looked from his wife to his arm in disbelief. 'Sandy…?'

She tutted. 'Well come on then, or we'll be there all night and the place will be full of drunks.' She strode into the hall, slipped on her heels and clacked over to the mirror to apply a coat of blood-red lip gloss which matched the soles of her shoes. 'This is so inconvenient,' she said, snatching up an oversized, blingy tote bag.

He followed her out and sat on the stairs as he tackled putting on his boots with his good hand. 'It's not exactly how I envisaged spending my evening either.' The injured wrist hurt with the slightest movement.

Sandy stood in the doorway tapping her foot, her lips pressed into a line. 'I'm not taking you to the toilet, mind.'

'I wouldn't want you to.' He noticed her red toenails peeping out of her sandals. For the first time ever, he thought his wife, despite her designer gear, looked cheap. He stood up and felt something drop from the back of his trouser leg – the tea towel. 'Oh, for goodness' sake, I'm covered in gravy.' Exhausted, he looked at Sandy. 'Please can you help me get into some clean trousers?'

Sandy glared at the stain. She blinked slowly and exhaled noisily through her nose. 'Let's just get to the hospital. It's hardly noticeable.' She gave herself a generous blast of perfume and clomped off down the drive, leaving Christopher coughing on a cloud of Versace Blue and struggling to lock up.

Two impatient beeps sounded from the car, making him drop the keys. When, he wondered, had Sandy developed such a hard streak? Perhaps it wasn't only the changing soft furnishings he'd failed to notice.

Chapter 28

Alison jogged over to the side of the car park and smiled, proud of making it all the way down to the dene without stopping. Hands on her knees and head down, she caught her breath while she waited for the other girls. The sound of tyres crunching over the pebbles announced Katie's arrival. She wiped the perspiration from her brow and waved to catch Katie's attention.

'Makes a nice change to get out of the office on a lunchtime,' Katie said, surveying Cherry Dene Hotel's impressive old architecture.'

'Perfect timing.' Alison checked her watch. 'They said it would be ready for twelve-thirty.' She pulled a packet of Wet Ones from her rucksack and wiped her face. 'I hope they let me in dressed like this.'

'You'll be fine. I'm starving – trying to cut down to get into my party dress, but it's killing me.' They set off towards the entrance. 'Sharon's on her way. She's full of hell. Apparently, her new office is awful.'

Inside, Alison sniffed the air and wrinkled her nose. 'Funny smell in here today.'

'Like lilies,' said Katie. 'It reminds me of going to visit my old Auntie Gladys in the home.'

As the bar area was empty, they had their pick of where to

sit.

Gavin strode over with place mats and cutlery. 'Good afternoon ladies, are you ready for your lunch?'

'Yes please.' Alison looked around the room. 'Have you had lilies in here?'

He grimaced. 'Oh God, no. Those things stink.'

'It does smell strange in here today,' said Katie.

Gavin looked up and tapped the air with his finger. 'I know… It'll be the freshener in the vacuum cleaner.'

'No, that's not it,' said Alison. 'It's more of an, erm… old people's care home smell.'

He splayed his hands and turned a full circle. 'Welcome to Cherry Dene Hotel – where old people come to die on a Sunday.'

The women laughed, then noticed his expression and fell silent.

'You're serious?' said Katie.

Gavin rolled his eyes. 'The ambulance is never away from the door. I'm surprised you haven't seen it. Why they all have to come here to have a heart attack's beyond me…'

'It's a little out of the way down here,' said Alison. 'Do you have a defibrillator?'

'Heavens, no. I don't want the responsibility of one of those contraptions.'

'They're easy to use,' said Katie. 'Pretty much automatic. It tells you where to stick the pads and when to press the button. I'm involved in producing the training videos at work.'

'There's nothing wrong with a good old thump to the chest.' He clenched his fist and mimed it like a professional.

'Let's hope we never have a heart attack down here,' said Katie.

Gavin disappeared and returned with three scented candles which he set down on the windowsill. 'Better not put these too close to the curtains,' he laughed. 'Please keep coming here. Some days it's like a morgue.' He arched an eyebrow. 'If I slip you a free drink, would you come in on a weekend?'

'Maybe I'll bring my husband down for a couple of drinks,' said Alison. Not that she felt like going anywhere with the old misery-guts at the minute.'

A waitress set down a tray of coffee and sandwiches. 'Enjoy, ladies.'

An elderly man with a Zimmer frame shuffled into the bar, accompanied by a lady with two walking sticks. They looked from the candles to the women, huffed and puffed their disapproval then shuffled back out, mumbling something about tea in the lounge.

Gavin watched their slow-motion departure with a barely disguised baring of his teeth. 'Give me a break, it's only blooming Monday,' he muttered under his breath. 'I'm sure it would be better for business if there weren't so many *old* folks around. I bet people turn back up the hill as soon as they spot the ambulance outside.' He stretched to the side and rubbed his back as he wandered away. 'It's always in an awkward space that they collapse in.'

Alison turned to Katie. 'Do you know, I can't remember the last time Martin and I went out on a date.'

'Do you need date nights when you've been together for so long?'

'We need something. He's been so ratty with me lately. He blames it on the upcoming Ofsted inspection and my sleep programme, but I can't seem to do a thing right.'

Katie looked at her, her head tilted to the side. 'You've threatened his security.'

'What do you mean?'

'He doesn't like change. You've changed all your routines – the housework, meals, your sleep pattern. And let's not forget the biggie looming on the horizon… your career.'

Alison shook her head. 'No, I don't think so. It must be something else. He started off very supportive.'

Katie twisted her mouth to one side. 'Don't you think it's

easy to be encouraging when you don't believe anything will really change?'

'But it —'

Sharon bustled in, her face like thunder. 'Sorry I'm late. It's all Billy's fault I'm stuck in the back of beyond.' Her 'new' office was an old prefab on the outskirts of the St Mary's hospital site. The building was old, but not in a traditional, well-preserved way – it was more, dilapidated. And rumour had it that it was haunted. 'It's taken ages to get here, and I was late setting off because no one could find the blasted keys. And then some bloke had a go at me for asking him to put out his cigarette.'

'Car keys?' asked Katie.

Sharon shook her head. 'Keys to the building. Can you believe it? Someone's got to lock up. Even when we go for lunch, which for some ridiculous reason, must be at the same time. One set of bloody keys.'

'What, as in keys to the office?' said Alison in disbelief.

Sharon hung her coat over the back of a chair. 'Yes. They're a right funny bunch… There's one woman, Sadie, who hates handing them over to me.

'As bad as Phyllis?' asked Katie.

'Worse, can you believe? And it's like stepping back in time. They have *paper* files all over the place. And don't get me started on the computers. The consoles are the size of a spaceship. It's like the office that time forgot.'

Alison thought back to Dr Smedley's computer, with its overheated fan whirring and blowing dust into her face and chuckled to herself. At least their office desktops had recently had a software update – even though it had caused lots of crashes. 'What can you do? It's the National Health Service. One of the finest in the world.'

They all burst into laughter.

'Sharon,' said Alison, 'do you think I'm serious about going back to university?'

Sharon shot Katie a sideways glance, as if she'd been set a trap. 'Yes, of course,' she said, her tone cautious. 'Well, I think your *intentions* are serious.'

'But…'

She gave Alison an awkward smile. 'You might get side-tracked…'

'What do you mean?' Alison looked at Katie, who seemed overly focused on stirring cream into her coffee. 'You agree, don't you?'

Katie pursed her lips. 'Hmm… I think you'll always prioritise Martin's needs. And I suspect he'll always have needs for you to prioritise.'

'Like a leaf on the wind,' mused Sharon.

They both turned to her.

'Being blown around, this way and that. I heard it in school assembly when I was a kid. I didn't understand it at the time.'

Alison felt blindsided. Had she become one of those 'I'm-going-to-do-such-and-such-one-day-never' type of people?

'I worry it might end up being a little late by the time you do it,' said Katie. 'No offence, but you and Martin aren't exactly poor. If you really wanted go, what's stopped you?'

'I had no idea I came across like that. How pathetic.'

Katie swallowed a mouthful of ham sandwich. 'You're not pathetic.'

'Maybe just a bit floundering,' said Sharon.

No one noticed Gavin hurtle past the door and down the corridor.

'Well it's about time I got my act together.'

'Yes, that's the attitude. You go for it,' said Katie.

It was only when a screaming ambulance pulled up outside and they heard a, 'For God's sake…' coming from the lounge, that they realised Gavin might need a hand.

The women dashed out to help, but – much to the relief of all three – two paramedics overtook them with a trolley and a grab bag.

One leg of an upturned Zimmer frame was sticking out of the lounge doorway. 'Stand clear...' said one of the paramedics.

'You don't know how long you've got left do you?' said Alison in a quiet voice. 'That could have been any one of us.'

'Pull yourself together,' said Katie. 'He has to be at least ninety.'

But, wondered Alison, does he have a one-day-never plan?

She had painted a couple of bananas in her mind's eye, to cope with yet another software crash that afternoon, when Boris from IT wandered into the office. Great, Alison thought, a friendly face. Last time she'd seen him, he was about to get married. She looked forward to hearing all about his wedding in Cyprus. He paused, scanned the room, counted the computers and groaned.

His shoulders slumped, he read out a reference number from the small tablet he carried around. Alison clicked on her email inbox to check the reference for the enquiry she'd raised with the help desk – and watched the screen crash before she found it.

'I'm looking for Alison Riley's computer,' he said in a flat tone.

'That's mine,' said Alison with a cheery wave. 'Perfect timing – it's crashed again. Oh, wait a minute, it's restarting.'

Boris wheeled over a chair and sighed heavily as he sat down.

'It's updating, yet again. It only gets to thirty per cent before crashing,' said Alison.

He turned his head slowly and looked at her with deadened eyes. 'Tell me about it.' He gave the screen a slow blink. 'They roll out update after update. At the same time, throughout the Trust. Without prior testing. He gritted his teeth, screwed his eyes shut and clawed at his face. 'They. Do. Not. Listen. To.

Us.' He held down the off switch to stop it restarting.

No-one in the office spoke. Those who could, worked, others stared at frozen screens. Young Hayley scuttled off to the ladies and didn't return until Boris had left. Alison felt she should try to lighten the atmosphere but was stumped for something to say. She opened her mouth to ask about the wedding, then thought better of it. After what seemed like an age, Boris got things running for long enough to work on the problem.

'Look at the state of this dinosaur.' He hammered the keyboard. 'Do you know, they want to upgrade the whole hospital Trust with new computers? Six. Hundred. Devices. Within a stupidly insufficient window of time.' He briefly stopped tapping to throw his hands in the air and glare at the ceiling. 'And they won't let me order the necessary equipment to carry out the task because there's no money left in the budget.'

Alison squirmed in her seat. 'Would you like a cup of coffee?' Boris's odd behaviour unnerved her. It wasn't like him at all. But there was something more disturbing niggling away at her... It was as if he was acting out how she sometimes felt inside. But he looked mental.

He stared blankly at the screen. 'My boss has been moved on. Two new managers – more money wasted. Neither with any IT experience.' He emitted a snort-laugh sound from the back of his throat, his knuckles whitened.

'Did he get a new job?' said Alison in an unusually high-pitched voice.

Phyllis glanced over at her and smirked.

Boris turned to face Alison, his eyes red-rimmed and dark shadows beneath them. 'No. He didn't deliver a project. That. Was. Undeliverable.' He turned back and resumed tapping.

A crisp voice sounded from across the room.

'What's she twittering on about?'

Phyllis's nostrils closed completely as she sniffed in a sharp breath. 'I said, I like my computer.' She was holding a Brazil nut between her thumb and forefinger.

Boris peered at her, then turned to Alison. 'She's like a squirrel with that nut.' He spoke in a low monotone. 'I'm going to leave this dump and find a new job.'

As Alison watched Boris implode, it was like watching a premonition. Boris was desperate to find a new job. She had the perfect solution to her own predicament just waiting for her to get started. She wondered why she had even allowed herself to become so stressed with it all. An image of the upturned Zimmer frame came to mind. Her anger towards Billy and Phyllis dissipated as she realised that, rather than waste time and energy hating them, she needed to stop talking about her plans and get cracking with them. Katie and Sharon were right.

Billy's office door banged off the wall and he stormed out. He glared around the room then spotted Boris and his expression brightened. He clicked his fingers. 'Right, come over here and sort out my computer. It's crashed again.'

Boris continued working on Alison's computer. 'Raise a ticket with the help desk,' he said through clenched teeth. 'I'm stowed off today.'

Billy tutted. 'Don't be stupid. You're already here.'

Alison noticed beads of perspiration appear on Boris's forehead. She also noted something she hadn't seen before in Billy – panic.

'Hurry up,' barked Billy 'I have to sign off the payroll.'

With a couple of final taps, Boris finished up and smiled at Alison. 'There, that should do it. Give us a ring if you have any more problems.'

He carefully wheeled the chair back to its desk and calmly walked towards Billy, knocking into Billy's shoulder on his way into the office. Leaving the door wide open he said, 'Right then, let's see.' He carefully raised his right leg and gave Billy's computer an almighty kick. He brushed his hands together as if to finish off a job well done.

Billy gawped at the computer debris scattered around his office.

Boris exhaled a sigh of contentment. 'There you go.' He turned to Billy and gave him a wide-eyed, broad grin. 'Fixed.' And off he went with a jaunty spring in his step.

Alison had a feeling they wouldn't be seeing Boris for a good while. She shivered, that could so easily have been her foot going through Billy's screen.

As soon as she arrived home, Alison clicked onto the university course webpage and gathered some information. Then she contacted them to request more, giddy with excitement at the prospect of it all coming together in the not-too-distant future.

That night, after dozing off within fifteen minutes of her head touching the pillow, she didn't stir for what she guessed must have been at least four whole hours. And she only awoke because of Martin's hog-like snoring. He was always the same after a couple of pints of Guinness, not that he ever believed her.

She fell back to sleep halfway through painting a banana. Next morning, she awoke with a scream, her heart banging in her chest.

Martin jumped out of bed straight into a Karate chop pose, his eyes peeled and scanning the room. 'Whasamatter?' He silenced the alarm clock.'

Alison breathed a sigh of relief. 'Sorry. I got such a fright. I can't remember the last time I awoke to an alarm.'

Martin pulled on his dressing gown. 'For goodness' sake.'

She got up, alert and smiling. 'Don't you think that sometimes, life's simply great?'

'Not lately…' He wandered off to the bathroom.

'I'll make the coffee,' she said, skipping down the stairs.

Chapter 29

The meeting with Judith had gone much as Christopher had expected. All she had needed was some advice and a little steering in the right direction.

The rent on the salon was steep, even for Earlby, and way above anything she could earn working alone. If Shirley was right about her old hairdresser, the property had sold below market value, so the new owner couldn't have a particularly high mortgage – must just be one of the greedy ones.

Still, her business could be a little gold mine with focus in the right places. It might also be the perfect establishment for Sandy to rent space in, at least to start off. As soon as Judith had left, he picked up the phone to tell her, but something stopped him.

He couldn't fathom what was going on with Sandy lately. One minute she wanted to set up a business, the next she was accusing him of being mean and practically sending her to the workhouse. He did wonder what she planned to do with the rest of her life. Surely, she wanted more from it than shopping for death-trap rugs and hairy cushions? Perhaps she'd lost confidence, being out of the workforce for so long. He frowned. Maybe not, there wasn't much that was shy and retiring about his wife of late.

His arm was putting. He stood up, walked over to the

window, then sat back down again. He loosened the Velcro on the splint. The fracture clinic had told him to rest it higher than heart level as much as possible to reduce the swelling, but it wasn't easy in the office. He spent five minutes grappling with a foil strip of Paracetamol and sent one ricocheting off the wall. He eventually managed to ease two more directly into his mouth, then sat holding his arm above his head while he waited for them to kick in.

Shirley tapped gently at the door and came in with a cup of coffee.

He looked up and smiled. 'I keep telling you, you don't have to knock.'

'Old habits.'

'And you don't have to bring me coffee.'

She looked offended. 'But Mr Brokely used to insist that I —'

'He had no right,' Christopher said quietly. 'And remember, I have my coffee machine over there.'

She turned and shot it a resentful glare. 'Anyway, you can't make coffee with your bad arm.'

'I can. It's automatic. I just put in a pod.'

As Shirley stepped towards the door, something crunched. She inspected the white powder beneath her shoe, then noticed the discarded strip of Paracetamol. She eyed the loose splint. 'They'll put you in a plaster if you don't keep that on…'

Christopher rolled his eyes and tightened the Velcro again. 'It's fine. Just a bit inconvenient.' He sipped the pale lukewarm fluid so as not to offend her. His stomach turned. 'Mmm, thank you.'

'I've got some Penguin biscuits in my drawer.'

'No thanks. Still on the diet.' He could kill for one, if for nothing else but to get rid of the taste of the coffee.

Shirley retreated from the office. Christopher imagined biting into a Penguin. He could almost smell the chocolatey biscuit, and taste that soft creamy bit in the middle. There was a clattering against the door. Shirley lumbered in with a hat stand.

Christopher's eyes widened as she clumped it next to his bad arm.

'It was Mr Brokley's.' She indicated a sling-like addition to the wooden stand. 'Rest your arm in this.' She gave a little smile of satisfaction at the sling she'd fashioned from her scarf.

Christopher did as he was told. 'It's perfect.' He coughed. 'Thank you.' If he'd been the emotional type, he might have acknowledged the lump in his throat.

Shirley disappeared and returned with some papers. 'Here's the latest list of Frank's appointments that you asked for.'

He looked in surprise at the long list of off-site visits. 'He's certainly been busy – though not in the office.'

Shirley shuffled from foot to foot. 'Actually, he and Mr Brokely used to conduct a lot of meetings off-site.'

'Thank you, Shirley.'

She returned to her own office, a look of approval on her face. He liked her. And she seemed to genuinely care about him, which he wasn't used to in the workplace. He'd never expect a secretary to run around after him, but he had to admit there was something comforting about her fussing, even if she couldn't make a decent cup of coffee to save her life.

He scanned the list. It didn't make sense for Frank to spend so much time out of the branch. It certainly wasn't within his remit. It seemed more like a thinly veiled way to skive. Old Brokely was known to be bone-idle. Frank must be stupid to think he could continue in the same way. By the time the travelling around was deducted, he was only working part time hours. If that's all he wanted, thought Christopher, he'd have to go onto a part time salary.

He unhooked his arm, stood up and felt his trousers slip down a touch. Grabbing them, he assumed he'd left the zip open and was surprised to find everything fastened up. They were simply too big. He pulled the waistband away from his stomach to inspect the gap. So that's why his shirts were constantly untucking themselves. He nodded in satisfaction. All this deprivation must be working.

As he walked downstairs to speak to Frank, he saw Martin at the indoor cash dispenser. He was tucking cash into his wallet as he turned and caught Christopher's eye. Christopher raised his hand in acknowledgement, but Martin averted his eyes and dashed off.

Such an ignorant man, he thought. Nothing like Alison. He'd only seen him on a handful of occasions, but he'd been rude every time. Alison had such a friendly personality, always happy to chat when he bumped into her in the park – apart from that first time, of course. He rubbed his brow and laughed to himself as he recalled the incident. Since then, he'd grown quite fond of the little catchups with Alison and Judith, and Haurice, too.

A flash of inspiration hit him. Perhaps a puppy would help Sandy come to terms with her empty nest. He pictured strolling in the park together. Maybe another Miniature Poodle – Oscar. She could walk Oscar over at lunchtime, and the three of them could get some exercise and have a catch-up with the others. It might cheer her up.

When Christopher got down to the savings accounts' advice desk. Frank was nowhere to be seen. He phoned Shirley to let her know he'd be working downstairs for a while. It was thirty minutes before closing when Frank returned, rosy-cheeked and looking pleased with himself. He spotted Christopher at his desk and froze.

'I'll see you up in my office in five minutes,' said Christopher. 'Bring your diary.'

He opened the door of the taxi with his good hand, the other supported in a sling beneath his suit jacket. He smiled at Sandy, she'd reverted to the strawberry blond she'd been when they first met. Such a welcome contrast to the more recent platinum. It had softened her appearance. She was glowing tonight.

She shot him a cheeky grin. 'What are you looking at?'

'My lovely wife, of course.' He watched her swing her beautiful legs out of the car, and then stand up with such elegance and finesse. She suited the new Louboutin heels. He tried not to begrudge their price tag.

As he closed the door, he saw Martin for the second time that day, heading towards the bar next door to the restaurant. Christopher knew Martin had spotted him, and he wasn't going to allow him to blank him again. 'Hello there,' he called over. 'Small world, isn't it?'

Martin started and turned towards him. 'Sorry –'

'Christopher – Henleys, pervert in the park, the gym...'

'Senior Head Office Quality Control Consultant for Henleys,' said Sandy in her posh voice.

Christopher cringed and shot her a please-don't-start-bragging look.

Martin gave a nervous laugh. 'Ah, yes.'

'I trust Frank's been helpful.' Two slippery types together, thought Christopher.

Apart from the times he'd seen Martin inside the bank, according to Frank's diary, he had met up with him offsite. Frank claimed it was difficult for Martin to get away from the school. Christopher suspected Frank was work-shy. He knew the type – high profile, low productivity. No wonder he hadn't wanted to go for a promotion. And as old Brokely had also been bone idle, it was little wonder the branch had been floundering. There was no place for a culture of low standards and lazy attitudes in his team.

Martin tilted his head. 'Frank?' He pulled out a tissue and wiped his brow. 'Warm tonight, isn't it.'

Sandy pulled her shawl around her shoulders.

Definitely something off with this bloke. 'I've seen you

chatting to him in the bank.'

'Aah, yes. Frank Budle.' Martin's smile was at odds with his narrowed eyes.

Christopher turned to Sandy. 'Alison's going back to university.' He took pleasure in the flash of anger from Martin's eyes.

Sandy yawned. 'Lovely.'

'Anyway, give my regards to Alison.'

Martin nodded and strode right past the bar he'd been heading for and off up a side street.

Sandy straightened her back and held her head up. 'Come on let's get inside.'

Christopher escorted her into the vestibule, where they waited to be seated. As a couple passed them on their way out, the man craned his neck to look at Sandy's cleavage. There'd been a time when he secretly enjoyed the envious looks he received from other men – when he'd been sure of her love. Sandy enjoyed the attention, even the daggers from the women whose husband's heads she turned. She smiled at the man.

He lowered his voice. 'Have some respect for his partner. And yours.'

Sandy pulled a face. 'You're jealous.'

'If you say so.' Oddly, despite being unsure of her love recently, he wasn't in the slightest bit jealous.

The Maître D'I escorted them to a table, where Emily and Simon were sitting, heads together and oblivious to the rest of the world. Emily's eyes glistened with love for her fiancé, while Simon had the grin of a man who'd won the lottery. He was winding a length of her hair around his finger as they chatted.

Although Christopher hated the thought of no longer being the man to whom Emily would automatically turn for support, if he had to be replaced, then he was happy it was to be by Simon.

The young couple jumped when Christopher and Sandy took their seats, as if they'd forgotten where they were.

Christopher felt blessed. He knew that few men had what he did, and he was grateful. He sometimes wondered what he'd done to deserve his life. He had no clue, but it must have been something good.

Simon stood up, kissed Sandy on the cheek and shook Christopher's hand. 'How's it doing?' he said, nodding at his other arm.

Sandy shot it a look of disapproval. 'It's inconvenient, to be honest. It could ruin the photographs.'

Christopher frowned at Sandy then turned to Simon. 'Not too bad, thanks for asking. It was a clean break, so just a splint for six weeks, and then hopefully it'll be fine for the wedding.' Christopher winked at Emily. 'Not that it could stop me walking you down the aisle.'

Emily kissed her father's cheek and shot him the smile that had made his heart melt since before she had teeth.

Sandy picked up the menu and then put it back down. 'Oh, Emily, you're going to love the gorgeous little bushes I've ordered for the entrance to the venue.' She outlined imaginary bushes in the air with her hands, her eyes twinkling. 'Decorated with tiny diamantes that will sparkle in sunlight.'

'But the entrance is already perfect,' said Emily. 'Understated but classy.'

'There was a footballer's wedding on mid-week, so I popped up to have a scout around. Oh, it was heavenly.' She pressed her hands together and looked up to the ceiling. 'All the special little touches.'

Simon kissed Emily's cheek. 'As long as you're there, nothing could make it more special than it's going to be.'

Christopher smiled, happy to see his daughter so content, also relieved she'd fallen for a good man.

Sandy laughed. 'You leave it to us girls, we know what we're doing, don't we, Emily?'

'What does Margot think about the bushes, Mum?'

Sandy twisted her mouth and raised her eyebrows.

'Sometimes I think we might have made a mistake with her. She can be a bit… thrifty.'

Christopher almost choked on his drink. 'Not according to the pile of invoices we've got.'

Emily looked at Christopher with huge, concerned eyes. 'Sorry, Dad.'

He felt like the meanest father in the world. 'I'm not complaining, darling. I think *she* should be suggesting these nice touches, without your mother having to gate-crash other people's weddings.'

'I quite enjoyed it. I saw the hair stylist and her team arrive. I nipped over and got one of her cards. Everyone's trying to book her at the minute.'

'But you and Emily have been with your hairdresser for years,' said Christopher. Won't she feel hurt?'

Sandy laughed and gave a dismissive wave of her hand. 'Everyone needs the absolute best for a wedding.'

Simon looked at Christopher and laughed. 'Do we have to have wedding hair, too?'

He pulled a face. 'Not likely.'

It was over dessert that Sandy said she and Christopher had some 'exciting' news. Finally, thought Christopher, she'd come on board with his career plans and wanted to surprise him when she told Emily. That's why she'd been so nice earlier, she'd stopped worrying. He looked at his wife and felt a surge of guilt for inwardly criticising her so much.

Emily would be pleased, too. He also felt remorse about all the time he'd spent away from home while she was growing up. A painful image pricked his conscience and jabbed his heart – Emily, her little eyes screwed up and her dark curls soaked with tears, as he'd prised her tiny arms from around his neck. If only he could turn back the clock. At least he'd see more of her in the future. He hoped it wasn't too late to make up for leaving her so much. And if they started a family, he was determined to be the best grandad ever. He imagined himself playing football with a tussle-haired toddler in the garden.

Sandy rubbed her hands together and grinned with glee, barely able to contain her excitement. 'Remember the Williams' house in California? We're buying it.'

Christopher felt like he'd been slapped. He opened his mouth to speak, but Sandy patted his leg to silence him.

'Which one was that again?' asked Emily.

'You know… They had the most fantastic pool. We went to a barbecue there one time – best house in the street. It'll need a new pool by now, but we can sort that out later.'

Christopher wiped his mouth with his serviette. 'Now hang on, Sandy. We've discussed this –'

She held up her palm to his face without looking at him.

He gently eased down her hand. He could feel his blood pressure rising and pulsating through his head.

'Mum, I can't remember it.' She shuddered. 'Ugh. I can remember the huge spiders, though.'

Sandy turned to Christopher, her eyes narrowed. 'Chris, don't be such a misery-guts.' She glanced at Emily and arched a brow – as much as she was able to after a recent Botox top-up. 'You know Dad… he can be such a stick-in-the-mud.'

Simon looked relieved when the waiter came over with a basket of bread.

He took out an electronic tablet. 'Are you ready to order?'

'Sorry, could we have a few more minutes, please?' said Christopher.

The waiter retreated to the kitchen.

'Right,' said Simon. 'Let's have a look at the menu.'

Christopher squinted at it. 'It's so blinking dark in here.' He switched on the torch app on his mobile phone.

Sandy giggled. 'It must be your age.'

'Dad's not old, Mum,' said Emily. 'Caroline at uni used to have a crush on him. She said he looked like Adam Sandler.'

Sandy let out a 'Pfft' sound and cackled. She ran a manicured nail down the drinks' menu. 'Let's have

Champagne.'

Christopher smiled at Emily and Simon. He couldn't look Sandy in the eyes. It felt stifling hot. He loosened his tie.

'Are you all right, Christopher?' Simon pointed to his hand. He hadn't been aware he was rubbing his chest.

'Dad?' said Emily, her eyes filled with panic. 'What's wrong?'

Sandy gave a slow blink. 'For goodness' sake.'

'I'm fine, just indigestion.' He smiled. 'Thanks, kids.'

'You work too hard, Dad.' Emily leaned across the table and stroked his hand. 'I've been thinking. Now I'm through university, and going to be out of the flat soon… Would you consider scaling it down at work? She looked at him, her eyes full of concern. 'I don't know what I'd do if anything happened to you.'

'I'm going to be around for a long time yet. I promise. And I am thinking of scaling my work down.' Tonight no longer felt like the right time to go into more detail. He felt Emily's hand relax on his.

Out of the corner of his eye, Christopher saw Sandy flinch.

'We could start playing golf together,' said Simon.

'Great idea. I'll dust off my clubs.'

Emily was grinning from ear to ear.

Sandy's mouth was pressed into a hard line.

Chapter 30

'What do you think of this tripod?' Alison turned her laptop towards Martin. 'Jack said I could use it both indoors and outside for my business.'

Martin peered at the image on her laptop. 'A *business*?' he laughed. 'But you know nothing about setting up a *business*.' He walked over to the hob where a lamb pasanda curry was simmering. 'Wow, you cooked.' He flashed her a wide grin and wiggled his eyebrows at her.

'I'm learning. Come back and listen to me, please.' She could barely contain her excitement as she gushed about YouTube, adverts and passive income.

'That's an awful lot of information to assimilate.' He gave the curry a stir and picked out a piece of meat. 'Mmm, nice.' He turned around to face her. 'It feels like it's one thing after another with you at the minute.'

'You complained about losing my income, so I'm trying to create another – even though that was never the plan.' She met his gaze. 'I don't recall you studying and working at the same time.'

He checked his watch. 'Lamb's still a bit tough. Do I have time to go for a quick gym session?'

'Stop ignoring me. Would you come here and look at this blooming tripod and tell me what you think?'

'I saw it.' He trudged back and leaned over her shoulder. She felt his heavy sigh against her neck. 'It looks okay. It's a tripod for a mobile phone. What can I say?'

'You could tell me if you think it looks cheap, or if you can spot any obvious bad points.'

'How would I know?' He sneezed. 'Has that cat been in?'

Alison pretended she hadn't heard him. Sammy had kept her company while she prepared the curry earlier. 'Because you see what the professional photographers use for the end of year photographs.'

'There's no comparison.'

'Fine, so it's rubbish. That's all I wanted to know.' D*ickhead.* She gasped.

'What now?'

'Nothing.' Never in the whole of her marriage, had she called her husband something so offensive, even in her head. She stared at the screen without looking at it, her racing heartbeat catching her breath.

Martin sat down and took hold of her hand. 'Alison, what's going on?'

'What do you mean?'

'All of this *restlessness.*'

She shook off his hand. 'Stop it. You're making me feel like I'm crazy.'

Martin sighed. 'We were content.'

'You sound like you're on a blasted loop. How many times do we have to have the same mundane conversation?' She threw up her hands. 'I'm miserable. Why don't you care?'

'Of course I care. You're exaggerating... You're not *miserable.*'

'Are you saying you don't want me to go to sleep, or study, so that I can make your life lovely again?'

Martin stood up. 'Don't twist my words.'

'You never expected me to go back, did you? What do you think the savings have been about?'

Martin shuffled awkwardly. He turned away then back and blew out a heavy breath. 'To be honest, I didn't. And nor did I believe you were foolish enough to leave a well-paid career to return to a teenage dream.'

Alison felt tears sting her eyes. 'Teaching was your teenage dream.'

'And I had the sense to pursue it while I was young enough to make it happen, without disrupting anyone else's life.'

'*The sense?* How about if *you'd* had the bloody, sodding, naffing *sense* to drop out to look after *your* children, while *I* continued with my career?'

He stepped towards her and reached out for her arms. 'Look at me. Take a breath. You're becoming irrational.'

She pushed him away. 'I can't believe what you're say–'

Someone hammering at the front door interrupted them. Martin shot away to answer it.

A sour-faced Gail pushed her way into the hallway. 'I've had enough. I can't take any more.'

Alison went to investigate the ruckus. 'Whatever's wrong?'

Gail thumbed over her shoulder to Robbie, who was standing on the doorstep chewing gum. Alison cringed, it sounded like someone walking through mud in Wellington boots.

'He's been evicted for non-payment of rent. Keith's gone AWOL again…' She threw her hands in the air and burst into tears. 'I can't take any more.' She dragged Robbie in by his ear.

'Steady on, Mother,' he shouted, as he tripped over the threshold.

'Robbie, shut up.' Gail looked from Martin to Alison and sneered. 'You and your perfect stinking lives. Well, it's your turn to have the hassle.'

Martin stood, flabbergasted.

Alison raised her hand. 'Whoa, hang on.' She forced a smile, at odds with the panic racing around inside. 'Let's have a cuppa and talk about it. Have you eaten?

'No, no.' Gail gritted her teeth. She went back out and hauled a dirty holdall up from the step.

Alison nudged Martin. 'Say something.'

'Don't bother.' The holdall landed with a thud in the hall. 'There's nothing either of you can say to make me change my mind.' She shot off down the drive, tearing at her straggly hair and laughing like a maniac. The smell of burning clutch filled the air as she screeched along the street.

A hissing noise sounded from behind Robbie. Sammy was staring at him from over by the hedge, his back arched, and lip curled, revealing a set of razor-sharp teeth. Robbie kicked the door shut.

'So, Uncle Martin and Auntie Alison, can I stay for a while please? Until Mam calms down.' He stood, a sweet smile on his face, his doe eyes pleading, then he cracked a bubble.

Alison felt like slapping his mocking face. She waited for Martin to speak up. Robbie was his brother's son, after all.

He simply turned to her and shrugged, then stepped towards Robbie and laid his arm across his shoulders. 'Of course you can, son. Come in.'

Alison shot Martin a murderous look which he appeared not to notice. 'Do you want some curry?' she said, following behind and digging Martin in the back of his ribs. He didn't flinch.

'Love some,' Robbie said, rubbing his hands together and grinning. 'You got any beer?'

Ten minutes later, Robbie was ensconced in the lounge, slopping beer and curry down his T-shirt as he watched football. Alison and Martin tidied up the kitchen. Or at least Alison did. Martin sat at the table, looking pale and drawn.

'Why does he have to stay here?'

'You heard Gail – to give her a break. She's going through a hard time.' He rubbed his chin as if checking for bristles.

After being so obtuse when it came to her own unhappiness, she felt a stab of resentment over his concern for

Gail. 'Why can't he stay with his dad? Or your mother?'

'He's here now, so we'll have to get on with it.'

No, not obtuse – pig-ignorant. 'This suits you, doesn't it? You think I'm going to be stuck here waiting hand and foot on him. Well I'm not. You'll have to speak to Keith.'

'Keith won't take him. He blames Gail for spoiling him and reckons Robbie needs to stand on his own two feet. It's because Keith never really bonded with him that Gail overcompensated.'

'Why are you defending her? She criticises you to the hilt. I've given you everything, yet you couldn't give a toss about me.'

'For God's sake, woman. Does everything have to be about you?'

Woman?

The roar of the football crowd blasted along the hall into the kitchen. Alison's knuckles turned white as she gripped the edge of the sink. 'I can't stand the bloody sound of sport on TV.'

'Robbie's not to know that, is he?'

'Why would he? He doesn't live here.'

'It's only for a few days. Gail will come around after she's had a break. Why are you reacting like a spoilt child? We've got plenty of spare rooms.'

Alison turned to face Martin. 'Because I know you'll leave me to do everything. I'm not looking after a grown man.'

The kitchen door opened, and Robbie walked in carrying his empty plate. He set it down on the bench top and belched. 'Aah, that's better.' He opened the fridge and took out another bottle, flicked the top onto the plate and swaggered back out of the kitchen.

'A couple of days and he's out,' said Alison. 'Or I'll be off.'

Martin laughed. 'Don't be silly. Where would you go?'

'Any bloody where.'

Chapter 31

Sandy glanced up from her *Beautiful Weddings* magazine and looked Christopher up and down. 'Why are you wearing jeans? You're going to be late for work.'

'I'm going in late this morning. We need to talk.'

She rolled her eyes. 'For goodness' sake, Chris. Not that again.'

'No, not my job, if that's what you mean. It was too late to talk last night when we got back from the restaurant. But we can't go on like this.'

'Like what? I haven't got a clue what you're on about.'

'I'll get to the point. I feel as if all you want me for is to pay the bills. You don't seem to care about me at all.'

Sandy scrutinised his face, as if she was choosing her words carefully. 'That's not true. I'll admit I've been more focused on money recently, but that's because I panicked when you wanted to drop your salary.'

He still didn't trust what she was saying. He nodded at the file containing the figures he'd brought home for her to read, abandoned under some mail on the end of the table. 'Did you even look at that?'

She shot it an irritated glance. 'I wanted to build up our property portfolio. Assets. We need assets.'

'What?'

'I was chatting to someone at the gym who works in a bank. He told me it's a good time to invest in property because the prices haven't yet reached their ceiling after the austerity years.'

'He works in a bank?' His instinct told him exactly who she'd been talking to. 'Frank Budle by any chance?'

Her eyes darted from side to side. 'Maybe.'

'Of course. It doesn't surprise me he hangs out at your gym. People with plenty of money to target. Did you know he flogs property as a side-line? He's not someone you should trust.'

'He didn't *target* me. You forget that I know him from *your* bank. What he said makes sense. But it's not about his properties. Look…' She reached for her tablet. 'I received this email from the Californian realtor.' She scrolled down the screen to the details of the William's house.

Christopher laughed in disbelief.

'This has got nothing to do with Frank Budle. The pound's holding okay against the dollar, and we don't know what'll happen when Brexit's all done and dusted. Now could be a good time to –'

Christopher held up his hand. 'I'm not interested in that house or the state of the pound. We aren't buying another sodding property while my arteries fur up and I brew a stroke.'

Her eyes widened. 'You're swearing. Anyway, don't I get a say in my own life?'

'Stop it. You're behaving like a money-grabbing bint.'

Sandy gasped in shock. 'A money grabber?' She shot him a wounded glance, then frowned. 'What the hell's a *bint*?'

He exhaled slowly and shook his head. 'Who knows…?' He had no idea what a bint was, or why he'd called her that – but she looked like one. He thought about what Alison had said about working. 'How about this…? When you go back to work, we'll save the money you earn and invest it in another property?'

'Don't be silly.'

'Silly? You working is silly? Or investing your salary is silly?'

'Stop it, Chris.'

'And what do you think will happen if I drop down with a heart attack or stroke? Who's going to pay the mortgage on all these properties you want to buy? Oh yes, I forgot, you've already ensured the will's up to date.'

She stood up. 'For goodness' sake. It's one house. And no one with any sense buys a property without making provision for such eventualities. The insurance would pay it off.'

Christopher stared at her, his mouth gaping. He laughed in disbelief. 'So rather than scale down my work and avoid the life-threatening illnesses, we should simply take out a bloody good insurance policy?'

Sandy stormed over to the other end of the room, tearing at her hair, then turned back to face Christopher, her face etched with anger. 'Don't twist my words.'

She strutted back over, rhyming off a list of men's names. Every one of them would have given their right arm to marry her. Cherish her forever. Worship the ground she walked on.

A burst of fury shot through him. 'Do you realise, there are some marriages where both spouses work fulltime? Some women don't have a partner and have to provide for themselves. Take Alison and Judith –'

She screwed up her face and made a 'pft' sound. 'What, you want me to work in an *office*? Or be a *hairdresser*?'

'No, you're not qualified to do either job. But you were a nail technician. Why on earth would you look down on these women?'

She made a hand-swirling motion in the air and opened her mouth to speak –

'And some women raise children *and* work – without the help of a nanny, or a cleaner.' He banged his fist against the tabletop. 'Women whose children don't go to a bloody expensive school, and who don't own one bloody holiday home, never mind two plus a sodding apartment in Durham, that the poor sucker paying for never gets a chance to set foot inside.'

'How dare you. I've sacrificed everything for you. To bear your child and cater to your every whim – even when I didn't feel like it.'

'When you didn't feel like it? What do you mean?' He grabbed the back of the chair as the floor moved. 'Oh, my lord.'

'No, I didn't mean that. Of course I didn't.' Sandy grappled at him. 'You're an extremely attractive man. You always have been.'

He held his hand over his mouth, appalled.

She tried to hug him – it was grasping and nippy.

Christopher batted her arms away. 'No wonder you couldn't give a toss if I work myself into an early grave. He looked at his wife. Who was this woman? 'You've sacrificed nothing.'

Sandy sniffed in a lungful of air. 'You should think yourself lucky I –'

The sound of her voice was muffled, like a speaker plunged into water. He wanted to laugh at her spiteful words, spat out of a once beautiful face, now a sneering, almost ugly mask.

'Well,' she said, hands on hips.

He blinked and tried to refocus, there must be something wrong with his eyes – her head resembled a lollipop on a stick.

'Say something.'

His voice dropped to barely audible. 'Why didn't you ever feel lucky?'

Sandy's mobile pinged. 'Look, we can't talk now. I have an appointment.' She picked up the folder and tucked it underneath a pile of wedding paraphernalia on the sideboard. 'I'll look at this tonight.'

Christopher plucked it out, sending the rest of the pile flying onto the floor. 'Don't bother,' he said, storming off to change into his work clothes.

He decided to walk to work – he'd probably crash if he

drove. As he banged the front door closed, his neighbour, old Mrs Graham called him over.

'Christopher, could you help me please? I've had this letter from the bank. It's gone bankrupt.'

Although he was desperate to stomp off and kick something, he smiled and wandered over to look at her letter. 'Oh, it's nothing to worry about. They're letting you know that the underwriters of the insurance you took out through the bank have gone bankrupt. But they're looking for another company to take over and they're informing you that you're covered until they find someone.'

'Oh, I'm so relieved. I thought we might lose the house.'

Christopher laughed. 'But you no longer have a mortgage. No-one can take your home away from you, don't worry.'

Mrs Graham hugged him and kissed his cheek. After the unpleasant start to the morning, her gratitude for such a small act made him feel warm inside. As he walked down her drive and set off along the pavement, a car door flung open, almost knocking him off his feet.

'Oh, I'm sorry,' called out a familiar voice from inside the vehicle.

Christopher bent down to peer inside. 'Hello, Judith. Weird to see you outside of the park. How are you doing?'

'Busy, busy. It's going much better.' She stepped out onto the pavement. Sorry, got to dash. Might see you and Alison later.'

His earlier anger dissipating, Christopher power-walked off to work, assuming Judith must be going to see one of the older ladies in his street. She'd said she had a few regulars from when she was a mobile hairdresser and who she didn't like to let down, even though she didn't have the time to make house calls any longer.

As Christopher disappeared around the corner, Sandy opened the door to Judith. 'Hi, come in. Thanks for calling by. I couldn't get over to the salon this morning.'

Judith stepped into the hallway. 'What a beautiful house you have.'

'Thank you. I see you met my husband, Chris,' Sandy said, nodding towards the pavement. 'I saw you chatting to him through the window after you pulled up.'

'Oh, Christopher...?' said Judith, looking shocked. '*You're* his wife?'

'I know,' said Sandy with a smug smile. 'You wouldn't put us together would you?'

'Not really, no. He's such a lovely man.'

Sandy shot Judith an angry glare. 'You mean I'm not?'

'Oh, no, sorry, that's not what I meant at all,' she stammered. 'I know him from the park. I walk my dog there on a lunchtime.'

'You're the hairdresser? I suppose you know this Alison, too?'

Judith looked as if she wasn't sure what the right answer was here. 'Yes, she exercises there. For her insomnia.'

Sandy rolled her eyes. 'I'm surprised she doesn't sleep like a log. Working and exercising. Chris said she's going back to study, too. Right little goody-two-shoes.'

Judith rummaged clumsily in her bag and pulled out an envelope. 'Here's what you asked for,' she said, handing it to Sandy. 'I'll get the changes updated online as soon as I can for next time.'

Chapter 32

By the day of Cynthia's party, Alison and the girls were ready for a good night out – a welcome reprieve from the daily grind, and an excuse to eat and drink their body weight in unhealthy fayre. And for Alison, it was also a break from Robbie. She thought she'd go mad if she had to spend one more night listening to football blaring from her once tidy lounge.

After they heard about the party, Billy and Phyllis turned more spiteful, ramping up the sniping comments and excluding Alison from more key departmental information. With Billy now unable to recall his emails from her, he had reverted to verbal abuse. But unbeknown to him, she was recording it all in her diary, which read like something from a school play yard.

Sharon was miserable in her 'back of beyond' office, as she now referred to it. She said that the stress of trying to cope with Cynthia freaking out about her age, as well as her difficult work colleagues, made her want to drink herself into oblivion. Katie was the only one who'd had a good week – she was ready to party for the fun of it.

As guests started to arrive at the venue, the atmosphere was light and happy. Sharon and Big Davey arrived in their best party clothes. Sharon tottered around on strappy silver stilettos and was wearing a jade halter neck dress with a swinging skirt. Big Davey, a heavy-set man with a quiff, was a dead ringer for a member of Showaddywaddy, in his drainpipe jeans and Teddy Boy crepe shoes. They went straight I to check everything was as it should be.

Just before they had left the house, Robbie had announced he was going out in town and staying over at a mate's place – no doubt not wanting to fork out for a taxi back. The news had cheered up both herself and Martin. For the first time in a good while, he'd made a fuss of her and even wolf whistled when he walked into the bedroom, to find her in her black dress and heels. It had felt nice when he'd taken her hand to escort her out to the taxi.

St Paul's had also had a glowing Ofsted report, which went a long way to improve the atmosphere at home. Martin was particularly pleased with the praise heaped on the senior management team for their exceptional leadership. He'd even made some headway with Gail and Keith. Robbie was going to move in with one of them on Monday. After that piece of news, Alison had slept for an amazing five-hour chunk.

The previous day, Billy had taken a swipe at her with a nasty insult, insinuating she must have cut back on her *drinking* because her eyes weren't so bloodshot. Only a week before, that type of comment would have made her want to throttle him to death.

She smiled to herself. Who would have thought 'painting' bananas would be life-transforming? Just musing about it produced an image of a banana in her mind's eye, sending a wave of calmness through her body.

As they waited to check their coats into the cloak room, Martin smiled at her. 'You look beautiful tonight – so happy.' Then in a more serious tone he said, 'I owe you an apology.'

Alison was taken aback. He did – for a few things, but she wasn't expecting one. 'Why?'

He splayed his hands and grimaced. 'As much as I hate to admit it, I've been a right prat lately. Sorry. I let the stupid inspection come between us.' He shot her a cheeky grin. 'And to make up for it, I've done the ironing.'

Alison reeled in mock shock. 'Crumbs, Martin.'

He guffawed. 'Crumbs?'

She shrugged. 'Don't know where I got that from.'

He planted a kiss on her lips and a little shiver ran up her spine. It had been a while since that had happened.

Martin cupped her face in his hands, his eyes twinkling as he gazed into hers. 'Seriously though, I do love you. I don't know what I'd do if I lost you.'

'Get a room you two.' Katie bustled in with a beautiful man on her arm. 'This is Connor.'

'Hi,' said Connor, flashing the most perfect set of teeth Alison had ever seen.

The four of them went into the party together in good spirits. Inside, Sharon and Big Davey beckoned them over to a table sprinkled with sparkly shapes and a bright pink halogen balloon, floating up from the middle. Twenty minutes later, the room was full of friends and family and the atmosphere was buzzing – aided by the flow of alcohol and eighties pop music blasting out from DJ Johnny's music system.

Katie pointed over to a table laden with presents and cards. 'Have you seen how many bottle bags are over there?'

The group craned their necks to look at the copious amount of alcohol.

'Hmm…' said Sharon. 'Maybe it'll wipe the scowl from her face. I've never known her be so snappy and nasty. She's been an absolute bitch to Ian. All he wants to do is make her happy, and she treats him like dirt. Her mobile pinged. 'Oh, they're here.' She dashed out to meet them, while DJ Johnny shushed everyone.

A cool chill blasted into the room, as Cynthia and Ian made their entrance to a chorus of 'Happy Birthday'. Cynthia clapped her hands to her face in mock delight.

'Uh-oh,' said Sharon. 'She's not happy.'

After three 'hip-hip hurrays', DJ Johnny spoke over the

microphone in his smooth DJ voice to ask everyone to grab a drink and toast the birthday girl. 'To Cynthia, on her big Four-O.'

The spotlights beamed onto a horrified Cynthia. A terrified-looking Ian steadied her as Cynthia appeared to stumble. He attempted a futile situation repair with a fake laugh and a joke about a cheeky vodka and Red Bull helping them to get their over-excited children settled for bed.

'They've been to Mr Soft Play to celebrate with the girls this afternoon,' explained Sharon. 'Apparently it ended in tears, with the kids going feral and kicking the poo out of each other.'

As Ian accompanied Cynthia around the hall to greet her guests, he had the look of a worried man, the strain of it all visible in his face. Sharon said he'd tried to persuade Cynthia to have a glass of her favourite Prosecco, which he'd left chilling in the fridge with Belgian truffle chocolates for their return from Mr Soft Play. But after spending her birthday surrounded by hyper kids, she'd insisted on vodka and Red Bull, even though it made her angry and argumentative.

'To be fair to Cynthia though,' said Alison, 'she's putting on a good act of being thrilled.'

Sharon eyed the gift table with trepidation. 'Wait until she sees all the fortieth birthday cards…'

Alison took a selfie of herself and Martin holding up their glasses in a 'cheers' and sent it to Jack and Chloe.

Jack sent one straight back – Chloe dancing round a pole in a dark, crowded room.

She frantically tapped out a reply.

Where are you? Who's Chloe with? What's she doing on that pole? Is she wearing shorts? It's only seven p.m. Is she drunk?

'Martin, look at this.' She pushed the screen right up to his face. 'They don't go out in the same crowd. Oh no, someone must have called him to collect her.'

He laughed. 'Jack's winding you up.'

A message pinged with an emoji of a fish dangling from the

end of a fishing line pinged straight back.

Don't worry, it's the end-of-term afternoon do at the Student's Union. She's fine. Going home soon. P.S. You need to get that tripod sorted out for your videos. Chloe and her mates have been doing them. She said they are okay but a bit wobbly.

Blimey, are people watching my routines?

Blimey? Jack texted, followed by four laughing emojis.

She thought she'd got away without a tripod for her last video by Blu Tacking her mobile to the bird table. A burst of pride caught her unawares. *Chloe and her friends were doing them?* She hadn't seriously thought anyone would watch them, never mind try them.

Martin put his arm around her shoulders. 'You have to let them go. You've done a good job; it's time to relax. Time for you.'

It was on the tip of her tongue to point out that that's not what he said when Robbie landed on them, but she decided not to spoil their night. 'I'll never stop worrying about them. Even when they've got good jobs and I'm a student – I'll still worry.' Alison noticed Martin's left eye twitch. 'But you're right about it being time for me. I've filled in my application form.'

He withdrew his arm. 'Let's not ruin the evening.'

'Ruin it? What did I say to ruin it?'

He leaned in and lowered his voice. 'Shh, people can hear.'

'Heaven forbid *I* upset random people by mentioning something good about *me.*'

He jumped up and clapped his hands. 'Right, who wants a drink?'

'I'll give you a hand,' said Big Davey.

Alison watched Martin scarper off to the bar. He could object all he wanted. There was no way she was going to hang around going crazy until she completely lost the plot, like poor Boris. As Martin talked and laughed at the bar with Big Davy, Alison thought she'd be more inclined to crash Billy Chapman's head through Martin's car windscreen than put her foot through a work computer.

Bill Hayley's 'Rock around the clock' cranked up, provoking a Pavlovian response from Sharon, who kicked off her heels and sprang into action. Big Davey shot her a smouldering look from his position at the bar then swaggered over, clicking his fingers and swinging his arm in time to the music. They did a hop-skip dance-walk towards each other, approaching the dance floor from opposite ends of the room. The crowd parted, darting out of their way, as Sharon and Big Davey got nearer to each other and their hop-skips gathered gusto. As soon as their hands touched, he started flinging her around like a cheerleader baton, to the delight of everyone watching.

'Wow,' said Katie. 'No matter how many times I see this I can't get over how much she trusts him not to drop her.'

A whooping, foot-tapping, hand-clapping circle formed around them.

'I love it when they get going,' said Alison. 'Proper hijinks.'

Cynthia scowled. 'Don't you think it gets a bit samey? Davey's piling on the weight. At least Ian's health conscious.'

'Why are you being nasty, Cynthia?' said Alison. 'Go home if you don't want to be here.'

'It's my party,' said Cynthia in a petulant voice. 'You're the nasty one.'

Alison edged away, ashamed she'd snapped, but not enough to apologise. She perused the room for Martin, who was nowhere to be seen.

Connor seemed to be thoroughly enjoying the show, and from the sparkle in his eyes when he looked at Katie, he was besotted. 'They're spectacular,' he said, as Davey twirled Sharon above his head. 'Nifty for an old bloke.'

Katie shot Connor a snarky look. 'Less of the old.'

The crowd cheered as Sharon's dress flicked up, revealing satin shorts covered in gold stars.

'For God's sake,' said Cynthia.

'They've been dancing for years,' said Katie. 'Ever since Big

Davey's Deejaying days.

Connor smiled at her, his eyes big and soppy. 'We could learn to do that.'

'The two of you are so gym-toned, you'd look amazing,' said Alison.

Katie hooted with laughter. 'Don't be daft. It takes years of practice.'

'So?' said Connor.

Katie shot Alison a panic-stricken glance. 'Erm, it's my back... That's why I do yoga.'

Alison pulled what she hoped was a 'give-him-a-chance' face. If Katie could get beyond the superficial stages of a relationship, she might get to experience the richness offered by a committed, long-term one, like Sharon's or her own – well, maybe her own at one time.

Sharon and Big Davey ramped up the fun for the finale. He flung her beneath his legs, she leapfrogged back over him and then hop-skipped into his arms in perfect synchronicity with the final note.

'I'm going to find out where they learned,' said Connor.

Katie grabbed his hand. 'Later. I'm parched, let's get a drink.'

Martin sidled up to Alison and squeezed her waist. 'I'm glad we came tonight. I do support you, you know.'

'Then please stop putting obstacles in my way.'

He took her hand and led her over to the table. 'Let's have a nice night. We can talk in the morning.'

Alison stopped. 'No, there's nothing to talk about. I'm going –'

Martin's mobile trilled. A look of concern crept across his face when he saw the name on the screen. 'Hello, hang on, I can't hear you properly.' He mouthed *Gail* to Alison. 'Do you want to speak to Alison?'

Alison sighed and held out her hand for phone. Martin shook his head and shrugged. 'Wants to speak to me...' he whispered. 'Probably looking for our Keith.' He stood up. 'Hang on, Gail, I need to go outside to hear you properly.'

He returned minutes later looking pale.

'What's wrong?'

'Keith's walked out – for good.'

'It's been on the cards for a while now.'

'I knew he was unhappy, but I didn't think things were that bad.'

'Really?' She wondered how he could know so little about his brother. 'He's been miserable for ages. She's a cow to him.'

Martin shot her an exasperated look. 'That's not helpful. She said he won't answer his phone. He's not picking up my calls either. I'll have to go and look for him.'

'He obviously doesn't want to speak to her. Tell her to call a friend.'

'Don't be unkind. She's in a state.'

Alison reached for her bag. 'Come on then.'

Martin touched her shoulder tenderly. His face softened. 'Stay. You and the girls have been looking forward to tonight. I'll get a taxi up to their house, find out what happened and go from there.'

'Typical of her to spoil our first night out for ages.'

Martin gave her a weak smile. 'Yes, I know.' He leaned in to kiss her cheek. 'You have a good time. I'll call when I know what's what, and I'll try to get back as soon as I can.'

When he'd gone, Alison called Gail. No answer. She didn't understand why Martin had shot off to listen to his sister-in-law's marital woes, yet he seemed unwilling to even admit cracks had appeared in his own marriage. Her stomach churned.

The party had lost its sparkle. *Get a grip*, she told herself. There was nothing she could do about any of this. She might as well try to enjoy the rest of the evening. Or at least not spoil it for anyone else. Cynthia was already trying her best to do that. Her irritation with poor Ian was growing, she'd snapped at him in public about checking his heart rate on his Fitbit. Alison felt sorry for him after he'd made such an effort with the party.

It was after Sharon and Big Davey had given it what for on the dance floor to another Bill Hayley classic, that Cynthia started sniping at Sharon, too, to the point that Sharon had dragged her off somewhere private to hash it out.

Connor set down a tray of drinks on the table. 'I think your friends are having a bust up out by the ladies.'

Alison and Katie shot out to investigate and found Sharon and Cynthia, spitting insults at each other in the corridor.

'What on earth's going on?' said Alison.

Katie stepped in between them, as Cynthia tried to jab Sharon's shoulder.

'She gets on my bloody nerves.' Cynthia bared her teeth. 'Showing off and making a spectacle of herself.'

'Listen to yourself, you stupid idiot,' said Sharon.

'Why the hell would you have bloody custom-made knickers if you weren't flaunting yourself? And at your sodding age.'

'They're dance shorts,' shouted Sharon. 'I'm wearing normal underwear underneath.'

'You and Davey... You go on as if your marriage is perfect. In your tidy little house, with your ridiculous oversized American fridge freezer. No wonder Davey's so fat.

'My Davey's *not* fat.'

Katie tried to steer Cynthia away, but she shook her off and stepped towards Sharon to resume her jabbing.

'Cynthia, what the heck?' said Alison.

She turned to Alison. 'And *you* can shut up. With your stuck-up husband and pathetic "I'm going to university" shit. You're spineless.'

Alison gasped.

Cynthia turned back to Sharon. 'I'll tell you what...' she ranted, '... you wouldn't have time to go dancing if you had kids. You've only got that fat lump because I don't want him. I could've had him like that,' she said, snapping her fingers. 'Still could.' She smirked, flicked back her hair and turned to leave.

Sharon launched forward, grabbed her by the hair with both hands and threw her up against the wall.

It took both Alison and Katie to prise Sharon's hands open and untangle her fingers. Sharon stood, clumps of knotted hair sprouting from her rings and bracelet.

Cynthia stumbled back towards the hall. All heads shot round as the door burst open and she appeared in the doorway swaying, a bedraggled mess. DJ Johnny killed the music and, mistaking the banging around for an important entry, turned the spotlights onto her again. She retched and vomited into the room, the sound of spattering echoing off the wood flooring.

There were a few gasps and the odd stifled giggle and then DJ Johnny said, 'Better out than in, lass.' Ian darted towards his wife with outstretched arms, as she slid down the door frame into a heap on the floor.

With the party coming to such an abrupt end, there was a clamour for taxis. Alison called Martin to see if he could pick her up on his way home. He didn't answer. There was nothing she could do but have another drink and wait her turn.

It was after midnight by the time she got in, tipsy and worried sick about Martin's whereabouts. *What if he'd gone into town looking for Keith and been mugged by a gang of drunks?* It was with a mixture of relief and irritation, that she found him snoring on the sofa, an empty brandy glass lying on its side on the carpet.

'I've been frantic with worry. You could've called me.' Not a peep. 'Well you can freeze down here on the sofa.'

As she headed for the stairs, guilt set in. 'Oh heck.'

Unable to leave him to perish in the night, she fetched her horsey blanket and one of her nicest nest cushions. He didn't stir when she toppled onto him as she eased the cushion underneath his head and tucked the blanket around him. She put her finger over her mouth. 'Shh,' she said, before clattering off to the kitchen. She returned with a glass of water and two Paracetamol. As she set them down on the coffee table, she noticed he was scowling, even though he was fast asleep. She reluctantly conceded that trying to help Keith and Gail must be wearing. Maybe she'd been a bit too hard on him.

He snorted and turned over, dribbling brandy stained drool over her cushion and blanket.

'Oh, Martin,' she whispered, her eyes brimming with tears. 'My horsey blanket.'

Before she knew it, she was sitting at the dining table with her laptop. Sniffling quietly, she logged onto her application form. It was difficult to make sense of it, what with the tears and effects of the alcohol. It didn't matter, she told herself, she'd checked it lots of times, along with the encouraging email she'd received in reply to her request for more information. Scrolling to the bottom, she took a deep breath and clicked Submit.

Alison stroked Sammy's head and watched the clouds floating across the sky as the effects of Paracetamol and caffeine kicked in. The gentle swinging motion of the garden seat felt almost hypnotic. She inhaled the fresh morning air, her head uncluttered and thoughts clear, despite her fading hangover.

A clatter from inside interrupted the peace. She could see Martin through the kitchen window. It looked like he'd dropped the kettle in the sink.

Alison stood up and wandered over to the window. Sammy stretched and jumped off the seat to follow her. She tapped on the glass. 'Bring your coffee outside, it's a beautiful morning.' Despite her bright tone, her stomach was churning. She had no regrets about submitting her application form, but she was dreading Martin's reaction.

He looked up and scowled. 'Shh.'

Sammy shot off.

After more clattering, Martin emerged with a mug, and a face like a pile of laundry. 'It's bloody bright out here.'

'How's your head?'

He'd crawled up to bed at some point during the night and slept upside down with his feet on the pillow. As soon as he sat down on the swing seat, he turned grey, got straight back up and plonked himself at the garden table.

'That thing makes me queasy.' He squinted at Alison through bloodshot eyes from beneath puffy lids. 'I feel rough as hell.'

'I left you some Paracetamol on the coffee table.'

He nodded and reached into his dressing gown pocket for the painkillers and washed them down with a mouthful of coffee.

'What happened last night?'

He shot her an indignant look. 'Nothing. What do you mean?'

'With Gail and Keith? You said you'd let me know. You didn't. I had to wait ages for a taxi home.'

He looked sheepish. 'Oh, yes, sorry. I meant to call you. I found Keith in The Butchers Arms in town. He's not going back – had enough apparently. He wouldn't tell me what's going on and neither would Gail. Waste of time.'

She had a feeling there was more to it. 'So why didn't you come back to the party? And why were you drinking Brandy when you got home?'

'You sound like my mother.'

Keen not to go off on a tangent, she ignored his insult. She ventured a nervous smile. *Get it over with. Start gently.* 'I've been invited to the course open day.'

He put his head back and groaned. 'Give me a break. It's far too early for that, and my head's banging.'

'It's half-nine. Anyway, I enquired, and they said I could

apply now. To start in September. But separately to that, last night –'

'For goodness' sake, Alison. It'll be an automated message. Don't get your hopes up.'

She felt herself rankle. *Don't bite, be nice.* 'No, it wasn't. They liked my curriculum vitae. They –'

Martin buried his hands in his face. 'You sent your CV? They'll think you're an idiot. There's a correct way to apply for a university place, you need to –'

Alison gritted her teeth. 'I know what to do. I sent it to find out if they thought I'd be wasting my time.' She shot him a stony sideways look. 'And, as I said, they liked it. But that's not all. Last night –'

He spread his hands, exasperated. 'Stop it. You're obsessed. I'll help you when the time's right. Now leave it. Please.'

Patronising sod. 'As I was saying… Last night I submitted it.'

Martin jumped up, knocking the chair over. 'You should have let me check it,' he stuttered.

She stood up to face him. 'So you could change it? To ensure I didn't get an interview?'

'Don't be stupid.' Martin raked his hand through his hair. 'You should've waited. This is *not* the right time.' He gave her a long, cold stare and stormed off.

Alison sighed and sat back down. Sammy leapt out of the apple tree then jumped onto her lap and purred.

'Well Sammy, that went well, didn't it?' She gave the ground a little push with her foot and set the seat off swinging again. 'But he's wrong. It's the perfect time.'

Chapter 33

'Where's that executive summary?' bellowed Billy from his office.

All eyes shot down.

Alison knew, as did he, that the hospital firewall had blocked anyone without special security clearance from opening the document, due to the software used to format it – the software provided by the hospital. Apparently, the girl covering Boris was dealing with the issue. Boris was on compulsory sickness leave, pending investigation into his violent attack on Billy's computer. According to Peggy, the girl wasn't far behind Boris in the 'going off her trolly' department.

Billy stormed out onto the office floor. 'Well? Where the hell is it?' He glared at Alison. 'Someone's head is going to roll for this.'

There was silence in the room, barring the nervous tapping of a pen on a table. Billy shot the tapping hand a murderous look. The pen clattered onto the laminate with a 'tck'.

'The hospital trust needs to save an extra two million pounds from April – on top of the five identified last year. And when they start cutting jobs, I'll have a list of candidates to give them.'

Something banged against the office door. There was no one to be seen through the glass windowpane. Another thud sounded. Billy snarled at the door. Alison got up to investigate.

'Hello there, er, Alison.' Peggy slid her mop over the toes of Alison's shoes. 'Mind your feet, pet.'

She retreated to her desk and cleaned her shoes with a tissue. Peggy's mop had made them dirtier than they were before.

Billy ranted on about inefficiency and lackadaisical attitudes.

'I think it's a simple backlog in the IT –' she started to say.

He glared at her. 'Get it.'

Everyone looked from Billy to Alison, wide-eyed with shock. Alison stared at him in disbelief.

'Well, don't just sit there, fool. Sort it.'

Alison opened her mouth to protest but found herself pushing back her chair, getting up and doing as he'd demanded. The short distance from the seat to the door felt like walking through treacle.

'Ooh, you look a bit pale, hinny,' said Peggy. 'Are you all right?'

The slop-slap of the mop continued as Alison struggled to find her voice. Peggy flashed her a suspicious look.

Finally, Alison managed a weak smile. 'Yes thanks, full of busy today.'

Peggy reduced her voice to a whisper and touched her nose with her finger. 'Menopause?' She looked from side to side. 'Don't worry, it'll pass in a couple of years.' She sighed and rinsed the mop in the bucket of brown water. 'Eeh, the things us women have to put up with.'

'No, not yet, thankfully,' said Alison with a fake laugh.

Peggy cackled and carried on up the corridor, leaving a dirty trail behind her.

Alison snuck into an empty office and dialled the IT helpline. She was put into a queue.

Peggy's head popped around the door frame.

Alison jumped up, startled. 'I thought you'd gone.'

'Hinny, you're a nervous wreck.' She tapped her nose again.

'I was gona say...' She checked the corridor then leaned back in and lowered her voice. 'There's trouble a-foot with the timesheets.'

'What do you mean?'

'Not sure, but something to do with too many days off and overtime. And here's me, had to get a second job because I can't get overtime for love nor money.'

Peggy disappeared before Alison could ask any more questions. She was about to follow her when she got through to the help desk. To her relief, the required document had got security clearance and would be sent to her straight away. Too humiliated to return to her own desk, she logged onto a computer where she was and managed to distribute it to the rest of the team. Fingers crossed they could all open it. She didn't check it, she had something more important to deal with.

She completed a grievance form, accusing Billy Chapman of harassment and bullying, using the information from her diary, which she could access through her documents on any trust computer. For transparency, she called Ashley before sending it to HR.

Ashley sounded unnerved. 'I understand what you're saying, but could I ask you to give him the benefit of the doubt, please?'

'You can't be serious.'

'Look, Alison, trust me, I'll sort this out. But please, don't do anything official yet. There are things going on behind the scenes that you aren't aware of.'

It seemed to Alison that wherever she was, there was always something more important going on, for which she had to push her own needs to one side. 'I'm sorry, Ashley. I was calling to inform you about what I'm going to do, not ask your permission.'

Alison ended the call and looked around her. The place had become a joke. Her DECT phone rang. It was Billy, demanding that she get back into the office. She informed him she was taking the rest of the day as annual leave. He said she couldn't, so she returned to grab her bag and clocked off anyway.

After changing into her jogging clothes, Alison wandered over to the park on shaky legs. She felt like running away. So she did, she ran and ran. The more effort she put in, the less shaky she felt. She ran down to and around the dene, and then most of the way back up, flopping down onto the grass at the clearing above the waterfall. Her chest heaved as her burning lungs sucked in air, the welcome spray from the cascading water cooling her face as she lay there.

'That was amazing.'

She sat up, totally spent, but completely relaxed. Looking up, she noticed a hollow in a tree and had an idea.

'Perfect.' She positioned her mobile phone in the hollow. The wood held it secure, as if it had been carved out especially. With the waterfall in the background and the sky peeping through the trees behind her, she recorded a Pilates warm down and posted it to YouTube.

She noticed that beneath one of her previous videos, there were fifty Likes. There was a comment below the video that said, *Love the cat.* 'Cat?' She scrutinised it and saw Sammy's head, peeping out from behind the garden Buddha. She checked some of the other routines. There he was – up a tree in one, and stretching his legs in another, as if he was trying to copy her. Alison laughed. 'Little tinker.'

She was still smiling when she got to her bench and took out her lunch. It had taken a battering in her rucksack. As she sat, picking at a squashed ham and tomato sandwich, Christopher ambled over.

He puffed out a weary breath as he sat down. 'Hi.'

Alison noticed how pale his face was. 'Are you okay? You don't look yourself today. Is it your arm?'

He smiled weakly and opened his lunch box. 'No, it's

healing well, thanks.' He was wearing the splint, but no sling. He picked out a salad sandwich and looked at it with disdain. 'I'm sick of low carbohydrate bread and fat free coleslaw. I mean, what on earth is in it anyway? I could ravish a cheese and ham panini.' He gazed into the middle distance and licked his lips. 'With a big, fat cinnamon swirl for afters.'

Alison dumped her lunch in the waste bin. 'Put that sandwich away. Let's go to Alessandro's.'

Christopher turned to her. 'I'd love to, but my obesity…'

'Look, you've lost a boatload of weight, you're exercising, and you said the other day that you're not drinking alcohol until the wedding.'

'Yes, but –'

'But nothing. We deserve a treat. Anyway, I've had a hell of a morning and I desperately need to eat stodge. And you look blinking great.'

He laughed and blushed at the same time.

She felt her cheeks flush up, too.

A piece of damp lettuce flopped onto the ground. 'You're on.' He aimed his sandwich at the bin. Like magic, it was snatched mid-air by a blurry shape. 'Haurice… Where did you come from? At least it wasn't a panini he swiped, like the little Westie.'

'I haven't seen Angus and his dad for ages,' said Alison.

'No, me neither.'

Judith appeared from the path behind the boat house. 'Haurice. That's naughty.'

The poodle looked up at Judith and deftly wolfed down the sandwich before she reached him.

'I'm so sorry,' said Judith. 'I'll get you another from the coffee kiosk.'

Alison's head snapped around. 'There's a coffee kiosk in the park?'

'Yes, behind the boat house. Not a huge selection, but fresh and quite nice.' She turned to Christopher. 'What about ham salad? Would that be okay for your diet?'

Christopher stroked Haurice's head. 'Don't worry about it. It was on its way into the bin. We're off to Alessandro's for a carb-fest. Do you want to join us?'

Judith seemed a little on edge. She checked her watch. 'I'd love to, but I have to get back to work.'

'How's it going?' asked Christopher.

'Okay, thanks.' There was a reticence to her tone. 'I expect you'll already know that.'

'Goodness, no. I don't check up on customers behind their backs. That wouldn't be ethical at all.'

Alison noticed the way Judith raised one eyebrow ever so slightly.

'How's your online presence? Alison's got hers up and running now, too.'

'I've started to post my Pilates videos,' said Alison. 'I've got some Likes. But I don't really understand it all. Jack's going to help me when he comes home for Easter.'

'That's a good start,' said Judith. 'If you can get enough people to like and subscribe to your channel, there's the potential to earn money from advertisers. Not that I'm earning yet,' she quickly added.

'Oh, I see. I usually skip the adverts when I watch other people's stuff.'

'If you let the advert finish, the person gets a small payment,' said Judith. 'Sorry, got to dash. Come on Haurice.'

Alison turned to Christopher, her mouth in and Ooo shape. 'So, if I get thousands of subscribers watching the adverts, I'll be rich?'

'Well, there's no guarantee, but there are some people who make decent money from it.'

Alison hauled her rucksack onto her back, and they set off for Alessandro's. 'Judith seemed preoccupied today.'

'That's what I was thinking. I hope it's not her landlady again. Greedy blighter.'

Alison giggled. 'That's where I'm getting the phrases from.'

He turned to her. 'Phrases?'

'Crikey, blimey…'

Christopher laughed. 'My dad used to go mad if he heard swearing. I had to use more "acceptable" language. It stuck. Emily once said I sound like an Enid Blyton character.'

Alison felt a surge of warmth as he spoke. 'Yes, you do.'

'Have you made a decision about university?'

She grinned. 'I've applied.'

'Fantastic.' Christopher was grinning from ear to ear. 'I'm so pleased for you. I know Martin wasn't keen.'

'He's furious.'

Christopher looked at Alison as if he was weighing up something. 'If you don't mind me saying, I thought he was being short-sighted. You're starting out on another secure career, and you must already have years in the NHS pension scheme. Yes, there'll be a three-year hiatus, but your next role will build upon the same pension, and eventually at a higher salary.'

'Exactly. I tried to get him to go into the bank with me to get an expert opinion…'

'I'm surprised he didn't get some advice while he was last there.'

Alison turned to him. 'When was he there? He usually does everything online.'

Christopher looked awkward. 'I recently saw him chatting to Frank, one of our advisers. Sorry, I shouldn't have mentioned it.' He coughed. 'I'm not in the habit of discussing clients to other people. I don't know what I was thinking.'

Alison felt stupid. She didn't want Christopher to think she was an idiot. She attempted to appear unconcerned. 'Oh, hang on… Come to think of it, he did say he'd been into Henleys. Hmm, I wonder if he's been checking out my figures. To be fair to him, he did look at my spreadsheet.' *Didn't trust it though, did he?* For the second time that day, she felt usurped. And furious with Martin.

'You should set up a website…or a blog,' said Christopher.

'That's what Jack suggested. He's going to help me with it when he comes home.'

Christopher pushed open the door to Alessandro's and sniffed the air as he stood back to let Alison through. 'Blimey, that's good.'

Alison giggled. 'Golly gumdrops, it smells scrumptious in here.'

They chose the window seat she and Martin had sat in, only this time, her companion was happy to be there. As she tucked into her panini, Alison felt enthusiastic about her plans, heartened by Christopher's encouragement.

He bit into his and the colour returned to his face. He sighed in contentment.

'You look one hundred percent better,' she said. 'See, you've been denying yourself too much lately.'

'It's not only the lunch. Martin isn't alone in disliking change. Sandy wants me to stay in my current job and buy another holiday home.'

Alison felt a shot of anger towards Sandy. 'What do you want?'

He nodded in the direction of the bank. 'To stay there. I love it. But the salary won't stretch to a detached Californian home with a huge pool. Not without selling the Portugal and Durham properties, which she also wants to keep.'

Alison flung her head back and guffawed. Then she saw Christopher's serious expression. 'Oh, sorry. I thought you were joking. That's a lot of properties.' *The bitch.* 'Well, you know what the answer is don't you…?'

Christopher looked at her with a blank expression.

'She needs to get a blinking job.' She regretted the words as soon as they were out of her mouth. 'I'm so sorry. That was rude of me.' The trouble was that he was so easy to talk to.

Christopher laughed. 'Hmm. I suggested she started up the

business she had always planned. Not for the income, but for her own career satisfaction. She was offended.'

Alison looked at Christopher's kind face. He was naïve for such a successful businessman. Perhaps that's why she felt protective towards him. 'Are you sure it was a real plan?'

He stared into his cappuccino, as if he was turning something over in his mind. 'I thought it was.'

'I don't understand her objections. The twins and I lived in a terrible flat above a take-away while Martin finished his studies. I had to get a job when they were babies.'

'That's inspirational.'

'We were married, a team. Well, we weren't married at that point, but we were still a family. I supported Martin and now it's his turn to support me. Why would one person work to provide for another who's capable of working, too?'

'I've never thought about it before. I was brought up to be a breadwinner. To look after a woman.'

Alison looked directly at him. 'Why? Because we can't look after ourselves and need a meal ticket?'

Christopher shook his head. 'I'm not a meal ticket.'

'No, of course not. I didn't mean to imply you were.' Alison washed down the last of her panini with a mouthful of coffee. 'Sorry.'

He brushed off her apology with a dismissive wave of his hand. 'Don't worry about it.'

'Marriage… It's not easy, is it,' she said with a nervous laugh.

'No wonder we need a good old Danish now and again.' He sighed and sunk his teeth into his cinnamon swirl.

She smiled at Christopher, but inside she was angry at the thought of selfish Sandy's privileged life. So much time to do whatever she wanted, without a care for her husband. How dare she make such demands on him when he'd worked his guts out to provide for her. And now he had to eat limp lettuce and dust sandwiches to put his health right. Poor bloke, she thought as she drained her cup.

Alison wasn't sure whether she was livid on Christopher's behalf, or simply jealous of his wife. In her opinion, Sandy had it all – a lovely, supportive husband, a big house and lots of money. An attractive, kind husband, a cleaner and no need to work. A fit, sexy husband, with the most striking hazel-flecked green eyes. *Those eyes. Why did they look so familiar?*

Chapter 34

As they turned into the lane leading down to Cherry Dene Hotel, Christopher looked over at Sandy and smiled.

'Here? I wish you'd told me.' Sandy stared out of the window in dismay. 'I would have suggested somewhere else. No one comes here these days. I haven't been for years.'

'They reckon the food's excellent here. You asked me to take you somewhere quiet for dinner.'

'It's a hotel, it won't be quiet. We can hardly have a private conversation in a public place like this.' Sandy rested her head against the headrest and blew out a sigh.

'Don't worry. Apparently, it's not busy during the week.' He couldn't seem to do anything right any longer. Christopher pulled into a parking bay and rammed on the handbrake. He couldn't face another row at home. It had reached the point where he dreaded leaving work.

He took her by the hand to go inside. 'I've booked us a table in the restaurant, but let's find the bar and have a drink in there first. It has a real fire.'

She walked inside without saying anything and didn't look up when the receptionist gave them a cheery welcome. Christopher compensated for her rudeness with an extra friendly, 'Hello'.

Sandy headed straight into the bar and over to a corner by

the fireplace. 'Let's sit here, out of the way.'

'See...' said Christopher, '...there's not a soul in here. Perfect.'

As Gavin approached the table to take their drinks order, Sandy dashed off to the ladies.

'Business meeting?' Gavin asked, flashing a toothpaste advert smile.

'No. A drink with my wife before our meal.'

Gavin shot Sandy's back a puzzled look then turned to Christopher. 'Really?'

Christopher glared at Gavin in disbelief. 'That's rather rude. Yes, she is beautiful, and you might well wonder what she's doing with me, but there's no need to be quite so obvious in displaying your thoughts.'

Gavin turned crimson. 'I'm so sorry...' he stammered. 'That's not what I was thinking at all.'

'You'd think I was a bloody gargoyle or something. Am I really that bad?'

'Absolutely not. You're an *extremely* handsome man.' Gavin dropped his pen.

Christopher turned cerise.

Gavin coughed. 'Please accept my apologies. I thought your wife was someone else. I certainly didn't mean to offend you.'

'Oh, right.' All this unpleasantness between himself and Sandy was spilling out into other areas of life. 'I over-reacted. I'm sorry.'

'No, *I'm* sorry.'

'Entirely my fault.' Christopher loosened his tie. 'It's warm in here.'

Gavin raised an eyebrow at the fire, as it crackled in the grate.

Christopher shrugged. 'My wife wanted to sit here.' He took off his jacket.

'I'll open a window.' Gavin gave a little smile then scuttled away. By the time he returned with the drinks, Sandy was back in her seat. She turned away as he set them down on the table. 'On the house,' he said before retreating to the safety of the bar.

Sandy shot a nervous glance at the bar. 'Why on the house? What did he say?'

'Nothing, it was a misunderstanding.'

She looked at Christopher's shirt sleeves and grimaced. 'You've got sweat patches.'

'Can we move to another table? I'm boiling.'

Her eyes widened. 'No, let's stay here, it's more private. Take off your splint – that'll cool you down.'

'Never mind.'

'Okay. No need to drag this out. Let's cut to the chase.'

Christopher splayed his hands and frowned. 'I beg your pardon?'

'I get it. You've moved the goal posts. You earn the money, so you get to do that.' She held up a hand to stop him interrupting. 'If we sell the Durham apartment, half that money is mine. We're not using it to prop up your pittance of a salary. And we're not taking out any loans. I don't want to be left with debt.'

Christopher felt a stab of indigestion. 'Left with? You'd think I was dying the way you're talking.'

Sandy tutted. 'Please stop rubbing your chest. I'm not falling for all that heart disease stuff.'

From their table, neither of them could see the look of panic on Gavin's face, or the wet glass shoot out of his hand. But they both jumped as it exploded on the floor.

A nervous Gavin popped his head around the side of the bar and peered tentatively at them. 'Excuse me. Did I hear you mention heart disease? I don't mean to intrude, but is everything okay?'

Christopher gave a fake jovial laugh. 'Yes, I'm fine thank you. Indigestion.'

'Good.' Gavin blew out a sigh of relief.

He assumed the poor bloke was trying to make up for the earlier misunderstanding with gushing attentiveness. He wished he'd stop, it was disconcerting.

Christopher turned his attention back to Sandy. 'Look, there's no need for drastic talk about division of property. Let's have a nice drink and start again.'

Sandy's shoulders slumped. 'Well, okay. So, you say we won't be any worse off…?'

Chapter 35

Alison was wearing her black leather shoes because of their metal heel tip to try to earth herself. According to a blog she'd found online, she had a build-up of static which needed to be dispersed. The metal tip could help. It didn't. She stumbled out of the lift following a particularly severe shock.

She was still rubbing her hand when she heard the trundle of Peggy's trolley. It was travelling along the corridor – unmanned. Peggy was nowhere to be seen. The trolley was going at a steady pace but was in danger of shooting straight into the office door. As it came towards her, Alison grabbed the end with both hands, planted her feet firmly on the ground and put her entire body weight into halting it. It stopped. Then she felt it push against her.

'What the hell...?' sounded an angry voice from the other end of the trolley. 'What are you doing, hinny?'

Alison looked around the side, to find Peggy's befuddled face peering at her from around the front end.

'Crikey, Peggy. Sorry, I couldn't see you for your mop. I thought your trolley was moving on its own.'

'He, he, he. Have you been on the drink?'

Alison straightened her blouse and wiped the perspiration from her brow with the back of her hand. She'd miss little Peggy when she left. When she left... A frisson of excitement fluttered around her stomach.

'Hey, have you heard?' Peggy surveyed the area and lowered her voice. 'Redundancies.' She touched the side of her nose and whispered. 'I'm watching my step. You never know who's looking over your shoulder.'

She smiled – it was usually Peggy doing the snooping. 'I'd heard a rumour. I don't think our jobs are in danger. I suspect they'll start with natural wastage – get rid of any posts that become vacant by changing the job descriptions, to create roles at lower pay grades. Or maybe divide work between existing members of staff.'

'You never know...' She checked the area again and pointed towards the office door. 'With a bit of luck, that miserable sod might get the boot. And good riddance to the big dollop,' she chuckled. 'Well, better get on...'

The trolley started up and then stopped again. 'Oh, hang on a minute. You know my other boss, don't you? Lovely little lassie. Jane, no, what's her name again. Come on Peggy, you're ganin doolalley... Judith, that's it. There's something up with her. Nasty landlady came in, and when she left, Judith was crying. Didn't see me, I was cleaning behind the washbasin. See if you can cheer her up if you see her in the park.'

'Her landlady sounds greedy by all accounts. Keeps increasing the rent.'

Peggy tapped the air with her index finger. 'I know what I'll do... I'll take her some peanut brittle to cheer her up. One of the grandkids brought it back from a school trip to Bamburgh. I can't eat it.' She stuck her finger in her mouth and continued talking, making it difficult to understand what she was saying.

Alison sucked in a sharp breath and reeled at the sight of a shark-like half-tooth. 'You should get that looked at by your dentist.'

'Whey no,' cackled Peggy. She pointed to a gap on the other side of her mouth. 'My Alf pulled that one out for me.' She gave an angry wave of dismissal. 'I'm not forking out for a blooming dentist when it isn't necessary. I'll tape the box back up – she'll never know it's been opened.'

As Peggy trundled off cursing peanut brittle, Alison thought about the redundancy rumours. Billy had been scaremongering about job cuts to bully people, but what if there was some truth in it? If she volunteered to go, would she get a severance package, she wondered?

She made a detour down to HR and came out grinning. Not only were the rumours true, they were going to look at voluntary redundancies first of all. The project hadn't yet been rolled out, but they'd given her the forms so she could have them ready when it was.

Alison checked to see if there was anyone around. There wasn't. She took off her jacket and shoes and placed them on the floor next to her handbag. Then she did three cartwheels down the corridor and three back up. She straightened herself up and called Katie and Sharon to invite them for a drink later. She suggested leaving their cars at work and taking a taxi down, as she had some exciting news to celebrate.

'Hi, ladies.' Gavin was standing behind the bar, carefully polishing a glass when Alison, Katie and Sharon walked in.

'That would be lovely, thanks.' Said Alison.

Katie walked over to what had become their table and dumped her bag on a chair.

Sharon flopped down. 'I wish it was Friday. If I have to listen to that lot at work twittering on about the rising price of potatoes once more this week, I'm going to swing for one of them.'

Gavin set down the bucket and flutes. 'I'm glad to see you ladies.' His cheeks flushed pink as he slid his eyes towards the corner table. He lowered his voice to a whisper. 'I made an awful faux pas earlier and need something to take my mind off it. But shh, I'd hate them to hear me.'

'Intriguing,' Alison whispered back.'

Gavin wiped his brow with the back of his hand in mock dismay. 'It was awful.'

Alison craned her neck. She could see the back of a woman. 'That's the lady with the chic clothes and perfect make-up. I recognise her hair.'

The others leaned over to check her out.

'She was having a go at him before. Reckons he's lucky to have her.' Gavin raised his eyebrows. 'She's lucky – he's one good-looking silver fox.'

The couple got up and everyone quickly looked away. Gavin tiptoed off to watch from the safety of the bar.

'Hello, there, Alison,' said a familiar voice.

She looked up to see Christopher walking over to their table. 'Hi,' she said, with a huge smile.

'You were right, it is nice in here.'

'Yes, lovely.'

Gavin was staring at Christopher's back and nodding.

'This is Sharon,' Alison said, indicating to her right. 'And you've met Katie before in Alessandro's.' Both women looked at him with doe eyes, as he flashed them a smile.

'And this is Sandy, my wife.'

Sandy gave Alison a tight-lipped smile.

Alison felt her heart banging against her rib cage. *What had she been doing in there with that Frank?*

They were all looking at her. Katie nudged her, and she realised she was staring at Sandy.

'Sorry… I was wracking my brains, trying to work out where I'd seen you before. I think it was in here one time.' Close up, she wasn't as stunning as Alison recalled.

Sandy's eyes grew round.

Christopher gave his wife a quizzical look.

She pulled at his hand. 'Nice to meet you all, we must dash to get to our table.'

As they walked off, Alison heard him asking when she'd

been there, and Sandy stammering something about wedding planning.

'Liar,' muttered Alison.

'Who?' said Katie.

'She was with that slimy bloke from the bank. I hope she's not cheating on Christopher.'

'Hmm. I'd stay well out of it if I were you,' said Sharon.

'But he's so *nice*.'

'Very *nice* indeed,' said Gavin. He gave a sigh of satisfaction and set about clearing the glasses from the vacated table. 'Mind you, he thinks he's batting above.'

'I'd bat –' said Katie.

'You'd have to get past me first,' said Gavin.

'Bit slim for my liking,' said Sharon.

Alison attempted a non-plussed shrug. 'Never looked at him in that way.' *If that woman was cheating on Christopher, she'd… What? What could she do?*

'Right, Alison. Tell us your exciting news,' said Katie.

Pushing her concerns for Christopher to one side, she tried to muster up her earlier excitement. 'Well, it turns out that the redundancy rumours are true.'

Katie gasped. 'I thought it was going to be something good.'

Sharon clapped her hand over her mouth. 'Oh no. We couldn't manage the mortgage on one salary.'

'No, don't worry. They're going to be seeking voluntary redundancies.'

Katie took a slug of her drink.

'Phew,' said Sharon. 'Those prefabs have never looked so good.'

'I'm going to apply. It would solve all of our financial concerns –'

'Martin's concerns. You don't have any,' said Katie.

'No, but it would be added security.'

Sharon narrowed her eyes at Alison. 'What does Martin think about it?'

Alison topped up the flutes. 'I'm going to tell him tomorrow. I wanted to celebrate with you two first. Not that it's guaranteed I'd get it. But if I hand in my forms quickly, I'll be ahead of the game.'

Katie was scrutinising her face.

'Why are you looking at me like that?'

'I'm surprised you haven't spoken to Martin first. Are you worried about what he'll say?'

Alison sighed. 'No, I think he'll be relieved. He's been so concerned about the money side of things.' She held up her hand. 'Yes, I know it's unfounded. But he's still getting used to my other bit of news.'

They both looked at her expectantly.

Gavin's ears pricked up over at the bar. 'Don't keep us in suspense, what is it?'

Everyone turned to him and laughed.

He shrugged and gave a dismissive wave. 'Don't look at me like that. You know I listen to everything. So, what is it?'

'I've submitted my application for university – for this September.'

Katie clapped. 'Excellent. I'm so proud of you.'

'About time,' said Sharon.

'Congratulations,' said Gavin. 'But will you still come in here when you're a student? Please.'

'Of course.' Alison was pleased she'd shared her good news with the girls first. This is what it should be like, she thought. The people you love celebrating with you.

'Let's have a toast. Katie held up her flute. 'To Alison, and her brilliant new life.'

As they clinked glasses, Alison was so happy, she felt like cartwheeling across the room.

Chapter 36

Alison buttered toast and replayed her latest YouTube video while she waited for Martin to come downstairs. Uplifted by her friends' encouragement the night before, she couldn't wait to tell him about the redundancies.

He wandered in, looked at the screen with a pained expression. 'Won't pay the bills though, will it?'

She studied his face. 'Oh dear, you look rough this morning. Didn't you sleep well?'

'Not particularly. It's all the work stuff going around in my head at the minute.'

'But the inspection's over.'

He reached into the cupboard for a mug. 'I meant, the come down. You know, after the build-up – months of endless pressure. Everyone's a bit low now.' He poured himself a coffee and yawned. 'Why are you so chirpy after a night out? By the way, I won't be able to give you a lift in, I'm leaving early today.'

'That's fine, I'll get the bus. I slept well last night – six-and-a-half hours. According to my sleep diaries, it's increasing by about five minutes a night. You should try my painting bananas exercise, might help take your mind off work.'

He gave a snort.

'Anyway, I've got some news that will cheer you up.'

Martin sat down and shot her a wary look. 'Are you sure about that? Whenever we discuss anything in the kitchen these days, we end up arguing.'

'Oh, don't spoil it, Martin. I wanted to share something I thought you'd be really pleased about. And I don't want to do that when Robbie's around to ruin it.'

'Sorry. Go ahead.'

'They're offering voluntary redundancies at work.'

'And…?' He picked up a piece of toast.

'If I take it, we'll have a bunch of money for when I go back to university in September.' Alison could barely contain her excitement. 'We'd be even better off than now.'

He put the toast down and pushed his plate away. 'But…'

'You said it was the money. A twenty-year redundancy package will more than make up for the extra year I would have worked.'

He reached over and placed his hands on hers. 'You're right, it would give us a huge safety net.' He smiled. 'I'd better get off to work.'

Something wasn't right. 'Martin, what's wrong? I thought you'd be pleased.'

'I am. I'm just… worn out. Everything keeps changing.'

Alison shook her head. 'So am I. I went out with the girls last night because I wanted to celebrate. I knew they'd be pleased for me.'

'It's not even definite.'

She pushed her chair back and got up. 'No, it isn't. But it's a realistic possibility. And anyway, we were also celebrating my uni application. They were really happy for me.'

He splayed his hands. 'And that's not a given either. You're constantly turning everything upside down for a load of half-cocked ideas.'

'Why do you have to be such a killjoy?' She filled the sink with soapy water so that he wouldn't see the tears she was struggling to suppress.

Martin trudged off to work without saying anything else.

Alison was too deflated to stay angry with him. Despite her tears, she wasn't sure she cared what he thought any longer. She felt more upset that he didn't seem to care that he'd spoiled her happiness. How could he hurt her like that if he loved her?

As she went upstairs, a sound startled her. She looked up, to find Robbie, standing on the landing in his underpants, scratching his lardy stomach and yawning.

'Is breakfast ready?' he asked, lifting his leg to pass wind. 'Aah, I needed that.'

'No, it isn't,' shouted Alison. 'And put some sodding clothes on, for God's sake.'

Robbie laughed. 'Alright, keep your hair on. Oh, did Martin tell you I'm staying a bit longer? Mam called him last night. She's having a new bathroom fitted, so I can't go back yet.' He wandered off.

Alison wobbled and had to grab the banister to steady herself. 'What about your dad's place?'

'He's gone on holiday to Spain and taken his keys with him.'

'Your grandparents —'

'Nope —'

She ran to get her mobile and call Martin. It went straight to answerphone.

Martin was incommunicado right up until half-eleven when he eventually returned one of Alison's many calls, but only to say he was stowed under with work and he'd explain about Robbie later. She worked through lunch so she could leave early and catch him before he left for the gym. But by the end of the day, she had worked herself up into such a frazzle, she couldn't face going home.

Finding herself at a loss for what to do, she clocked off and wandered down to Cherry Park, calling at the Newsagents for a Cadbury's Fudge and a packet of liquorice shoelaces. As she wandered through the park, she passed the little cottages situated at the far side bordering the dene. One of them had a for sale board up. She sat on a bench and thought how lovely it would be to look out onto the park every day, and she wished she could pick up her lovely house and move it there.

Something nudged her leg. 'Hello, Haurice.'

Judith wasn't far behind. 'Hi,' she said on reaching them. 'It's strange seeing you here at this time of day. I would have walked straight past if Haurice hadn't stopped.'

A little white Westie dog in a tartan coat hurtled past, followed by a man in a T-shirt. He smiled and said 'Hello' to them.'

Once he'd got past, Alison turned to Judith. 'Do you ever see that other man with the Westie dog?'

Judith shook her head and shrugged. 'Can you narrow it down a bit?'

Haurice wandered off for a sniff around.

'Wears lots of clothes, even in mild weather? Dressed for the Antarctic.'

'That was him, just now.'

Alison craned her neck to look at him. 'No, it can't be…'

'Didn't you hear about it…? It was disgraceful. He tripped and bashed his face – the only bit of him not covered. Nearly bled to death. Apparently one of the old doctors at the health centre over the road had prescribed too much blood thinning medication. It was in the newspapers. Dr Smelly, or something.'

'Smedley? How did I miss that?' She clapped her hands. Haurice shot back over to her, then he trotted off again when he realised she had nothing for him.

'Apparently, the medication makes you feel cold. The GP is being investigated.'

'Thanks for that. It's really cheered me up.'

Judith shot her a wary look.

'Not the accident… The doctor being exposed as an

incompetent fool.' She recalled Peggy's concern for Judith. 'Anyway, I'm pleased to see you. I was wondering how your business was going?'

She tilted her head to the side and pursed her lips. 'So-so.'

Alison felt her hand move. Haurice had sneaked back and managed to gently steal a liquorice shoelace. He scarpered and stopped a few metres away to eat it.'

'Oh, I'm so sorry,' said Judith.

'It's fine, but I hope he doesn't choke. They aren't easy to chew. Like eating plastic.' She offered the packet up to Judith.

'Thanks.' She took one and tried to bite a piece off. 'You need sharp teeth for this.'

'Business is only so-so? Isn't it going as well as you'd hoped with the extra stylists?'

Judith averted her eyes. 'Can I be honest?'

She was a little taken aback by her serious tone. 'Yes, of course.'

'I'm not sure I can trust you.' Judith scuffed at the grass with her shoe.

Alison coughed on a piece of liquorice. 'Why?'

'Because of your friendship with Christopher.'

She stared at her, flummoxed.

Judith sat down. 'Well, for all I know, you might repeat whatever I say to him. And of course, he'll tell his wife.'

'Sorry, I don't understand.'

'He offered to give me business advice, knowing fine well it was unethical given that his wife's my landlady. The least he should have done was to disclose that information.'

'You're joking? Your greedy landlady is Christopher's wife?'

'I feel scammed.' She shook her head. 'I even thought about reporting him. I'm sure that kind of thing isn't allowed.' Haurice returned and sat by Judith's feet. He peered up at her with worried eyes. She tickled him under his chin. 'Mammy's okay, don't worry.'

Alison was reeling. Surely lovely, honest Christopher

couldn't be married to someone so horrible. He couldn't be a scammer. It was too much to bear. 'But he told me Sandy doesn't work, and that she wanted to open a beauty salon.'

Judith attached Haurice's lead. 'It's funny. I used to think you and he were married.'

She made a high-pitched laughing sound. 'What a strange thing to think. Mind you, I was surprised when I saw him with Sandy recently. She seemed so brassy.'

'Hmm. Just shows you. You can't always trust appearances.'

Haurice licked Alison's hand then led Judith off across the park.

Alison remained on the bench, dumbfounded.

She was still feeling flummoxed as she drove home. That all changed quickly when she pulled up on the car and heard the music blasting out of her house. All the windows were open. Even her bedroom window. She dreaded going inside but knew she had no choice but to face it head on. Sammy sidled up as she went to unlock the door. He meowed and brushed against her legs, as if to bolster her.

The stench of cigarette smoke hit her as soon as she stepped inside. Sammy scarpered.

Robbie and two of his friends were sprawled in the lounge, dirty plates, takeaway containers and empty beer cans covering every surface.

He glanced at her and looked away. 'Martin's working late.' He inhaled on his cigarette and blew out a string of smoke rings.

Alison was shaking. 'It's "Uncle Martin". Robbie, I can't begin to tell you how disappointed I am.'

He sighed.

She pointed to his friends. 'You two need to go.'

They ignored her.

'Now,' she screamed. She turned to Robbie. 'And you, get

my home cleaned up.'

Robbie rolled his eyes. 'You're such a nag.' He reluctantly got up and pulled on his trainers. 'Come on, let's get out of here,' he said to the others.

After they'd gone Alison looked around her filthy lounge. She picked up a half empty can and threw it against the wall where it spilled its contents down the paintwork.

Hyperventilating, she called Martin.

'I can't hear you, I'm on the treadmill, can't understand what you are saying.'

The equipment whirred in the background. 'Get off the bloody, sodding thing.' Her knuckles whitened as she sank her nails into the palm of her hand.

'Can it wait until I finish my work-out?'

Alison covered the mouthpiece with her hand while she tried to control her tears of fury, and noticed her palm was bleeding.

'Alison?'

Faltering between sobs, she told him what had happened. 'Martin, I can't stand it.'

'Try not to upset yourself. It's only for a few more nights.' His footsteps continued to pound on the belt.

'No. I don't want him under our roof a moment longer. I'm going to call Gail and tell her to come and get him.'

'Don't do that. I'll speak to her. He's my brother's son, I'll sort it out. I'll go to see her in person, after I finish here.'

Fury shot up from the pit of Alison's stomach and jabbed the top of her skull. 'Get off that blasted treadmill.'

'Calm down. You're becoming hysterical.'

'If you don't go right now, so help me, I'm going to storm round there and pull her stupid head off.'

'I'm on my way.'

The line went dead.

Alison stared at the phone in disbelief. What had happened to her marriage? It was as if everything she'd always counted on was sinking in quicksand. The phone trilled while it was in her hand. Relieved, she wiped her eyes. 'Martin?'

'Alison?' said Doreen. 'Robbie's turned up here. Would you come and pick him up? He's drunk, and I'm not having it.'

'No, Doreen, I will not. Call his parents.'

'Well, I have never in all my life –'

This time, it was Alison who hung up.

It was nearly ten o'clock when Martin returned, weary and tetchy. 'She's not budging. He dumped his gym bag on the floor. 'We're stuck with him.'

Alison stared at her husband, unable to fathom his attitude. 'Of course we aren't. We were doing Gail and Keith a favour. Robbie isn't our responsibility. Apart from anything else, he's an adult.'

Martin rubbed his eyes with the palms of his hands. 'Oh, I hate this.'

She stepped towards him and gently touched his arm. 'So do I. It's damaging our relationship. We seem to do nothing but argue these days.'

'No, not that. Well, that as well. I hate all this...' He splayed his arms. 'Coming home to aggro from you.'

A gasp caught her breath '*Me?*'

'Yes. I could count on you, Alison.'

'What the –'

'Now all you do is complain. Whining about your job, me, our family. You've no interest in the home any longer.' He noticed the beer-stained paintwork and the can lying on the floor. 'Let me guess. You threw that can at him?'

'I didn't. I threw it at the wall when he'd gone.' Her mind was reeling. 'There's no way I'm allowing Robbie to verbally abuse me.'

Martin closed his eyes and sighed. 'So now it's abuse. Strewth.' He went to leave the room then turned back and looked at her through cold eyes. 'Robbie's staying at my mother's tonight, but he'll have to come back tomorrow.'

'No chance.'

'Gail's a basket case at the minute. She's not fit to deal with him. Keith's washed his hands of him.'

'She's having a kitchen fitted, she can't be that bad.'

He flopped into an armchair. 'Actually, I need to ask you something.'

Alison looked at him in trepidation, dreading what he might say next.

'It's just that… I have a reputation to think about. People are talking about your videos. Do you really think a deputy head teacher's wife should be jumping around, on YouTube?'

She threw her head back and guffawed.

'It's not funny. And Lycra's so unforgiving on a middle-aged woman. Would you consider giving them up? Please?'

She continued laughing and laughing until her stomach hurt. Eventually, she stopped and wiped her eyes. 'I have a better idea. How about I simply give up being a middle-aged deputy head teacher's wife?'

Chapter 37

'It's smashing to see you.' Christopher set down a mug of coffee next to Emily. It was a joy to have her visit him at work. She'd never been able to do that before. 'Do you have to dash off?' He checked his watch – eleven thirty. 'Fancy an early lunch?'

'Sorry, I'm meeting Mum to go through nail colours for the bridesmaids.' They both laughed. 'I know… Mum reckons it will spoil the colour scheme if anyone wears the wrong shade.'

He laughed. 'Cherry Dene Hotel? Over coffee with Margot?'

Emily gave him a quizzical look. 'Where? She's never mentioned that place.'

Christopher felt something sink inside. 'Must have been one of Mum and Margot's meetings.'

'Could be, she doesn't include me half the time. You wouldn't think it was my wedding.' She took a sip of coffee. 'Mmm, this is nice.'

He nodded at his coffee machine. 'Only got it working again this morning. Somehow, the fuse fell out. It was strange because it's a sealed unit. I had to buy a whole new power lead.'

Emily had started to doodle on a Post-it-note. 'Dad… Are you and Mum okay?'

The question caught him off-guard. 'Yes, of course we are.'

'It's just that you both looked a bit peeved with each other in the restaurant –'

'Oh, that was nothing. We'd had a bit of a disagreement about the William's house and –'

'Well that's not all. This morning, when I was having a look at Mum's new wedding shoes upstairs, the door to one of the spare rooms was open… I saw your slippers in there, and your dressing gown was on the bed.'

Drat. He'd slept in there since they'd had words on their return from Cherry Dene Hotel and she'd accused him of interrogating her. 'Ah, well… I had too much to drink last night. Mum complained about my snoring and said she couldn't afford to lose her beauty sleep so close to the wedding.' He hated lying, but he didn't want to give Emily more cause for concern.

She sighed. 'You know, Dad. This wedding's getting out of hand. We never wanted a big affair.'

He shrugged. 'You know your mum. She wants to spoil her only daughter.' He took a sip of coffee. 'So do I.'

There was a quiet knock and Shirley's head appeared around the door. 'Would you like…' her voice trailed off as her gaze fell on their cups. With her foot still in the door, she clattered something down outside and came into the office with a plate. '…a caramel shortbread?'

Christopher followed her gaze, as she glanced over at the coffee machine, puzzled. *Aha.* He gave Shirley a little smile. 'It was the fuse, would you believe?'

Shirley had the look of a mischievous child who'd been caught red-handed. 'I'll just, erm…' She tiptoed away and closed the door quietly behind her.

Emily walked around the desk, perched on the arm of his chair and kissed the top of his head. 'I do appreciate it all. But I only ever wanted a small, intimate do, with our close friends and family.'

Christopher looked up into his daughter's eyes and felt his

heart melt.

'I love Simon. But you do know no one can ever take your place, don't you? I'll always need my dad. I've loved you working nearby for a change.'

'Well, I've got some good news. I've been given the opportunity to stay on here, as manager.'

Emily shrieked with glee. 'That's fantastic. She reached over for the plate of biscuits. 'Have one of these to celebrate.'

Christopher eyed the caramel shortbread and grimaced.

'Get one Dad. And that's another thing. Your pre-diabetes has gone, but you're still wasting away.'

Christopher patted his stomach. 'There's a way to go before I –'

Emily picked up a square and shoved it into his mouth.

He closed his eyes and bit into the caramel. 'Mmm. Seriously though, are you saying you aren't looking forward to your wedding?'

'I've started to dread it. It's costing a fortune. And Mum wanted the Californian house. To be honest, I can't even remember the place.'

Christopher held up his hand. 'Firstly, we can more than afford your wedding. Wanting a small do and *saying* you want a small do because of the cost are two completely different things. And secondly, we're not buying that blinking house.' He banged the desk with his fist. 'I'm sick to death of hearing about it.'

'Sorry.'

He was gutted – he'd never shouted at Emily before. 'No, *I'm* sorry.'

Emily looked at him, her eyes wide with concern. 'But you are having to make cutbacks because of me. And you're so stressed these days. What's more, you've got all these properties, but you never get to stay in them.'

Christopher sighed and turned towards his daughter. 'That's what I was saying to Mum.'

'Dad, please take the job. I know you had to work away when I was little, but I want you around in the future.' She threw her arms around him and burst into tears.

'Don't you worry. I'll be here for a long time yet.' Fury hurtled around inside him. This should be one of the happiest times of Emily's life, yet she was miserable. Sandy had spent months planning the wedding, no expense spared, but her love of money was ruining everything. 'Emily, have you noticed a change in Mum lately?'

She sniffed and loosened her grip. 'No. But I've been so worried about you since you got pre-diabetes and high blood pressure. I don't want you to die. I want my children to have a grandad.'

Christopher blinked back his own tears. 'Emily, I'm healthier than I've been in years. I'm not going to die.'

'But all this…' she went over to her bag and pulled out her wedding file. It thudded as she clonked it onto the desk. 'You have to work so hard to pay for it all.'

He laughed. 'It's a size, isn't it…'?

'Tell me about it, I have to carry it around.'

'Listen to me. I have an excellent salary. We have money in the bank, and we can afford this. Maybe not a house in California, but we can certainly keep Casita Emilia.'

'Dad get rid of it. And either sell or rent out the Durham flat.'

'Hmm, Mum wanted to keep that one for staying over in town now and again.'

'Then she'd better get a job, like the rest of us. I'll never put Simon through what Mum has put you through.'

He blew out a silent whistle. 'That's a little harsh… Your mum has devoted her life to looking after us.'

Emily blushed. 'Yes, I know. I'm being a bitch.' She walked back to her seat. 'But women can work too, you know.'

Christopher looked at his daughter with pride. 'Simon's a lucky man.'

'We're both lucky. I couldn't have wished for a more wonderful husband.'

What he would give to hear Sandy talk about him like that. Or at least at one time, he wasn't so sure any longer. 'I hope neither of you ever lose that feeling.'

Emily looked at her father as if she was going to say something but changed her mind. She pulled a tissue from her pocket and blew her nose. 'I love Mum. But sometimes…' She paused and walked over to the window.

'What's wrong, love?'

She chewed the corner of her mouth. 'This sounds awful… But sometimes, Mum reminds me of a clique of girls in my old sixth form.'

He looked at her, puzzled. 'Girls like Mum?'

'They didn't want to carry on studying. But they didn't want to work in a rubbish job either. They'd go out in Newcastle, to nightclubs – the ones where only the men with plenty of money could afford to go.'

'Emily, what are you insinuating?' A frightening image of seedy night spots flashed into his mind – lap-dancing clubs and worse.

'Oh, nothing bad. It's just, those girls knew they were pretty. And they knew where to meet a wealthy boyfriend.'

'Your mum was working when I met her.'

'In a posh hotel.'

Christopher thought back to the plush spa, and the restaurant he'd never have afforded to eat in had it not been paid for by work. 'That was a coincidence. It could have been anywhere.'

'Thing is, Dad. They wanted to settle down as quickly as possible – all married with children now. Not a pound earned between them.'

He was shocked and disappointed that Emily could think of her mother in such a disrespectful way. 'Your mum was nothing like those girls.'

'She once told me where the Newcastle United footballers go out in town, and suggested my friends and I –'

The room moved out of focus. He grabbed the edge of the desk.

'Dad…?'

Get a grip, man. 'You didn't need a rich husband and neither did she.' Taking a deep breath, he stood up. 'Come on, let's go for a Panini and a Danish pastry. You're right, I'm thin enough.'

Emily grinned and dropped the file back into her bag.

'But will you do one thing for me please?'

'What's that?'

'Put your foot down with Mum. It's your wedding and I'll be vexed if it isn't the one you've dreamed of.' He laughed. 'Especially as I'm paying for it.'

She kissed his cheek. 'Thanks, Dad. I love you.'

As he popped through to tell Shirley he was going out, he heard Emily talking in a firm voice on her mobile. 'No, Mum. Thank you, but we're not having the bushes with the fairy lights. I love the entrance the way it is.'

An memory of Sandy floated into his mind – she was sitting looking beautiful on a stool in the hotel bar on the night of the awards. He'd put his award down on the bar while he ordered a drink. She admired it. He remembered how discombobulated he felt when he caught sight of her beautiful skin through the thigh-length split in her evening dress, as she slowly crossed her legs, her manicured feet showcased in exquisite stilettos. And how his knees buckled as she turned her striking eyes towards him and flashed a perfect smile.

Chapter 38

'Psst!'

Alison peered up the stairwell. There was no one around.

'Psst! Over here.'

She took a tentative peek around the side of the stairs. No one. Her heart was thumping. She'd heard one of the offices on this floor was haunted.

'Here, man, for God's sake. Joan, er whatsit… Alison, are you blind?' Peggy popped her head out from beneath the stairs.

'Oh, it's you, Peggy. Good grief, how do you fit under… Never mind.'

Peggy nipped out to survey the surrounding area. 'There's trouble looming.' She pointed to the ceiling. 'That lazy lump up there.'

Alison stepped in closer. 'Tell me what you know.'

Peggy dragged a bucket and mop from beneath the stairs and doused the mop head in the water. The shank was taller than her by at least a foot-and-a-half. 'I can't.'

'Go on, please. I won't tell anyone.'

Peggy looked at Alison as if she were stupid. 'Are ye deef? I said, I can't. I don't know.'

Alison's excitement evaporated. 'Aw, I thought you were going to give me good news.' She jumped back as the mop licked the toes of her shoes.

'Mind yer feet,' said Peggy. 'Well, I did accidentally overhear what's-her-name in erm Human whatsit, on the phone. But she saw me and shut the door. Cheeky mare – as if I would eavesdrop. Anyway, I heard snippets through the door. Mind that wood's thick.' She peered up the stairwell again. 'It's something to do with that oaf. He's in trouble.' She arched a brow and nodded at Alison. 'You mark my words.'

An ear-piercing alarm sounded from the floor above.

'That's us, it's continuous.' Alison sniffed the air and scanned the area for smoke.

Peggy threw down her mop and darted upstairs.

'No, you never go *into* the fire zone. Come on, we have to evacuate.'

People from surrounding offices bustled out, bringing with them an excited vibe, fuelled by the opportunity to escape from their desks.

Peggy caught up Alison near the exit. She was carrying a mug. 'I'm not standing out there without a hot drink. It's the beverage bay.' She was wearing the beverage bay fire blanket around her shoulders. 'Bin on fire, would you believe? I put it out with the water from the kettle.'

As they made their way to the car park, a kerfuffle sounded behind them, accompanied by twittering and grumbling.

'I've got you,' said a breathless, scrunchy voice.

Alison turned to witness Billy, frantically trying to free himself from Phyllis's vice-like grip. The sound of a screaming siren grew nearer.

'Get off me, woman,' said Billy.

Phyllis gazed up at him as she scuttled along by his side, her eyes glistening with adoration. 'I'll never let anything happen to you.'

Dorothy approached Billy. Phyllis blocked her. Billy pushed past Phyllis.

Rick Shannon appeared in a Hi Viz fluorescent yellow waistcoat, holding a clipboard. He instructed everyone to line up according to their base office, then proceeded to count people and tick them off his list.

'When can we go back inside?' said Billy. 'I heard the fire's out.'

Rick shot him a long-suffering look. 'We have to wait for the stand down.'

A fire engine screeched to a halt in the car park, and a team of firefighters in black and yellow gear jumped down from the rig and jogged into the building, with a fire hose.

Billy watched, his face dead-panned with jealousy.

Women jostled to sneak a look at the hunky heroes.

He turned to Dorothy. 'I've got one of those suits in the house. I look better in it than they do.' He stepped towards her and said in a low, throaty voice. 'Would you like me to show you sometime?'

Dorothy shot him a wary look and darted over to her own office line.

'I would,' said Phyllis, her eyes glazed over.

Rick Shannon approached Billy with his list. 'Where's the rest of your staff?'

'Sickness leave.' Billy looked down. He scuffed the ground with his shoe and launched a pebble across the car park.

'Ow,' came a cry from another line.

'There's a virus going around.' He rubbed his nose and nodded over to a couple of the other, extra-long lines. 'We've got a few in on overtime during annual leave from other offices.

'Why can't I get any blinking overtime?' piped up Peggy.

'You get away to your own line,' said Billy.

'Keep your hair on.' Peggy sauntered over to the steps at the back of the fire assembly point to join two other cleaners, both holding mugs and cocooned in fire blankets.

'Why *have* we got so many people off work?' Alison asked Billy. 'I haven't noticed anyone complaining of feeling unwell in the office.'

'That's confidential information.' He marched over to Rick and demanded to go inside. When he wasn't allowed to, he stomped over to Alison and informed her she'd have to work late to make up for lost time.

She only just managed to stop herself from slapping his face. As she shook with rage, she had a better idea. Thinking back over recent weeks, she realised there'd been an unusually high number of staff covering others who were off sick. Billy had looked nervous when Rick questioned him about the staff list. Perhaps Peggy was right, maybe he was up to something.

Alison sidled away from the others and called Ashley. Knowing that he wouldn't give her any information, she told him she was concerned about her office environment, in view of the number of people who had gone off on the sick recently. He didn't sound surprised but said he would look into it. She glanced over at Billy and smiled to herself.

Rick made an announcement – it was to be at least another thirty minutes before the building would be cleared for entry. The firefighters had to go into the ceiling panels to check the electrics. There was nothing to explain the cause of the fire. But he assured them they'd find the culprit. And someone's head would roll.

Alison watched a wide-eyed Phyllis slope over to a waste bin and drop a little box into it. Edging away from the area, she spat on her hands and rubbed them in a frenzied fashion, then wiped them on her skirt, leaving black smudges. Alison glanced at Billy and chuckled.

She wandered over to sit on the wall at the edge of the carpark and decided to sort out access to her savings account while she waited. A pleasant young man in a Scottish call centre helped her reset her account. After the recent difficulty with the login process, she nearly fell off the wall when she got straight in.

There was one pound in it.

Chapter 39

Alison held her mobile in front of her face and screamed into it. 'Calm down? Calm? Bloody? Down?'

People were craning their necks to look at her from their lines.

She was hyperventilating. 'It's empty. Empty.'

Billy wandered towards her across the car park.

She squared up to him. 'Take another step towards me and I swear I'll knock your stupid head off your shoulders.'

He pursed his lips, executed a heel turn and slinked off.

Martin was garbling down the line.

'You're not making sense.'

He puffed out a shaky breath. 'I moved it.'

'You what…?' Alison raked her hand through her hair.

He made a high-pitched laughing sound. 'I thought about what you'd said about scammers –'

She paced around in a circle. 'Scammers? What scammers? I never mentioned scammers.' She went dizzy and had to crouch down to breathe. 'We've been *scammed*?' A million scenarios fast-forwarded through her head, all of them ending in not going to university and working with Billy Chapman and Phyllis until she died.

'Alison,' shouted Martin. 'Listen to me. We haven't been scammed. You couldn't get into the account. As a precaution,

I had a chat with Frank Budle –'

'And he told you to swipe your wife's university fees?' Her voice had almost reached the pitch of a low-flying aircraft. 'I *knew* he couldn't be trusted.' She spun around and glared in the direction of the high street and Henleys. 'I'm going to knock his block off.'

'Shush. I transferred the money into another account.'

'You what? Which one? The holiday account?'

There was a pause. 'No... A new one.'

'But I haven't signed anything. How could you empty a joint account and open a new one without me? And why the heck didn't you speak to me first?'

The fire fighters jogged back across the car park and hopped up onto their rig.

Rick Shannon gave the go ahead to re-enter the building, and everyone started to filter inside. Except Phyllis, who hung back and cocked her ear in Alison's direction.

'Sod off, weirdo,' screeched Alison.

Phyllis scuttled over to Billy, who side-stepped around her.'

Alison didn't move. Billy gave her a wide berth and avoided eye contact as he passed.

Rick approached her all macho-like, legs in the gait of John Wayne, arms bent, as if he couldn't get them near his torso because of the size of his biceps. 'Could you make your way inside? I need to speak to everyone.'

She turned her head slowly and looked at him with deadly eyes. 'With due respect, Mr Shannon, if you mention the word "chock" to me one more time, I will –'

Rick held up his hands and stepped back. 'In your own time.' He hot-footed it after the others, muttering, 'Never, in thirty-two-years...'

Getting through the afternoon was excruciating – every minute felt like an hour. No one came near her desk. She couldn't get the image of the account balance out of her mind.

When she finally got home, she was relieved to see Martin's car outside. She strode up the drive, resolute. First things first; Martin was going to transfer the money into her account. She was the one who'd be charged with the fees. It was her course, and she was going to ensure she was in full control from now on.

Alison's gaze was drawn to the front bedroom window. Music blared out as usual. The smell of marijuana wafted down, sending fury shooting through her veins. Martin's next job was to sort out his nephew.

And if he didn't agree with either of those things, he could leave. She'd had enough. As she opened the door, a crash sounded from the kitchen. Alison dropped her bag and keys on the hall floor and ran in. She was met by a terrifying scene – Gail, lunging at Martin's throat with a fork. Rave music thumped through the ceiling.

'Get away from my husband.'

Gail turned and sneered at her. 'Some husband.'

She grabbed Gail by the hair, pulled her off Martin, and eased the fork from her clenched hand. Then she turned to Martin. 'What happened?'

Gail glared at Alison. 'Oh, for God's sake, don't stand there looking all innocent. "Look at me… I have the perfect life. I'm going to university." You're pathetic.' She snatched her glass of wine and took a swig. 'You… "Ooh, my twins are at university and going to become the bees' knees." Makes me sick.' She threw her head back and cackled at the ceiling. 'But you're not going to university now, are you…?'

Alison turned to Martin. 'What's she on about?'

Gail went to flop down onto a stool but missed and fell in a heap on the floor. 'Tell her. Tell her, you spineless moron.'

'Shut up,' said Martin, his face deathly pale.

Gail scrambled up and reached over for more wine. She calmly took a swig then turned to Alison. 'Do you remember that time you two broke up?'

'We've never broken up,' said Alison.

'Stop it, Gail,' said Martin. 'Don't mess with my marriage because yours is on the rocks.'

Gail flashed Alison a spiteful grin. 'After you trapped him with your sprogs.'

Martin shot over to Alison's side and placed a possessive arm around her shoulder. He pulled her face around to look at him, his grip a touch uncomfortable. 'She's lying. She's been blackmailing me. Threatening to tell you lies if I didn't give her money. I'm sorry, I had to use our savings.'

The room started to spin. Alison tried to focus on him, unable to make sense of what he was saying. 'Blackmail? About what? You gave her our holiday savings?'

He was shaking. 'I can explain.'

Gail threw her head back and guffawed. 'It's a drop in the ocean to what you owe me.'

Martin shot her a vicious glare. 'You've had years of bleeding Keith dry. You've never been short of money.'

He turned to Alison, his eyes pleading.

She looked from Gail to Martin as the information registered. 'No,' she whispered. 'My fees…?'

Gail clanked the glass against her teeth as she took another glug. 'You must remember… When you and Martin had split up and he was with me. When he said you and he were *over*?' She spat out the last words.

Alison felt the floor move beneath her. '*Over*?' she whispered, searching Martin's face for proof Gail was lying. She tried desperately not to cry – not in front of Gail.

'No, Alison… It's not true.'

'Twenty years of missed child support. But don't you go thinking that's the end of it.'

Martin turned to Gail. 'Why are you doing this? You got your money.'

'And then when he left me pregnant…' Gail jabbed her

finger at her. 'You and your bloody sprogs. You had to trump me, didn't you…? And I was left with the booby prize. Stupid Keith. Stupid, puppy-dog Keith.'

Alison's heart pounded as she tried to make sense of Gail's words. Her legs buckling, she reached for the wall. Her eyes pleaded with Martin, willing him to convince her it wasn't true, to reassure her their life together hadn't been one big lie.

He dropped his gaze. 'It was a stupid fling, that's all.'

'Liar,' screamed Gail.

Alison took her glass from her and emptied it down the sink. 'Time for you to leave.'

Gail laughed.

She opened the cupboard door beneath the sink and pulled out a roll of black refuse sacks. 'And take your son with you.'

In silence, she calmly walked upstairs and into Robbie's room. She snatched the spliff from his mouth. It sizzled as she dropped it into his beer can.

He jumped off the bed and grabbed the can and stared in dismay through the hole in the top. 'What do you think you're doing, woman?'

She tore a bag from the roll and threw it at Robbie. 'Get your stuff together.' Alison started bundling his possessions into another bag.

'Don't touch my…' He grappled around the messy room, trying to salvage his belongings before Alison sent them crashing without discrimination into the bag.

She tied a knot in the plastic, then straightened up and blew a strand of hair off her face. 'Get your rubbish and your trashy mother out of my property.'

Robbie's belongings clanked off each stair as Alison booted the bag down to the front door.

'My stuff,' he shouted. 'Be careful.'

Back in the kitchen, Martin and Gail were hissing insults at each other. She gently but firmly grabbed the back of Gail's neck with one hand and the waistband of her jeans with the other and pulled her off the stool. One of Gail's wedged shoes dropped on to the laminate as Alison ousted her from the house. Robbie stumbled out with his bin bags and old holdall. Alison picked up and hurled Gail's shoe outside, it landed on top of a bag with a crack.

The frame rattled as she banged the door shut. She straightened her shirt and leaned against the hall wall, finally allowing the tears to come.

There was an almost audible silence coming from the kitchen. She dried her eyes and walked in. Martin was cowering on a stool. Seeing her calm expression, he puffed out a breath. 'What the hell was all that about? The woman is mental.' He rolled his eyes, climbed off the stool and went over to the sink.

Alison followed him with her eyes as he filled the kettle. *Who is this man?* 'That weekend – you stormed off to your mother's because the twins were teething, and you –'

'I was under pressure at university… My exams, I –'

'They needed something to soothe the pain. But on the way to the pharmacy, the wheel of the pushchair got stuck in a drain.'

He reached into the cupboard for two mugs. 'What's that got to do with –'

'I tried to call you but couldn't get a signal. I had to leave them alone in a back lane to get through to you – but you didn't pick up.'

His hand shook as he spooned coffee into the mugs. 'It was a lot to cope with. I needed a break. Come on, let's not rake over the past.'

'They were alone and crying, anything could have happened to them. We needed help. A stranger had to rescue them – because you'd run away.'

'I didn't *run away*. And you were so miserable…'

'My parents had died,' she said in a small voice.

He looked away. 'At least I had stuck by you.'

'No, you didn't. *I* stuck by *you*. You abandoned us. And you

294

cheated on me.'

'Can't you at least try to understand how I was feeling?'

Alison laughed. She pulled out a stool and sat down. 'How much did you give her?'

Martin avoided looking at her as he noisily stirred milk into the mugs. 'We'll make it up.'

'Leave the coffee. How. Much?'

He stood facing the wall. 'Twenty thousand.'

'She gasped.' The blow felt physical. It was worse than when she'd thought scammers had taken the lot, at least they'd have been faceless thieves. 'Did you know about Robbie from the start?'

Martin sat down, still unable to meet her gaze. 'Yes. But she was dating Keith and pretended he was his. Apparently, Keith has suspected a while – something Gail said during a row when she was drunk. Afterwards, she told him she'd wanted to hurt him and that it wasn't true.'

'Why would he keep something like that to himself?'

'He was planning his escape. He waited until he had his finances in order and somewhere lined up to live.' He shook his head. 'Can you believe he'd even seen a solicitor. Calculating so-and-so, he –'

Alison cackled. 'Don't you dare criticise Keith. It's you and Gail who are in the wrong here.' She squinted at him. 'Did your mother know?'

He looked away. 'Apparently she always suspected.'

'She did take my hair ornament, didn't she?'

'I think so. But what could I say? Alison, you've no idea the pressure I've been under. One wrong word from me and it could all have come out.'

'So you let them pick on me. And then take my money and future?'

Martin frowned. 'That's a bit dramatic. You've got me. I've got my job. In fact, you've done well from my salary.'

'They must all think I'm such a fool.'

'To be honest, it didn't help you telling them we'd saved for your fees. It was like Gail had won the lottery. Greedy cow.'

It suddenly dawned on her. Her locked account. 'You messed with my login details, didn't you? I didn't forget them at all.' She got up and paced around. 'You let me think I was stupid.'

Martin puffed out a heavy breath. 'It was a temporary measure. Frank Budle –'

'Him again.'

'I mentioned I needed to transfer funds for a while. I said I wanted to surprise you – do up the kitchen, and then replace the money in a few months. He said I could get you locked out and move the money.'

Alison ran the cold tap and splashed her face with water. 'It's like a bad dream.' Never, had she imagined Martin could deceive her like this.

'I wouldn't care, he charged me fifty quid for the advice.'

She shot around. 'He works for a bank. He can't do that. Does Christopher know?' Her heart sank. She hadn't wanted to believe he knew about Sandy owning Judith's salon. She'd been stupid.

'Frank's not crooked. And don't go telling tales to goody-two-shoes Christopher. Look, the bottom line is that it will take longer to get the fees saved up again.' He shrugged. 'If you still want to go in a couple of years, we can think about financing it. Somehow. I have ten thousand left.'

'*You* have?'

'We have. I meant *we*…' He looked up to the ceiling and exhaled slowly. 'You know, it's such a relief to get it all out in the open. She can't do any more harm. We'll be fine now.'

Alison laughed. '*Fine?* We'll never be *fine* again, you moron.' She leaned against the sink and let out a guffaw. '*Fine.*' She laughed so much she could barely breathe.

'All right. Calm down. It's not that funny.'

'You're right –'

He jumped off the stool and reached out to hug her. 'Of course I am.' He smiled at her, his head tilted and a patient look in his eyes, as if he was calming an over-wrought child. 'You'll see, we'll be –'

She pushed him away. His touch made her skin crawl. 'I mean, you're right, it's a relief.' She looked at his pathetic face and felt a stab of compassion. He had no idea what he'd done. 'I feel like a heavy weight's fallen from my shoulders.'

He paled. 'What do you mean?'

'I'd like you to leave.'

'Don't be silly –'

'Tonight. After you've transferred the rest of the money into my account.' She went to leave the room then turned back. 'Don't just stand there. Pack a bag and get out of my house.'

It was Saturday morning, so there was no rush to get to work. There was a lot to sort out, but for now Alison lay in bed, staring into the darkness. She had no idea what time it was, but it had to be the early hours of the morning because she felt rested, as if she'd had her first good chunk of sleep of the night. She briefly thought about painting a banana, but there was no need, she felt calm and cosy. She'd get up shortly if she didn't doze back off.

The previous evening's events replayed in her mind. It was like watching a screen in the distance, she felt numb. No, not numb, it was quite pleasant – like she was floating in a bath of warm relief. She knew she wasn't going to get back to sleep, better get up.

Alison opened the bedroom door to a stream of bright daylight. She went back into the bedroom and reached into the bedside drawer for her mobile. Nine o'clock. She'd slept for eight and a half hours.

There were five missed calls and a load of texts from Martin. Ignoring them, she skipped downstairs, made herself a cup of coffee and went into the garden, still in her pyjamas. As soon as she sat down on the swing seat, Sammy appeared and jumped up beside her.

She breathed in the morning air and smiled. The landline sounded indoors, but she ignored it and continued to swing and smile. Sammy purred by her side.

Chapter 40

Christopher opened his wardrobe door. His shirts and trousers hung in neat rows, as usual, but something seemed different. He couldn't put his finger on it. It was the same in the study. Not a thing out of place, but something not quite right. It was all too neat. As if the contents of everything had been removed, tidied, and put back the same, only neater.

Ever since Alison had mentioned seeing Sandy at Cherry Dene Hotel, and Sandy had accused him of interrogating her about it, he'd been unable to quell his growing suspicions that she was having an affair. The more he thought about it, the more sense it made – Sandy lying about not having been to the hotel recently, the barman's shock that he was her husband, and the big one of course, her resistance to him moving back home permanently.

He could hear her bustling around downstairs. As he wandered into the lounge, Sandy looked up from straightening a pile of wedding magazines and smiled. Christopher did a double take at the duster in her hand.

'What? What are you looking at?'

'You're dusting…'

'You'd think you'd never seen me tidy up.' She started to polish the mirror above the fireplace. 'Have you had a haircut?' It was as if she couldn't stand still.

'Not recently. Do I need one? I was going to wait until just before the wedding.' He watched as she went from one chair to another plumping cushions.

'Sandy, could you sit down for a minute?'

She continued busying around.

'Please, I need to speak to you.'

She picked up the remote control and flicked through the television channels, not pausing long enough to discern the programmes. 'What about?'

He took a deep breath. 'Are you having an affair?'

Sandy choked out a guffaw. 'What? Don't be stupid.'

'So why did you lie about being at Cherry Dene Hotel with Margot? Please, don't deny it.'

She paused and turned to him, hands on hips. 'Look, I couldn't tell you… I was with Frank Budle – sounding him out about money for the Californian house.'

Christopher felt a mixture of relief and betrayal. 'So, you weren't cheating on me with another man, just with our finances…'

'Nonsense. It was you who said gathering information was a good thing, when you were putting me out to work.'

He could feel himself rankling. 'This is entirely different. He's my employee for one – I don't want him knowing about my personal business. But worse than that, is that you went behind my back, and about something I'm completely against.'

Sandy gave an irritated shake of her head. 'You're overreacting.'

The evening news flashed up on the TV screen. The presenter started to say something about property prices in and around Earlby. Sandy zapped it off.

'Not interested in that for your portfolio?' said Christopher, his tone flat.

'Don't be sarcastic.'

'Surprised you haven't asked Frank about local property, since you're so pally with him.'

Her eyes widened. 'Now you're being ridiculous.' She sniffed the air. 'Why are you wearing aftershave? Where've you been?'

The question disarmed Christopher. 'What? Work.'

'You seem to be making a lot of effort for work.' She picked up a newspaper and slapped it onto the table. 'Was it for your park date with the dowdy sisters?'

'Where on earth is all this coming from?'

She screwed up her face as if she had bitten into something sour. 'And look at your arm. It's still not right.'

He stretched it out. 'I can almost straighten it properly.' He rubbed it. It still ached, but he didn't dare mention that.

Sandy bustled out to the kitchen and started banging doors and clattering dishes.

'What's wrong with you tonight?' he called after her. He switched the TV back on. 'You should look at this, Sandy,' he called. 'Something to discuss next time you see Frank.... A dodgy solicitor conning old people out of their houses when they go into nursing homes.'

She shot back into the lounge. 'Why watch that stuff? Misery and pessimism.' She switched it off.

'Shirley was on about something like that.' He clicked it back on, but it had finished. 'I've missed it now.'

Sandy made a 'pfft' sound and picked up an ornament to polish. 'What would Shirley know?'

'Buying them up for ridiculously low prices, she said.'

Sandy tutted. 'Idle gossip.'

He sighed. 'Have I done something wrong?'

'You think you're so important, don't you?'

'What on earth...?'

'With your job and your suits. You've no idea...'

'Sandy, what the heck...?'

'It's a mess.'

'What is?'

She looked out of the window then dashed to the cupboard

under the stairs. The vacuum cleaner cranked up and she swept back into the room. 'Move your feet,' she said, knocking them out of the way with the foot of the machine.

Christopher got up and pulled the plug out. 'Has something happened? You're all flustered and tearing around.'

She flung down the vacuum cleaner and flopped onto an armchair. 'I've got a wedding to organise and time's running out.' She blew a strand of hair from her face. 'And this house is a mess.'

He looked around at the gleaming surfaces. 'It's spotless.'

She screwed up her face. 'Oh, stop mithering on and man up.'

'Man up?'

You never put a foot wrong, do you? Mr bloody perfect.'

'What?'

'First the decent job goes. You're already walking in the park like some old codger. Next thing, you'll be in tartan slippers and smoking a pipe.'

He glanced down at his leather moccasin slippers. 'You're not making sense.'

'The only thing wrong with me, is you. Pulling the rug from beneath my feet. Coming back and messing around at the bank. Changing everything.' She turned and pointed at him. 'I could have married –'

'Yes, the whole world knows this already...' He shot her an angry glare. 'Lately, Sandy, I wish you *had* married some other poor sod.' The words tumbled out before he could stop them.

Sandy burst into tears. He rushed towards her, but she jumped up, grabbed her bag and shot out of the house, the screech of car gears filling the air as she tore off down the road.

Christopher stood at the window, staring at the empty space on the drive where her car had been. Emily's comments about the sixth-form girls came to mind. *Surely not, not Sandy.* Looking around the lounge, he realised something for the first time. Their house was like a show house, not a home.

And his marriage… Was there a word for a show-marriage? *Yes*, he thought with a wry smile. *A sham.* Was that the word he was looking for?

Chapter 41

Alison was drinking a cup of decaffeinated coffee in the lounge. She glanced around the room – it had taken her the whole of the day before to clean it, but it was almost back to normal. She'd had to close the door on the room Robbie had been using, that was a project for the following weekend.

She'd ignored Martin's calls since he left on Friday night, but she knew she'd have to speak to him soon. She hadn't yet mentioned anything to Chloe and Jack, or to Katie and Sharon. She needed time to process it all. It would have been easy to ask the girls to come round for a Prosecco cleaning party – no doubt they would have supplied lots of sympathy and support – but she wanted to start as she meant to go on. If she was going to be alone, she had to learn to rely on herself first.

The washing machine beeped, signalling the end of the cycle. She went through to the utility room and pulled out the sheets from Robbie's bed. Even though they'd been on a hot wash, she could still smell beer and cigarettes on them. It might have been her imagination, but it didn't matter, she decided – they were going in the dustbin.

Alison opened the back door and tripped over Martin, sitting on the doorstep in a crumpled T-shirt and scruffy jeans. She dumped the sheets in the bin and grudgingly allowed him into the house.

'Thank Goodness.' He went over to the fridge. 'Do we have any beer? I've been out there for ages, I'm parched.' He picked out a can. 'Great.'

'Come and sit down, we've a lot to get through.' She noticed his shoulders slump.

'We don't have to trash through it all again, do we? I think it would be much better to talk about the future.' He pulled out a seat and took a long drink.

'I agree.'

'Listen, I've been doing a lot of thinking over the weekend. Maybe counselling would help.' He looked at Alison with hope-filled eyes.

She shook her head. 'I don't think that's necessary.'

'Well, you might not think so now, but it could fester inside. It'll be no good if every time we disagree about something in the future, you bring up my misdemeanour.'

Alison felt a surge of sympathy for him. 'Oh, Martin. You don't understand.' She smiled gently. 'I'm sorry, I haven't changed my mind. We need to talk about how to tell jack and Chloe first.'

He reached across the table and took her hand in his. 'You're still angry, I can understand that. But the worst is over. We can survive this.'

She spoke softly. 'I'm not angry. I was. It seems as if I've been angry for as long as I can remember. But not any longer.'

He frowned. 'I expect you've had no sleep since I left –'

'I'm sleeping great.'

Martin withdrew his hand. 'Alison, don't be like this.' He sighed. 'I know you're just trying to punish me. It was a fling.'

She stood up and walked over to the window. 'I don't care any longer. And it wasn't only that, anyway. It's taken this to make me realise that you've always put me at the bottom of your list of priorities.' She watched Sammy climbing up the apple tree. 'I'm to blame as much as you, I allowed it. Everything was always about you and your reputation?'

He sighed. 'No, it wasn't.' He pulled a white paper bag from his pocket and handed it to her. 'I've told Mam it was unacceptable what she did.'

Alison took the bag and peered inside. She went dizzy. Tears pricked her eyes at the sight of the tiny diamantes. 'Why did she take it? Why didn't you get it back for me?' She leaned against the sink and gently held it in the palm of her hand.'

He looked at her, pain etched across his face. 'It's beautiful. Like you. I'm so sorry I let them get away with so much. Please forgive me.'

She pulled a sheet of kitchen paper from the roll and wiped her face. 'Anyway, it's done now. She narrowed her eyes at him. 'You were sitting on the back doorstep. Why weren't you at the front door? You didn't knock.'

He splayed his hands and stuttered. 'What difference does it make?'

'It was so no one could see you, wasn't it? In case I refused to let you in.'

Martin banged his palm against the tabletop. 'You're just looking for things that don't exist.'

'I'll speak to Jack and Chloe tonight. As far as I'm concerned, we can split the equity in the house and what little savings are left, minus my university fees – I want those before anything is divided up. I won't seek financial support from you, if you don't from me. You'll have more to lose, as I'd get half your pension to date. I've heard that's what happens these days, but we can check with a solicitor first if you want to. You've got a lot more in your pot than I have in mine, so I can't imagine it would be worth your while fighting me. I want to keep any redundancy money I might get. As you've pointed out, I'll have no salary for three years.'

Martin was standing, aghast. 'Alison, stop this. I get it, you're angry. I know I did wrong. But you've made your point.'

She walked to the back door and opened it. 'You need to go now.'

He reluctantly stepped outside. 'I'll come back tomorrow. Things might seem different by then.' He leaned in to kiss her cheek, but she turned away.

'Here, give this to your mother.' Alison handed him the bag with the hair comb.

He stared at it. 'I don't understand.'

'I don't want it. It's not the same.'

He searched her face with tear-filled eyes. 'But it's your beautiful wedding comb. It's precious to you.'

She shook her head. 'It was. But not any longer.'

Chapter 42

The corridor was empty as Alison wandered towards the exit. It felt light and airy – and so did she. Despite the terrible mess her life had turned into, she was sleeping better than she had in years. Lately, she could recall painting bananas only twice. She smiled to herself. When she did the exercise, she could smell and taste them. She loved painting bananas. And she'd had to think hard to work out how many times she'd awoken during the night lately. She didn't know, and it didn't matter.

She'd been to see Michelle for the last time. A lot had changed since she'd first attended the sleep clinic. 'Once you let go of trying to sleep, you sleep more,' she heard Michelle's voice say. She'd let go of a lot more than chasing sleep. There was one final telephone consultation in a couple of weeks to wrap it all up. At the start of the programme she'd never have believed how much she'd improve.

As she walked past a patient waiting area, someone called her name. She recognised the voice and looked around, her heart pounding. The sight of Christopher walking over to her caught her breath.

He seemed genuinely pleased to see her. 'Hello. Fancy bumping into you here.'

She was about to smile when she remembered – Judith's revelation, Frank, Christopher in cahoots with Sandy. 'Hello,' she said, keeping her tone as cool as she could.

He gave an exaggerated swing of his arm. 'Look, just about better.' He pointed to a double door with a Physiotherapy sign above it. 'Going for a check-up and X-Ray to make sure it's healed properly. I think they'll discharge me after today.'

'That's good news. Perfect timing for the wedding.'

'How are you? I've missed you in the park recently. I haven't seen Judith around, either. I thought about texting you, to make sure you were okay, but it wouldn't have been ethical to get your number from your account records.'

She laughed out loud. 'Very funny.'

He looked at her, perplexed.

He was a good actor, she'd give him that. 'I'm fine thank you. Michelle reckons I'm fixed.'

'Brilliant. Sweet dreams from now on for you and Martin.'

She felt her blood pound around her body. 'Hardly. But you wouldn't think about that when you're flouting the rules to line your own pockets, would you?'

'Alison, I don't understand. You seem cross.' He raised his eyebrows. 'Are you annoyed with *me*?'

'Please don't insult me with lies. I wasn't surprised Frank was a crook, even Sandy. But you —'

'Hang on a minute.' Christopher gently took her arm and led her over to some seats away from the main waiting area. 'I'm sorry but I haven't got a clue what you're talking about,' he said gently. 'Is it to do with when you saw them at Cherry Dene Hotel? Please tell me, were they… together?' His face was serious, his eyes intense. 'It has crossed my mind.'

She almost believed he really didn't know. He seemed so earnest, his eyes so honest, so kind… She gasped. 'They were your eyes…' She stared at him, her mouth open.

'You've completely lost me.'

'You helped me. You freed the wheel of the pushchair from the drain cover…' He couldn't possibly be in cahoots with Sandy. That young man had gone out of his way to help her —

he was too nice. 'I knew I recognised your eyes.'

Christopher's expression changed as the penny dropped. He laughed. 'Well I never... Yes, I was up for a rugby union at the university. You were on the way to the pharmacy for teething gel with your twins. Martin had gone off in a huff.' He frowned. 'But why you're angry with me?'

'Yes. I thought I'd made a friend in you, Christopher, but when I heard that Sandy was Judith's landlady, I –'

'You heard what?'

'Judith told me. And what with Frank taking payment from Martin for telling him how to hide my university money. I was hurt Christopher. I have to tell you, Judith may even have reported you.'

He wasn't listening. He was staring straight ahead, his hand over his mouth.

Alison touched his arm. 'You really didn't know, did you?'

He slowly shook his head. 'Not an inkling.' He turned to her. 'Thank you for telling me.'

'I'm sorry. I wish I'd come to see you now. I should have checked before assuming the worst.'

He looked at her, his eyes now full of sadness. 'What else could you think? I'm sorry.'

A nurse came out of the Physiotherapy Department and called his name. He stood up and straightened his jacket.

Alison wanted to wrap her arms around him and make him feel better. But she didn't. She smiled up at him. 'I hope it's good news with your arm. Take care Christopher.'

'You too, Alison.'

He smiled and disappeared through the doors with the nurse. As they closed behind him, she felt a tug on her heart.

Going into work after seeing Christopher, wasn't easy. Alison wished she could have escaped down to Cherry Dene Hotel with Katie, Sharon and a bottle of Prosecco. But it was a workday, so that was that. Thankfully, when she got there, Billy and Phyllis weren't around.

There was an official looking letter on her desk. She hoped it might be in connection to her complaint about Billy. It wasn't. It was much better than that – her redundancy application had been approved.

Alison sat reading the letter over and over. She would have liked to have been able to tell Christopher, but that wasn't to be. She looked around the quiet office as she tried to assimilate the idea that her days there were numbered. Even if she didn't get her place at university, the money would give her time to think about what to do next.

She logged on to her emails. There was one from Ashley, asking to see her straight away. Ignoring it, she grabbed her DECT phone and wandered down to the canteen for a coffee. She had taken annual leave for her hospital appointment and was back early. She had time to grab a coffee before her caffeine curfew. As she clipped the lid onto her cup, the phone rang. Ashley. He wanted to see her now.

'I'm about to have a coffee before I start work.'

'Bring it with you.'

Alison assumed it was to discuss her leaving date. He was quick off the mark, given that she'd only just received the letter. She didn't mind – it would be good to draw a line under her job, along with other things. It felt like packing up to move. Sorting through what to take, and what to leave behind. There wasn't that much she wanted to keep – her children, friends and her share of the finances. It all felt rather organised and civilised. She walked along to Ashley's office at a relaxed pace, rather than at the walk-dash tempo she usually employed for hierarchy.

Ashley smiled at her. 'Grab yourself a seat.'

'Is it about my redundancy package?'

'Kind of.'

She took out her diary and pen from her bag. 'That's great,

I'm keen to agree a date so that I can sort out my finances until I hear about university.'

'University?'

'Yes, I've applied to study physiotherapy in September.'

'Oh… The thing is, I was hoping to persuade you to stay.'

'But my redundancy application has been accepted.'

'Yes, I know. But we're short-staffed. Billy has gone on extended leave, and I wanted to offer you the chance to act up.'

'Does this have anything to do with my grievance?'

'No, that's still being processed.'

'Good job I'm not scared to come to work, isn't it? I expect some people might be.'

Ashley raised an eyebrow. 'Well anyway, Billy won't be back for a while.'

'Is he ill?'

'I'm not at liberty to say.' He smiled. 'It would be an excellent opportunity for you. Look good on your curriculum vitae.'

'Not for physiotherapy.' Alison looked at Ashley, so encouraging about this opportunity, yet completely dismissive of her actual plans. 'Are the rumours true about him fiddling sickness leave and selling overtime for a fee?'

Ashley steepled his hands and squirmed in his chair. 'No one has been accused of anything at this stage.'

She'd known something was amiss the day the fire alarm had gone off. Peggy had given her an update since then. Apparently, a select few, had been taking it in turns to go on sickness leave and then taken annual leave to come into work on overtime. All paying Billy a fee to organise it. 'So, when money is involved, he's in trouble, but the bullying can go on the back burner?'

He shook his head, his brows knotted together. 'No, no, not at all. That is a separate issue. I can assure you your complaint is being taken seriously.' He smiled at her again. 'The extra money would no doubt come in useful for when you do eventually go back to university.'

The words *back to university* sounded tiresome. She'd been saying them for years. She wondered if people did an inward eye-roll when she mentioned it. Well not any longer. 'There's no "eventually" about it. If you remember, I did that job temporarily before Billy. It didn't do much for me or my curriculum vitae back then, did it? You didn't want me for the permanent post.'

'Ah, yes. I remember. But there's nothing to say you wouldn't be successful next time. Billy was a stronger candidate on that occasion.'

'No, he wasn't. He took ownership of someone else's hard work and passed it off as his own. Apparently, he was renowned for it.'

'I don't think it's fair to accuse someone of something when they aren't here to defend themselves.'

'He's a lazy, bullying liar. And he once told me he only had two GCSE's.'

Ashley's eyes widened. He rifled through some blank pieces of paper before re-composing himself. 'Well, if we can get back to my offer of a temporary promotion for you.'

'No thank you.'

He gave her a terse smile. 'Alison, the service is under immense pressure. We need you to step up.'

'You decided that I wasn't good enough last time. I don't want to do it again.'

'The service comes first.'

'It used to, but not any longer. Offer someone else the chance to work their socks off, and then dismiss them in favour of a cheating dollop of poo.'

Ashley gawped at her.

She stood up to leave. 'Thank you for the offer, but no thank you. It's high time I "stepped up" for myself.'

As she walked along the corridor, Alison felt weightless. She couldn't remember the last time she'd felt so liberated. She strode into the office with confidence, her integrity, for once intact.

After work, Alison called into Alessandro's for a coffee. Despite everything that was going on, she felt younger and more energised than she had done in years. As she bit into a Danish pastry and gazed out of the window, she saw a familiar figure leaving the bank, a mobile phone clamped to his ear. Poor Christopher, she thought, he must be having a dreadful day.

Alison felt a twinge of sadness as she wondered what would happen if Chloe or Jack got married. Thoughts of awkward wedding days filtered into her mind – herself and Martin estranged, Gail on his arm, his conceited mother making nasty comments. Whatever the situation was, she'd do her best to make their weddings wonderful.

Watching Christopher disappear down the street, she felt tears sting the back of her eyes. She should have gone to him. He'd rescued her all those years ago, but she'd let him down when he needed help. She wondered if his marriage would survive. She hoped not, he deserved better than Sandy.

Chapter 43

As Christopher strode away from work, he was still trying to get hold of Frank. Sandy wasn't answering his calls either. After the devastating morning, the day got worse, starting with an ashen-faced Shirley appearing at the office door, holding the local newspaper.

'Have you heard about Frank?'

Christopher had looked up from his computer screen, expecting to hear news of Frank's return to work following a cold virus. 'No, hasn't yet called to say when he'll be back. But I need to speak to him as soon as he does.'

'It's about something else.' She'd tentatively set down the newspaper on his desk. 'I couldn't believe it.'

The news article had shocked him to his core. 'Crikey,' he'd said as the gravity of the situation hit him. A picture of Frank, Frank's wife and another man, all looking hard-faced and gangster-like, stared up at him, beneath the headline, "Local trio scam old people out of their homes."

Christopher had read out the article on automatic pilot. 'I don't believe it. "*Local banker, Frank Budle, acted as a broker, charging investors a fee to hook them up with his solicitor cousin, to buy property at a discounted price. His wife, manager of local care home, Patricia Budle, would recommend the cousin to prospective residents and their families, who wanted a quick sale to secure care home fees.*"

Despicable. What kind of monsters could rob old people like that?'

'I never liked him,' Shirley had said.

Christopher closed his eyes. And thanked the heavens he'd called Head Office as soon as he'd left the Physiotherapy Department, and before this news had broken. It had been a precautionary call, in advance of further investigation. He'd told them what Alison had said about Frank. In normal circumstances, he'd have spoken to Frank himself first, but his gut instinct told him that not only would it be true, but probably worse than helping customers prevent spouses from getting into their accounts.

His stomach was churning. Why wasn't Sandy picking up? He silently prayed that she hadn't bought Judith's salon through Frank. Strictly speaking, she wouldn't have done anything illegal. But still…

'Oh, dear Lord. It says here Frank cherry-picked potential buyers from among our clients. I need to get back onto Head Office…'

By the end of the afternoon, Henleys' press office had released a statement condemning Frank's activities, but Christopher hadn't been able to contact either Frank or Sandy.

He dropped his briefcase on the hall floor. 'Sandy, where are you?' He knew she was home, her car was on the drive. He went through to the kitchen, took a glass from the cupboard and poured himself a large gin and tonic. 'Sandy, where are you?' he called. 'He poured her a drink, too.'

No answer.

He carried the drinks through to the lounge and shook his head in dismay at the three-piece suit. With even more new cushions on it, it was beginning to look like a sheep pen. 'For goodness' sake,' he said, hurling two of them onto an armchair. He sank into the sofa and took a long drink.

It had been a huge relief that Henleys had been able to release a press statement. It was going to take some sorting out, but transparency was of the utmost importance. He switched on the television to see if there was anything on the News.

The sound of snivelling from the hall made him jump.

Sandy stood in the doorway, her shoulders hunched and her eyes red-rimmed. She was clutching a blue file.

'I take it you've heard?'

She remained in the doorway, rooted to the spot.

Christopher got up and gently took her by the arm. 'Why on earth haven't you answered any of my calls?'

She allowed him to lead her to the sofa. She perched on the edge and looked at him with fear-filled eyes. 'I think I've done something silly. She grasped the file. 'I was thinking of the future.' She gave him a sideways, shifty glance. 'A safety net, just in case. It was Frank's idea –'

A feeling of foreboding engulfed him. 'He helped you buy Judith's salon, didn't he?'

'She looked down at her feet and nodded.

'Look, Frank and the others are in big trouble. But it doesn't have to mean that you are.'

She handed him the file.

'At least legally.' He couldn't look at her. 'Fleecing Judith is another matter. But we'll deal with one thing at a time.'

'I was building it for us…'

Christopher leafed through the file. He felt the space around him expand. It was a dossier of properties. He looked at his wife in disbelief. 'These must go back years…' His voice tailed off.

'Frank said…'

'Did you know what he was involved in?'

He watched her get up and start pacing around the room. The way the light reflected off her Chanel belt made him feel sick. 'Four properties? You knew you were benefitting from the misfortune of four families?'

'As you said, it was legal and above board.'

'All in your name. Purchased, no doubt, at the expense of little old people, backed into a corner by crooks?'

He glanced up from the file to his wife. 'Sandy, is this a running away fund? Were you preparing to leave me one day?'

She gasped. 'No. I told you, it was for us.'

'Four properties I knew nothing about. And half of everything we own together. Was that the plan?'

How could he not have realised? 'You must have been devastated when I wanted to stay at this branch,' he said quietly. 'There I was, going on about spending more time with you. No wonder you panicked.'

'I told you, I wanted to build something for our future.'

'What future? The one where I wanted to be with you, and you wanted me as far away as possible?'

She reached for his arm. He pulled it away.

'Don't be like that, darling,' she said, with a sickly-sweet smile.

A laugh caught the back of Christopher's throat. Her eyelash extensions reminded him of Daisy the Cow from a childhood story book. The more he stared at her, the more docile she looked.

'Stop it,' said Sandy through plump lips. 'Look, I'm sorry. I should have told you.'

'Where on earth did you get the money from?'

'I saved for the first deposit. And sold some bits of jewellery I didn't wear —'

'That I'd bought you? No wonder you were so delighted whenever I gave you jewellery. You saved?' He laughed again. 'You mean you withdrew money from our account and secretly banked it elsewhere?'

She shot him a snarky look and ignored the accusation. 'Then I carried on saving. Once I had the first one, I invested some of the revenue from the rent into the next one. So, you see, I earned it.'

He started to laugh uncontrollably. 'What an idiot I've been.' He looked directly at her. 'You're as bad as the other three. You're a thief.'

'I'm not. It's all there.'

'A running away portfolio.' He guffawed.

'It's not funny, Christopher. I don't want to be tarred with the same brush as those people.'

He wiped away a tear. 'No, it isn't funny. It's tragic. Of course, legally, as we're married, I own half. You do know it works both ways, not just for wives, don't you?'

Sandy's eyes widened. She started to say something then stopped herself.

'Clearly not. Don't worry. I want nothing to do with your ill-gotten gain. Stealing from little old people, who'd worked their whole lives for what they had. You, on the other hand, don't know what work is.' He looked at her as if seeing her for the first time. 'You always said you could have married any number of men. Why me? Was I the easiest prey?'

Tears spilled down her cheeks. 'Christopher…' She moved towards him, her arms outstretched. 'I love you.' Her tone changed. 'What are we going to do? It's all over the news.'

He stood up. 'I don't know. I need to get back on to Head Office. I have to tell them about your involvement.'

'No, you can't,' she shrieked.

It had been humiliating enough the first time. This latest debacle didn't bear thinking about. He shot her an angry look. 'Apart from hurting vulnerable people and destroying the bank's good name, you may have ended my career.' Christopher waited to be connected. He tapped the file. 'You, lady, need to get yourself some legal advice. About this. And us.'

Chapter 44

Despite the heartbreak and upheaval, since Martin and his belongings had gone from the house, Alison had slept a solid seven to eight hours a night. She felt amazing, awaking each day full of energy and with a zest for life. She had attracted comments about how great she looked from just about everyone she knew. Katie even thought she'd had a skin peel.

Michelle had discharged her from the sleep clinic, announcing she was 'fixed'. Alison had worried that, without the safety net of the programme, the insomnia might return. But so far it hadn't. And with each night that passed, she felt increasingly confident it wouldn't. In any case, she knew that sleep was usually only a banana away.

The phone calls and texts from Martin continued at stalker level. He was languishing in a rented apartment with Robbie, which he described as a living hell, while Gail waited for him to move into her house, despite Martin's insistence that that wouldn't be happening.

Alison no longer cared what they did.

It was a Saturday morning when the letter dropped onto the hall mat. An offer of a place to study at Northumbria University – that September.

She sipped her morning coffee and read the information booklet from cover to cover, like an excited child on Christmas morning.

Her mobile was red-hot from the numerous calls she'd made. Chloe and Jack were both delighted. Although upset about the break-up, they were doing all right. Chloe said that she and Jack had already talked about the possibility she and Martin might split up. Chloe said she'd always reminded her of 'a trapped bird in a gilded cage.' They hadn't been so accepting of Robbie as a stepbrother and remained furious with Martin. Alison was sure they'd forgive him, eventually. He was their father after all. And he did love them.

Katie and Sharon were coming around that evening to help her celebrate with Prosecco and a takeaway. But that was hours away. She sat at the kitchen bench, desperate to do something, but not sure what. In the end, she ventured up into the loft to hunt out her old anatomy and physiology books. Then she got on her laptop to research the latest journals and articles. She went from one thing to another, too restless to do anything for more than a few minutes.

Finally, she pulled on her trainers. She grabbed her rucksack and set off down to the park to sit on her bench and read the information for the umpteenth time. But when she got there, she still couldn't settle. She wandered over to the kiosk for a coffee, her eyes darting around – at the dog walkers, the children playing on the football pitch, the little lake – something was missing. She felt thrilled but all in a spin.

After she'd finished her coffee, she jogged down the path towards the dene to try to disperse some of her energy. Who would have thought during the sleepless years that she'd have so much of it? She was laughing to herself as she ended her run with a loop of the miniature lake, flopping down, sweating and out of breath, on her bench. She still felt out of sorts, unable to put her finger on what was wrong.

'Hello there, Alison,' said a familiar voice.

Her heart leapt. She shot around, to find Christopher walking towards her. She jumped up, pulled her letter from her pocket and waved it at him. 'I got in.'

Christopher clapped his hands together and gave her a wide grin. He didn't need to ask what she was talking about. 'Fantastic.'

She giggled, as she jumped up and down like an excited child.

He picked her up, swung her around and planted a big kiss on her cheek. 'I can't tell you how delighted I am for you.'

She blushed then staggered back to the bench. 'I'm so glad you're here, I was itching to tell someone.'

'Me, too. I couldn't be happier for you.' His eyes twinkled with pride as he looked at her.

Alison noticed he was thinner, not unhealthily so, but he looked different. 'Are you all right?'

He gave a dismissive wave of his hand. 'Yes, absolutely fine. I've had stuff going on at home, that's all.'

'Of course, the wedding preparations.'

'Not just that.' He took a deep breath and exhaled slowly. 'Sandy and I have decided to split up. You can imagine what it was about. It wasn't only Judith's salon she'd bought. By the way, Sandy refunded some of the money and has reduced her rent.'

'That's good of her.'

He shot her a dubious look. 'It took a bit of arm-twisting.' He smiled again. 'On the positive side. I didn't lose my job.'

'That's a relief.' Alison felt selfish. Behaving like an over-excited child, while Christopher was going through such a terrible time. All the same, her heart was beating so fast she thought she might pass out. 'I am sorry about you and Sandy.'

'Don't be. It's for the best. It's my fault as much as hers.'

Alison looked at him in shock. 'Oh, I see. It's none of my business, I didn't mean to pry.'

'No, no. There's no one else or anything like that. I meant, I've been wrapped up in my work for so long, I had no idea we weren't happy.' He sighed. 'I think I was fooled by the façade.

When it came down to it, we had no substance.'

'Blimey.' What were the chances that they were both going through the same thing at the same time?

'If I hadn't had the health scare and had to think about downscaling my work – and salary – I would never have realised.' Christopher shook his head. 'I didn't have an inkling we were such a superficial couple. I don't think I ever knew her properly.' He looked up at the sky and laughed. 'Actually, I didn't know her at all.'

'I understand completely.' Alison started to laugh, too. 'I thought Martin and I had a rock-solid foundation – we were drowning in quicksand.' She gave an almighty guffaw and clutched her stomach. As she screamed with laughter, her whole body shook. She could barely breathe.

Christopher put his hand gently on her shoulder. 'Please don't cry? Here, take this handkerchief.'

Alison sat up. 'I'm not crying,' she squeaked. 'Our split…' she said between hoots, '…it's the best thing that could have happened to me. I had no idea I'd become such a wimp.'

He looked at her, his expression one of confusion. 'You're not a wimp. I think you're one of the most admirable women I've ever met.'

As she took the handkerchief, their hands touched, and the strongest shock to date crackled through her.

'Crickey.' Christopher rubbed his own hand.

'Did you feel that, too?' she asked.

'It rattled my fillings.'

She touched the metal rubbish bin next to the seat. Nothing. 'Wow.' She looked at Christopher in amazement. 'I think you've grounded me.'

He chuckled. 'Always pleased to be of service.'

Alison looked into his striking-green eyes. Her stomach lurched. She wiped her own eyes. The handkerchief smelled of him – she wanted to keep it.

It seemed an age before either of them spoke.

'Alison, would you like to join me for a coffee and a Danish pastry?'

'I would like that very much,' she said, her mouth stretching into a smile so wide it hurt.

As they stepped through the gates of Cherry Park, an image flashed into her mind – herself, holding her mother's hand as they ambled in to feed ducks. A surge of love flooded through her as another image floated in. It was her mother again, but this time it wasn't a memory – she was smiling down on her and Christopher. And then she felt the warmth of Christopher's hand as he gently took hold of hers.

The End

Dear Reader,

Thank you so much for reading *Painting Bananas.*

I hope you enjoyed reading it as much as I enjoyed writing it. If you did, I'd really appreciate it if you could spend a few minutes leaving an honest review on Amazon or Goodreads (it can be as short as you like).

I would also love to hear what you thought about *Painting Bananas*, so please feel free to drop me a line via the addresses below to let me know. And, if you'd like me to let you know about new releases and special offers, you can sign up for my Newsletter via the email address.

My online homes are:

Email: contact@amandapaull.co.uk
Website: http://www.amandapaull.co.uk.
Facebook: www.facebook.com/Apaullfiction
Twitter: https://twitter.com/Apaullfiction

Best wishes,

Amanda

A Note from the Author

Although *Painting Bananas* is a fictional story, I have taken creative license to use some real places in fictional ways, such as Newcastle and Durham, while other places are completely made up.

As far as characters are concerned, they are all fictional, except for the sleep nurse, Michelle. I have to admit that there may be a little bit of myself in Michelle. The character Peggy the cleaner, was concerned about children being trapped in a cave. This was loosely based on a real news item from a couple of years ago, which was about a different sporting team. There was no reference to any real people. I wanted to use it because I knew of someone who did actually believe that the driver had driven his coach full of kiddies into a cave, and it made me giggle.

Nick Shannon, the fire officer, is based on all the fire officers I have encountered over nearly twenty years of mandatory annual fire training updates. I love their talks, and the way they adore fire doors and absolutely hate door chocks.

About the Author

Amanda Paull is the author's pen name, which she chose in order to keep her writing separate from her day job. She is a former teacher and, more recently, a nurse.

Amanda writes Women's Fiction novels and Romantic Comedy short stories and novellas. Although all her stories are works of fiction, she finds that ailments and hospitals do tend to creep in.

Today Amanda is a full-time author and lives in the North East of England with her husband.